A FUTURE
AND A HOPE

A FUTURE
AND A HOPE

a novel

DAVID MATHEWS

Ambassador International
GREENVILLE, SOUTH CAROLINA & BELFAST, NORTHERN IRELAND

www.ambassador-international.com

A Future and a Hope

ISBN: 978-1-62020-830-4

eISBN: 978-1-62020-836-6

This is a work of fiction. Names, characters, and incidents are all products of the author's imagination or are used for fictional purposes. Any resemblance to actual events or persons, living or dead, is entirely coincidental. Any mentioned brand names, places, and trademarks remain the property of their respective owners, bear no association with the author or the publisher, and are used for fictional purposes only.

Cover Design & Typesetting by Hannah Nichols
Ebook Conversion by Anna Riebe Raats
Author Photo by David Denney

AMBASSADOR INTERNATIONAL
Emerald House
411 University Ridge, Suite B14
Greenville, SC 29601, USA
www.ambassador-international.com

AMBASSADOR BOOKS
The Mount
2 Woodstock Link
Belfast, BT6 8DD, Northern Ireland, UK
www.ambassadormedia.co.uk

The colophon is a trademark of Ambassador, a Christian publishing company.

To everyone who, at one time or another,
ever doubted the goodness of God.

ACKNOWLEDGMENTS

I would like to give a shout out to Jeff Edwards and Edwards Drive-In / Dashboard Diner, 2126 Sherman Dr., Indianapolis, Indiana, for providing the real-life inspiration behind the 50s-style diner in this book. You really do serve the best tenderloins and onion rings.

I greatly appreciate my senior pastor, Dr. Jon Young, for taking time from his busy schedule to read the manuscript and review it for theological content and accuracy. You have a true servant's heart.

I am deeply indebted to my editor, Daphne Self, who, with all the skills of an experienced surgeon lobotomized my brainchild, but in the procedure saved its life.

I am thankful for my wonderful wife, Donna, who is the love of my life, my best friend, my sister in Christ, and my partner in capital "A" adventure. Were it not for your encouragement, input, and patience, this story would never have been written.

Most importantly, I am grateful to my Lord and Savior Jesus Christ, Who died on a cross to pay my sin debt and rose again to give me the hope of eternal life. Thank You for loving me with Your everlasting love and having a plan for my life that is for my good and not my harm.

PART ONE

CHAPTER ONE

FIRST CONTACT

THE SHARP JANGLE OF THE bell pierced the library-like quietness of Baxter High School's main hallway. A moment later, as if choreographed, doors flung open and rivers of students and sound poured from classrooms, flooding the corridor and displacing the echoes and emptiness. Against the swirling sea of academia, students somehow managed to navigate back to their lockers with the skill of a driver facing the oncoming traffic of a one-way street.

A loud "Wahoo!" arose above the cacophony of noise. Dodging bodies with the agility of an All-American running back, an exuberant Caleb Sawyer zigged and zagged his way through the hordes of humanity at high velocity.

From the safety of his classroom doorway, the biology teacher bellowed his usual "Where's the fire, Sawyer?" to which the speeding senior responded with his usual "Sorry, Mr. Hartsock!" but with little noticeable reduction in miles per hour.

He meant no disrespect. It's just that, after sitting through class after class from morning to afternoon, his pent-up energy simply needed a safety valve.

"Hey, dude!" The sound of B.J. Martin's voice accomplished what Mr. Hartsock could not. Caleb eased off the throttle, executed a tight U-turn in the middle of the hallway, and cruised back to his best friend's locker. He shot B.J. a wry look.

"Don't you know it's Friday, man? Freedom calls!"

B.J. scrambled to unload his books. "What time you gotta be back here for the Jamboree?"

"Coach says six-thirty. Dressed and on the field by seven." He grimaced. "Not a good idea to be late for the first game!"

"You got time to go to Edwards first?" B.J. asked.

"I've got some things to do at home, but I can be there around five-thirty. But just long enough to grab something to eat. What time you gonna be there?"

B.J. buried his face in the locker. "Five, maybe. Fills up pretty early on game nights. Want me to save you a seat?"

Caleb didn't reply. He stared down the hallway.

B.J. repeated his question without looking up. "Want me to save you a seat?"

Still staring, Caleb answered absentmindedly, "Uh, yeah . . . fine."

B.J. disengaged himself from his locker, and glanced up quizzically. "Hey, Einstein! Did I lose you back there somewhere?" He spelled it out slowly for his friend. "Do. You. Want. Me. To. Save. You. A. Seat?"

He followed Caleb's gaze.

About fifty feet down the hall, Ellie Thompson stood in front of her locker loading books into her backpack. With beautiful brown eyes, a nice but somewhat shy smile, and long wavy auburn hair that bounced when she walked, she was just the kind of girl that turned heads.

"Ellie Thompson?" B.J. shook his head incredulously and gave an evil grin. "Out of your league, pal!"

Caleb snapped out of his trance. "What do you mean, 'out of my league'?" He squared his shoulders. "How do you know she's out of my league?"

"Well just look at her. She's gorgeous! *And* a straight 'A' student. Might even challenge Monica Stedwell for class valedictorian."

Caleb snorted in disbelief. "How could you possibly know that? Did she tell you her GPA or something? I heard she pretty much keeps to herself and hardly talks to anybody."

B.J. threw up his hands defensively, "Hey, all I know is that Jaimee Starrett volunteers in the records office, and she just happened to see her grade transcripts on Miss Johnson's desk the first day of school."

"And why don't you think I'd stand a chance with a gorgeous, straight 'A' student?" Caleb pressed.

B.J. smirked. "I'm just trying to keep you away from her so I have a better chance myself!"

Caleb feigned offense. "Aha! The truth finally comes out! Some friend you are!" He playfully punched his friend in the arm.

"Ow!" B.J. rubbed the spot gingerly. "Well, she definitely isn't gonna be easy to get to know. Chris Miller was hitting on her the first day of school and got shot down big-time! So did Kenny Wilson. I mean, I've heard she's okay and all. Not stuck up or anything. But it's almost like she doesn't want anyone to get close to her."

"You gonna take somebody else's word for that?" Caleb raised one eyebrow. "How do you know that's true unless you talk to her yourself?"

B.J. stared sheepishly at his shoes. "I tried. And got nowhere." He looked up and added, "Just like everybody else!" Staring down the hall at her, he sighed wistfully, "She sure is a challenge."

Caleb resolutely planted his feet. "Well, I happen to like a challenge! And I don't give up so easily." With all the false bravado he could muster, he announced, "With her kind you gotta keep things light and easy. Slow and steady. And have patience. Lots of patience! That's how it's done, bro." Patting B.J. on the back, he glanced down the hallway. "Wish me luck!"

His friend shook his head. "Okay, pal. Your funeral!" Caleb turned and headed in Ellie's direction. B.J. called after him, "But don't count on me being there for it!"

Caleb glanced over his shoulder and shot his friend a confident grin.

"I'll give you a progress report at Edwards!"

The sharp jangle of the bell pierced the ghost-like fog in Caleb Sawyer's brain. A groan emanated from somewhere deep within his body. A thought pierced the haze like a laser beam. *That sound was annoying!*

For the next forty-five minutes he would be confined to a school desk with no chance for early parole. Not that he hated learning. He just loved the idea of freedom more. Perhaps he was a kinesthetic learner. Another thought materialized with greater clarity. *What if this bell signaled the end of last period?*

That would change everything! Funny that he couldn't distinguish between the two.

Caleb blinked and opened his eyes. It was not the cold, harsh florescent lights of the classroom that assaulted his eyes, but the warm, soft rays of the early morning sun. And that teeth-grinding sound was not the bell in the school hallway, but the alarm clock in his own bedroom. With great effort, he rolled onto his right side, managed to locate the offending timepiece, and put it out of its misery.

He struggled upright in bed. The fog was almost gone now. He glanced at the clock. It was eight o'clock Saturday morning.

Somehow he'd forgotten how hard it was to get up the morning after a football game. However, if he didn't get a move on, he'd be late for work. He begrudgingly surrendered to the inevitable, and climbed out of bed. After stretching his slightly sore muscles, Caleb began to dress.

He liked his job at the Pet Palace near the Southridge mall. It was a really fun place to work. Stocking shelves, mopping floors, and cleaning cages wasn't all that much fun, but the joy of interacting with the puppies and kittens more than made up for those other responsibilities. Last year, Karen Waters had come into the store and teased him mercilessly for being such a big softy. But he hadn't let it bother him at all. Instead, he'd talked her into buying a Yorkie.

Caleb ran a comb through his sandy-brown hair, and grabbed his wallet and keys off the nightstand. Then after glancing at his rumpled bedding with the best of intentions, he headed downstairs for a quick breakfast. His parents were already at the table, along with his ten-year-old pest of a sister, Cassie.

His mother greeted him with her usual morning cheerfulness. "Glad to see you up. How's my Cherub today?"

Thankfully she only called him that at home. No matter how old he was, or how much trouble he got into, he would always be her little angel. After all, weren't moms supposed to feel that way about their kids?

Managing a "G'morning" he plunked down at the table and began to shovel frosted cinnamon cereal into his mouth.

"How's my Cherub this morning?" Cassie mimicked her mother. "I'm glad to see my little Poopsie-Whoopsie Bear at the table!" She giggled at her own cleverness. Instead of his usual response he tousled her hair. He was sure there would be many more opportunities for revenge.

"Quit it, Caleb!" She pulled away, still giggling.

His father glanced up from the morning paper. "I heard you had a pretty good game last night, son. Sorry I got back from Columbus too late to catch it."

"That's okay," Caleb managed, his mouth full of cereal.

"How many yards did you end up with?"

"I dunno. Thirty or thirty-five I guess. Only four catches, though. Main thing is we won."

"Not bad for the Jamboree. You can count on us being at all your regular-season games," his father promised.

"Last night coach was trying out different receivers. But he said I ran some really good routes and he noticed my blocking is improving. I should get more playing time against Cairo next week."

"Keep this up, and we may get to see you play at UGA next fall!"

Caleb laughed at his father's encouraging tone. He was only an average high school football player in an average small-town football program. Even if he did try out as a walk-on for the SEC powerhouse Bulldogs, realistically there was no chance he would ever make the roster, let alone take the field in storied Sanford Stadium on game day. One thing he knew for sure, "Rudy" Ruettiger he was not!

Besides, he had no real desire to pursue the sport after graduation. He would be content to cheer for the team from the student section.

His mother changed the subject just as he inhaled the last of his cereal. "I didn't get to ask you last night how school went this week. Anything interesting happen?"

For as long as he could remember, she had never failed to ask that question at the end of each school week. He glanced at the clock over the kitchen sink and stood up, draining the last of the orange juice from his glass. "Um, nothing this week."

The look his mom gave made it perfectly clear that his succinct reply had not satisfied her need for conversation. He fumbled for a lengthier and more appeasing response. "Mr. Hartsock told me to slow down in the hall again yesterday."

Failing this latest attempt at meaningful dialogue, he planted a grin on his face and a kiss on her forehead.

He grabbed his jacket which hung by the back door. "I'll be late for work. Bye!" Then he fled the house and headed for the Pet Palace.

No reason to mention his encounter with Ellie Thompson the previous afternoon. That game hadn't ended as well as the one on the football field.

———

For most of the students at Baxter High School, it was lunchtime on the Wednesday after Jamboree weekend. But for Caleb, it was lunchtime on the Wednesday after Ellie Thompson's brush-off. Today, as usual, he sat at the round cafeteria table with B.J. and some of their friends. He didn't feel much like joining their animated conversation which, when combined with the loud chatter of the other forty or so circles in the cavernous cafeteria, assaulted the ears of anyone entering through the heavy double doors from the relative hush of the corridor beyond.

He tried participating but resigned himself to the role of listener. When that proved difficult, he let his mind drift back to the subject of Ellie. For the past four days he had not been able to get her out of his mind. The unpleasant memory of their awkward Friday afternoon encounter had not diminished in the least. He'd determined that the best course of action to engage Ellie into conversation would be to ease into the situation by approaching her as nonchalantly as he knew how. Lighthearted conversation and chit-chat was sure to do the trick. That was the idea, but then he'd discovered that Ellie didn't much care for lighthearted conversation and chit-chat. Instead, she'd avoided his direct gaze, and when she'd replied, it was to the back of her locker or into her backpack. Maybe she was just shy. Extremely shy. No. It wasn't shyness.

She hadn't been shy so much as she'd been evasive. As if she were guarding a secret she didn't want to reveal. Maybe it was something about herself, or about where she came from—wherever that was. He thought back to his conversation with B.J. He had basically said the same thing about her. A thought crossed his mind, one that assuaged his bruised ego and offered a sliver of comfort. At least she hadn't treated him rudely like he'd anticipated.

And while she hadn't been exactly friendly, she hadn't shot him down either. At least, not like she'd shot down Chris Miller or Kenny Wilson. Or even B.J., for that matter. She'd ended his attempts at conversation by making some excuse for having to be at some appointment somewhere, and then she'd scurried off. No sir, that didn't qualify as being shot down. Not in the technical sense. He shook off his thoughts and returned to the present.

B.J. and his other friends were still going strong. Thankfully no one seemed to notice his withdrawal from the conversation. He let his gaze drift around the cafeteria. A group of cliquish cheerleaders sat isolated at their usual table. So did some of the nerds. Several of his teammates, along with their girlfriends, had pushed two tables together and were huddled up as if on the football field, loudly engaged in teenage testosterone-filled braggadocio. The rest of the cafeteria was abuzz with students coming and going; some in the food line, some seated, some heading for the tray-return window. Caleb's gaze swept past the table in the far corner of the room, and then returned to it.

Four girls sat there, each keeping to herself. One of them was Ellie. She was reading what looked like a newspaper, and seemed to be oblivious to the chaos around her. His heart skipped a beat.

What was that he felt? Fear? Was he actually afraid of her? A twinge of embarrassment shot through him. Maybe she really *was* a challenge, even to someone like him. Or could it be that he wasn't as good at making friends as he thought? He forcibly slammed the door on the creeping tentacles of doubt and self-loathing that were trying to force their way into his mind. He would have to give it another try. After all, he'd told B.J. he wasn't one to give up easily.

He would make good on that boast. He would see this thing through with Ellie Thompson, come what may! Caleb grabbed B.J., who was in the middle of an animated debate with Jenny Bristol over who had the better movie resume, Tom Hanks or Denzel Washington.

"I'll see you in class B.J. There's something I have to do before fifth period."

B.J. stopped talking. "What do you hafta do before class?"

"Nothing important. Just gotta talk to somebody, that's all." He stood up and grabbed his tray.

"Okay. See ya!" B.J. turned back to Jenny and picked up the debate right where he'd left off.

Kelli Anderson, who had been sitting across from Caleb, looked up quizzically. "Anything wrong, Caleb? You seem pretty quiet today."

A hot flush spread across his face, and he hoped it didn't show. Leave it to Kelli to notice his introspection. "Nothing's wrong. Just thinking about . . . things, I guess."

He hastily retreated from the group and headed toward the far corner of the cafeteria. Two of the other three girls at Ellie's table had already left. He took a deep breath. For the first time, he noticed that she wasn't dressed quite as nicely as most of the other girls in school. Not that it mattered to him. What a person was on the inside was far more important that what they wore, or how they looked.

Ellie didn't notice him standing across the table from her. She was buried in her newspaper.

"Mind if I sit here?" Caleb's mouth suddenly felt dry.

Ellie glanced up, and a look of recognition crept across her face. She shrugged. "Be my guest. It's a free country." She smiled ever so slightly, as if worried her tone had been too harsh. Then she dove back into the paper.

"Thanks." Leaving an empty chair between them, he sat down, and cautioned himself, *Take it easy, Caleb. Give her some space. Be patient.*

He sipped his Coke, hoping the carbonation would alleviate the dryness in his mouth. After shooting a sideways glance at the other girl across the table, he took a bite of his sandwich and silently watched Ellie for a minute. She was looking at the job listings.

"Looking for a job?" He had to start somewhere, and that was as good an opening as he could come up with at the moment. When she glanced up at him, he was reminded of how beautiful she was.

"Yes."

"How's it going?"

"I'm not having any luck." She returned to her paper.

Apparently she was going to give him only the bare minimum reply to his questions. Nothing more.

Undaunted, he continued. "I guess there just aren't very many jobs in a small town like Baxter."

A hint of resentment crept into her voice. "It's not that. All the other kids grabbed them before I got here." She looked down again.

"Yeah, I see what you mean. I never thought about that before. Must be hard being in a new school and a new town. I mean, I've never had to deal with anything like that. I've always lived here. Got my job when I was a sophomore." He stopped and grinned, "I guess that makes me part of the problem, huh!" He detected a slight smile from her. Not much of one, but it was enough to keep him going. "Have you tried any of the stores at the mall?"

"I've looked everywhere." The other girl at the table got up to leave.

Caleb thought about his dad's insurance agency. While he knew his dad didn't have anything, the other businesses might. "What about the businesses downtown?"

Exasperation filled her brown eyes. "I've tried there. I've tried the grocery stores, the restaurants, the drug stores. Even the gas stations!"

Still trying to be helpful, he added, "What about Cairo? Have you looked over there? Of course, that would mean going over to the enemy."

This time, he was sure of the smile. But it quickly disappeared. She hesitated, as if embarrassed. "I don't have any way of getting there."

Caleb was running out of ideas. "Couldn't your mom or dad take you to work?"

Ellie stiffened noticeably, and began collecting her things. "I . . . I have to go." She looked uncomfortable. "I have some things to do before fifth period."

As he scrambled for what to do next, a still small voice seemed to whisper in his ear. She pushed back her chair and stood up. He had to talk fast. "If I hear of anything, I'll let you know."

"Thanks." She managed a nervous smile.

"I'll be praying that God will give you the perfect job."

She stopped and stared at him, eyes wide.

"Why would you even do that?" she asked suspiciously. "You don't know anything about me!"

Taken aback, he wasn't sure how to respond. "Well . . . you're right. I don't know anything about you." He paused. A shot of boldness flowed through him. "But God does. He knows all about you, and He knows what you need."

Her eyes narrowed and grew cold. The wall he thought he'd been tearing down brick by brick was suddenly back up again, and higher than ever. "Well I don't believe that!" She spat out the words loudly.

Kids at the surrounding tables turned and looked at them. Embarrassed by the unwanted attention, Ellie quickly sat down next to him and lowered her voice. "Listen, if God knows what I need, then why did He let my father abandon us soon after I was born?" He could see pain in her eyes. "And why would He allow my mother to die when I was only seven? Seven! Do you have any idea what that did to me?"

Caleb stared back at her in stunned silence. This time, he was at a loss for words. "I . . . I'm really sorry you had to go through that." He fumbled for anything comforting. "It must be awfully hard for you to—"

"I don't want your sympathy!" Ellie cut him off sharply.

She leaned forward so no one else could hear. "All I want is for people to leave me alone. Just leave me alone!" Tears welled up in her eyes. She got up hastily and grabbed her backpack.

Then she rushed out of the cafeteria, leaving her tray and Caleb behind.

CHAPTER TWO

TWO COATS AND ONE HORSE

WEEKDAYS WERE PRETTY BUSY FOR Caleb. Especially Wednesdays. After a full day of classes, it was two hours of football practice, home for a quick shower and supper, and then off to church youth group from seven o'clock to eight-thirty. The youth meetings were great. About twenty-five or thirty kids came each week. They'd play ping-pong or Foosball for a while, and then sing a few songs and listen to a talk from the youth pastor before breaking into smaller discussion groups. Each week he'd leave early enough to pick up some of the other kids who didn't have rides, including B.J., Kelli Anderson, and her younger sister Krystal. While a ten-year old Hyundai sedan with over a hundred thousand miles, hail damage, and one different colored door wasn't exactly a teenage boy's pride and joy, it was a blessing his parents were able to provide for him.

Following the youth meeting, and after dropping off his friends, he drove home, passed on his usual evening snack, and went straight up to his room. He did a backwards flop onto his bed—one that might have set a school record had it been in the high jump pit—completely forgetting his promise not to do that. It was because of that exact maneuver that his previous box spring had been forced into an early retirement.

But tonight, Caleb didn't think about eating snacks or keeping promises. His latest encounter with Ellie consumed his thoughts. Lying on his back, fingers laced behind his head, he stared absentmindedly at the nearly invisible crack in the bedroom ceiling. It had been difficult explaining to B.J. in fifth period what had taken place between him and Ellie in the cafeteria. How many other kids had witnessed the awkward exchange? He didn't relish the idea of having to explain it to anyone else. What had he learned from her so far?

That she was desperate for a job.

That her dad had abandoned her and her mother had died when she was seven.

That she was hurting, and isolated, and angry at God.

But why did she need a job so badly? Who was she living with now? Where did she move from? And why did she move here just before her last year in high school? Replaying the events over and over in his mind, he sought to discover where he had gone wrong. He was certain the Holy Spirit had prompted him to tell Ellie that he would pray for her and that God cared about her. But he had been unprepared for her response. The flash of anger followed by the hurt in her beautiful brown eyes haunted him. It seemed he had touched on the reason why she kept to herself, why she wanted to keep everyone at a distance. It was obvious she was deeply wounded.

Who wouldn't be? To never know one parent, and then to lose the other one at such a young age would be devastating to anyone. He even understood why she might want to blame God. Despite her not wanting his, or anyone else's sympathy, he felt sorry for her. She was blaming and rejecting the only One who could offer her the hope and healing she truly needed.

He prayed softly, "Lord, please be with Ellie. She's had a tough time, losing her dad and mom. Show her how much You love her. And show me how I can help her find You." He started drifting off to sleep. "And please provide a job for her . . . one right here in Baxter."

Caleb didn't see Ellie all day Thursday. While he didn't have any classes with her, he usually caught a glimpse of her in the hallway between periods, or at lunch. Could she be sick? No. Most likely she was intentionally avoiding him. On Friday, instead of eating lunch in the cafeteria, he carried his tray outside to the "Senior Suite."

A dozen or so students dotted the eight picnic tables that were scattered randomly around the grassy courtyard reserved for the upperclassmen. Caleb selected an unoccupied one farthest from the others and sat down. Today he didn't feel much like eating with his friends in the cafeteria. Or even being around anyone for that matter. He wanted to be alone to think. And to pray. He had no idea how long he'd been sitting there when someone called his name.

"Caleb?"

He looked up. Ellie stood at the far end of the table. His heart pounded in his ears. "Uh . . . hi."

She glanced around uncomfortably, as if to make sure no one was within earshot, before speaking hesitantly. "I didn't mean to . . . to lose it the other day," she apologized.

For some reason, her terse statement sent his spirits soaring. "That's okay."

"I mean, I wasn't really angry with you. I know you were just trying to be nice."

Some of the self-assurance that had fled him returned. "You'd be surprised how many nice kids there are here at school." He thought of B.J. "You just need to give them a chance, that's all."

The pain flickered in her eyes again.

With a sheepish grin, he added hastily, "Of course, of all the nice kids here at school, *I'm* the nicest!"

She arched her brow skeptically. "Oh, really?"

"Sure. Just ask anybody!" For the first time he heard her laugh. It was the most beautiful sound he'd ever heard, and he would never forget it.

She shook her head. "I'll take your word for it." Then she grew serious again. "Look, I'm really not as bad a person as everyone thinks I am."

"I don't think you're a bad person at all," he reassured her, desperately wanting her to sit down so he could talk with her. "Care to join me for a minute?"

Recalling her opening comment from their last meeting, he motioned to the empty bench across the table. "Be my guest. After all, I recently heard somewhere that it is a free country!"

Ellie rolled her eyes. A faint smile threatened to reveal itself. "Well . . ." she hesitated. "Okay. But only for a minute."

She placed her backpack on the table between them and sat opposite him. "Look, here's how I see things: I'm stuck in Baxter for a year, okay? After graduation, I'm out of here! I really don't have time to make friends."

"A lot can happen in a year, you know!" He tried to be encouraging, but she didn't take the bait.

"Most of you have grown up together here. I'm the outsider. The new kid on the block. Anyway, I need to focus on my grades. And working all I can."

He fished around in his brain for something to say. "Still no luck with the job search?"

"Not yet. But I'm not going to give up. I can't afford to." She paused. "Where do you work?"

It was the first time she had actually asked him a question. Maybe the wall was beginning to come down again. "At the Pet Palace near the mall. I work there only a couple of nights and on Saturdays, though. Because of football. My parents bought me a car last year, but I have to pay for gas and repairs and stuff. It's not much of a car, but it gets me where I need to go, you know? Plus, I'm saving a little money for college expenses. That's why the job. What about you?"

"Well, I'm uh . . . I'm saving for college, too." She offered no further details.

"Where are you going?"

"University of Georgia, I hope." She looked around as if she wanted to leave.

"Me too! My parents are covering my tuition and room and board, but I have to pay for everything else. I applied in August, but I haven't heard anything yet. When did you apply?"

She hesitated long enough that he began to fear he'd said the wrong thing again.

"I um . . . I haven't yet." She stared at the table for a moment, then looked up directly at him. The hurt had returned to her eyes. "You're so lucky to have parents who are able to pay for college."

A million questions raced through his mind, but he checked himself.

Remembering how guarded she could be, he resisted the urge to ask who she now lived with. He was grateful for the little she had already shared.

Before he could figure out how to respond, she announced, "Hey, I really need to go." Ellie stood up and grabbed her backpack. "But I appreciate the chance to clear the air."

"No problem." A thought occurred to him. "Hey, listen. Some of us hang out at Edwards Drive-In on Saturday nights. If you don't have anything to do, maybe you could join us." Then, in case she might need more convincing, he added, "They've got really good food!"

"I doubt if I'll be able to make it. Once I find a job, I'll be working all the time." She started to walk away, but turned around. "Thanks for the offer, though."

Her smile, and the bounce of her auburn hair as she walked away warmed him in a way he had never known before.

––––––––––

Another week went by. Uneventful compared to the previous one. Caleb saw Ellie only in passing in the hallway on several occasions. They had exchanged a polite "Hi," but nothing more. He constantly thought about their interaction at the table in the Senior Suite. *She had approached him!* And she'd actually sat down and engaged in a brief conversation. That was the furthest anyone in school had been able to get with her—a fact about which he couldn't help feeling a little bit of pride.

During Wednesday night youth group, he shared the details with B.J, who seemed genuinely impressed.

"Just be careful, Caleb," he cautioned. "It's easy to let someone like her change you. You gotta admit, you've been pretty preoccupied with her lately. And that challenge thing? You know you don't have to prove anything to me."

"Yeah, I know, I know. But thanks for the warning, anyway." He grinned sheepishly. "I promise I'll try to control myself in the future."

––––––––––

Sitting through economics class and listening to Mr. Grossman drone on and on in his monotone voice had never been a particularly enjoyable exercise for Caleb, but one required for graduation. As he absentmindedly doodled in the margins of his class notes, he allowed his mind to wander to Ellie Thompson.

What was so mesmerizing about her?

Was it her looks? Her eyes? Her hair?

She was very attractive.

Or was it that she was a bit of an unknown, and therefore mysterious?

Perhaps it was the cold, hard fact that she was a real challenge, one which he had been so eager to tackle. Or could it be that he was actually falling for her?

No, he couldn't allow himself to go there.

Since giving his life to Christ back in the eighth grade, he had committed to putting Jesus first in everything he did. That included his social life. Two years ago, Tony Sonnenberg, his youth pastor, had spoken to the group about honoring God in their relationships. Caleb had been one of many who had voluntarily signed a pledge, based on the "unequal yoke" principle of Second Corinthians, to not only remain sexually pure until marriage, but to only date other Christians who were seeking to obey the Lord in their daily lives. While that commitment had narrowed the field considerably, he was determined to keep his promise. He had dated a number of girls since, but none steadily or too seriously.

No, he couldn't let himself fall for Ellie. But he wished he could somehow convince her to join his group of friends. They were all decent kids, and he was sure she'd fit in. If she'd only open up and give them a chance.

He began piecing together the threads of information he had extracted from her in their two brief conversations. She was hurting from the loss of her parents, and wanted to be left alone for the most part. She wasn't here by choice, and couldn't wait to graduate and get away from Baxter. Didn't want to make friends. Didn't have time. She wanted to go to Georgia, but hadn't applied yet.

Why not? Most kids had already applied to college and many had already been accepted. What was that she'd said? *"You're so lucky to have parents who are able to pay for college."*

That must be it! Whoever she was living with must not be in a position to help her financially. Maybe they made too much for her to qualify for federal assistance but not enough to help her themselves. No wonder she was in desperate need to find a job and work as much as possible. Right then and there, he determined to pray consistently for her. That she would find a job, find lasting friendships, find healing from the hurts of the past. He ignored his surroundings and prayed silently in his seat.

Saturday morning Caleb went to work and asked his boss, Mr. Pruitt, if he would be willing to hire any more help. As expected, the answer was "no." He already had ten people on the payroll, including Caleb and four other part-time high school kids. Later that night, he and three carloads of friends went to Cairo to play miniature golf. For the first time in a couple of weeks, he was able to put Ellie out of his mind and participate wholeheartedly in the laughter and horseplay. How they managed to survive an evening which involved golf clubs and golf balls without hurting someone or breaking something would remain one of life's little mysteries.

Afterwards, they drove back to the Dairy Shack in Baxter for ice cream. As the group of friends sat on the patio under the red and white striped umbrellas, defending their putt-putt scores, and debating who cheated and who hadn't, he couldn't help but wish that Ellie was there. She would have enjoyed the evening.

On Sunday morning, he and his family went to church. The red brick building with white trim sat on a hillside overlooking the town. Its tall white steeple could be seen from several miles away. His dad was one of the deacons and a "greeter," so the family usually arrived there early enough for him to meet people entering the building.

As soon as they arrived, Cassie dashed away to find her friends, a giggling gaggle of girls. Caleb went down the hall to the youth room and plopped down onto one of the old sofas lining the walls to wait for B.J., Kelli, and his other friends. After the youth hour was over, everyone gathered in the main auditorium for the morning worship service.

Following the songs, announcements, and offering, Pastor Murphy got up to preach. His sermon text was from the Gospel of Luke, the third chapter, and his subject was "The Fruit of Repentance." Caleb listened with interest.

John the Baptist, after living in the wilderness and receiving the word of the Lord, came into the countryside near the Jordan River, proclaiming that people everywhere should repent so that their sins could be forgiven. When people came to him seeking to be baptized, he told them to produce fruit in keeping with their repentance. The pastor explained that people who have genuinely repented of their sins will demonstrate that inward change by the way they live their lives. The people who came to John wanted to know what this looked like, so he gave them some examples: those with two coats were to give one to someone who had none, and they were to do the same with their food; those who collected taxes were to deal honestly and not steal by taking more than was lawful; and those who were in positions of power, such as soldiers, were not to use violence or make false accusations against those under their authority, and were to be content with their pay. As usual, it was a good sermon. But this morning, one phrase in particular stood out to Caleb: *"Anyone who has two coats should share with the one who has none, and anyone who has food should do the same."*

Following lunch and an afternoon of playing hoops with some of the guys at B.J.'s house, Caleb returned home, loaded some leftovers and snacks onto a plate, and retired to his room to finish some homework that he had intentionally neglected until the eleventh hour. He was in the middle of solving a calculus problem when the phrase from the morning's sermon returned: *"Anyone who has two coats should share with the one who has none, and anyone who has food should do the same."*

He pulled open his nightstand drawer, withdrew his Bible, and turned to Luke chapter three. He read the eleventh verse over and over. What did it mean for him? He had several winter coats and three or four light-weight jackets. Was he supposed to give some of them to someone who had none?

He couldn't think of anyone he knew who didn't already have a coat. Or food, for that matter.

"Lord," he prayed, "what are You trying to tell me? Who am I supposed to help?" He ended his prayer and finished his homework.

As he brushed his teeth and stared into the mirror, it suddenly hit him. The person God was telling him to help was Ellie! And it wasn't a coat she needed, it was a job. But he didn't have two jobs.

"Think, Caleb, think!" he urged himself as he slipped under his covers. Through no fault of her own, Ellie couldn't find a job, one she desperately needed in order to pay for college. But his parents were paying for his tuition. All of it. Plus room and board. His job was just for gas and oil, and spending money. What should he do, give up his only job for her?

He'd have to park his car and cut out all the fun at Edwards, and the bowling alley, and the Dairy Shack, and everything! He couldn't touch what was in the bank. That was designated for incidentals while he was at UGA.

"Lord, I don't have an extra job to spare. Are You telling me to give up my *only* job so Ellie can have it?" That didn't seem right. Besides, his parents would never agree to that. He hadn't even told them about her yet. He lay quietly for a while.

His mind drifted back to a few years before during a Wednesday night youth meeting. Once every quarter, instead of the usual program, Tony would schedule a Christian movie night, complete with popcorn, snacks, and sodas. On this particular night they had watched the movie *Sheffey*. Shot mostly in the Carolinas, it told the story of Robert Sheffey, a circuit-riding preacher who traveled the Appalachians on horseback during the mid to late 1800s, preaching and serving mountain folks wherever he could. He was a determined man of God, known for getting answers to his prayers.

In one of Caleb's favorite scenes, Mr. Sheffey came across a poor family whose horse had just died. But they didn't have any money for another one. He got down off his mount and began to pray that God would provide for their immediate need. Looking up at his own beloved horse, he knew he already had the answer. There was no need to pray. He gave his own horse to the needy family, and soon after that, God provided him with another ride.

He was certain he knew what God wanted him to do. He would give up his job and let Ellie take his place. Then she would have to acknowledge that God cared about her and that He answers prayer!

But how would his parents react? And what would *he* do for work?

He recalled Tony's words following the movie, "Whenever God tells you to do something, He'll always provide what is necessary to complete it. It may not be obvious, or easy, but He will provide."

―――――――――

"Dad, you got a minute?" Caleb paused in the doorway of the home office where his father was paying bills.

"Sure thing! Come on in." His father shuffled some papers to one side of the desk as Caleb entered the windowless room and plopped into the cane-backed chair facing him. "What's on your mind?"

Four days' worth of thought and prayer hadn't shown him how to approach the subject.

"I wanted your advice about something." Better to ease into it gradually.

"I'll give it my best shot." His father folded his hands across his stomach and leaned back in his chair. "Shoot!"

"Um, there's a situation at school I wanted to discuss with you. See, there's this new girl in the senior class. She just moved to Baxter this past summer. I found out she lost both her parents when she was very young, and she's still hurting from that. I think that's part of the reason why she doesn't want to make any friends. She needs a job so she can go to Georgia next year, but there's nothing available here in town." He paused to catch his breath. "And she doesn't have a car. I thought that since you're a member of the Chamber of Commerce, you might have some ideas about that."

His dad looked at him with a twinkle in his eye. "Ideas about what? The car or the job?"

"About a job, Dad!" he laughed. "She's been looking since they moved here, but the other kids have all the part-time jobs locked up." He waited for his father to reply.

Always careful to think before he spoke, his father took his time. "No jobs, huh?" Caleb shook his head. "Sounds like a community problem to me. We can't expect Baxter to grow if there aren't enough jobs here. Tell me, is her family able to help with expenses?"

"I don't know the details. I mean, I'm not sure who she's living with. She doesn't really open up to anybody. But from what I've learned, if she doesn't get a job, she won't be able to go at all."

"Well, there are other options besides going to Georgia this fall. What about the community college instead? It's less expensive, and she could live at home to save on room and board."

"I don't think she can even afford that."

"What about the option of waiting a year or two? By then she should be able to find something and save enough to at least get in."

His father's line of questions made him feel woefully unprepared for this discussion. He hoped his lack of knowledge wouldn't jeopardize the desired outcome. "I'm not sure about any of that. It never came up. But I know she's desperate. I'm grateful that you and mom are able to cover my tuition and room and board. But Ellie doesn't have that option. She's on her own, and it's not looking very good at the moment. I've been doing a lot of thinking about it. And praying, too. Dad, I'm convinced God wants me to give her my job at the Pet Palace."

He waited for the reaction, but none came. Instead, his father leaned forward, put his elbows on the desk, and clasped his hands.

Several moments passed before he spoke. "Hmm. How did you arrive at that decision?"

Caleb told him everything he knew about Ellie and how God had spoken to him. The words poured out. When he was through, he thought he'd done a pretty good job presenting his case.

"I think that's great, son." His father looked pleased. "I'm proud of you for being so sensitive to God's prompting. I'll agree that her needs seem to be greater than yours at the moment." He paused. "But what about your car? And your bank account? What you've saved so far won't last long once you're on campus."

Caleb wanted to say "But God will provide," but that sounded a bit presumptuous.

"I thought I might start up my lawn-mowing business again. I heard some of my old customers aren't happy with their current service."

"Okay, I'll go along with that, for the moment. But let me ask you a more important question. Why is it that you are so interested in helping this young lady?"

Caleb wasn't quite sure what he was driving at. "Well, um . . . to help a person in need. To show God's love. You know, the 'fruit of repentance' that Pastor talked about on Sunday."

His father looked at him for a long time, and then spoke slowly and gently. "Could it also be that you're hoping she'll be attracted to you once she hears you've given up your job for her?"

A burning heat rose in his face. "I . . . I don't think that's the reason, Dad. Honest! I really *do* want her to see how much Jesus loves her. And that He answers prayer." He feared his words sounded insincere.

"That's wonderful, Caleb. I believe you do. But how would she know that's why you're doing it? Can you see how she might think otherwise?"

Caleb considered that for a moment. "Yeah, I see what you mean. If she thinks I did it because I like her that might keep her from seeing the truth."

"That's right, son. Anytime we do something for God, we need to first check our own motives, and then make absolutely sure we do it in such a way that He gets all the credit."

Caleb could feel his cause slipping away, and with it, his enthusiasm. He was sure his dad was angling for him to keep his job.

"Do you suppose there's any way you could arrange it so that she wouldn't know how the job became available?"

Caleb couldn't believe what he'd just heard. "You mean you'd be okay with me quitting if I could do that?"

His father got out of his chair, walked around the desk, and placed a hand on Caleb's shoulder. "Caleb, I'm going to level with you." There was pride in his voice. "I believe your heart is in the right place. I can see you've put a lot of thought and prayer into this decision. You're convinced it's what God wants you to do." He smiled broadly, "If—and I mean *if*—you can work it out with your boss so that she won't know what you've done, I'll support you one hundred percent!"

Caleb had always looked forward to weekends. Two days with no school, Friday night lights, Saturday hanging with friends, Sunday church and a well-deserved rest. But this week, Saturday couldn't come soon enough. He planned to go to work and talk to Mr. Pruitt about giving his job to Ellie. Friday seemed to drag by unbearably slower than ever. He soldiered through biology and calculus, but economics was absolutely excruciating. Even study hall couldn't end fast enough today.

When the final bell rang, mercifully putting an end to the torture, Caleb exploded from his last period class into the sea of students filling the hallway.

"Wahoo!" He sprinted to his locker before Mr. Hartsock could station himself in his classroom doorway for the mandatory warning. He hurriedly threw some books and things into his backpack and headed upstream to B.J.'s locker. "Hurry up, dude! Let's get outta here! Time's a-wastin'!"

B.J. glanced up and tried his best to imitate the biology teacher. "Where's the fire, Sawyer?"

Caleb grinned. "Just hurry up, will ya?" B.J. took his sweet time before they left the building together.

Caleb's four-cylinder sedan laid down some rubber on the way out of the parking lot, risking a fine and suspension of school driving privileges.

That evening, as the Bearcats took the field for pregame warm ups, Caleb glanced into the stands. Mom, Dad, and Cassie sat near the top of the visitor's bleachers. He smiled inside his helmet. They could always be counted on to be there. As the teams prepared for kickoff, he surveyed the student section. Baxter was well-represented tonight.

He searched through the sea of blue and white. A twinge of sadness overcame him when he didn't see Ellie there. Of course she wouldn't be at a football game. She was probably home studying. Or out looking for work. For a moment he imagined her right in the middle of the crowd, cheering for him along with the rest of the student body. Then, embarrassed for allowing those thoughts into his head, Caleb turned his attention back to the field as the referee's whistle signaled the start of the contest.

Saturday morning came all too early for Caleb. After silencing his alarm, he lay in bed for several minutes, taking inventory of the aches and pains his body had accrued during the previous night's game. His left elbow was bruised where he'd taken a hard hit from the crown of an opponent's helmet. The defensive back had timed his hit just right, and the ball had popped loose before Caleb could safely tuck it away. It was the first time he'd dropped a pass this season, and he was determined not to let it happen again. His thoughts turned to his work. Today he would talk to his boss about letting Ellie take over his job. Following the discussion in the office, his father, had shared Caleb's decision with his mother.

At first, she had strongly opposed the idea of letting her son give up his job, especially for a girl he'd met only a few weeks earlier, and about whom he didn't know very much. But his dad had convinced her to go along with it, and she'd finally come around, albeit somewhat reluctantly.

Climbing out of bed, he wondered how he should approach Mr. Pruitt about the subject. As he dressed for work, several different scenarios ran through his mind.

It was five minutes to nine when he pulled into a parking space in the nearly empty lot in front of the Pet Palace. After clocking in and hanging up his jacket, he sought out the owner. He located him in the pet food aisle, inspecting a partial skid of puppy food.

"There you are, Caleb. Could you put up the rest of this skid? Aaron didn't get around to finishing it last night."

"Sure, no problem." Caleb grabbed one of the twenty-five pound bags and started stacking them neatly on the proper shelf. He turned toward Mr. Pruitt, but he had already disappeared around the corner.

First chance I get, Caleb promised himself.

The next opportunity didn't present itself until nearly one o'clock that afternoon. The store had been exceptionally busy all morning, and he had been given the tasks of keeping an eye on the puppy playpen near the front of the store, helping customers find various pet-specific products, and cleaning up a massive spill in aisle seven, thanks to a six-year old brat in serious need of a good spanking.

Toward the end of his lunch break, Caleb walked past the office and noticed his boss was alone behind the desk. The heavy wooden door was partially open, so he rapped lightly and stuck his head into the room.

"Uh . . . Mr. Pruitt?"

The man replied without looking up from his paperwork. "Yes? Come in."

Caleb stepped through the doorway into the tiny office and hesitated.

Mr. Pruitt glanced up. "Hello, Caleb. What can I do for you?"

"Do you have a minute? I need to ask you a big favor."

His boss paused, and then nodded and motioned for him to sit down. "Sure. Have a seat."

Caleb sat down in the worn padded chair in front of the desk.

Mr. Pruitt repeated his question. "What can I do for you?"

Caleb quickly prayed for the right words to say. "Well, I've worked here for almost a year and three months now. It's been a great job, and I really like it here." His tongue seemed to stick to the roof of his mouth. He wished he hadn't left the can of Sprite sitting on the lunchroom table. "This is really a great place to work," he added.

Mr. Pruitt tapped his fingertips impatiently on the desk. "Caleb, if you're leading up to asking me for a raise, I'm afraid I can't help you. We're on a pretty tight budget, as you know. And I just got notice that the insurance premiums for the full-time employees will be going up starting next month." He picked up the correspondence he'd been reading and waved it as evidence. "There's really nothing I can do for you at this time. I'm sorry."

"Um, Mr. Pruitt, I'm not here to ask you for a raise. I'm very happy with what I'm being paid now. You're very fair about that. I wanted to ask you to consider letting me give my job to someone else."

Mr. Pruitt frowned. "Give your job to someone else?" He shook his head. "I'm not sure I follow you. If you like it here, why would you want to quit your job?"

Caleb took a deep breath and launched into the reason for his request.

When he finished, Mr. Pruitt leaned back in his chair and drummed his fingers thoughtfully on the desk. "That's very generous of you, Caleb." He shot him a knowing look. "Of course, it certainly won't hurt your chances with the young lady, will it?"

Caleb blushed. His dad had been right about sending mixed signals. He would have to do this the right way, or not at all. "I don't want her to know how the job became available. In fact, the only way I can go through with this is if she doesn't find out that I quit so she could take my place."

Mr. Pruitt looked at him with admiration. "I don't believe I've ever heard of a more generous offer. But I'm curious about one thing. If you're not doing it to impress this girl, just why are you doing it?"

Recognizing the opportunity God was giving him, Caleb explained how the Lord had spoken to him through the Bible verse about the two coats, and the circuit-rider giving away his horse. He shared how he had sought his father's advice before following through on his decision.

Mr. Pruitt listened intently, and with deep interest. Then, after asking several questions about Ellie, he promised to interview her for the job without divulging Caleb's secret, and praised him for being so kindhearted. "I'm really going to miss you around here, Caleb," his boss lamented. "You've been an exceptional worker. I wish more of my employees had your character and heart. The world would be a better place because of it." He smiled, stood up, and extended his hand across the desk to the embarrassed youth. "Good luck, young man!"

Caleb scrambled to his feet and grasped the hand offered to him. "Thank you, sir." As he left the office, he nearly ran over Megan Harris. The part-time employee startled noticeably.

"Sorry! I didn't see you," he apologized quickly. She glanced nervously at him, and without a word spun on her heels and hurried away. Now that was odd. What was she doing outside Mr. Pruitt's office? And what had she overheard?

Shoving those questions aside, Caleb returned to the break room and cleaned up his lunch leftovers. His spirits soared. A deep sense of satisfaction in knowing that he'd done the right thing flooded his heart. Soon Ellie would have the job she so desperately needed, and maybe then she could acknowledge God's goodness and love for her.

With a smile on his face, he left the lunchroom and clocked back in for the rest of his shift.

CHAPTER THREE

I QUIT!

MONDAY COULDN'T COME FAST ENOUGH for Caleb Sawyer. All Sunday afternoon and evening he wondered when he would get the chance to talk to Ellie, what he should say about the job opening, and how she would react to the good news. In bed that night, he finally grew weary of rehearsing the endless possibilities, and came to the conclusion that it would be best if he just waited for the right opportunity, and then let the moment take care of itself.

Decision made, he rolled over, turned out the light, and fell asleep. He awoke Monday to the heavy rumbling of thunder. As he was getting dressed, raindrops began pattering against his bedroom window, and by the time he arrived at school and parked in the senior lot, it was coming down in sheets. Making a mad dash for the nearest entrance, he hydroplaned into the building. The other students had also brought puddles in with them.

Were it not for the anticipation of seeing Ellie, this would have been the perfect day to stay home in bed. Even the prospect of going through the day with wet clothes and frizzed-out hair didn't dampen his spirits in the least. But Ellie apparently wasn't at school, and it nearly drove him crazy. Between classes, he kept an eye on her locker, and waited for her in the cafeteria, but she never showed up.

She must be sick. He would have to try again tomorrow.

She wasn't at school on Tuesday, either, and by noontime Caleb could stand it no longer.

In the lunchroom, he asked around until he found Tanya Combs, who rode Ellie's bus. She told him where Ellie lived. He was a little uncomfortable about the whole thing, but chalked it up to nerves and suppressed the feeling. After football practice he would stop by her house to see if she was okay, and to tell her about the job opening at the Pet Palace.

As soon as practice ended, he showered in the locker room and changed back into his school clothes. Normally he showered when he got home, but tonight he didn't want to show up at Ellie's smelling like an old pair of sweaty socks. Pulling out of the senior parking lot, he headed across town.

Driving past his father's insurance agency, Caleb made his way through the downtown district. As he waited for a traffic light, an uneasy feeling prodded at him. Brushing that aside, he continued down the main street until he reached Ellie's neighborhood. The area had the reputation for being an undesirable place to live. The houses were small, and many were in need of some type of repair or maintenance.

By now the uneasiness weighed heavily on him.

He pulled into a convenience store parking lot to figure out what was going on.

It was as if the Holy Spirit were holding up a red STOP sign in front of his face. Caleb remained in his car outside the quick mart and prayed out loud. "Lord, what are You trying to tell me? Am I not supposed to be here?"

For a few minutes, he reflected on his plans. Might she still misconstrue his true motive if *he* were the one telling her about the job opportunity? Was this really any different than coming right out and saying that he had given up his job for her? Conviction filled his heart. No, he was *not* supposed to be here!

Caleb pulled out of the lot and headed back the way he'd come. On the drive home, he recalled being uneasy about going to Ellie's house even when he first thought of the idea that afternoon. But he had ignored the warning then, too.

By the time he pulled into his driveway, he had formulated a new plan. He would recruit B.J. to tell Ellie about the job! At school Wednesday, the two friends joined up in the cafeteria at noon, and after going through the food line, carried their trays outside and sat down at an unoccupied picnic table.

Caleb told B.J. how he had started for Ellie's house the night before to tell her about the job opening at the Pet Palace.

B.J. shook his head in disbelief. "I can't believe you did that. Not too smart, Caleb. What in the world were you thinking?"

"I'll admit, it wasn't the brightest idea I've ever had. Anyway, I never made it over there." He shared how God had prompted him to turn around and not be the one to tell her about the job.

"Well, at least that proves you're not totally hopeless . . . yet! No telling how she would've reacted if you'd shown up at her house uninvited."

"Yeah, pretty stupid of me, huh?" Caleb suddenly felt foolish.

"Probably saved yourself a lot of embarrassment, too." B.J. rubbed it in a little. "I seem to recall you saying something about trying to control yourself."

Caleb grinned sheepishly. "I know, I know. But I couldn't help it! She hasn't been in school for two days, and I was worried about her."

B.J. tilted his head to one side. "You expect me to buy that?"

"Okay," Caleb admitted, "the truth is, I couldn't wait to tell her about the job!"

"I think you'd be much better off if someone else did that. I mean, then you wouldn't have to worry about Ellie misunderstanding your intentions and all."

Caleb jumped through the opening his friend had just created. "Would you tell her for me, B.J.? After all, you're my best friend. And the only one I've really been able to talk to about this thing."

B.J. hesitated, and took a long sip of his Sprite. "I don't know." He paused reflectively. "She didn't give me much of a chance that one time I tried talking to her, remember?"

"Yeah, I know," Caleb pressed. "But this is different. She's really desperate now, and you'd be doing her a big favor. And me too. Come on! I'm sure she'll be grateful for the tip. Besides, how else is she going to hear about it if someone doesn't tell her? Mr. Pruitt isn't going to put a 'Help Wanted' ad in the newspaper!"

B.J. sighed and gave in. "Alright, alright, bro. I'll do it." He shot his friend a sly look. "Of course, this just may cause her to end up liking me instead of you, ya know!"

Caleb jokingly grabbed at his friend across the table, but B.J. pulled away and laughed hard enough that a dribble of Sprite came out of his nose.

"You know that's not why I'm doing this," Caleb insisted. He paused while B.J. wiped his face with his napkin. "We both signed the 'equal yoke' pledge, remember? I'm not trying to get her to like me so she'll go out with me. Right now she's hurting inside, and she needs to see God's love demonstrated in a real way. Maybe then she'll loosen up enough to make some friends. I'm pretty sure there's a lot of loneliness behind that mask she wears."

"Yeah, you're probably right," B.J. replied soberly. "I'm sure it would be good for her to make some friends." Then he grinned mischievously, "But, if she's going to make some friends, it might as well be us!"

Caleb wadded up his sandwich wrapper and threw it at B.J. "You're impossible!"

This time, the dribble of Sprite became a gusher.

Caleb found it hard to concentrate in class that afternoon. Harder than usual, that is. He passed Ellie in the hall between fifth and sixth periods, but resisted the temptation to say anything more than a passing "Hi." No need to risk doing anything that might negatively impact B.J.'s chances with her. But he was glad to see her back at school.

After last period, as he was putting away his books, he glanced down the corridor in the direction of Ellie's locker in time to see B.J. walk up to her. Part of him wanted to stick around, but he couldn't bring himself to watch, so he grabbed his jacket, closed his locker, and headed for the parking lot to wait for his friend. He'd get the full scoop on the way to B.J.'s house.

It was a while before B.J. emerged from the building and headed toward Caleb's car. He opened the door and slid into the front passenger seat.

"Well?" Caleb blurted out as soon as B.J. shut the door.

"Well what?"

"How'd it go?"

"How'd *what* go?" B.J. gave him a puzzled expression.

"Oh, so we're going to play the 'Let's Make Caleb Wait' game again, are we?"

B.J. chuckled. "It's way too easy messing with you, dude."

"Come on, man, what did she say?"

"Well, I asked her if she was looking for a job. And do you know what the first thing she said was? 'How'd you know about that?'"

"Oh, man," Caleb groaned. "What did you tell her?"

"I told her I'd seen her looking through the paper in the cafeteria. You know, that day she yelled at you to leave her alone."

"But *I'm* the one who told you she was looking for a job. In fifth period, remember?"

"Yeah, I know. But I did see her reading the paper that day. It wasn't a lie, Caleb! I just sort of, you know, combined both bits of information into one statement, that's all. What was I supposed to say, 'Caleb told me'? You did want me to keep you out of this, didn't you?"

"Yeah, okay, okay. So how did she respond when you told her about the job?"

B.J. apparently wasn't finished with having fun at Caleb's expense. "She seemed genuinely grateful," he began, in all seriousness. "In fact, she was *so* grateful, that right there in the hallway—in front of everybody—she *kissed* me and said I could be her boyfriend if I wanted to!" He looked over at Caleb and burst out laughing.

Caleb grabbed him and put him in a headlock.

Another weekend rolled around. Another academic week in the rear view mirror. Another gridiron clash in the headlights. This week, Baxter High faced its toughest challenge of the season, the Arlington Tigers. The rival school had been to the Georgia state semi-finals the past two years.

Oblivious to the main hall's chaos, Caleb loaded his backpack for the weekend. He was looking forward to the Baxter marching band spaghetti dinner, and so focused on the game, that he almost didn't hear his name called.

"Caleb?"

He looked up, surprise showing on his face. "Hey, Ellie!"

"I thought you'd like to know that I've got a job interview tomorrow morning." She smiled. "Finally!"

Caleb was pleased that she had gone out of her way to share the information with him. "That's great! Um, where at?"

He felt a twinge of guilt for pretending he didn't know the answer.

"The pet store down by the mall."

"You mean the Pet Palace?"

"That's right. The Pet Palace." She looked at him quizzically. "But didn't you say that's where you worked?"

He'd forgotten that one minor detail. "Well, I . . . I used to work there." He struggled to choose his words carefully. "But I decided I could, you know, maybe do better mowing lawns. I used to run my own lawn-care business before I worked at the pet store. For about two years. Now I'm focused on building my client base again instead."

His answer seemed to satisfy Ellie. "Oh, okay. Well, I just wanted to let you know that you can stop looking out for me now. Hopefully, that is! I don't have the job yet."

Caleb grinned broadly. "I don't mind looking out for you at all!" As soon as the words were out of his mouth he winced. Did he really just say that to her? But instead of the negative reaction he half expected, she rolled her eyes, and tried somewhat unsuccessfully to stifle a laugh.

"Well, anyway, thanks for thinking of me." She hesitated. "Or should I say, thanks for praying for me?"

Caleb was floored.

"Maybe there *is* something to that, after all." A momentary sadness filled her eyes. "At least for you, there is."

He swallowed hard, unable to find anything to say. Ellie started to walk away, but stopped and turned back to face him.

With a sincerity that surprised him, and a smile that engulfed him, she added, "Good luck tonight! I hope you have a good game."

The spaghetti dinner was a big success. Well over two hundred people attended the meal to show support for the Baxter Bearcats football team. Caleb sat with his parents and sister, along with a teammate and his family. Following the meal, the players suited up in the locker room and boarded the bus for the ride to Arlington. Three other buses, loaded with cheerleaders and students, many with homemade signs, fell in line behind the team bus. Fifteen or twenty cars, mostly full of students, completed the caravan.

Upon arrival at Arlington High School, while the rest of the entourage headed for the bleachers or the hot dog stand, the football team sequestered itself in the visitor's locker room for a quick pep talk by the coaching staff. Caleb could tell this game meant a lot to them. In Coach Davis' six seasons at Baxter High, his teams had played the Tigers four times, and had lost each time.

"Baxter has never beaten this team," he told the players gathered around him. "But tonight, the past means absolutely nothing! We start this game tied with our opponent zero to zero. They've won four games, but so have we. They're undefeated, but so are we. Whoever plays the hardest, the best, the smartest, will win this contest. Give it everything you've got, gentlemen. Leave everything on the field. Tonight is *our* night!"

Caleb loved these pregame speeches. They always reminded him of the line from the "Win one for the Gipper" speech given by Notre Dame coach Knute Rockne:

> " . . . sometime when the team is up against it and the breaks are beating the boys, tell them to go out there with all they've got and win just one for the Gipper."

If it was the last thing he did, Caleb intended to do just that for Coach Davis tonight.

The team huddled for the usual cheer, and then ran out onto the field to prepare for battle. There was an electricity in the stands as the game began. Even though the Tiger fans vastly outnumbered them, the Bearcat faithful were loud and proud tonight. Baxter won the coin toss and elected to receive. Following the opening kickoff, the Bearcats offense went three-and-out, and punted. The Tigers took over on their own thirty-nine yard line, and methodically marched sixty-one yards on thirteen plays, scoring on a two yard dive over center by Arlington's big fullback.

On the next offensive series, the Bearcats managed to move the ball pretty well, and picked up several first downs, including one by Caleb who caught an eleven yard pass off a slant pattern. The drive stalled at the opponent's twenty-nine yard line, however, and facing a fourth and two, they opted to go for it rather than to attempt a long field goal. Stopped inches short, the visitors turned the ball over on downs.

The rest of the half see-sawed back and forth. Both teams moved the ball well, but failed to score. The Baxter defense rose to the challenge and kept the Tigers out of the end zone again. At half-time, Coach Davis was effusive with his praise. They were only down by one score, and he was confident they could overcome that deficit. After making some minor adjustments on offense, he sent the team back onto the field believing that they had won the first half.

The second half became a bruising battle of stamina. With thirty-four seconds remaining in the third quarter, the Baxter kicker split the uprights for a twenty-four-yard field goal, and the visitor stands erupted.

But on the ensuing kickoff, Arlington's heftier front line began to show its superiority, and their running game took over. They ground out yard after yard, moving the ball down to the Bearcat nine-yard line, and scored on a naked bootleg that had everyone fooled.

Behind fourteen to three midway through the fourth quarter, the Bearcats put together a nice, long drive of their own, moving the ball down to the Tiger fifteen-yard line. On first and ten, Richie Davenport, the quarterback, called for a play-action pass.

The plan was for the tight end to run a short up and in pattern to draw the defensive linebacker with him, while Caleb, at wide receiver, was to curl under him and head downfield against one-on-one coverage. As soon as the ball was snapped, Caleb executed a flawless route, and streaked down the right sideline, a step ahead of the defensive back. Richie unloaded in his direction, but was hit just as he released the ball. It hung in the air, giving the safety time to sprint over from the middle of the field. Caleb had to slow up a bit, and as he leaped high, both defenders sandwiched him when he was fully extended.

Something popped in his side as he crashed to the turf along with the two defenders. The ball fell incomplete in the end zone. Caleb lay dazed on the field. With each breath there was a sharp pain in his rib cage. He thought he heard the Tiger defenders apologize, but then things became fuzzy.

When the cobwebs finally cleared, Caleb found himself sitting on the bench, minus his helmet and shoulder pads. One of the assistant coaches and the athletic trainer tended to him. His head ached, and his ankle throbbed from the awkward way he'd landed on it. But it was his ribs that hurt the most.

The trainer suspected a possible hairline fracture, and as a precaution applied ice and a wrap to Caleb's torso. Much as he wanted to get back into the battle, his night was over.

He tried to pay attention to the game. The Bearcats had scored a touchdown following the injury time-out, but the Tiger defense controlled the rest of the game. Although Baxter managed a thirty-one yard field goal with one minute and thirty-eight seconds left on the clock, Arlington held on to win fourteen to thirteen.

Following the game, his parents drove him to the Emergency Care Center in Baxter. Thankfully, the x-rays showed no rib fractures, but he had sustained severe bruising to the muscles on his left side. After wrapping his torso with a large ace bandage and prescribing some pain medication, the on-call doctor sent him home to get some rest. When he gingerly climbed into bed that night, it wasn't the ribs that hurt as much as the idea of being unable to play football for a while.

―――――――――――――――

"Dude! You gonna stay in bed all day?"

Caleb looked up from his laptop as B.J. came into his bedroom. "Hey, man! What are you doing here?"

"What do you think? I come bringing good tidings of great joy to my best friend, that's what. And an appetite for pot roast."

Caleb knew what kind of damage B.J. was capable of at the dinner table. "Yeah, well that's just fine, pal. But please leave me some seconds this time, will you?"

B.J. laughed.

"And whatever you do, don't make me laugh! It hurts when I laugh."

"Okay, I'll try not to." B.J. looked at the ace wrap peeking out from under Caleb's pajama top. "Where does it hurt?"

"Where *doesn't* it hurt? I still have a mild headache, but it's better than yesterday. The good news is I don't have a concussion or any fractured ribs. But I've got a big bruise on my left side, and it's really sore. Plus my right ankle is sprained, but I can still walk on it some. "

"Ouch! You really got beat up pretty good. Tough break."

Caleb told B.J. about the game, and how long he'd likely be sidelined from playing football.

Just then his father appeared in the doorway. "Dinner is served, gentlemen!" he announced.

Caleb gingerly got out of bed and hobbled downstairs for the Sunday meal. After dinner, B.J. hung out with the wounded warrior for about an hour.

Caleb told him how Ellie had initiated the short but pleasant conversation with him Friday afternoon. "And get this, B.J. She thanked me for praying about a job for her."

"Seriously?" His friend asked incredulously.

"No joke. We need to really pray for her," he added. "She's definitely hurting inside. I see it when I talk to her. But I think she's beginning to warm up a little."

"Maybe we can recruit Kelli and Allison and some of the other kids at church to begin praying for her, too," B.J. suggested.

"That's a great idea! Why didn't I think of that?"

B.J. shot him a wicked grin. "Probably because you've gone all gaga and giddy and . . . and googly-eyed over her!"

"You promised not to make me laugh!" Caleb protested weakly, holding his side.

Caleb didn't go to school on Monday. To appease his mom, he stayed home one more day to recuperate. Tuesday morning he felt well enough to drive to school. His right ankle ached a bit as he drove, especially when braking. But it wasn't too bad.

After parking, he made his way into the building with a noticeable limp, and was immediately greeted by a large number of well-wishers who all asked how he was doing. At first he didn't mind the attention, but by lunchtime he'd grown weary of explaining everything to everyone over and over again.

Entering the cafeteria, he headed for the food line, and reached the stack of empty trays just ahead of Ellie. He grabbed two trays, and handed her one.

"Thanks." She smiled politely. They began selecting items off the `a la carte menu as they moved down the line. "I heard you got hurt during the game Friday night."

"Yeah, I got banged up a little," he grinned. "But I'll live." He grabbed a bowl of fruit and a ham salad sandwich.

"I didn't see you in school yesterday. How are you doing?" Ellie asked as they slid their trays toward the cashier.

Could she have actually missed him? He'd grown tired of answering all the questions, but for some reason he didn't mind answering hers. "Well, I'm pretty sore. I've got a sprained ankle and some banged up ribs. And a big purple bruise shaped like Barney the Dinosaur."

She looked straight at him and laughed out loud. Her eyes sparkled in a way he'd never seen before. And they captivated him. Captivated him so much that he slid his tray right off the end of the counter and onto the floor.

───────────────────

"Okay, you can stop laughing now," Caleb pleaded. "It's ancient history!" He and Ellie had just sat down across from one another in the Senior Suite. She was still thinking about the tray incident a few moments earlier, and every so often stifled a laugh.

"So I made a first class fool of myself in front of the entire student body." He looked at her sheepishly. "You happy?"

Ellie put her hand over her mouth. "I'm sorry!" It didn't sound like she meant it. "But that was just about the funniest thing ever! If somebody caught that on their cell phone, they'd win *America's Funniest Home Videos* for sure!"

"Well, Terry McGinley didn't help any when he slipped on the grapes!"

They looked at each other and laughed together.

"I guess now everybody knows how much of a klutz I am." Caleb was positive he'd be hearing about this for a long time to come. He changed the subject. "Did you have your interview Saturday?"

Ellie held up her hand as she finished the bite she'd just taken. "Oh, that." She wiped her mouth with a napkin. "Yes I did. And I got the job!" She looked both relieved and happy, and he was relieved and happy for her. "I work Thursdays and Fridays four o'clock to closing, and Saturdays from ten to seven. I start day after tomorrow."

"That's fantastic! I'm really glad for you." Caleb took a swig of his soda and silently thanked the Lord for answering his prayers.

"What about your lawn-care business?" Ellie wanted to know. "I guess you won't be pushing a mower for a while, will you?"

"Not for a couple of weeks anyway. But it's all good. God's in control of things."

Ellie cocked her head over his last comment. "You always seem so . . . so confident about God. How can you be so sure of things like that?"

"Well, I guess it's because I have a personal relationship with Him," he began. "And He's proven His love and faithfulness to me time and again."

"What do you mean by 'personal relationship'?" she asked.

Ellie listened politely as he explained to her how he had accepted Jesus as his Savior at the age of thirteen, and how God had been with him from that moment on, keeping His promises, speaking to him through His Word, and answering his prayers.

"I'm glad that all works for you," she commented, "but I've never had reason to believe in God myself. If He does exist, I picture Him as this . . . this 'distant deity' who sits up there and watches us self-destruct.

He doesn't seem to care about our problems. If He does, then why doesn't He step in and do something?" Her question seemed genuine this time. The anger she'd expressed when he first mentioned God to her several weeks ago was gone.

"He did step in! That's what Christmas is all about. And the cross!" Ellie remained silent. As she quietly processed his reply, he stole a glance at the time. Fifth period was about to begin.

After they returned their trays to the kitchen, Ellie said goodbye and headed off to class. Caleb was thankful for the opportunity to share his faith with her. As he walked back to his locker to grab his books, it struck him that this was the first time she'd hung around for an entire conversation.

He was confident that real progress had been made in tearing down the brick wall that existed between them. And he was thrilled about that. Even sitting through Mr. Grossman's boring economics lecture later that afternoon failed to suppress his surging spirits.

═══════════════════════════

Caleb may not have been able to play, but he could still support the team. He watched his teammates scrimmage before heading home. Youth meeting was tonight. He quickly changed clothes and stopped on the way to church to pick up B.J., Kelli, and her sister. During prayer time, he told the group of twenty-four how he'd been able to share his faith with Ellie during lunch.

"Would you all pray for her?" he requested. "She needs to see how much God cares about her. And pray that she would see her need for Christ."

On the way home, Kelli spoke up from the back seat. "Caleb, you can count on me to pray regularly for Ellie. I'll try to reach out to her at school, too. She's in a couple of my classes."

"Thanks, Kelli," he replied gratefully.

On Thursday, as difficult as it was, Caleb intentionally avoided Ellie. He wanted to give her some space after their lengthy lunchtime conversation the previous day. But on Friday, eager to find out about her first afternoon at the Pet Palace, he stopped her in the hallway and asked if she'd like to have lunch with him.

"Thanks for the invite, but I can't today. I need to spend the time studying for my English composition test."

"No problem. I just wanted to find out how things went last night."

"Last night?"

"Yeah. Your first night at work. How'd it go?"

"Oh. Pretty good," she told him. "I think I'm going to like working there."

That was all he was able to get out of her before she had to go.

Saturday came, and Caleb and his father spent most of the day working on his car. The oil needed changing, as did the plugs and wires, and the front wheels needed new brake pads.

His dad insisted on doing the oil change and brake job himself. Around one o'clock, his mom called them in for lunch.

As they were washing up in the half bath off the kitchen, she pointed to the table. "Caleb, there's an envelope for you on the dining room table. I think it's your paycheck."

Caleb wiped his hands on the towel hanging next to the sink, and went into the dining room, completing the hand-drying process on his pants. He picked up the envelope with the Pet Palace paw print logo in the upper left hand corner, and tore it open. Inside was his final paycheck and a handwritten note from Mr. Pruitt. In it his former employer reiterated his praise for the work ethic and thoughtfulness of his former employee. He concluded by saying that if another position ever opened up, Caleb would always be welcome to come back and work for him.

There was a P.S. under the signature: "Please accept the enclosed gift as my way of saying thanks, and use it toward your college needs."

Caleb looked at the pay stub. In addition to the regular amount for the hours he'd worked, there was an separate line-item gift of $500.00.

After lunch, they went back outside to finish up the preventative maintenance on the Hyundai. Around four o'clock, with the repairs completed, and his chariot deemed roadworthy again, Caleb texted some of his friends to see if they were going to be at Edwards later on. B.J. replied that he had to work, but others responded affirmatively, so after cleaning up and changing clothes, he headed for the diner.

As he entered the red-and-white 50s-themed restaurant, the pleasant smell of fried food greeted him. He glanced around the interior. Some of his friends already occupied the corner booth near the back.

He walked past the pictures of James Dean, Elvis Presley, and Marilyn Monroe on the wall next to the take-out counter, and popped a quarter into the restored original jukebox. After selecting the Coasters' "Yakety Yak" from the "100 Greatest Hits of the 50s" play list, he pulled a chair up to the already crowded booth, and ordered a tenderloin with everything, a side of onion rings, and a draft root beer.

No better place to be on a Saturday night. As the friends joked and laughed and plowed their way through a mound of onion rings and seven or eight songs on the jukebox, he found himself wishing that Ellie could have joined them. If only she could see how much fun she was missing. Anyway, she was at work now. And socializing was not something Ellie Thompson had any interest in. But he could always hope that she might change her mind. Or that he could change it for her.

He would see her on Monday and talk to her then he promised himself.

Monday morning Caleb arrived at school ten minutes earlier than usual so that he could speak with Ellie. He'd given her plenty of space the past four days, but he wanted to ask how things had gone at the Pet Palace on Saturday.

He hung around his locker and pretended to straighten up the perpetual mess of books, papers, jackets, and gym clothes that always made closing the door a spectacle, while keeping an eye out for her. Soon he caught sight of Ellie's bouncing auburn hair coming down the hall. He gave her time to open her locker and hang up her jacket before heading in her direction.

"Hey, Ellie!"

She glanced at him. Her eyes grew cold, and she turned back to her locker without a word.

He tried again. "I um . . . how was your first Saturday at the Pet Palace?"

"I don't want to talk to you!" She spat the words into the depths of her locker.

Stunned, Caleb stood there. He hadn't been prepared for that type of reception. "Is there something wrong?"

She pulled her head out of the locker and stared straight at him. Her usually beautiful brown eyes were narrow, smoldering slits. "How can you even stand there and ask me that?" she demanded. "Did you really think I wouldn't find out?"

"I'm . . . I'm not following you." Confusion swirled in his head. "Wouldn't find out about what?"

"Don't play dumb with me, Caleb Sawyer!" Her voice drew unwanted attention from passing students, but she didn't seem to notice or care if anyone heard her. "I know all about it! What you did to get me on at the pet store!"

So that was it! She knew.

"Oh, you found out about that." Crimson crept into his face. Still, her reaction seemed way over the top, considering the sacrifice he'd made for her. Why should she be so upset about the kindness he'd shown?

But then, B.J. had labeled her a challenge at the start of school, hadn't he? Was he ever right!

"Yes I did. And I can't believe you'd do something like that!" Ellie glanced around and lowered her voice. Her tone changed from anger to hurt. "You had me convinced you were a really nice guy, Caleb. I thought you were different from most of the jerks around here." The hurt became bitterness. "But you aren't, are you? All that talk about God, and prayer, and Him being in control and everything. That was just a pack of lies, wasn't it? God didn't get me this job. *You* did!"

Caleb winced. "You weren't supposed to know about that. I didn't want you to find out. Honest! You've got to believe me."

"Of course you didn't want me to find out. Caleb, how can I believe anything you say after this? You're a hypocrite and a liar!"

"I'm really sorry you feel this way about it. I was only trying to help you, Ellie." A hard knot grew in his stomach.

Tears formed in her eyes "I don't want your help! Or your sympathy." She turned away and swiped at the tears with her sleeve. Then she closed her locker, picked up her book bag, and looked at him one last time. A deep sadness that just about crushed him laced her voice. "Caleb, I really thought you were different. I really *wanted* you to be different!" She paused. "Now, I just want you to leave me alone. Like everyone else. Just leave me alone, okay?"

She rushed off down the hall, still brushing at her tears.

CHAPTER FOUR

ONE BIG MISUNDERSTANDING

CALEB WAS TWENTY-FIVE MINUTES LATE to first period world history. After the scene at Ellie's locker, he ducked into the boys' restroom and escaped into one of the stalls. With the door closed, he retreated into the churning chaos that bubbled and boiled in his brain.

"What just happened?" Realizing that he'd spoken these words out loud, he quickly glanced under the stall dividers. To his relief, there was no one else there.

He took a deep breath and replayed the events of the last five minutes. He needed to figure out what had gone wrong. How in the world did she find out? Certainly Mr. Pruitt wouldn't have said anything to Ellie about their arrangement. Who did, then?

The only other person who knew anything was B.J. But he'd been very careful when telling Ellie about the job opening. No matter. He'd find the source of the leak. Somehow.

Why was she so angry about what he did? It didn't make sense. Hadn't he given the idea a whole lot of thought? Sought his dad's advice about it? Even prayed about it? He'd been so sure his actions would in some way help Ellie understand God's love for her.

"Dear Lord," he began, looking up at the ceiling, "where did I go wrong?"

What came to mind was something his youth pastor had written on the white board during a group discussion several months ago, "We should ask and seek the answers to five questions when determining God's will for a particular situation. One. What is God's Word telling me? Two. What is the Holy Spirit telling me? Three. What are godly counselors telling me? Four. What are the circumstances telling me? Five. What is my heart telling me? If we're surrendered to God, and the answers all line up, then we can be confident that we're doing the right thing."

He'd done that. And the answers had all pointed him in the same direction. A sense of reassurance and a peace washed over his troubled heart. As he sat alone in the stall, he prayed silently, *Lord, if I've done the right thing—and I honestly believe that I have—then it's up to You to work this all out. For Your glory.*

He left the stall, and stood at the sink. Splashing water on his face, he recalled the words of an old song his mother used to sing around the house when he was a little boy:

"I believe the answer's on the way, I believe the Lord has heard me pray;

'Cast not away your confidence,' saith the Lord our God.

Now by faith in Him alone I stand, Firmly held by His almighty hand;

Fully trusting in His promise, Praise the Lord!"

Caleb emerged from the restroom and entered the deserted hallway. He went to his locker to get his books. "I don't understand what's going on, but please help me trust You, Lord," he whispered quietly. "Don't let me lose my confidence in You!"

Then he walked into world history class, and into the middle of the Crimean War.

When the bell rang, Caleb made a beeline to B.J.'s locker. On the way he passed Chris Miller in the hallway. Around school, Chris had the unsavory reputation for being short-tempered, crude, and full of himself. He'd also been the first one to attempt flirting with Ellie at the beginning of the year.

"You really got roasted good, dude!" Chris shot him an evil grin. "Welcome to the burn unit!"

Apparently he'd witnessed Ellie's take-down of him an hour ago. Or heard about it second hand. Incidents like this usually spread across Baxter High's student population faster than a prairie fire in a Kansas windstorm. Caleb caught up with B.J. at his locker. His friend had a strange look on his face.

"Dude, what happened before school? I heard you and Ellie really got into it!"

Caleb groaned. He'd have to deal with this all day, and he dreaded the thought of having to explain it. "She found out, B.J. Somehow she found out about what I did!"

B.J. looked at him wide-eyed. "No way! That's bad news, man. But how?" He tilted his head to one side. "You don't think *I* told her, do you?"

The accusing words died on Caleb's lips. No need to accuse his best friend and hurt their long-time relationship. "No, I don't think you told her. But somebody did!"

"Mr. Pruitt?" B.J. wondered. "He's the only other person who knew about it, right?"

Caleb recalled his last paycheck with the very generous gift attached. "No, he wouldn't do that. I'm sure of it."

B.J. closed his locker and looked at his friend. "What are you going to do about it?"

Caleb wasn't sure what he was going to do about it. He couldn't very well talk to his former boss. That might come across as questioning his integrity. "I guess I've got only two options. Leave her alone like she wants, or get her to tell me how she found out. Somehow."

B.J. grimaced. "I vote for numero uno, pal! After the way she dissed you in public like that, you think the other one's a good idea?"

Caleb didn't think it was a good idea. Not a good idea at all. But he had to find out!

The week progressed slowly. Way too slowly for Caleb. Thankfully, by Wednesday the scuttlebutt around school had begun to die down a bit. Chris Miller, however, continued to sneer at him every time they passed in the hallway, and had even recruited Kenny Wilson and Adam Spencer to join his snarky team.

Caleb was beginning to understand why many kids dread the thought of going to school. His friends did their best to be supportive. They attempted to maintain the usual lighthearted banter, but although he participated in the conversations, he knew they were tiptoeing around the subject. That evening, he didn't much feel like going to youth group, but his parents urged him to go anyway. During snack and game time that night, Kelli pulled him aside from the rest of the group.

"I talked to Ellie in Biology this afternoon," she informed him.

"Oh yeah? How'd that go?"

Kelli hesitated. "Well, not so good. I was just trying to be friendly to her and engage her in conversation, but she made it pretty clear she wasn't interested."

"I guess she wasn't kidding when she told me she just wanted people to leave her alone."

"So, are you going to leave her alone?" Kelli gave him a teasing glance.

Caleb grinned broadly. "What do you think?"

"Not a chance!" Kelli laughed. "I know you too well, Caleb Sawyer. Then neither will I."

Thursday and Friday dragged by. When the bell rang ending the misery that was the school week, relief flooded through him. This had been one of the most difficult weeks that he could remember. What was it that Ellie had said right before fleeing the scene in tears?

"I really wanted you to be different!"

Those words stung more painfully than her plea to be left alone. Now, it seemed as though the Great Wall existed between them, along with a mile-wide moat filled with all sorts of vicious, hungry creatures. He'd permanently blown it with her this time. Ruined any future chance to show her how much God loved her. And ruined Kelli's and B.J.'s and everybody else's chances to do the same.

Caleb spent the weekend wrestling with his thoughts and feelings. Finally, unable to keep them to himself any longer, he confided in his mother on Saturday evening. While he often solicited advice from both parents, when it came to deep personal feelings, it was easier to talk to his mom about things of that nature. She listened patiently as he shared the mixed emotions he was experiencing as a result of his last encounter with Ellie.

"Caleb, my only advice is for you to trust the Lord, and if possible, seek some type of closure with her."

"That's not gonna be easy, Mom," he groaned. "I'm not sure I even want to tackle that task."

"I don't expect it will be easy, but you don't want the tension between you to remain and fester, do you?"

"No, I suppose not." He sighed heavily. His mother was right, of course. He must attempt to tie up the emotionally raw loose ends that still existed between him and Ellie in a mutually satisfactory way. "But how do I go about doing that?"

His mother smiled at him. "When the time comes, God will show you the way." Before praying with Caleb, she gave him Romans 12:18 to claim as his motivation.

If possible, so far as it depends on you, live peaceably with all.

He pondered that verse when he went to bed, and committed to giving it his best shot. Amazing how much lighter he felt, as if a weight had been lifted from his shoulders.

———————————

As Caleb drove to school Monday morning, he wondered how he was going to communicate his desire for proper closure. Ellie had left little doubt that she was just fine with leaving things the way they were. But he had to at least try.

"*If* possible, so far as it depends on you," he told himself.

Since emotions were still running high for both of them, and to avoid the risk of another humiliating confrontation, he decided to stick a note on her locker door. That way she could either respond to it or tear it up, whichever she wished. But at least he would have made the effort. During study hall, he drafted the note on a sheet of college rule notebook paper. After several edits and rewrites, he felt confident that he had stated his intentions as clearly as possible:

> Ellie, you said you wanted me to leave you alone, and I will respect your wishes. But I don't want to go through the rest of the year feeling like I have to avoid you all the time, either.
>
> I'd at least like to clear the air so there are no hard feelings on either side. I'm not asking for a second chance at a friendship.
>
> I know that's not what you want. I'm just asking you for a chance to end things on a positive note, so we can at least be civil to each other and move on with our senior year. If you agree to this, meet me at Edwards Drive-In tomorrow after school at 4:00. That should give you time to think it over. If you're not there, I'll take it you're not interested, and I promise not to contact you again. ~Caleb

He folded the note into a small square and wrote her name on the outside. As soon as the bell rang, he dashed to her locker, hoping to get there before she did, and wedged the note into one of the vent slots in the door so only a corner was visible. Then he hurried back to his own locker to wait. Soon Ellie came down the hall toward him. He pretended to be rummaging through his mess as she passed behind him.

He peered out of the corner of his eye. She stopped at her locker, and dialed the combination. As she pulled open the door, she caught sight of the note peeking from the vent. She pulled it out and started to unfold it.

And that's all Caleb stayed around for.

Slamming his locker door, he quickly darted off in the other direction before Ellie had a chance to read his note. Caleb intentionally avoided any contact with her for the rest of that day and the next. He waited until she had come and gone at her locker before going to his. He stayed out of her way in the cafeteria, hanging out with his friends at their usual table instead.

As Tuesday wore on, a knot formed in his stomach every time he thought about going to Edwards after school. She probably had torn up his note after reading it anyway—maybe even after seeing who it was from—and he was ninety-nine point nine percent certain she wouldn't be at the diner. As faint as it was, he still held on to that hope.

On the way home from school that afternoon, Caleb told B.J. of his intention to meet Ellie at Edwards in an hour.

"Seeking closure's not a bad idea," his friend agreed. "I'm all for that. But realistically, what are the chances of her showing up?"

"Realistically?" Caleb gave B.J. a look of resignation. "Slim to none."

"Hey, I admire you for making the effort, though," B.J. said as the car pulled into his driveway. "And I really do hope she shows up. I'd sure like to know how she found out that you got her the job!"

Caleb took his time driving to Edwards, which was a mile from the high school in the opposite direction. It was usually pretty empty this time of day, especially during the week. Plenty of time for a quick, private conversation before people started showing up for supper around five-thirty.

He pulled into a parking space off to one side, and entered the diner through the stainless steel and glass double doors with the words *Edwards* etched on each one. The little silver bell above the door jingled its usual friendly greeting. He glanced around the red and white decorated room, and saw that there were only three customers in the place.

Good, he thought. *Fewer distractions.*

He selected a booth near the back of the diner that offered the most privacy and sat down facing the front door. The waitress brought a menu and a glass of water to his table.

"Welcome to Edwards," she announced cheerfully. "Do you know what you'd like or do you need a few minutes to look over the menu?"

"Actually, I'm waiting for someone. I'll order when they get here."

"Sure. Take your time. I'll check back later." She smiled and then turned and walked back to the kitchen.

Caleb checked the time on his cell phone. It was three forty-nine. He repressed the feeling that this was going to be a complete waste of time. Even if she didn't show, he'd given it his best shot.

No regrets. At least he'd get a good meal out of the visit.

The little bell above the door jingled, jerking him out of his thoughts. He glanced up at the front door, heart pounding in his chest. False alarm. One of the customers was leaving the diner.

He drew a deep breath and exhaled slowly. "Please, Lord, let her show up," he prayed, "so I can end this thing in a way that honors You."

He sat there until his phone showed eight after four. The bell jingled again, but it turned out to be one of the cooks arriving for the evening shift. By four fifteen, he was ready to tell the waitress he'd changed his mind about ordering. He just wanted to get out of there and go home. He'd done all he could.

With a sigh, he slid out of the booth and zipped up his letter jacket with the big "B" on the back. He turned to walk up to the counter. His feet froze to the floor.

Ellie walked toward him. To say that he was surprised would have been the understatement of the year.

She approached the booth hesitantly. "Sorry I'm late," she said in a subdued voice. "It took longer to walk here than I thought."

He kicked himself for forgetting that she didn't have a car. "That's alright. I didn't mind waiting." He motioned toward the table. "Care to have a seat?"

"Okay." There was no emotion in her voice. Ellie slid into the booth and placed her backpack on the red faux leather bench next to her.

He quickly removed his jacket, tossed it on the other bench, and sat down facing her.

"I'm glad you came." He managed a slight smile, but she failed to return it.

"Look, Caleb, I'll come right to the point. I'm only here because you asked for a chance to clear the air. I guess I at least owe you that much."

"Well, thanks anyway for giving me the opportunity," he replied, grateful for her presence. "I don't like having bad blood between me and anybody else. I'd like to get things resolved and move on."

"I'll agree to that." She sounded a bit like a lawyer hashing out a business contract. "So, what is it you want from me?"

"Well, I'm uh . . . I'm really confused about a couple of things. First, why are you so angry about what I did? And second, who told you about it?"

Ellie stiffened and raised her eyebrows incredulously. "Seriously? Why shouldn't I be angry with you? You lied to your boss! You got someone fired! Just so I could have the job! You don't see anything wrong with that?" She glared at him. "And then on top of that, you have the nerve to pretend like it was all just an answer to your prayers!"

Caleb was gobsmacked. "Wait a minute. You're telling me I lied to Mr. Pruitt and got somebody fired?" He frowned. "What are you talking about?"

"Come off your high horse, Caleb!" Exasperation tinged her words. "I know all about it, so you can quit pretending now. Are you going to sit there and deny that you framed another employee to get Mr. Pruitt to fire him? Just so I could have his job?"

Caleb couldn't believe his ears. "Where in the world did you hear that?"

As she was about to answer, the waitress came back to the table with another menu and glass of water.

He turned back to Ellie and repeated his question. "So where did you hear that?"

"From one of the other employees who saw the whole thing."

He sat in stunned silence, his mind a tornado of thoughts. He desperately tried to grab a hold of anything that made sense, but so far, nothing did. He shook his head in bewilderment. "Who said that?"

Ellie hesitated, as if she didn't feel comfortable revealing her source. "Megan Harris. Saturday in the break room. She told me you planted some store items in an employee's coat. Somebody named . . . Adam Zuckerberg, or Zuckerman, something like that. And then you told Mr. Pruitt that he was stealing from the store. Just to get him fired."

"Megan Harris told you that?"

"That's not all!" Ellie sounded like a prosecuting attorney about to reveal a piece of evidence in a criminal trial. "She told me the real reason why you left, too. When Mr. Pruitt learned what had really happened, he fired you! Then he tried to get Adam to come back, but he didn't want to after what you did to him."

Caleb couldn't believe the extremes Megan had gone to in order to get him in trouble. All he could manage was "I don't believe it!"

"I didn't want to believe it at first, either." She narrowed her eyes suspiciously at him. "But then I remembered how much you wanted me to have a job, and how you said you'd quit the Pet Palace to go back to mowing lawns. Well, it all started to add up."

Caleb shook his head. "But Ellie! Nothing she told you is true! Not one word of it!"

"Then why did she say Chris Miller would back her up?" she shot back.

"Chris Miller?"

"Yes, Megan said if I didn't believe her to go ask him, and he'd confirm it. And when there are two witnesses who agree . . . " Ellie's voice trailed off. "At first she didn't want to tell me how I really got this job, but then she thought I ought to know the truth. She didn't want to see me get hurt any more. Actually, she was very nice about it."

Caleb ran his hands over his face in disbelief. Megan must have overheard his conversation in Mr. Pruitt's office and used the information to turn Ellie against him.

He took a long, slow breath. "I'm beginning to see the picture now. But I never dreamed she'd do anything this crazy!"

"What do you mean?"

"Ellie, let me tell you what really happened. Adam Zuckerman was a junior who used to work at the Pet Palace. But his dad got a job with

Boeing, and they moved to Seattle . . . a year ago last June! That's when I was hired to take his place. You can ask Mr. Pruitt. He'll verify all that."

Ellie didn't look convinced. "Well, if that's true, why in the world would she make up such a wild story like that?"

"I've gotta tell you about Megan Harris. I don't like badmouthing anyone, but you need to know this. Let's just say that she tried really hard to get me to, um . . . to go out with her about a year ago when I first started working there. But I wasn't interested in her at all because I signed a pledge at church to date only other Christians. Besides, she's got a pretty nasty reputation around school, if you know what I mean. But she kept hitting on me and doing everything she could to change my mind. She wouldn't take no for an answer! So, I finally had to sort of—you know—put her in her place to get her to stop. I thought she was over it, but I guess she's had it in for me ever since."

"But what about Chris Miller?" Ellie demanded suspiciously.

"I wouldn't worry too much about Chris."

"Why not?"

"Because he's Megan's current boyfriend."

"Her boyfriend?"

"Yeah, you can ask anyone. And they'll tell you he'd do just about anything she asked him to do. He's really not much different than she is, you know." Caleb paused to give Ellie time to process everything. Then he gave her a sideways look across the table. "You know the kind of person he is. I heard he was hitting on you the first day of school."

"Oh, that!" Ellie rolled her eyes and held up her fingers just inches apart from each other. "I came this close to slapping him."

He wished he could have been there to see her publicly shame the beast.

"He's so disgusting," she added.

Caleb decided not to mention how Chris had been treating him lately. There was no point in that. "You know what I think? I think Megan fabricated that whole story just to get back at me for turning her down. And she used you to do it. And she must have heard that Chris hit on you. I'll bet she blackmailed him into going along with her lie."

Ellie was quiet for a minute. "Well, that does all seem to fit, I guess." Then she presented her last piece of evidence. "But tell me this, if none of that is true, then why didn't you deny it when I first accused you? Why did you say you didn't want me to find out about it if it's all just a big lie? Hmm?"

All this time Caleb thought she was mad at him for giving up his job, when actually it was because she thought he'd lied to Mr. Pruitt and gotten Adam fired. No wonder she was so angry. But now he was backed into a corner. He could see no way around revealing what he had wanted to keep secret. It was time to tell her everything.

"I guess I'd better start from the beginning." He took a deep breath. "Ever since you told me you were looking for a job, I've been praying that God would provide one for you. Then I came across a verse in the Bible that says if we have two coats, we're to give one to somebody who doesn't have any. I figured I had two jobs, one at the Pet Palace, and one mowing lawns. And you didn't have any. So I prayed about what to do. I was reminded of a movie I saw once where a man gave his horse to a family in need. After that, God supplied another horse for him. So I decided to give up my job at the Pet Palace and go back to mowing lawns."

He smiled wryly. "Of course, I could have given you the mowing job, but I didn't think you'd appreciate that as much."

Ellie tried unsuccessfully to stifle a laugh.

"I tried to keep it a secret," he continued. "That's why I had B.J. tell you about the job instead of me. I didn't want you to misunderstand my intentions."

She sat quietly and avoided his eyes. Instead she stared at the table, fidgeting with her glass of water. "I . . . I don't know what to say." She sounded subdued and humbled. "I can't believe you did that for me. Giving up your job for someone you hardly know. Someone who hasn't been . . . .who hasn't been very nice to you at all."

Her eyes filled with tears, and he suddenly felt badly for her.

"Ellie, I never expected anything like this to happen. I'm awfully sorry for the pain I've caused you!"

She looked up at him in amazement and shook her head sadly. "Caleb, you shouldn't be apologizing to me. I'm the one who should be apologizing to you! I never should have doubted you in the first place. It's just that, well . . . I've never really had a good reason to trust anyone before." She paused and wiped her eyes with the napkin on the table. "I'm sorry for getting so angry with you."

An awkward silence filled the void until she looked straight into his face and pleaded, "Can you forgive me for even thinking that you could do such a terrible thing?"

Caleb exhaled slowly and smiled. "Sure! No problem." He reached across the table and put his hand on hers. She stiffened at his touch, but then relaxed and let his hand remain on hers. "Ellie, do you remember when I told you that I was the nicest kid in school?"

She nodded.

He paused for effect, and then gave her one of his patented mischievous grins. "Well, do you believe me now?"

The pent-up tension between them vanished, and Ellie burst into laughter. "I'll take your word on that!"

Several people came into the diner and took a nearby booth, distracting Caleb for a moment. Some of the dinner crowd was arriving a little early. Glancing at his phone, he saw that it was almost five o'clock.

The waitress returned to their table for the third time. "Are you ready to order yet, or do you still need more time?" She pursed her lips, and then chewed her gum furiously.

If he hadn't known her from all the times he and his friends had eaten there, he would have thought she was getting irritated.

Turning to Ellie, he asked, "Would you like to get something to eat? I mean, if we're going to be moving on and everything, we might as well do it on a full stomach!"

She laughed lightly, and then grew serious. "Well, actually, I think maybe I should be going."

His heart sank.

She picked up the menu laying in front of her and studied the pictures. "But the food does look pretty good." Flipping her auburn hair to one side, she tilted her head and looked up at him. "What would you recommend?"

Nearly an hour and a half later, with the ice half-melted in their glasses, and only a few traces of tenderloins and onion rings remaining on their white ceramic plates, he and Ellie still occupied the red booth farthest from the front door. The place was nearly full now, and the sounds of mealtime conversations and 50's music filled the air. They had talked about work, and school, and what their plans were after graduation.

Caleb learned that Ellie was very artistic, and liked to spend her time outdoors doing pencil sketches of buildings and landscapes around town. She said she enjoyed the peace and solitude those settings provided, but promised to show her drawings to him some time. Her dream was to major in drawing and painting, providing she could get into college.

When he asked how the application process was going, she told him she'd recently applied for federal aid, and would be applying for a partial academic scholarship to UGA. But if those means of assistance fell through, she might have to sit out a year, work to save up more money, and consider going to a community college instead.

Caleb told her he planned to major in architectural engineering with a minor in computer programming. He confessed to having difficulty maintaining focus in some subjects, but the hands-on approach to those two disciplines seemed to hold his attention.

During a lull in the conversation, he glanced at his cell phone. "Six thirty? Man, the time sure went fast!"

Ellie looked startled. "I really do need to be going this time!" She picked up the backpack beside her on the bench.

Caleb quickly wiped the table with his napkin and stuffed it into his glass. Then he grabbed his jacket and picked up the check left by the waitress.

"I've got this," he said matter-of-factly.

"Thanks! That's very nice of you." Ellie smiled.

After paying the tab, Caleb held the door open for her as they exited the diner. "Do you have a way home, or can I give you a lift?" he asked, hoping she would choose the latter.

"Oh, I don't mind walking," she replied, rather quickly. "I'm used to it by now."

As he began to mentally calculate the distance she'd have to walk, she added, "Some other time, maybe."

Caleb nodded, and then said goodbye before heading toward his car.

"Hey, Caleb?"

He stopped and turned at the sound of Ellie's voice.

She took a few steps toward him. "You once told me that God cares about me. Well I never believed that before. But now . . . " she hesitated. "Now you've given me a reason to think about it."

Those words were like heavenly music to his ears. All he could think to say was, "Well I'm glad!"

She closed the distance between them. "I told you I really wanted you to be different, Caleb." She suddenly reached out and put her hand on his arm, sending a zinger throughout his body. "And after tonight, I can see that you are!"

Then just as suddenly, she turned and hurried away, leaving him standing alone in the middle of the parking lot with the lingering memory of her sparkling brown eyes and her warm, soft touch.

Wednesday dawned bright and beautiful for Caleb. The fact that it was hump day failed to diminish his renewed enthusiasm for life this particular morning. Silencing his alarm, he lay back in bed, and allowed his mind to drift back to the conversation at Edwards. He was still amazed that Ellie had even shown up, and was eager to tell B.J. and Kelli and the rest of his church youth group about the breakthrough that had taken place. God was working, for sure!

He rehashed the lies that Megan Harris had so meticulously crafted to turn Ellie against him. How could someone be so cruel and vengeful? She must have known that her deception would be exposed, and that the intricately woven threads of her lies would eventually come unraveled.

Perhaps a person so miserable and desperate for attention simply wouldn't care if she were found out. In spite of the pain that Megan had inflicted upon him and Ellie, he felt sorry for her. And for Chris Miller as well. Before he got out of bed, he prayed that they would both come to know the forgiveness and freedom that he'd found in

Jesus Christ. He prayed the same for Ellie. Then he thanked God for the results of the previous evening.

So far as it depends on you, live peaceably with all.

No matter what the future held, it was satisfying to know that he'd done everything he could, and that a very difficult matter had come to such a peaceful resolution. At least between him and Ellie.

Throughout the next few days at school, he kept his distance from Ellie, figuring that might allow her time to recover from the raw emotions of Tuesday night. On Wednesday night, the other kids at youth group were energized when they learned how God had worked in diffusing the tense situation.

"I'll try again to reach out to her at school," Kelli promised him. "Maybe I could invite her to sit with us at lunch."

"That would be great, Kelli, but could you hold off on that for a few days? Let's give her a little space first."

"Sure. I can wait until sometime next week, if that's okay."

"Perfect!" He put his index finger and thumb together and gave her the "okay" sign.

Caleb was back on the Bearcat sideline Friday night as his team took on the Greenview Giants. The previous week, the team had dropped its second game of the season, losing to Grant County in overtime, and this week the Bearcats suffered a humiliating defeat at the hands of the Giants, denying them a chance for post-season play.

It was agony for him to stand idly by and watch his teammates get manhandled by their opponent. He ached to be out there with them.

It had been three weeks since being injured in the Arlington game. His ankle was fine and his ribs were healing nicely, but the doctor said it would be another week before he could start practicing with the team again. Hopefully, he would be ready to play in time for home-coming against Madison Central in two weeks.

On Monday morning, Caleb stopped Ellie in the hallway before school to see how work had gone that weekend.

"So . . . did you confront Spiderwoman about her intricate little web of lies?"

Ellie laughed and shook her head. "Not yet. I haven't figured out the best way to deal with her. I don't want any drama at work. That might jeopardize my job."

Later Caleb joined his friends at their cafeteria table. Talk about a fight that had broken out behind the bleachers during Friday night's football game was the main topic. Caleb hadn't heard about that.

"What happened?" he inquired eagerly. "Who was involved?"

"You're not going to believe this," B.J. told him, "but it was between Chris Miller and Kenny Wilson."

So his antagonists were beginning to self-destruct. While he didn't wish ill will or revenge on anyone, he couldn't help but think, *what goes around comes around!*

He glanced over at the corner table which Ellie usually occupied. She was busy writing something on a stack of papers. He decided to go see what she was doing.

He picked up his tray and zigzagged his way around the intervening tables toward her. "Okay if I join you?" Without waiting for an answer, he set his tray down next to her.

Ellie looked up from her writing and shrugged. "If you want, sure." She resumed her writing, but added, with a poorly disguised grin, "It's a free country!"

Caleb took the seat to her left. "Well what do you know? She talks and writes and tells jokes and everything!" He watched her for a moment. "Is that an application you're filling out?" The temptation to tease her got the better of him. "Don't tell me you're applying for a new job already!"

She looked up and laughed. "Not a chance! I love my job . . . it's the people I can't stand. I saw that on a T-shirt at an outlet mall once." She seemed more relaxed than he had ever seen her before.

He leaned over and noticed the red and black University of Georgia logo on the letterhead. "UGA application?"

"Remember that academic scholarship I told you about at Edwards? That's what this is. I'm hoping to send it off later this week."

Caleb recalled how much she was counting on this kind of financial aid in order to get into college, and offered his encouragement. "I'd say there's an awfully good chance you'll get one. I mean, with grades like yours, it should be a no-brainer . . . pardon the expression!"

Ellie ignored his anemic attempt at humor and frowned at him. "How do you know what my grades are? Mid-term report cards won't be out for another two weeks."

Caleb quickly explained how Jaime Starrett had accidentally seen her grade transcripts in the records office on the first day of school.

Ellie shook her head. "It didn't take long for that to get around, did it?" She shot him a wary look. "So what else does everybody around here know about me?"

"As far as I know, that's all. Do you think you'll get a full scholarship?"

"I seriously doubt it. They have only a limited number to offer, and there are hundreds of applications each year, most with better grades than mine. I'd be happy to get even a partial scholarship. Then if I get the federal assistance I've applied for, and with the money I hope to have saved by then, I should be able to at least pay for my first year. But that's a lot of 'ifs'!"

Caleb risked asking a question that had been on his mind since their first meeting. "I remember you said I was lucky to have parents who could pay for my education. I do consider myself very blessed that way." He hesitated. "Listen, Ellie, I don't mean to pry or anything, but . . . isn't there anyone who can help with your tuition?"

She was quiet so long that he began to wonder if he'd made the wrong decision by asking. But then she took a deep breath and looked him squarely in the eye. "Caleb, I've never been one to open up about myself to other people. I'm a very private person, as I'm sure you know by now." She flashed an embarrassed little grin. "I've gone through a lot of stuff in my life, and I've always handled it by keeping to myself as much as possible. For protection, you know?"

Ellie waited for him to respond, but when he remained silent she continued. "But I have to admit, I get so I can't stand it sometimes. That's hard to believe, right? I mean, here's this girl who pushes everyone away, and then wishes she had someone to talk to. Makes me sound kind of crazy, doesn't it?"

She seemed alone not crazy, and hurting, and afraid inside. A deep compassion for her welled up inside. If only she could see what God was willing to do for her—what He had done for her!

"No, you don't sound crazy to me. But you might feel better if you were to . . . " He thought back to their rendezvous at the diner. " . . . if you wanted to clear the air."

Ellie quirked an eyebrow. "Clear the air? You mean like you did at Edwards?" She sighed. "I'm sure that wasn't easy for you, either."

He saw what appeared to be admiration creep into her eyes. "I really respect you for doing that."

The bell signaling the end of lunch period interrupted Caleb's reply. Just when they were beginning to make progress! He didn't want this conversation to end here. No telling when—or if—he'd have another chance like this. "Time to go."

Ellie gathered the application papers and slid them back into the manila folder in her backpack.

Caleb stood up and stacked the trays together. "I'll take care of these. You go ahead."

"Thanks." She gave him a sweet smile. "I'll see you later."

That afternoon in Mr. Grossman's sixth period economics class, Caleb occupied his assigned seat but his mind was occupied elsewhere. He thought about how Ellie had started opening up when they were cut short by the bell.

Lord, please give me another opportunity like that. I know patience is a fruit of the Spirit, but sooner than later would be greatly appreciated!

He was sure God had a sense of humor. When the final bell of the day sounded, Caleb shot out of the seventh period and sprinted down the hallway toward his locker.

"Where's the fire, Sawyer?" The familiar cry of the exasperated biology teacher rose above the growing din that filled the corridor.

"Sorry, Mr. Hartsock!"

He dialed the combination on his locker and tugged repeatedly on the handle. With one definitive yank the jammed door with #134 on the front flew open, and several books, a ball of gym clothes, and a half-empty bottle of sport drink rushed out to eagerly welcome their owner home.

B.J. came up behind him as he tried to reload the items back into the limited space. "You need two lockers, bro! You oughta see if Karen will rent you half of hers."

His friend bent over and picked up a tightly folded piece of paper. "You dropped something."

"No kidding!" Caleb retorted, his head buried inside his locker.

"No, I mean this must have fallen out of your locker. It has your name on it." Caleb straightened up and looked at the small white object in his friend's hand.

B.J. scrutinized the tiny square of paper. "Looks like a girl's handwriting." He sniffed at it. "Smells like a girl, too!"

"Gimme that!" Caleb grabbed the note out of B.J.'s hand and stuffed it into his jeans pocket.

"Hey, aren't you even gonna read it?" his pal queried. "It might be something important. Like a marriage proposal or something."

"Shut up!" Caleb took a backhanded swipe at his friend, who managed to duck just in time. The pair left school in Caleb's car. After dropping off B.J. at his house, and denying countless requests to investigate the contents of the note that was burning a hole in his pocket, Caleb pulled back into the school parking lot to go watch football practice. But before exiting his car, he pulled out the note and unfolded it.

The handwriting looked familiar. He'd seen it before. On a scholarship application, maybe? Checking to make sure his windows were closed, he read it out loud:

> Caleb, you had the courage and decency to ask me to meet with you so we could 'clear the air' between us and move on with our senior year. You have proven to me that you have a lot of integrity, and that you are someone I can trust. That's not an easy thing for me to say. But I don't want to go through the rest of the year feeling like I have to avoid your

questions all the time, either. Unlike you, I *am* asking you for a second chance at a friendship. I know that's what you want. If you agree to this, meet me at Riverside Park in the gazebo tomorrow after school at 4:00. That should give you time to think it over. If you're not there, then I'll just have to keep after you until you show up! ~Ellie

CHAPTER FIVE

FLYING HIGH UNTIL THE WINGS FALL OFF

SCHOOL ON TUESDAY WAS A real drag for Caleb. His classes—even the few he normally looked forward to—were nothing but a line of unavoidable obstacles that had to be cleared in order to get to four o'clock. Time seemed to pass at a fraction of its usual pace, as if he were in the Twilight Zone or something. When the academic agony came to a merciful end, it was all Caleb could do to keep within the speed limit, both in the Baxter High hallway and on the road to B.J.'s house. After dropping off his friend, he drove to Riverside Park, one of several municipal green spaces in Baxter located across town from his subdivision and next to the Flint River near Ellie's neighborhood.

Rain began to fall as his two-tone sedan with the hail damage cruised slowly down the main road of the park, winding its way to the small parking lot near the river's edge.

Caleb parked close to the gazebo. He sat in his car and watched the water drops trickle down the windshield. A glance at his cell phone confirmed that he was almost twenty minutes early. As he waited for Ellie to arrive, he wondered what she would reveal about herself. He was glad she had initiated this meeting. That meant she was feeling more at ease with him.

He opened the dash compartment where he had stashed her note, and read through it for the twelfth time. *"You have proven to me that you have a lot of integrity, and that you are someone I can trust."*

Somehow reading those words in her own handwriting meant more to him than if she'd texted them. Of course, she wouldn't have done that. She didn't have his phone number, nor he hers. But he hoped she would soon feel comfortable enough to share that information with him, also.

Through the raindrop distorted glass of the passenger side window, he saw a lone figure in a hooded rain jacket hurrying toward him on the walking path adjacent to the road he'd just traversed. It was Ellie, and she was carrying a flat object wrapped in what looked like a plastic garbage bag.

He exited his vehicle and made a dash for the gazebo, as though his speed might somehow save him from a few more drops of rain. He made a mental note to keep a spare jacket in his car from now on.

Ellie ducked into the gazebo. "I'm glad you're here. I wondered if you would show up at all, with it raining and everything."

Caleb arched his eyebrows as high as possible. "What? And run the risk of you hounding me until I did? Not a chance!"

She broke into laughter. "Oh, that! You know I would have, too! Have you been waiting long?" She flipped back her hood and shook the water off the plastic-wrapped package in her hand.

"I got here a little early. Came straight from B.J.'s house. His is the last stop on his bus route, so I usually drop him off after school."

"That's decent of you. I'll bet he appreciates it." Ellie smiled approvingly. "So I guess you really are one of the nicest guys in school after all!"

"That's *the* nicest, Ellie. *The* nicest!" He couldn't resist correcting her.

She laughed again. It was quite becoming of her. "I'll take your word for it!" She gave her package one final shake and removed an artist's sketchpad from the plastic bag. "I brought some of my drawings to show you like I promised. Although this weather makes the paper a little damp."

The two of them sat down at the picnic table in the center of the gazebo. For the first time they sat on the same side. Ellie opened the sketch book and began showing Caleb some of her art work. He immediately recognized some of the locations that had inspired her drawings: the courthouse clock tower on the town square, the memorial statue at the entrance to Veteran's Park, St. John's Church with its two-hundred-year old architecture, the gazebo in which they were sitting.

It was obvious that she was a very gifted and talented artist, and he was quite impressed. "Has Mrs. Sinclair seen these?"

"No. They're just for me. It's kind of therapeutic, I guess. I go somewhere and draw when I want to get away from things." She grew introspective. "From certain people, I mean."

Caleb felt he should pursue that further, but something else popped into his mind instead. "Do you have any more of these drawings?"

"I've got stacks of them at home. Mostly pencil and charcoal sketches, but some watercolors, too. I've been drawing for as long as I can remember. I don't have some of my earlier ones, though. I've moved around quite a bit, and a lot of them have disappeared over the years."

"I think you ought to show them all to Mrs. Sinclair. She might be able to help you get an art scholarship or something. I'm sure she has connections with the art world, or at least she would know how to pursue that."

Ellie looked a little skeptical. "I don't know. I've never thought they were anything special. I just live in the moment, and draw what I see and feel." She paused for a moment. "Do you really think they're good enough to show her?"

"Are you kidding? I mean, I'm no artist or anything. Me, I can draw only stick figures!" Ellie laughed at his self-deprecating humor. "But I think these drawings are good enough to sell! Anyway, Mrs. Sinclair would be the one to tell you how good they really are." Then he added, "Don't sell yourself short, Ellie."

"Thank you for believing in me, Caleb." She sounded genuinely grateful. "I guess I don't have much self-confidence when it comes right down to it."

He wondered if her past, to which she had alluded, had anything to do with that. "When you said you draw to get away from certain people, did you mean the people you live with now?" As soon as the words left his mouth, Caleb feared he'd replaced them with his foot. But surprisingly, Ellie's only reaction was a sigh.

"Yes. They're definitely one of the reasons. But I'm not sure there's time to go into all that."

Caleb gave her a reassuring shrug. "I don't have anywhere else I need to be!"

She smiled, and then focused on the sketchbook on the table in front of them.

"Caleb, I don't like talking about myself. There are things in my past that are, well . . . painful for me to remember." She stopped suddenly, and then turned to face him. He could have sworn there was a twinkle in her eye. "But then, I did ask you to meet me here, didn't I?"

For the next two hours, surrounded by a gray shroud of falling rain, the only two people in Riverside Park sat huddled together under the gazebo. Perhaps it was the downpour that provided Ellie with the privacy needed to open up to Caleb. Her story came spilling out like long-held-back water suddenly released from a dam.

"I was born in Hickory, Virginia. It's just a wide spot in the road, really. My mother was eighteen at the time and not married. My father . . ." Ellie stopped as if the word was bitter to her taste. "My father abandoned us before I turned two. I don't remember him at all."

Caleb shook his head. "How did your mom manage? I mean, being that young and single and everything."

"She did the best she could. Her family completely shut us out of their lives. They wanted nothing to do with us, so she pretty much raised me without any help. I remember a babysitter while she was at work, but that's it. She worked as a waitress and a motel maid to support us. But then she was diagnosed with leukemia and passed away at the age of twenty-five. Just before my seventh birthday. Her name was Katherine."

Caleb empathized with her. "That must have been very difficult for you. Who took care of you after that?"

"Well, none of my relatives wanted the responsibility, so they tossed me into the state welfare system. I was shuffled between several foster care facilities. That was a nightmare!" Ellie gazed at the curtain of rain surrounding the gazebo. "I recall living in an orphanage for about two years before they placed me with three different families in Virginia. Then, when I was fourteen, I moved in with a foster family in Charlotte. But after a year of being physically abused, I was removed and placed with my current foster parents. Their names are Tony and Beverly Markle. They moved to Charleston when I was sixteen. Then four months ago they suddenly pulled up stakes and moved here. Just before school started. They won't tell me why."

Caleb could see the hurt in Ellie's eyes and could hear the pain in her voice as she talked about her life. He wished there was some way he could have learned about it without having her relive the past. Now he understood why she was so careful to avoid others. Keeping this to herself all these years must have been nearly unbearable. But the fact that she had chosen to confide in him was not lost on Caleb. He silently thanked God for her willingness to open up, but feeling the weight of that responsibility, also asked for the wisdom to know what to do about it.

Ellie suddenly looked embarrassed. She glanced sideways at him. "I'm sorry! I didn't mean to carry on like that."

"Don't apologize," he reassured her. "I'm glad you shared that with me. I think I understand you a little better now."

"Well, thanks for listening, anyway. I haven't met too many guys who cared about listening, especially to a girl. They usually only cared about—well, you get the picture." Caleb nodded, and she continued. "But you're different. I don't mean just about listening. You really care about people, don't you? And you have a . . . a confidence that isn't put-on or fake."

It was a good thing that Ellie was not omniscient. "Ellie, all that bragging about me being the nicest guy in school, you know I'm just trying to be funny, right? Truth is, I'm really no different than anyone else. The Bible says we're all sinners, and I'm just like everyone else when it comes to that. If you see a difference in me, I hope it's Jesus you're seeing. When I gave my life to Him, He made me a new person, and that's why I've changed. Anything in me that's good comes from Him."

"Well, you're one of the few people I've ever met who actually practices what he preaches. I wish I had your confidence about life."

"Any confidence I have is not in me, Ellie. It's in Christ! And His love for me."

Ellie contemplated his words. "I know you really believe that. And I'm happy for you. I wish I could believe that, too. But I honestly don't understand something. How can I believe that God loves me when He allows bad things to happen to me? Can you explain that?"

"I don't claim to have all the answers. But I do know that all the bad and evil in this world exists because of sin. God created a perfect world, but we're the ones who messed it up."

"Then why doesn't He do something about it?" she asked in all sincerity.

Caleb thought carefully before answering. "He did, Ellie. God didn't just say 'I love you'. He proved it! Do you know what John three sixteen says?"

Ellie rolled her eyes. "Yes, everybody knows that one." She grinned. "Even me! I went to Sunday School when I was in the first grade. But I've never really had much use for the Bible. Not since my mother died."

"'For God so loved the world that He gave His only Son.' That's just one of many. 'But God shows his love for us in that while we were still sinners, Christ died for us.'"

"You ought to be a preacher!" she teased. Then she grew serious again. "But isn't it easier to believe all that when you've had a good life? I mean, you have two parents who care about you. You have a nice family, and a home, and lots of friends, and your way paid to college, and a car. What about people like me who haven't had any of that? People who've lost someone close to them, or who've experienced awful things in their life, or who've never had anyone love them. It's not as easy for them to believe in God the way you do."

"Do you know Allison Wentworth? She's a girl in my church youth group who lives with her grandma and grandpa. Both her parents were killed in a traffic accident when she was thirteen. But that didn't stop her from believing in God. Don't be fooled by appearances, Ellie. A lot of us have suffered loss in one way or another, and we still believe that God loves us. In some ways, those difficult experiences make His loving-kindness more precious than ever!"

Ellie looked puzzled. "You said 'us'. How would you know? Your life seems just about perfect from where I'm sitting."

Caleb smiled, but the old familiar sadness crept in. "I do have a lot to be thankful for, that's for sure. But I've experienced loss in my life, too."

"What kind of loss?" Ellie seemed almost afraid to ask.

Caleb paused and took a deep breath. "I lost my brother when I was ten."

Ellie's eyes widened. "You . . . you had a brother? But I thought it was just you and your sister."

"It's just the two of us now. But I had a brother named Calvin, who was three years younger than me. We were up north one summer on vacation, visiting my cousins. One day we all went swimming in Lake Michigan. My brother wandered off down the shore a ways and chased a beach ball into the water where there were no lifeguards. The undertow swept him out before anyone could reach him, and he drowned. He was only seven."

Tears welled up in Ellie's eyes and trickled down her cheeks. "Caleb, I don't know what to say. I had no idea! I'm so sorry!" As she wiped her eyes with her sleeve, he resisted the urge to put his arm around her. "Why didn't you tell me this before?"

"Ever since you told me about losing your mother, I've wanted to tell you I understand how you feel. But I was afraid you'd think I was playing on your sympathies. You know, to get you to like me. Besides, it's not something my family talks about much."

"The hurt never completely goes away, does it?"

"Not completely, I guess. I know I'll always miss him."

"How did your family handle his . . . his loss?"

"Well, there were a lot of tears and sadness for sure. It still hurts when I think about losing Cal. But three months before he drowned, he gave his life to Jesus, so we know he's in heaven. That's very comforting.

Beyond that, I'd have to say it was God's love and grace that carried us through. I remember the preacher at his funeral read a verse that says we shouldn't sorrow in the same way as those who have no hope."

"No hope of what? Of seeing their loved ones again?"

"I think so. We miss them because they're gone. But for the Christian, it's only a temporary separation." Caleb could see that Ellie was profoundly impacted by this. She remained quiet and reflective for some time.

Ellie finally broke the silence. "So, I guess what you're saying is I can still believe God loves me no matter what bad things have happened, right?"

"Yes, and that other people care about you, too."

She smiled warmly, and placed her hand on his forearm. "I know you do!" Ellie hastily withdrew her hand and blushed noticeably.

Caleb added quickly, "I didn't mean just me." He grinned, "But that includes me! You know Kelli Anderson, don't you?"

"The girl who sits at your lunch table?"

"Yeah. I've known her since third grade. I drive her to youth group every Wednesday night. She's one who'd like to make friends with you."

"I know. She's talked to me several times at school, but I'm afraid I wasn't very nice to her." Ellie was apologetic. Then she asked shyly, "Do you go out with her?"

"Kelli? No! Well, not any more, that is. I dated her a few times last year, but we're just good friends now. Besides, she has a boyfriend, Aaron Johnson."

"Oh!" Was that relief he detected in her voice?

The two talked a while longer, waiting for the rain to let up. When it showed no sign of abating, Caleb glanced at his phone. It was getting late.

"We probably ought to be going. I don't think this rain is going to stop any time soon. May I drive you home?"

Ellie hesitated. "Thanks, but I live only five blocks from here. I'll be alright."

Caleb persisted. "Yeah, but what about your drawings?" He grinned. "I know you won't melt like the Wicked Witch of the West, but I'm not so sure about this!" He tapped the sketchbook with his forefinger.

Ellie laughed. "Okay. You convinced me!"

After wrapping her sketchbook in the garbage bag, the pair dashed to Caleb's car, where he held the passenger door open for her. Driving the half mile to her house, he could tell she was nervous, and he assumed it was because she was ashamed of the lower class neighborhood in which she lived.

Caleb pulled his car to the curb in front of a small bungalow in obvious need of repair.

"Here, let me get that door for you." He started to get out of the car, but Ellie quickly stopped him by placing a hand on his arm.

"No, I'm fine! Really." Caleb hesitated indecisively. She forced a smile. "I . . . I'm just not ready for you to meet my foster parents, that's all. But thanks for the lift home. And thanks for listening to me."

"My pleasure. See you at school tomorrow?"

"Sure. See you tomorrow." She got out and dashed up the crumbling sidewalk. He waited until she had entered the house and closed the door before he drove away from the curb.

The remainder of Caleb's week went incredibly well.

For one thing, Ellie seemed almost happy to see him, smiling and greeting him with a "Hi Caleb" as they passed in the hallways between classes.

On Thursday, much to his surprise, and at the invitation of Kelli, she joined his group of friends in the cafeteria. She didn't say much, but that was okay by him. The fact that she put forth the effort was a huge breakthrough as far as he was concerned.

And when Megan walked past their table on her way to the tray return line and saw Ellie enjoying herself with him and his friends, well, the look on her face was priceless!

Then to top it off, his doctor cleared him to begin practice with the team on Monday. That would give him four days to prepare for homecoming. Yes, the week was going incredibly well.

Friday night, Caleb traveled with his teammates to nearby Colquitt to play the Chargers. The Bearcats disposed of their win-less opponents, thirty-five to twenty. Coach Davis was happy to hear that Caleb would be back with the team on Monday, and promised to start him with the other seniors for their last homecoming game.

How much playing time he got would be determined by how well he reintegrated with the first string offense during those four days of practice.

The weekend flew by, and on Monday following lunch, Ellie pulled Caleb aside in the hallway to tell him that she had confronted Megan at work on Saturday.

"What exactly did you say to her?" he asked eagerly.

"I told her that her little web of lies didn't work, and that you and I both know the truth." She seemed very confident today.

"And how did Little Miss Muffett react to that?"

Ellie grinned, "All she said was, 'So what? You wanna make something of it? You gonna tell Mr. Pruitt?'"

"Well, are you?" he queried. "Going to tell Mr. Pruitt, I mean. Somehow I can't see you getting into it with her."

"Hey, buster! I can handle myself if I have to! I've dealt with worse than her before, believe me! But, no. I'm not going to tell Mr. Pruitt. I don't want him to think he gave this job to a drama queen."

"So how did it end?"

"Well, I said she might as well give up because we're onto her, and she can't hurt either of us anymore."

Caleb gave her an amused look. "And I'll bet that went over about as well as using a bowling ball in an egg toss contest!"

Ellie laughed out loud at his analogy. "Actually, she said I haven't heard the last of this. And neither have you! But I'm sure that was just an empty threat to save face. I think she was just blowing smoke and had to have the last word."

He was not convinced that Ellie was right about it being just an empty threat. Megan was not known for letting go of things quite that easily.

———————————————————————

On Tuesday, Caleb's euphoria hit some heavy turbulence, and he went into a tailspin. He was at his locker between second and third periods, when he happened to glance down the corridor in Ellie's direction. Chris had stopped and was arguing heatedly with her.

From where he stood, he couldn't hear what Chris was saying, but whatever it was, he could tell that Ellie was terribly upset by it. Other kids were giving the pair a wide berth, or watching from a safe distance.

Leaving his locker ajar, Caleb sprinted toward them in time to hear Ellie shout, "Leave me alone!"

As she tried to turn away, Chris reached out and grabbed the strap of her backpack and spun her around. "Don't turn away from me!" He cursed at her.

Caleb came up behind Chris and yanked him away from Ellie. "Back off, Chris!"

The forcefulness of his own voice surprised him, and startled Chris, who took a step back to collect himself.

Caleb turned to his friend. "What's going on, Ellie? What's he done?"

Ellie's reply was an emotional mixture of anger and tears. "He told me to leave Megan alone . . . said if I got her fired, he'd make me wish I had never messed with her."

Caleb turned on Chris. "Why don't you let your girlfriend fight her own battles? She's a big girl, now."

Chris got in Caleb's face and cursed him, too. "Why don't you mind your own business, punk." He gave Caleb an unexpected shove that nearly knocked him to the floor.

Caleb raised both his hands, palms outward. "Whoa, dude! Dial down the aggression, okay? We can handle this thing without getting physical."

"There's no 'we' here! This doesn't involve you," Chris snarled. "It's between me and her."

"That's where you're wrong. It's between Megan and her. You have nothing to do with it!"

By now a half-circle of students had gathered to watch the show.

"I told you to mind your own business!" He shoved Caleb again.

But this time Caleb stood his ground, and issued a final warning. "Don't put your hands on me again, Chris!"

Chris got in his face again. "Or what? What are you going to do about it?"

He was trying to goad Caleb, but Caleb wasn't taking the bait.

"I thought so!" Chris spat out the words with unconcealed contempt. Then he turned his back on Caleb and began to threaten Ellie again.

Caleb reached out and grabbed Chris' arm. "Hey, that's enough! I said this is between—"

Chris spun around and sucker punched him in the jaw, knocking him into the row of lockers with a loud bang. Then he pounced before Caleb could recover, and the two fell to the floor, wrestling and throwing punches.

"Fight! Fight!" The shout rose above the normal hallway noise.

Kids came running until the corridor was blocked in both directions. Caleb tried to get Chris into a headlock to avoid being struck in the face and stomach, but Chris, who was broad shouldered and nearly forty pounds heavier, was able to land a few blows.

Finally, Mr. Templeton, the school security officer, and Mr. Green, the calculus teacher, pushed their way through the crowd of students and managed to pull the boys apart. Caleb's nose was bleeding, and Chris had an angry abrasion on one cheekbone.

"Show's over, kids!" Mr. Templeton's voice boomed above the crowd.

The onlookers slowly dispersed. Turning back to the two combatants, he directed his attention to Caleb. "What's this all about?"

Caleb caught his breath. "He was harassing Ellie Thompson and put his hands on her. When I tried to pull him off, he shoved me, and then he punched me."

Mr. Templeton turned to Chris. "Is that true?"

"That's a lie! I was only having a conversation with her, and he came up behind me and grabbed my shirt. Yeah, I pushed him away. But then he punched me in the face!" Putting on an act worthy of an Oscar nomination, he gingerly touched his cheek and winced pathetically. "I had to defend myself!" Then he added, "See how much taller he is than me? It wasn't a very fair fight!"

Mr. Green eyed the heftier youth somewhat skeptically. "No, it probably wasn't. In any case, I think we need to continue this conversation in the Administration Office. You two have caused enough of a disruption to the educational process for one day." Mr. Templeton put his hand on Chris' shoulder and spoke firmly. "Let's go!"

Chris shrugged off the officer's touch, and scowled to show his displeasure, but went along with the other three to the school office.

After spending nearly an hour in the inner sanctum of the Administration Office, Caleb and Chris were released to join their respective classes in progress, with the warning that any further contact between the two would result in a call to the local sheriff's office requesting their removal from school.

Once the incident had been thoroughly investigated, they and their parents would be notified of the proper disciplinary action which, they were informed, could range from a write-up to a week's suspension.

At lunch, the cafeteria was buzzing with gossip about the fight. Rumors were flying faster than the fists that started them. Some had Caleb starting the fight to impress Ellie Thompson, while others had Chris blindsiding Caleb, who had to defend himself.

When Caleb walked through the double doors and got in the food line, a palpable hush descended over the room. He tried to ignore the stares and whispers, and began selecting his à la carte items as the crescendo of lunchtime conversations returned to its normal level.

He hadn't even sat down at the table before his friends were all over him about the incident.

"Caleb, are you all right?"

"What really happened?"

"I've heard all sorts of things!"

He gave them the abridged version of the incident. He noticed Ellie wasn't at their table, or the one in the corner, either.

He leaned toward Kelli, who was sitting next to him, and lowered his voice. "Have you seen Ellie? She was pretty upset."

"No, I haven't. Maybe she's in the Senior Suite today." He quickly scarfed down his meal and went outside to look for her.

She was not there. Knowing that she preferred solitude in times like these, he concluded there was only one other place to which she might withdraw.

Entering the quiet, carpeted room of the school library, Caleb looked around for Ellie, again ignoring the stares and whispers. He spotted her sitting in the corner, with her back to him, at one of the cubicles—a long countertop against the back wall with partitions separating the individual spaces.

He slipped inconspicuously into the empty cubicle next to her without her noticing. "Ellie!" he whispered in his best undercover voice.

She startled. "Caleb!" Then, realizing her voice was too loud, she leaned around the partition and whispered almost inaudibly, "Are you all right?"

"I'm fine. What about you?"

"I'm okay now. It took me a while to calm down, though." She paused. "I spent all of third period in the bathroom!"

He could identify with that escape tactic.

"I've never skipped class before."

"I don't blame you. You were pretty upset," he sympathized.

"So, what happened in the office? Are you in trouble?" She seemed worried. That was reassuring.

"Don't know yet. They're going to let us know about consequences once they finish the investigation."

"But you shouldn't be disciplined at all!" Ellie's reaction forced her to lower her voice again. "Chris is the one who started it."

"I know. But his account is, um . . . a little different than mine."

"What do you think they'll do?"

"I don't know. Mr. Green said it could be anything from a write-up in our student files to a week's suspension."

"A week! But that would mean missing homecoming Friday night, wouldn't it?"

That possibility was not lost on Caleb. "Yeah. But I hope it doesn't come to that. That would really hurt."

"Well, there were lots of eyewitnesses. They can prove you're telling the truth." She tried to sound encouraging.

"Don't forget, some of those eyewitnesses are Chris' friends. They'll take his side if asked. But most kids won't talk at all in situations like this."

Just then the librarian came over to remind them that there was to be no talking in the cubicles, and pointed to the signs posted in each to reinforce her position on the matter. Caleb whispered a "sorry" and got up to leave.

Ellie grabbed his arm. "Let me know as soon as you hear something, okay?" she whispered.

Caleb gave her a thumbs up.

"And thanks for standing up for me." With her beautiful brown eyes sparkling, she gave him her best smile yet. "It's nice knowing that someone as wonderful as you cares about me."

As he left the library, Caleb was smiling himself. It was nice knowing that someone as wonderful as Ellie cared about him, too!

Wednesday afternoon, during his sixth period economics class, a student volunteer from the office interrupted the lecture to hand Mr. Grossman a note. The teacher read it, and then walked down the row of desks to where Caleb slouched at his desk. Mr. Grossman leaned over and whispered, "You're wanted right away in the office."

Several nearby students let out an audible "Uh-ooooh!" as Caleb packed up his notes and left the room.

So this is it. He headed down the empty corridor to the Administration Office near the front of the school. In a few minutes he would learn his fate.

Any other week he would have gladly accepted a suspension. But to miss homecoming would only make it that much more difficult.

With his heart pounding, he pushed open the door to the outer office and approached the counter. The secretary had him take a seat on the worn vinyl bench outside the principal's office. He waited there for what seemed like an hour, but the clock told him it had been only ten minutes.

Finally the door opened and Chris emerged with a very unhappy look on his face. He scowled at Caleb as he passed and stormed out of the office without a word. His body language confirmed Caleb's worst fears. Chris had been suspended.

Mr. Abernathy, the school principal, stepped through the doorway. He motioned for him to enter. "Caleb?"

Caleb silently prayed for strength as he arose and entered the office.

The security officer sat to one side. Mr. Abernathy closed the door and offered Caleb the seat facing his desk. Then he took his place in the high-backed executive chair behind the imposing dark mahogany desk. He put his hands together and silently studied Caleb. An old-fashioned mantel clock that sat on the credenza under the window quietly ticked in rhythm to his heartbeat.

The principal took a breath and began. "Caleb, I'm sure you know why you're here." Caleb nodded. "I first want to say that here at Baxter High School, we have a very strict policy against physical violence. Fighting of any sort will not be tolerated. We simply cannot have these kinds of disruptions to the educational process. It's spelled out very clearly in the student handbook you sign at the beginning of every school year. As a senior, I'm certain you know that by now."

Caleb replied meekly, "Yes, sir."

"Good. Then you know that the consequences for such actions, depending upon the circumstances, warrant anything from a write-up in your permanent student record to a one week suspension from school, with no participation in school-related activities for that period of time. Do I make myself clear?"

"Yes, sir." He feared the worst.

Mr. Abernathy glanced over at Mr. Templeton, who nodded in silent agreement. "That being said, Mr. Templeton and I have reviewed the security tape of the incident in which you and Mr. Miller were involved on Tuesday morning in the main hallway."

Caleb had forgotten about the monitors strategically placed in the classrooms and halls throughout the building.

His principal continued. "From what we observed, Mr. Miller instigated the entire confrontation and was clearly in the wrong. It appeared you were trying to diffuse the situation, and the attack was totally unprovoked. You had every right to defend yourself. And Miss Thompson, I might add." He turned to the security officer. "Mr. Templeton, would you care to add anything to what has been said?"

"Just that I would encourage Mr. Sawyer here, as I did with Mr. Miller, to avoid contact with each other as much as possible. We don't want a repeat of what happened on Tuesday, do we?"

"No, sir!" Caleb replied adamantly. "I didn't want it to happen in the first place."

"We know you didn't, Caleb," Mr. Abernathy interjected quickly. "You've been here three and a half years now, and I've never known you to be involved in an incident like this before. Unlike Mr. Miller. Besides, it seems totally out of character for you."

Caleb was thankful for that kind of reputation, but he was anxious to hear about his consequences. The administrator must have sensed that.

"As to the consequences, we have suspended Mr. Miller from school and all related activities for a period of one week. As for you, since you were involved in a physical altercation, we are required to place the report in your permanent student file. But we have noted that you were not at fault, nor were you able to avoid the unfortunate incident. There will be no disciplinary action taken against you."

Caleb let the air slowly escape from his lungs with an audible "whoosh."

"I'm sure you're relieved." The principal smiled and glanced at Mr. Templeton, who grinned broadly. "You didn't want to miss homecoming, did you?"

"No, sir! That would have hurt worse than being suspended."

The two men chuckled. "Well, I guess that about wraps it up. Young man, you're free to go."

Caleb quickly got to his feet and shook hands with Mr. Abernathy across the desk.

"Thank you, Mr. Abernathy." He turned and shook hands with Mr. Templeton.

"Oh, one more thing, Caleb."

Caleb turned to the man behind the desk. "Sir?"

"Do your best to beat Madison Central Friday night will you?"

He heaved a sigh of relief. "I will! You can count on that!"

CHAPTER SIX

FACING THE OPPOSITION

EDWARDS DRIVE-IN WAS PACKED AND loud, even for a Saturday night. So packed that customers were lined up outside, waiting for tables to become available. And so loud that it was difficult to hear the person across the table, let alone the jukebox.

Most of the customers were Baxter teenagers, and most of the conversations were about the Bearcats' come-from-behind victory over Madison Central the night before. George Edwards, the owner of the diner, had pledged a complimentary meal to any Bearcat player should they win, and Caleb, along with most of his teammates, had shown up to claim their freebies.

"Nice game, Caleb," Mr. Edwards congratulated him as he personally delivered the free food to the wide receiver. "That was some game-winning toss you made."

Caleb nodded appreciatively. "Thanks! I'm usually on the other end of our pass plays. Coach sure knows when to call a trick play, doesn't he?" He pointed to one of his teammates sitting opposite him. "But don't forget about Nick here. We wouldn't have won if he hadn't caught my pass."

As he celebrated the win with his teammates and friends, Caleb wished Ellie could have gotten off work to be there. He'd been surprised to see her at the game, and he was flattered to learn that she had switched hours with another employee so she could watch him play. Tonight he found himself missing her.

Throughout the day on Monday, Caleb and his teammates exchanged fist bumps and high fives with the other students for their win over Madison Central. He felt like a celebrity surrounded by adoring fans—minus the autograph seekers, of course.

The only downside to the day was that he didn't see Ellie at school.

Tuesday morning before first period, he caught sight of her at her locker,and stopped by to see if she had been sick. But as he approached, she turned her face away from him.

"Hey, Ellie! I didn't see you at school yesterday. Were you sick?"

"I'm fine today," she replied, her face still buried in her locker.

There was more to her absence than a simple twenty-four-hour flu bug. She must have sensed his thoughts because she added, "Really, I'm fine! I just didn't feel well yesterday, that's all. Congratulations on the win Friday night."

"Thanks." He leaned against the locker next to hers, and spoke firmly but gently. "Okay, Ellie. There's something bothering you, isn't there? What's up?"

For a second he thought she was going to tell him to go away. After all, she was pretty good at letting a person know when she was through with a conversation. But instead, she turned and faced him. A bruise darkened her left cheekbone, and her eyes were a bit red and puffy, like she'd been crying.

"What in the world happened to you?"

She hedged a little as she spoke. "I uh . . . I had an accident at work Saturday. Ran into the edge of a door, that's all. No big deal."

He didn't buy that explanation. "Come on, Ellie. That's not what happened, and you know it!"

For a split second, anger flashed in her eyes, and then, just as suddenly, the sadness he had often seen replaced it. Suspicions whirled in his mind.

"Did Megan Harris do that to you?" He wouldn't put it past her at all. "Because, if she did . . . " he let his voice trail off.

Ellie glanced briefly at him. "It wasn't Megan." She turned away again.

"Who, then? I know you didn't get that bruise by running into a door." He attempted to lighten the tension. "Ellie, you're really not that good of a liar, you know."

The corners of her mouth upturned slightly, and then flat-lined again.

The owner of the locker that was acting as Caleb's prop arrived at that moment, so he stepped back and circled behind Ellie and posed the question again from the other side. "Then who was it?"

Ellie glanced up and down the hallway, then lowered her voice so that only he could hear. "I'll tell you at lunch, okay?" she whispered. "Meet me in the Senior Suite."

"Okay, I'll be there." He looked at her bruise again. "You sure you're okay?"

This time she managed a smile. "Yes, I'm okay. I'll see you at lunch." She closed her locker and headed off to class.

Throughout the morning, Caleb caught himself speculating as to who had inflicted the mark on Ellie's face. If not Megan, then who? To his knowledge, no one else at school had any motive for striking her.

Then again, Megan could have manipulated one of her friends to do the dirty deed, just as she had coerced Chris. Usually he did not harbor resentment toward others, but today he wrestled with feelings of bitterness. Only he didn't know whom to be bitter with.

By lunch time, he was so worked up about it that his appetite had fled. Instead of going through the food line, he went straight out to the courtyard to wait for her. About ten minutes later she came out with her tray and walked around the picnic table to sit next to him.

"No lunch today?" she asked, noticing he had no tray or food.

"I'm not hungry." He fiddled absentmindedly with a loose pine knot in the wooden table top.

She popped open her can of soda. "Caleb, you're not a very good liar, you know!"

He looked up sharply and caught her trying to hide a grin. His pent-up tension evaporated. "Okay, I had that one coming. I'll admit, I've been pretty steamed about this all morning."

"Well, you can set your mind at ease. It doesn't involve anyone here at school."

"It doesn't? Then who . . . " He stopped, recalling their rainy day conversation in the park. "It wasn't your foster parents, was it?"

She didn't respond, but he could tell from the look in her eyes that he'd struck pay dirt. "Which one?"

Aware of the harshness in his voice, he back peddled and approached her with a gentler tone. "Ellie, I really need to know what happened."

Ellie let the air slowly escape from her lungs. "It was my foster mother. We got into another argument. Sunday night. And it escalated into a shoving match. And then she hit me with her fist."

Anger welled up in Caleb. "That's assault, Ellie! You could have her arrested for battery." He tried to keep his voice under control. "Did you call the police?"

"No. I don't want to go that route. It would only make things worse."

"I don't understand. How would reporting that make things worse?"

Ellie glanced around to make sure no one was within earshot. She lowered her voice. "Do you remember at the park when I told you I've lived with the Markles for two years now?" Caleb nodded. "Well, in that time things have gone from bad to worse."

"What do you mean?"

"The only thing they care about is money. Tony—I can hardly bring myself to refer to him as my foster father—Tony does handyman work, but only when he feels like it. Which isn't very often. Beverly works part-time for minimum wage as a cashier at the convenience store on Seminole Street. The rest of their income comes from the state. It's supposed to be for my care, but most of it goes for alcohol and drugs. For them, I mean. Not for me."

"Well, I assumed that," he snorted, hoping to lighten the mood. "Have you ever turned them in?"

Ellie sighed. "I called protective services on them twice, but both times they were able to hide their addictions and convince the caseworker that I was the problem."

"How'd they manage that?"

"Caleb, you have no idea how good they are at the art of deception." Ellie's voice was filled with frustration. "When the authorities investigated, both of them concocted these elaborate stories and even went as far as to provide false evidence to convince them that I am this deeply disturbed and rebellious troublemaker at home."

"Did anything ever come of those investigations?"

She shook her head. "Nope. Nothing. Unless you count my foster parents' threats of physical harm if I ever turned them in again."

No wonder she was so nervous when he had driven her home. She was not only ashamed of her home life but afraid of what might happen if he met them.

"Have you ever thought of just . . . leaving?" he suggested.

"I've run away three times. Twice when I lived with another family in Charlotte, and once last year in Charleston when I was with the Markles before we moved here. But each time the police picked me up off the streets and returned me to them." She paused. "Caleb, can you see why I had trouble trusting you at first?"

Too numb to reply, he nodded.

Defiance crept into her voice. "But I'm older now, so I'm not afraid to try it again. But my plan now is just to hang on until I turn eighteen. Then I'll be emancipated and finally out of the system. And rid of them for good!"

Caleb thought about this for a moment. "When's your birthday?"

"December nineteenth." Then she added triumphantly, "Only six more weeks from today!"

"But where will you go?"

"I don't know. The homeless shelter on Hawthorne, maybe. Even if it's under a bridge, it'll be better than where I am now!"

Caleb's heart ached for her. It was hard to hear her talk like this.

He tried putting himself in her place, but was unable to comprehend what she must have to endure every day. He wished there were something he could do for her. Anything at all.

"Ellie," he chose his words carefully, "would you allow me to pray that God would provide you with a place to live? I don't mean the shelter or a bridge, but a nice place. A house?"

As she considered his offer, he wondered if their discussions about God's love had made any impact on her. Her response provided the answer.

"Caleb, when you first told me you'd pray that I would find the perfect job, I didn't believe in that. But then I saw how God answered your prayer by telling you to give one of your two jobs to me." She shot him a wry grin. "You don't happen to have two houses, do you?"

Caleb laughed heartily. "No, I'm afraid I don't. But God has the perfect place for you. Not only here in Baxter, but in heaven, too. Do you know what Jesus said about heaven?"

Ellie shook her head.

"I learned a verse in Sunday School way back when. John fourteen, six says, 'In my Father's house are many rooms. If it were not so, would I have told you that I go to prepare a place for you?'"

Ellie tilted her head thoughtfully to one side. "Funny you should bring that up. I've been thinking about heaven lately. Remember when I told you my mother used to take me to Sunday school when I was in the first grade?"

Caleb nodded and she continued. "Well, she used to tell me the same thing. I can still remember some of it." She smiled. "Do you know what I think? I think my mother might be there right now. In heaven, I mean."

Caleb's heart skipped a beat. "Wouldn't you like to know how you can go there, too?" he asked hopefully.

Ellie hesitated. "I need more time to think about that. It's a lot to process. But maybe we can talk about it again some time."

Caleb smiled. "That would be great, Ellie! Whenever you're ready." He reiterated his original offer. "So . . . can I still pray with you about a place to live here on earth?"

The sparkle in her laughter was only surpassed by the sparkle in her eyes. "Sure, Caleb, I'd like that very much!"

School returned to normal once again for Caleb Sawyer.

Ellie was now a regular at his friends' table in the cafeteria, enjoying the lighthearted banter with the others. Although somewhat quiet at first, it wasn't long before she began participating in the conversations. He'd known she would fit in and be accepted by his friends, and he was thrilled to see her open up to the group in general, and to Kelli in particular.

Ellie needed another friend besides himself, and he was confident that Kelli would be a good one for her.

Chris had served his week-long suspension and was now back in school. Apparently choosing to follow Mr. Templeton's advice, he kept his distance from Caleb.

The mocking comments had stopped, and when the two passed in the hall, he avoided eye contact with Caleb. Even Megan seemed to have cooled her jets a bit, according to Ellie.

Although the two girls still worked the same shift on Saturdays at the Pet Palace, Megan refused to talk to Ellie at all, a snub that suited the brown-haired beauty just fine.

Caleb reconnected with a few of his old lawn care customers, and once football season ended, he was free to mow lawns not only on Saturdays but after school on weekdays as well. He was relieved that his college savings account would finally begin growing again. He wanted to tell Ellie about his acceptance letter to UGA. It had come in the mail two weeks earlier, but he chose to withhold the news from her. She was still waiting on responses to her academic scholarship and enrollment applications, and he didn't want to discourage her in any way.

One mid-November Friday, Caleb was at his locker exchanging textbooks between classes, when Ellie hurried up to him.

"Caleb, guess what?" She sounded out of breath.

He glanced up and noticed the big smile on her flushed face. "Well, whatever it is, it must be awfully good news."

"It is! Mrs. Sinclair is taking some of my drawings to an art show in Columbus this weekend, and she thinks I stand a good chance of placing high among the competition," she gushed.

Caleb could not remember a time when Ellie had ever gushed before, and it certainly added to her attractiveness. "That's great, Ellie. Congratulations!"

"And that's not all. The best part is that the judges are all art instructors from UGA's College of Fine Arts! Wouldn't it be wonderful if I won my division, and they offered me the scholarship I applied for?"

If anyone needed encouragement, it was Ellie. After all she'd been through in her life, she could use some positive news. He silently prayed that she would garner the attention of the judges. But no matter the outcome, it was good to see her excited about something for a change.

When last period ended, Caleb danced his way down the hall with the usual "Wahoo!" As he and B.J. headed out of the building, they made a detour past Ellie's locker, where she was packing for the weekend.

"Hey, Ellie, do you have time to hang out at Edwards after work Saturday night?" Caleb asked.

"Well, I'd like to." She hesitated. "But I don't have a way to get there from work. The bus goes only between the mall and my house. Edwards is in the opposite direction."

Caleb was undaunted. "Then I'll pick you up from work. How's that?"

"I don't get off 'til nine." She frowned. "Is that too late?"

"Not at all!" he exclaimed, unable to curb his enthusiasm.

Her look of appreciation was not wasted on him, or B.J, who razzed him about it all the way home from school.

Saturday evening, Caleb sat in his car outside the Pet Palace. He'd left his friends back at Edwards to pick up Ellie at the end of her shift. B.J. and Allison had just announced to the group that they were now officially an item, and he had chided his best friend for not telling him the news first. As he waited for Ellie to get off work, he imagined how much she would enjoy hanging out with the others, and wondered how she would react to the news.

It was some time before she emerged from the pet store and headed toward his parked car. He could tell immediately from the look on her face that something was wrong. Reaching across the seat, he pushed open the passenger door and she slid in beside him.

As soon as the door was closed, she turned to him, distraught. "I think I'm about to lose my job, Caleb!" She sounded close to tears. "What am I going to do?"

Caleb was stunned. His mind raced. "What happened?"

"Mr. Pruitt called me into his office just before I clocked out and said he suspected me of stealing from the store."

Shock rocked him. "Stealing? Why would he accuse you of stealing?"

"He said he was in the employee break room and noticed some store items sticking out of the pocket of my work apron hanging there. He asked if I had the receipt and I didn't."

"What kind of items?"

"Small things. A dog collar, a chew toy, stuff like that."

"What would you want with things like that? You don't even have a dog."

"Exactly! I don't have any use for those things. Caleb, I didn't put them there!"

"I know you didn't," he said reassuringly.

Ellie put her hand on his. "Thank you for believing me, Caleb." She looked relieved.

"But I can't imagine that Mr. Pruitt would fire you based solely on circumstantial evidence like that," he exclaimed.

"Well, he said that things started disappearing shortly after I began working for him. Inventory keeps coming up short all the time. And get this, he said someone told him they suspected it was me. This person thought they saw me slipping things into my pocket."

"Megan?" Caleb wondered out loud.

"Who else could it be?" she lamented. "Nobody else has anything against me, as far as I know."

"What did Mr. Pruitt say he was going to do?"

"He told me he would look into the matter thoroughly and let me know his decision next week."

"I could go in and talk to him for you if you like," Caleb offered.

"Thanks, but I don't think that would do any good. After all, Megan has worked there over two years. And the thefts have occurred only since I was hired."

"I see what you mean."

"It doesn't look good, does it?"

"I'm afraid it doesn't," he agreed reluctantly.

"Would you pray for me?" Ellie pleaded. "I don't know what I'll do if I lose this job."

Delighted with her request, Caleb readily obliged. *She's come a long way from not believing in this kind of thing.*

He took her hand and prayed out loud. "Dear Lord, You know the truth. Please help Mr. Pruitt discover what's really going on. And help Ellie not to worry about it. You've got this under control. In Jesus' name, amen."

"Thank you, Caleb." She was noticeably relieved.

"Would you rather I take you home instead of to Edwards?" he asked considerately.

"Home? No, it's too stressful there." He shot her a concerned look and she quickly added, "I'd rather go to Edwards. I'm starved!"

After they arrived at the diner and secured their food, Caleb was relieved to see her jump right into the gang's conversation-in-progress as though nothing had happened. But as he drove Ellie home that night, he asked how things stood with her foster parents.

"Well, the situation hasn't improved at all since I got into it with Beverly. The tension's been building, and to be honest with you, it's just about unbearable! I'm not even sure I can hang on until my birthday."

"Until then, is there somewhere you can go so you don't have to spend any more time at home than necessary?" he asked.

"Well, like I told you before, I spend a lot of time around town drawing pictures. And I go to the public library sometimes, especially when the weather's bad. Or I might get a coffee at McDonald's or Wendy's. Being at work has helped take my mind of things, too." She paused. "That is, until now."

As Caleb drove home after dropping her off, he couldn't shake the heaviness of heart he felt for her. Even with the recent positive social interactions, her life was still marked by pain and misery. And in spite of all his efforts to help, he felt totally inadequate. As he pulled into the family driveway, he determined to talk to his youth pastor about it in the morning.

Following the Sunday morning worship service, Caleb sat down with Tony in the youth leader's small office, and explained Ellie's home situation to his mentor.

"I feel so helpless sometimes," he confessed. Shrugging his shoulders, he added, "What more can I do?"

Tony pondered his dilemma for a moment. "Why do you feel like you have to do anything at all?"

Caleb wasn't prepared for that question. "Well, I guess because God has used me before. Why shouldn't He use me now?"

His youth pastor smiled. "Caleb, I'm glad you're willing to let God use you. Don't ever get over that. Always be ready to do what He directs you to do." He paused. "But do you think God is limited to using only you in this situation?"

Caleb thought about that. "No, I suppose not. But I always seem to be right in the middle of everything, though."

"If that's where God has placed you, then great," Tony encouraged him. "Just be sure you're there for His purposes, and not your own." He paused to let Caleb think on that statement. "Do you catch my drift?"

Caleb looked down at the floor and grinned sheepishly. "Yeah, I hear what you're saying. I've asked myself that question several times." He looked up at Tony. "But I really do want her to see that Christ is the answer. She's come a long way since I first met her. If only she'd give her life to Him."

"Caleb, that's what all of us who are praying for her want. But sometimes we can unintentionally get in God's way. We think we have to fix the problem, when it's not ours to fix. Let God provide the answer. He doesn't always use the same methods, you know. Don't box Him in. He's infinite. Give the need to Him, and then step aside and watch Him work it out."

"Do you think I've gotten in the way?" Caleb wanted to know, needed to know.

"That's not for me to say," Tony replied. "That's between you and God. But sometimes we face problems that are beyond our ability to solve. They're not meant to discourage us, but to get us to trust Him more. That way, when He provides the answers, He gets the glory, and we get our faith increased."

"Well, I want God to get the glory," Caleb assured him. "And I definitely could use more faith!"

Tony laughed. "We all could." He placed his elbows on the desk and leaned forward. "Caleb, you're doing a wonderful job demonstrating the love of Christ to Ellie. God knows your heart, and I'm convinced your efforts will be rewarded. Why don't we pray about the situation before you go? Is that okay with you?"

"Sure." The two bowed their heads.

"Father," Tony prayed, "thank You for putting the desire in Caleb's heart to reach out to Ellie. We see evidence of You working in her life already, and we pray that You would resolve her crisis at home in such a way that will show her how much You truly love her. And use all this to bring her to a saving knowledge of Your Son, Jesus. In His name we pray, amen."

Caleb felt lighter in his spirit as he left the office. The battle was no longer his to fight. It belonged to the Lord now.

On Monday, Ellie shyly announced to the lunch group that Mrs. Sinclair had just informed her that her drawings had won the blue ribbon in the Columbus art competition over the weekend. One of the judges had even expressed interest in seeing more of her work, and the art teacher wanted her to bring in the rest of her portfolio.

As the friends congratulated her on this achievement, Caleb saw the pure joy in her eyes. But as the week progressed, Caleb noticed Ellie becoming more and more anxious. He tried his best to encourage her, but it was obvious that she was having a hard time awaiting Mr. Pruitt's decision.

Come to think of it, his job was not without its troubles, either. Although he'd been doing his best to drum up new business, so far he had been able to line up only two regular customers, one former client and one new one. That was a far cry from his earlier heady expectations, and nowhere near what he needed for income.

On Tuesday night he voiced his concerns to his father, even expressing doubts as to whether the decision had been the right one or not. His dad reminded him of his reason for returning to the lawn care business, and reassured him that God would work all things out for good.

Following the pep talk, Caleb was struck by how truly blessed he was to have such godly mentors in his life.

Wednesday evening, Caleb prepared to go to youth group. As he stepped out of the shower, he heard his cell phone beeping. When he saw the name of the caller, his heart skipped a beat. It was Mr. Pruitt.

With trembling hands, he accessed the voice message:

"Caleb? This is Mr. Pruitt at the Pet Palace. I'd like for you to come in to the store tomorrow afternoon at 4:00 if possible. I have something I need to discuss with you in my office that's of a rather urgent and private nature. If you can't make it, please call me back and we can make other arrangements. Otherwise I'll expect you here at four. Thanks!"

Caleb replayed the message twice, trying to read between the lines. This undoubtedly had to do with the accusations against Ellie, and her future at the Pet Palace. All sorts of thoughts ran through his mind as he drove to pick up B.J.

What should he say about Ellie?

How well did he really know her? It hadn't been until recently that she had even opened up to him.

While it didn't seem to fit her character, what if she really was stealing from the store?

Throwing suspicion on Megan would be the perfect cover if she had been caught red-handed. He suddenly felt ashamed for allowing those thoughts into his head.

Although he couldn't be one hundred percent certain that Ellie was innocent, he had to believe the best about her. For her sake.

Who else did Ellie have to stand up for her but him? And who else did Ellie have to trust in but him?

If he didn't believe her, she would probably never trust anyone again. Especially God!

Although he couldn't recall the exact reference, a verse in First Corinthians popped into his mind, *love bears all things, believes all things, hopes all things, endures all things.*

How could he ever expect Ellie to put her trust in God's love if he was not willing to demonstrate it himself?

No, he had to believe that she was innocent of that which she was accused. She had given him no indication of dishonesty.

Throughout his Thursday morning classes, Caleb debated whether or not to tell Ellie about Mr. Pruitt's phone message, especially since his former boss had referred to the matter as rather private. However, at lunch, it was Ellie who made the decision for him.

"Caleb, could I talk to you alone?"

"Sure. When we're done eating I'll walk you back to your locker."

After returning their trays, the two walked slowly together down the half-empty hallway. "I can tell you're worried about something," he began. "And I'll bet I know what it's about."

"Caleb, I got a call from Mr. Pruitt last night asking me to meet him in his office this afternoon." She looked at him with sad eyes. "I have this feeling he's going to let me go, and there's nothing I can do about it."

Caleb started to say that maybe he could do something about it, but thought better of it. "Ellie, all you can do is tell him the truth, that you had nothing to do with the missing inventory, and that you have no idea how those items got in your pocket. He has to know anyone could have put them there."

"But it's my word against this other person's. Who do you think he's going to believe? The new girl or the long-time employee? He has no choice but to let me go."

They reached her locker, and she dialed the combination. "I really needed this job, Caleb. It was fun working there. Now I don't know what I'm going to do."

It was difficult standing there and seeing her so hopeless. "At least let me drive you to the Pet Palace after school," he insisted. "I can give you moral support, if nothing else. What time does he want to meet with you?"

"Four. And yes, I'd like you to come with me. I need all the support I can get."

"He said to meet you at four?" he asked.

"Yes. Why?"

Caleb hesitated. "Ellie, Mr. Pruitt left me a message last night, too. He asked me to meet him this afternoon in his office. At four."

She looked at him with questioning eyes. "He did? I don't get it. Why would he ask you to meet him? And why the same time as me?"

Caleb shrugged. "I'm not sure. I thought he wanted my opinion of you. Or something like that."

Ellie raised her eyebrows. "And what were you planning to tell him about me?"

He caught a hint of lightness in her tone. "The truth. That I don't believe you would do anything like this. I mean, I haven't known you very long, but I think you're an honest person." He couldn't help breaking into a broad grin. "Sometimes a little too honest!"

Ellie rolled her eyes. "Thank you for having faith in me, Caleb. It means a lot!" She let out an audible sigh of relief. Then tears welled up and she placed her hand on his arm. "I really needed to hear that from you right now."

After school, Caleb and Ellie dropped B.J. off at his house.

"It seems like you and your Christian friends are all part of one big happy family," she commented, as soon as they drove away.

Caleb glanced at her. "Well, in a way, we are. When I gave my life to Jesus, I became God's child. So I guess you could say that makes every other Christian my brother or sister."

"But aren't all people God's children?"

"Well, God's creation, maybe. But not God's children. He loves everyone, and died for everyone, but the Bible says that to become His children, we have to receive Jesus as our Savior."

"What does that mean, exactly?" Ellie queried. "I've heard that before, but I guess I've never fully understood it."

"Well, I'm not very good at explaining things." He grinned. "I don't know. Maybe it's a guy thing." Ellie laughed. "But I'll try. The Bible says all people are sinners, and the penalty for sin is death. But God sent His Son to die in our place, so that whoever believes in Him wouldn't have to die but could have eternal life instead."

Ellie held up her hands. "And that's it? That's how we get to heaven?"

Caleb nodded, keeping his eyes on the road.

She shook her head. "But it seems too simple. Too easy."

"I don't think it was easy for Jesus to suffer the way He did. He took all of God's wrath meant for us. And it cost Him His life."

Ellie tilted her head to one side. "And all I have to do is believe that?"

"Well, not just in your head, but with your heart. Admit that you've sinned, believe that He died in your place, and ask Him to forgive you and make you a new person."

Ellie remained silent as they turned into the mall parking lot.

As they pulled into a space in front of the Pet Palace, she turned to him. "Caleb, would you mind praying about this meeting for me?"

He met her worried gaze. "Sure, Ellie." He took her hand in his and directed his next few words toward heaven.

"Caleb, good to see you again." Mr. Pruitt extended his hand, and Caleb fumbled for it. He nodded in Ellie's direction, "Miss Thompson." Motioning to the two chairs in front of them, he added, "Please, have a seat."

The two sat side by side facing him. The owner of the pet store came around the desk, shut the door, and returned to his chair.

"I'm sure you both have a lot of questions about this meeting," he began, "so I'll get right to the point. I asked you here because this involves both of you. Miss Thompson, as you are aware, there have been an unusually high number of items missing from our inventory recently. I've been watching the store front, but I haven't detected any suspicious activity on the part of our customers. So naturally, I began to suspect an employee—as distasteful as that idea is to me. Then, based on a tip I received from another employee, I found several items in a store apron hanging in the break room, which, as you know, turned out to be yours. When you were unable to provide a receipt, I had no recourse but to suspect you of the thefts."

When he paused to take a breath, Ellie spoke up, her words pouring out like an accused criminal's final plea. "But Mr. Pruitt, like I told you before, I don't know how those items got in my apron. What would I want with them anyway? Besides, this job is too important to me to risk everything by stealing a few petty items. You have to believe me! My reputation is the only thing I have. If you take that away from me . . . " her voice faltered, "then I have nothing left."

Caleb admired her for the way she stood up for herself, and sensed this was the time to lend his support. "Mr. Pruitt, um . . . I'd like to add to what she—"

His former boss stopped him in mid-sentence with a raised hand. "Caleb, I have an idea what you're about to say, but there's really no need for it." He turned to Ellie. "Miss Thompson, I hired you based solely on Caleb's recommendation, and in the short time you've worked here, you've proven to be one of my most conscientious employees. So when I found those items in your apron, I didn't want to suspect you, but I had to investigate the matter. And I have. This past weekend I went through the employee lockers. I have the master keys, of course. And what I discovered surprised me, to say the least. I found the rest of the missing items in one person's locker." He paused and looked at the two anxious faces in front of him. "That locker belongs to Miss Harris."

It took a moment for the truth to sink in.

Caleb let the air escape from his lungs and shot a sideways glance at Ellie. Her mouth was agape in stunned disbelief.

Megan had attempted to repeat the lie used before to turn Ellie against him. But this time, it wasn't with words alone.

Mr. Pruitt continued. "Tuesday I confronted her with the evidence. She denied any complicity, and even had the audacity to accuse you of planting the items in her locker. Of course that would have been impossible without the key. But it was entirely possible that she planted the items in your apron, since it was hanging out in the open for anyone to access. That, coupled with the fact that she was the one who made the accusations against you in the first place, convinced me of the truth. Therefore, as of this past Tuesday evening, Miss Harris is no longer employed here." His tone became conciliatory. "Miss Thompson, I deeply regret the trouble this incident has caused you. You have my sincere apologies, and I hope we can put this behind us and move forward together."

Ellie swallowed and found it hard to speak. "Thank you."

Mr. Pruitt turned to Caleb. "Now, young man, you're probably wondering why I asked you to this meeting. Am I right?"

"Yes sir."

"Well, I said this involved both of you, and it does. With the departure of Miss Harris, I'm afraid that leaves me one employee short. So . . ." he flashed a rare grin, "I was hoping you'd be able to come work for me again. I'd sure like to have you back, Caleb."

Caleb picked his jaw up off the floor. Out of the corner of his eye he could see Ellie nodding at him furiously. For a split second, the thought of his nearly nonexistent lawn care business flashed across his mind. Then it was gone. "Mr. Pruitt, I'd love to come back and work for you. That would be great! Just great!"

They stepped out of the office and as soon as the door closed behind them, Ellie threw her arms around Caleb's neck and gave him the hug of his life. When she finally pulled away, her eyes were wet with happy tears.

"Oh, Caleb, can you believe it?" she exclaimed, eyes wide with amazement. "Can you really believe it?"

Dazed, he shook his head like a bobble-head doll. "What just happened in there?"

Ellie laughed. "Don't you know? I'll tell you what happened in there, mister!" She took his face in her two hands and gazed intently into his eyes. "God answered your prayers, Caleb Sawyer. That's what!"

He stared back into her brimming, beautiful brown eyes, and felt the warmth of her palms on his cheeks. He wanted to kiss her. Instead, he took her hands in his.

"You're right, Ellie. This is definitely an answer to prayer," he agreed emphatically. "Isn't God good?"

Her smile assured him. "Yes, I can see that, now." Then she added, "But so are you, Caleb. I'm so lucky to have you in my life!"

"No, Ellie," Caleb protested, "I'm lucky to have you in my life."

"Well, I say I'm the lucky one," she insisted playfully.

He broke into a grin. "Nope, I'm the lucky one."

They stared at each other for a moment, and then, as if on cue, replied in unison, "Well, aren't we the lucky ones!" before cracking up.

Glancing at the wall clock, Ellie blurted out, "Hey, guess what? I've got a job to go to. I'll see you later, okay?" Without waiting for a reply, she turned and started toward the break room at the end of the short hallway. But then she stopped, and came back to him. "Thank you for everything, Caleb. You're amazing!"

Ellie put her hands on the back of his neck, stood on her tiptoes, and kissed him. Embarrassed, she blushed deeply and took a step back. "See you soon!"

Then she rushed off to clock in for work, leaving Caleb stunned, but happy as he stood frozen in the middle of the back hallway of the Baxter Pet Palace.

CHAPTER SEVEN

A PLACE FOR ELLIE

"YOU MEAN SHE KISSED YOU? She actually kissed you?" B.J.'s eyes grew wide as he stared at Caleb.

One of the broadest grins ever threatened to overtake Caleb's face.

"Pipe down, Einstein!" he hissed, glancing up and down the hallway to be sure nobody had caught the outburst from his flabbergasted friend. "I don't want it to get around, okay?"

B.J. barely lowered his voice. "Sure, bro, sure." He leaned in closer. "I mean, what guy in his right mind would ever want it to get around that he was kissed . . . by only the most beautiful girl in the entire southern half of the United States."

"Hey, careful, pal," Caleb fired back. "If I told Allison what you just said, she'd sink your battleship before you even knew you were hit."

The momentary look of panic on his friend's face was repayment enough for all the torment he'd taken from B.J. over his relationship with Ellie.

"No fair. That's not fair!" B.J. grabbed Caleb around the neck.

They scuffled until they banged into the row of lockers with such force that the noise drew the attention of nearby students.

Laughing, Caleb grabbed his books, slammed shut his locker, and headed off to first period class, but not before ruffling his friend's hair one last time.

Caleb had always looked forward to Saturdays, but he now had a new reason for anticipating the start of each weekend. He would be spending eight hours with the girl who had so thoroughly captured his attention, and whose attention he enjoyed.

Ellie had been relegated to the role of cashier at the front of the pet store, and while he spent most of his time between the back store room and stocking the shelves, it was still a thrill to see her behind the checkout counter, and occasionally catch her smiling at him. And the small raise Mr. Pruitt had given him certainly didn't hurt things either.

Caleb finished arranging the end cap display he'd been working on most of the morning and glanced at his watch. It was almost lunch time. That meant a half hour with Ellie in the break room.

As they sat facing each other across the worn and scuffed tabletop, Ellie told him that her troubles at home had not improved.

"They're really making life unbearable for me," she confided. "Things seem to be getting worse every day. I'm really grateful for the hours here. Not just for the income, but for the escape."

"Still no idea where you'll go when you turn eighteen?"

"No, not yet." She sighed and stared at her food.

"Well, don't give up. I'm praying about that for you. In fact, the entire youth group is."

Ellie glanced up quickly at him and frowned. "I'm not sure I like the idea of everyone knowing all about my home situation."

"Don't worry," he assured her. "They don't know the details. Just that you need a place to live."

"Well, I guess that's alright. I do appreciate their concern."

Following work, in order for Ellie to spend as much time away from home as possible, Caleb took her to Edwards to meet up with the other Saturday night regulars. After a couple of hours at the diner, he drove her home.

"Hey, what are you doing tomorrow morning?" he asked as he turned onto her street. "If you're not busy, would you like to come to church with me? That would give you a few more hours away from home."

She thought about it for a minute, and then politely declined. "I appreciate the offer, but I don't think I'm quite ready for that. But don't give up on me just yet, okay?" she pleaded.

Caleb borrowed a line which he had memorized and grinned, "Well, to quote someone who wrote a note I once found stuck in my locker, '*If you're not there, then I'll just have to keep after you until you show up!*'"

After she stopped laughing, Ellie turned to him. "All right, I promise to come next week. How's that?"

During the teen Bible study hour Sunday morning, Caleb shared how God had been answering the group's prayers for Ellie. The kids were eager to hear how He had spared Ellie's job and restored Caleb's at the same time, and they renewed their commitment to pray for a home for her. During the main worship service, Caleb couldn't help but wish it was next week.

He pictured Ellie meeting some of the kids for the first time, and imagined what it would be like having her sitting next to him in the pew. Did she have anything nice to wear? While most kids dressed casually, some chose to dress up, and hopefully she wouldn't feel out of place. His church family would welcome her no matter what she wore.

After all, he reminded himself, *God doesn't judge people by their appearance, but by their heart.*

When the service was over, Caleb felt a bit remorseful that he hadn't been able to focus on Pastor Murphy's message. He was an interesting preacher who was usually able to hold Caleb's attention.

As the congregation filed out of the sanctuary, Caleb rejoined his parents in the foyer. They were talking to one of the elderly widows in the church, Cora Williams. "Miss Cora," as she liked to be called, was nearly eighty-years old, and lived alone. Yet here she was, one of the most faithful members of the church, still driving herself to services each Sunday morning in her big, old Buick, rain or shine.

He caught the tail end of their conversation.

"Now you be sure and let me know if you hear of someone," she insisted, kindly poking her cane at his father.

Caleb saw the twinkle in her eyes, and wondered how a person with that many years and that many wrinkles could have such lively, energetic eyes.

His father laughed. "You can count on it, Miss Cora. I'll keep my eyes and ears open."

"What was that you were talking to Miss Cora about?" Caleb wanted to know as they drove home.

His mother turned around to face him in the back seat. "Miss Cora is looking for a boarder," she replied.

"A boarder? You mean, like a renter?"

"Yes, something like that. She said it gets lonely in that big old house, and she could use someone to help out a bit. It's getting hard for her to keep up such a big place. But she made it clear, as only she can, that she's not ready to move out just yet."

Cassie eyed her big brother and piped up in her usual obnoxious way. "I know someone who would be perfect for that place. Caleb!" She broke into annoying giggles. "Then me and my friends could have lots of sleepovers in his old room."

Caleb made a grab for his younger sibling and came away with her hair bow. Keeping it away from her, he stuck the frilly pink thing in his hair and looked in the rear view mirror. "Do you think this looks better on me or her?"

"Mo-o-om!" Cassie tattled, "Make Caleb give back my bow."

He tossed it back at her before either parent could respond. "Here, Squirt, you can have it. I don't look good in pink anyway."

Cassie stuck out her tongue at him and pinned it back into her hair.

Caleb looked at his father, "Dad, what kind of person is Miss Cora looking for? Someone in our church?"

"Not necessarily," he replied, glancing at his son in the mirror. "Just someone who's a little younger and has the energy to help her keep up the place. Nothing major, like maintenance or mowing. Just light housework, that sort of thing."

"Caleb knows how to vacuum and dust real good," Cassie volunteered.

He squinted at the pest sharing the back seat with him. "And if I move out, just who do you think will be stuck with all those chores at our house?"

As Cassie silently contemplated his question, Caleb looked out the side window and chuckled to himself. It wasn't much of a challenge engaging in a battle of wits with an impulsive ten year old.

That afternoon, after doing some homework, Caleb lay on his bed and stared absentmindedly at the crack in the ceiling. Later on, he would go to B.J.'s for some three-on-three basketball and homemade cookies. But right now, he was thinking of Miss Cora and her big house.

It was a lovely old house, the kind that has seen lots of good living over the years. Set back on a large corner lot, it had great curb appeal. The wrap-around porch with the gingerbread trim and white porch swing. The dark green shutters against the white lapboard siding covered with innumerable coats of paint. The well-manicured flower beds and large shade trees in the yard. It was the kind of house he would have loved to grow up in. The kind of house that makes for great childhood memories.

Not that his family's modest Cape Cod was a bad place to live or anything. It was very comfortable, and just as well kept as the old Victorian. Only it was a smaller house on a considerably smaller lot.

Later as he drove to B.J.'s, a thought kept nagging at him. But for the life of him, he couldn't figure out what it was. He'd had that unsettled feeling before, like he was supposed to do something.

When he arrived at B.J.'s, he pushed it to the side and got out of his car. If it really were that important, he'd eventually remember what it was. After two hours of friendly half-court hoops, and a half-dozen cookies, Caleb returned home and packed his things for school in the morning. He was preparing for bed when the feeling returned.

It wasn't until he crawled into bed and turned out the light that the thought escaped from the shadowy recesses of his mind.

That was it! Miss Cora was looking for a renter. Ellie was looking for a room. Could it be that simple? When he had prayed about a job for Ellie, the answer had been right under his nose. Now he'd been praying about a place for her to live. Was this the answer he and the youth group had been looking for?

He remembered Tony's encouragement to step aside and let God work it out. He'd been doing that. Praying, and waiting on the answer.

But was this it? The timing seemed to be perfect. What should he do?

The questions spun around in his mind like a Midwestern tornado. The more he thought about the idea of Ellie moving in with Miss Cora, the more excited he got. Knowing it would be nearly impossible to fall asleep, he got up and went downstairs.

His father was still up, reading in his living room recliner.

"Dad?" Caleb stepped through the doorway. "Can I talk to you?"

"Sure, Caleb." He closed his book and placed it on the end table. "What's on your mind?"

Caleb sat down on the end of the sofa closest to his father. "It's what Miss Cora said this morning about wanting someone to live with her. And about Ellie." He told his father how desperate Ellie was to get away from her foster parents, and how Miss Cora's need of a boarder might be the solution.

The conversation seemed very similar to the one they'd had when he wanted to quit his job.

After hearing him out, his father agreed. "The timing of Miss Cora's announcement might well be an opportunity for Ellie to look into."

"That's what I was thinking. But what should I do?"

"Well, perhaps you could call Miss Cora after school tomorrow and see what she has to say about it," his father suggested.

The following morning, Caleb waited at Ellie's locker. Soon she entered the building along with the other bus arrivals. She hadn't finished dialing the combination before he gave her the news about Miss Cora's available room.

Ellie hung up her jacket and organized her books for the coming school day. "What kind of person is this Miss Cora?"

"She's one of the nicest people I know," he told her. "She's a widow in our church. Close to eighty, I think. But I'm sure you'd really like her."

"Do you think she'd mind having someone my age living with her?"

"I'm sure she wouldn't mind at all once she gets to know you."
Caleb paused. "The truth is, I haven't talked to her about it yet. I plan
to after school today."

"What about the rent? I'm not sure I can afford anything right now."

"I don't know what she's asking. But why not see if she's at least
willing to meet with you first?" Caleb urged. "You've got nothing to
lose. Besides, if this is the answer, that will all work out."

Ellie smiled. "Alright. I'll talk to her. Let me know what she says, okay?"

As soon as he got home from school that afternoon, Caleb called
Miss Cora and explained Ellie's situation. The elderly woman had a
number of questions herself.

"What kind of a person is this young lady, Caleb? Is she responsible?
Trustworthy?"

"Yes, I can vouch for that," Caleb assured her. "She works with me
at the Pet Palace. Our boss said she's one of his most conscientious
employees. And she's very honest."

"That's good to know. But is she neat and tidy? And what about
noise? Is she loud like most teenagers?"

Caleb couldn't help but chuckle. "I've never seen her room at home,
but she's very organized at school. And she's on the quiet side. She
keeps to herself much of the time."

"Well, I do have some concerns about her age. Seventeen is mighty
young. I don't know." Miss Cora hesitated.

"She'll be eighteen in a few weeks," he added, hoping that detail
might influence her decision.

"Well now, that changes everything doesn't it?" He caught her lighthearted tone. "Alright, Caleb, I don't know this Ellie friend of yours,
but based on your recommendation, I'll agree to meet with her. Can
you bring her by on Wednesday? Say around four-thirty?"

"Yes, that's perfect, Miss Cora." Caleb could barely contain his enthusiasm. "We'll see you then."

The bell-like tones of the door chime brought back pleasant memories to Caleb. As a child, barely able to reach the lighted button beside the old dark-stained mahogany front door, it had been a thrill to activate the Big Ben-sounding peals that echoed deep within the cavernous old Victorian home at 401 East Pine Street. Time had not diminished the doorbell's appeal, and he felt the familiar twinge of expectation as he announced their arrival.

Through the leaded glass panes he could see the blurred image of Miss Cora approaching. Even the metallic turn of the deadbolt, and the squeak of the brass knob were invitations to his ears.

"Come in, come in!" Beaming with all the Southern charm and hospitality for which she was known, the diminutive white-haired old woman motioned them inside.

He and Ellie stepped across the threshold. The scent of old wood and fresh ginger assaulted their senses. Although it had been a while since he had been in the house, Miss Cora had apparently not lost her touch as a gracious hostess, and Caleb found himself salivating for the warm gingersnaps he was sure were awaiting on a tray in the kitchen.

Miss Cora closed the door. "So this must be the young lady you told me about."

"Yes. Miss Cora, I'd like you to meet Ellie Thompson. Ellie, this is Miss Cora Williams."

"How do you do?" Ellie politely shook hands with the widow.

"It's nice to meet you," Miss Cora responded. She motioned toward the next room. "Please, won't you both come in and sit a spell?"

She led the pair into the front parlor where she offered them a seat on the large sofa with the chintz fabric. Then she seated herself in the high-backed wing chair set at an angle to the coffee table in front of them. As the elder and younger females exchanged introductory pleasantries, Caleb allowed himself a look around the room.

Not much had changed over the years. The large pieces of furniture were perfect for the old house, serving as reminders of a bygone era. The large front windows were framed by heavy, swag draperies with antique-white sheers underneath. The original fireplace with its smoke-stained brick was the ideal setting for the old German mantel clock, which was still operational and keeping good time.

Family portraits, all neatly framed and lined up side-by-side, flanked the timepiece. The old varnished wood floor with the heavy wool area rug completed the step back in time. The only thing that had changed, he noticed, was the color of the walls. The faded rose-print wallpaper had been stripped and replaced by a relatively fresh coat or two of a neutral paint.

When Miss Cora excused herself to fetch some refreshments, Caleb turned to Ellie. "So, what do you think of Miss Cora?"

Ellie's eyes lit up. "She seems like a very nice person," she began, "very pleasant and friendly. Kind of old-fashioned, but in a nice sort of way . . . like I'd expect a grandmother or great-grandmother to be."

"What about the house?" he asked.

"It's beautiful. I love old houses. They have so much to offer. So much personality." Her eyes swept the room. "I could see myself living here."

Those words were music to Caleb's ears. The tinkling of ice in glasses turned their attention to the doorway. Miss Cora entered, carrying a tray with three tall glasses of lemonade and a plate of fresh, warm gingersnaps. Caleb smiled, grateful that some things never change.

After enjoying the refreshments and talking a while longer, Miss Cora showed them the rest of the house. The front parlor, a formal dining room, a large kitchen, and a half bath occupied the first floor. The upstairs consisted of three good-sized bedrooms and two bathrooms. The guest bathroom down the hall boasted a black and white tile floor, and a beautiful old claw foot tub with a curtain hung from a suspended oval shower rod.

Although showing its age, the house was clean and tidy, and had been well maintained over the years. The guest room for the boarder was the largest of the three bedrooms. Painted a soothing pale blue, it had a double bay window with a bench seat overlooking the side yard with its colorful dogwoods and stately oaks. While the closet was modest, the room itself contained a double bed with brass head and foot boards, a nightstand and lamp, a dresser and mirror, and a small table and chair.

Caleb's ears perked up when Miss Cora mentioned that the room came furnished. That thought never occurred to him.

The trio went back down the banister staircase and out onto the front porch. Caleb and Ellie took a seat on the white porch swing while Miss Cora chose the padded wooden rocker.

Ellie gleefully tested out the swing. "I love porch swings," she blurted out happily. "One of my favorite childhood memories is of my mother and me swinging on one much like this. Only I think it was green. And a little bit wider."

"My husband and I bought that one about ten years ago at a garage sale," the widow reminisced. "Somewhere south of Chesapeake, I think. Got a good deal on it, too, if my memory serves me correctly." She smiled, and the wrinkles spread out across her face. "It sat in the garage for about a year before Henry cleaned it up and hung it there. I always wanted a porch swing."

"What's this?" Ellie's fingers traced the outline of a heart carved into the right arm of the swing. Caleb leaned across her to see what she was referring to.

"Oh, that." Miss Cora giggled like a schoolgirl. "Henry carved it with his pocket knife on our wedding anniversary. Which one I can't remember." She leaned forward and pointed a finger at the artwork. "That's our initials. See the 'H.W.' and the 'C.W.'?

It was cute watching the elderly woman blush at the memory of the romantic occasion.

"Aw, that's so sweet." Ellie ran her hand over the initials. "Have you used this swing much?"

"Oh my, yes! We spent many wonderful evenings on that swing. Before he passed away." A momentary sadness crossed her face, but then she smiled. "But I'm grateful to the Lord for the seven years He allowed us to enjoy this swing together."

"That's about how long I got to enjoy swinging with my mother." Ellie paused. Then, with a seriousness that took him by surprise, she confessed, "I need to be more grateful for the short time I had with her."

Miss Cora nodded in agreement. "Amen, child. Be thankful for the time God gives you. I've lived a lot of years, but the truth is, whether it's seven years or seventy years, it all goes by way too fast. The Bible says our life is short, like a vapor which appears for a little while." She waved her hand in a circle. "And then . . . poof! It vanishes away." The old woman settled back in her rocker.

"Thank the good Lord eternal life is as long as this life is short," the old woman smiled sweetly. "I had fifty-one wonderful years with my Henry. And now two without him. But our separation is only temporary, just like this life. It's just a drop in the bucket compared to eternity."

Toward the end of the visit, the widow asked Ellie if she was satisfied with the living arrangements. After assuring Miss Cora that the house was perfect, Ellie reluctantly raised the subject of rent.

She began to explain her financial situation, but the elderly woman stopped her with an uplifted hand. "You needn't go into all that, my dear," she said gently. "Caleb's told me a little about your plight already. Let me ask you this, though." She stopped her slow rocking and leaned forward. "Are you willing to help out with the housework? Things like dusting, vacuuming, laundry, that sort of thing?"

Ellie seemed to be caught off guard. "Oh, uh . . . well, yes, of course. I've done household chores since I was a kid. And I've always done my own laundry."

"What about cooking? Might you be able to help with that?"

"Yes. My previous foster mother had me prepare an entire family meal once a week. I wasn't too happy about it at the time, but the experience taught me how to follow a recipe and how to cook. I actually enjoy it now."

Caleb wondered what this line of questioning had to do with rent, but Miss Cora wasn't finished yet. "And what about company? Would you be willing to sit on that porch swing and keep a lonely old woman company from time to time? Not every day, mind you. I know you have your own life to live. But on occasion, perhaps?"

Caleb caught the twinkle in Miss Cora's eye.

"Miss Cora," Ellie replied, with a sweet smile, "I would consider it an honor to sit and talk with you. Whenever you want. I'm sure there's a lot I can learn from you. And I would be happy to help you with whatever housework needs to be done. Meals, too. Whatever you need. Only . . . " she hesitated, " . . . only I'm not sure if I can afford the rent. I do have a job, but it's only part-time, and I'm trying to save enough for college next fall. What are you asking to rent the room?"

"Rent? My dear, I'm not looking for a renter. I'm looking for a boarder."

"I'm not sure I understand what you mean," Ellie asked, a puzzled expression on her face. "Is there a difference?"

"Oh my, yes. At least, as far as I'm concerned, there is. A renter is someone who pays me rent money. A boarder is someone who doesn't." She paused to let this sink in. Then she chuckled. "Honey, I don't want your money. Goodness, no. You keep that for college. Besides, God has already provided my needs through Henry's Navy pension. I want you to live here in exchange for helping me around the house, that's all. Why do you think I was asking all the questions about housework?" She shook her head wearily and sighed. "I can't seem to keep up with the cleaning and cooking like I used to."

The fire returned to her eyes, and she added a feisty exclamation point by thumping her cane on the porch deck. "But I'm sure not ready to move into that old folk's home any time soon!"

Caleb and Ellie laughed in unison. Somehow, he couldn't picture Miss Cora living anywhere but in this big old house, and driving that big old car. Ellie thanked the older woman profusely. With tears in her eyes, she promised to do everything she could to lighten the kind-hearted woman's burden.

They said their goodbyes and were walking down the front sidewalk to Caleb's car when Miss Cora called out to them with an afterthought reminiscent of the famous disheveled TV detective, Columbo. "Oh, just one more thing."

The pair stopped and turned to face the diminutive firebrand. "Just so you know, in my house, there's no smoking, drinking, or cursing. And no loud music."

The following Sunday morning, Caleb was up extra early. He dressed and ate breakfast with the family, and then left in his car to pick up Ellie for church. He was so excited that she was finally coming, and that his parents would finally get to meet her. The other kids had been thrilled to learn in youth group Wednesday night that God, in answer to their prayers, had provided a safe place for her to live. Caleb had offered to be present when Ellie talked to her foster parents about moving out, but she had thought it would be best if she talked to them alone.

To her surprise, they had agreed to let her move out any time, so long as she maintained her legal residence with them until her eighteenth birthday, something she was more than willing to do. They had also promised to file her emancipation paperwork at that time.

Caleb pulled over to the curb outside the Markle's small, run-down house. Its roof was missing several shingles, and one gutter was hanging loose at the corner. The once-white fence out front was a weather-beaten grayish color, and several pickets were askew or missing completely. The lawn was a tangle of weeds and dandelions, and in desperate need of a good haircut. No wonder Ellie hadn't wanted anyone to know where she lived. He could only imagine what the interior of the house was like. If it were maintained—or rather ignored—like the exterior, it must be a miserable place in which to live.

As he got out and walked around the front of his car, the front door opened and Ellie stepped out onto the crumbling stoop. He stopped, and stared. She was wearing a shimmering silvery-gray dress, with simple but elegant lines. She wore matching low-heeled shoes and carried a small white clutch purse in one hand. Her shining auburn hair was brushed neatly and pinned back on both sides, framing her face in a way that made her skin glow in the morning sunlight. He had never seen her in anything but worn jeans and T-shirts, or a Pet-Palace work shirt.

He was stunned at how beautiful she looked.

Ellie came down the sidewalk toward him and smiled. "Good morning!"

"You look . . . amazing!" He was suddenly aware that he was staring at her, and blushed.

She laughed at his awkwardness. "What's the matter, Caleb Sawyer? Are you surprised at how well I can clean up?"

She twirled around in a circle like a runway model.

His face grew even hotter. "No," he stammered, "it's not that. It's just that, well, I've never seen you wear anything like that before."

Apparently, she enjoyed his discomfort. "Well, I would have worn it to school, but I thought it might make me look uppity or something. Besides, I'm not interested in attracting attention to myself." She looked herself over, smoothing out her dress. "Do you think it's okay for church, though?"

Caleb looked at his polo shirt and blue jeans and felt grossly under-dressed compared to the beauty standing in front of him. "That's fine," he reassured her. "A lot of girls wear dresses on Sunday mornings. And some of the guys even wear sport coats and ties." He hesitated. "I didn't dress up because I wasn't sure what you'd be wearing."

Ellie smiled appreciatively at him. "That was very thoughtful of you, Caleb. I figured I'd better wear it just in case. Actually, it's the only dress I have." She eyed his outfit. "But you look great just the way you are."

"Thanks." Relieved that the wardrobe issue was settled, he opened the passenger door for her and she got in.

Caleb couldn't remember when he'd ever had a better time at church. He introduced Ellie to his mom and dad, who were in the lobby greeting people as they arrived. Cassie was already with her friends somewhere in the classroom wing of the building, but she would join them later for the worship service in the auditorium.

They made their way down the central hallway to the youth room, where the other teens went out of their way to welcome Ellie. Kelli and Allison pulled her aside, which allowed Caleb a chance to talk with B.J. and Aaron, and some of the other guys. Before the class began, he introduced her to Tony and his wife, Amanda, who both expressed their delight to finally meet her.

Later, during the congregational singing in the main service, Caleb shared a hymn book with Ellie. They stood with Allison and B.J. on one side, and Kelli and Aaron on the other. His church, like many other churches, sang a mixture of contemporary songs and older hymns. Lyrics of songs not in the hymnal were projected on the screen behind the platform. Ellie picked up the melodies very quickly, and proved to have a very good singing voice.

Pastor Murphy preached about Jesus' parable of the rich man and Lazarus in Luke sixteen. He pointed out that from the world's perspective, the rich man had everything going for him, while Lazarus was poor, diseased, and an outcast in society. But that changed when both men died. The rich man died and was buried, whereas Lazarus died and was carried. He declared that those who reject Christ in this life enter eternity alone, and spend it tormented alone in Hell, while those who accept Christ are ushered triumphantly into eternity, where they will be with Jesus and all the other believers forever in paradise.

During the message, Caleb glanced at Ellie sitting beside him. She was listening intently, hanging on to every word. Sensing his look, she returned it with a smile.

Following the service, Caleb walked Ellie to his car.

"I really enjoyed your church," she announced, as they drove back to her house. "Everyone was so friendly. I think I understand now what you meant when you said they're like family. The people all seem so happy."

Caleb spoke while looking at the road. "It's kinda like a family reunion every Sunday. But that doesn't mean everything's perfect all the time. Remember what I told you about Allison? She lost both her parents in a car wreck. I lost my brother. We still have the same struggles and heartaches as everyone else, but we have each other to share our burdens with. Then there's the Lord, of course. He carries them as well. That's why Christians can be joyful even if their circumstances aren't very good."

"The preacher was good, too," Ellie commented, changing the subject a bit. "I think it's ironic that the poor man went to heaven instead of the rich man. I take it the moral of the story is that it's not what you have or do in this life that gets you to heaven, but what you believe in. Am I right?"

Caleb glanced at her. "Well, yes. Only I don't think it's *what* you believe in, but Who you believe in. I heard a guy on the radio say there are a lot of cultural Christians in the world. People who have a belief system that accepts the ideas and teachings of Christianity, but don't have a personal relationship with Jesus Himself. It's the difference between knowing about Jesus, and actually knowing Jesus. They believe that what He said is true, but they don't act on that belief and accept Him as their personal Lord and Savior." He paused and shot her another glance. "Do you see the difference?"

She tilted her head to one side, and then looked across the seat at him. "Yes, I think so. It's that idea of believing with your heart and not just your head, right?" She wagged a finger at him. "See, I didn't forget what you told me."

They shared a laugh as the car pulled up to the rundown house that would soon be a part of Ellie's past.

Monday was moving day for Ellie, and both she and Caleb could barely wait for school to conclude for the day. They had talked to Miss Cora after church, and she had promised to have the room ready that afternoon. B.J., Allison, and Kelli had offered to help with the transition. Ellie had been a tad uneasy about them meeting her foster parents, and seeing the dilapidated house she had called home for the past five months, but was so grateful for their kindness that she had accepted their help.

Allison's grandfather was even loaning his old pickup truck for the move, as long as Allison did the driving. The teens were meeting at Ellie's house at four. She'd told them at lunch that most of her things were packed and ready to load. In addition to a number of boxes and suitcases, the only furniture she was taking with her was a large trunk where she kept her artwork and supplies, and an old flat-topped oak desk she used as a drawing table.

Caleb was anxious to meet the Markles. Ever since the rainy day when he'd first taken Ellie home, he'd been curious to see what they were really like. He had pictured Tony Markle as a short, balding man with a perpetual two-day stubble on his face. The hair around his ears tinged with gray and in as much need of a haircut as the lawn out front. Yellowed and crooked teeth and a large beer belly. Slovenly dressed in an old wife-beater and stained jeans. Someone as undisciplined and careless about his health and appearance as he was about the rest of his life. As for Beverly Markle, he had pictured her as an overweight, brutishly grim woman who marched around the house in hair curlers, house robe, and worn slippers, yelling and cursing all the time.

Caleb pulled up to the curb outside the dilapidated house ahead of his friends, who were being picked up by Allison in the truck. The first thing he noticed was that the yard had been recently mowed, and the picket fence had been hastily mended.

A dented trash can, minus the lid, peeked around the back corner of the house. The long necks of a number of beer bottles flowed over the rim. The Markles were apparently attempting to put their best foot forward for the movers.

As he approached the front concrete stoop, he saw that the doorbell was missing. Only the red and white low-voltage wires protruded from the hole that marked its former location. He knocked on the dented metal door and waited, fully expecting Ellie to greet him. It turned out to be Tony Markle instead.

Mr. Markle was nothing like he'd imagined. Taller than Caleb by a couple of inches, and very thin, he possessed a full head of dark, slicked back hair and a neatly trimmed goatee. He was impeccably dressed and sported a gold chain around his neck and an expensive watch on his wrist. He could have been a slick lawyer or politician from all outward appearances.

With a big smile and grandiose gesture he welcomed the teen into the house. "Come in, Caleb. Welcome!"

The man extended his hand, and Caleb shook it politely.

"Thank you." Caleb stepped into the small, dimly lit living room.

"It's so nice to finally meet you." His tone struck Caleb as overly friendly. "This is Ellie's mother, Beverly."

Mrs. Markle stepped out from behind her husband. Ellie had never called her "mother" before, and no doubt would have cringed to hear him use that term. *Just another part of the charade*, he thought.

Mrs. Markle was as much a surprise as her husband. She was slender with short blonde hair, average looking, and fairly well-dressed. "Pleased to meet you, Caleb," she said, with a surprisingly pleasant voice.

It sounded as though she really meant the words.

"Ellie's told us so much about you." She offered her hand, and he shook it obligingly.

"It's nice to meet you, too." The words almost stuck in his throat. He hoped they didn't betray the feelings he was experiencing at the moment.

Had he not known the truth about the pair, their friendly manner would have been totally believable. There was nothing in the way they presented themselves that would suggest that they were lazy, ill-tempered, mean-spirited abusers of alcohol, drugs, and the foster care system. Maybe they were unaware of what he knew. More likely, they didn't care.

This meticulous facade was no doubt why they had been able to hide their vices, and why they had been able to convince the authorities of their worthiness as foster parents, while maintaining Ellie's worthlessness as a foster child.

The old saying "you can't judge a book by its cover" came to mind. How many times had he passed people on the street or at the mall whose appearances suggested they were upright, moral, hard-working decent citizens, when in truth they could have been dishonest, violent thieves, or child abusers?

Ellie appeared from the hallway, and rescued him from the awkwardness of any further dialog. "Oh, hi, Caleb." She looked back and forth between the three already in the room. "I see you've already met my foster parents."

"Yes, we were just getting acquainted with this nice young man," Mrs. Markle cheerfully interjected before he could reply.

Ellie shot her foster mother a barely disguised look of contempt, and motioned for him to follow her. "Can you help me carry some boxes to the front porch?"

"Sure. That's why I'm here." He grinned, and then turned to the Markles. "Nice to meet you both."

He followed her down the dingy hall to her tiny room.

Ellie shut the door and turned to him with a look of total disgust on her face. "Oh boy, they're really laying it on thick today," she spoke in a half whisper, as if afraid of being overheard. "Do you see how charming they can be? If you could only see how they are when nobody else is around. They make me sick to my stomach!"

Caleb was taken back by the vitriol in her voice. No doubt they were very different people when not trying to impress someone, and no doubt very cruel and hard on Ellie. But for someone who had been taught to treat all authority with respect, whether deserved or undeserved, he wished she could find it in her heart to forgive them. Unchecked bitterness would only hurt her, and he didn't want that to happen.

If she only knew You, Lord, he thought, *then she would know what forgiveness is all about.*

He tried his best to alleviate her anger. "Ellie, I know they're putting on their best behavior just for me. But don't let it get to you. By tonight, they'll be out of your hair for good, won't they?"

His words seemed to refresh her like a splash of cool water. She smiled at him. "You're right. I'm sorry. I didn't mean to sound like an angry—" she caught herself. "Well, you get the idea."

"I understand how you feel," he acknowledged. "But that's all behind us now. Anyway, we've got to get you moved in with Miss Cora."

The brown-eyed beauty straightened up from the box she was sealing and looked at him with renewed appreciation. "You're such a good influence on me, Caleb."

As he stared self-consciously at the box in his arms, she added, "I'm so lucky to have you in my life."

"No, Ellie, I'm the lucky one, remember?"

They looked into each other's eyes and timed their responses. "Well aren't we the lucky ones!"

Laughing, they carried the boxes through the living room and out onto the stoop. Tony and Beverly sat on their living room sofa, smoking cigarettes and watching them silently. Neither lifted a finger to help. Once the others arrived in the pickup, it took the moving crew all of twenty minutes to clear out Ellie's things, including the desk and trunk.

"What about the bed and dresser?" Caleb asked. "Do those go or stay?"

"They stay. Tony insists they have to remain in order to maintain my legal residence here."

"I think I'd question the logic behind that reason," Caleb smirked.

"I don't believe it for a minute, either." She looked disgusted. "They just want to make sure they get my money as long as they possibly can."

Caleb couldn't believe how anyone could be so selfish and cruel. "Aren't you even going to challenge that?"

"No. At this stage of the game, I just want out, that's all."

When the pickup and sedan rolled up in front of the big white house on Pine Street, Miss Cora came out and stood on the front steps to welcome them.

It didn't take long to move everything upstairs into the large blue bedroom that was now Ellie's new home. As they were making the last trip up the wide staircase, the smell of banana bread wafted up from the kitchen.

"You all might as well get ready for a snack," Caleb prepared his friends. "I've never been inside this house without being offered something good to eat." His words proved to be prophetic. Upon their return to the first floor, they were met with a tray of warm banana nut bread, and coffee and tea.

CHAPTER EIGHT

A NEW CREATION

THE CHANGE IN ELLIE THOMPSON was dramatic. Now free from the daily stress of her former home life, she grew more relaxed and personable. Her friendship with Kelli and Allison began to bloom, and it wasn't long before she felt at ease with the kids at the round table in the school cafeteria. It was as if she'd grown up with them.

Although still possessing a hint of shyness, a quality Caleb found quite attractive, she was quicker to smile now, and seemed to have more self-confidence. Other students apparently noticed the change as well, and soon it was not uncommon for her to emerge from a classroom conversing with someone as they walked down the hallway between classes.

Still a bit reserved, she wasn't usually the one to initiate a conversation. But she didn't shy away from one, either, as she once had. This newer, friendlier version of Ellie caught the attention and inspired the hopes of a number of male students, much to Caleb's chagrin. While he knew he had no claims on her romantically, he still felt a twinge of jealousy whenever he saw her walking down the corridor talking to another guy.

He was glad to see her emerging from her self-imposed shell, and was happy for her sake that she was becoming more sociable. Still, he couldn't help feeling a sense of relief whenever she told him that she'd declined another guy's advances. In fact, she seemed to take particular delight in informing Caleb of another potential suitor whom she had, as kindly as possible, turned away.

He wondered if her comments were meant to be subtle hints to get his attention. But the fact that she confided in him was a great source of comfort and encouragement to the young man with the big heart. Another source of encouragement was the fact that Ellie had begun to attend church regularly. Each Sunday morning, she rode with Miss Cora in the big old, well-maintained Buick across town to the red brick building on the hillside overlooking Baxter. The little white-haired lady believed in being punctual, which to anyone else would have been called early. That usually gave Caleb and Ellie a few minutes to talk before the other kids arrived in the youth room.

"Caleb, I can't begin to tell you how wonderful it is living in that big old house with Miss Cora," she exclaimed. "It's like night and day compared to what my life was like before. No drama or conflict of any sort. Just peace and quiet." She paused. "That lady has got to be the kindest soul on earth."

"You're right about that. And I'm glad it's working out for you," he responded. "Isn't it amazing how everything just kind of fell into place? I mean, the timing of it all and everything. You've got to admit, it's a God thing."

"Yes, I can see that," she acknowledged with a smile. "But then, you had a lot to do with it too, Caleb. I mean, if you hadn't been so persistent with me, I never would have gotten this far. Thank you for sticking by me."

He grinned sheepishly and shrugged. "What's a friend for?"

She batted her eyes at him in a playful manner. "Just a friend?"

Her question sent an electric charge throughout his body.

"What do you mean?"

"I thought we were becoming more than just 'friends'."

Caleb's heart pounded in his chest, and for a moment he was afraid she could hear it as well. "I know what you're saying. I feel it, too. I think we both do." He fought for the right words. "Ellie, I'd like nothing more than to pursue that kind of relationship with you. Believe me, I really want to! But . . ." his voice trailed off. He just couldn't bring himself to finish the thought.

Ellie finished it for him. "I know. It's that promise you made to God, isn't it?"

He nodded silently, unable to speak.

She placed her hand over his and smiled. "Well, Caleb Sawyer, I wouldn't want you to break your promise."

He looked at her in amazement. "You wouldn't?"

"Of course not. Especially to God! One of the things I really like about you is that you keep your word. That's very important to me. And attractive, by the way. Don't ever change that about yourself, okay?"

Her openness gave him a surge of encouragement.

"I'll try not to." He grinned slyly. "But you sure make it hard, sometimes."

Ellie blushed. "Then I'll try not to."

They both laughed.

Tony came into the youth room, followed by Kelli and Aaron and several other kids. When Ellie got up to talk to Kelli, Caleb exhaled slowly. The room had gotten pretty warm there for a minute.

⎯⎯⎯⎯⎯⎯⎯⎯⎯⎯⎯⎯⎯⎯

That afternoon, Caleb stopped by Miss Cora's before going to play basketball at B.J.'s. He wanted to finish the conversation they'd started at church that morning.

Sitting on the porch swing with Ellie, he thought back to one particular statement of hers. "Ellie, this morning in the youth room you said something about being where you are because of my persistence, remember?"

She nodded. "If you hadn't kept after me none of this would have happened. And I wouldn't be where I am today."

"Well, what I wanted to say is, I don't really want you to stay where you are."

Ellie looked puzzled. "What do you mean? You don't want me to stay with Miss Cora?"

"No, that's not what I meant." He laughed off his awkward statement. "What I'm trying to say is, I hope you don't stay where you are spiritually."

She stared at him. "Oh. You're talking about me becoming a Christian, right?"

"Yes." He turned to look her squarely in the face. "Ellie, there's nothing I want more than for you to give your life to Christ. You see, it's really not my persistence that's gotten you this far. It's His. Jesus has been pursuing you all this time." He caught his breath. "You see that, don't you?"

Ellie was silent for a moment. When she spoke, he could tell the words came straight from her heart. "Yes, I do see that. In fact, sometimes I think I can actually feel His love." She smiled shyly. "Just like I can feel yours."

Caleb's face flushed and his pulse quickened. His fingers traced the heart carved in the arm of the porch swing as he formulated his response. "Ellie, as much as I'd like to tell you how I feel about you right now, I can't. It's not the right time. I've been trying to let God's love show through me. But sometimes I'm afraid my feelings have gotten in the way."

"Caleb, you *have* shown me God's love. I'm very grateful for that. And if it makes you feel any better, I've been doing a lot of thinking about what you've been saying to me. About becoming a Christian, I mean."

"That's wonderful! But Ellie, you can't make that decision to please me, or anyone else. It has to be because *you* see your need for Him. You have to want Him for yourself."

"I know. When I get to that point, I'll make the decision for the right reason. I promise." She gazed off into the side yard with all its wonderful shade trees. "But I'm not quite ready yet."

Her last statement drove a stake through his heart.

Sensing his disappointment, she turned to him. "I just need a little more time, that's all."

"Well, I guess you're the only one who would know when you're ready," he conceded. "But just remember this: the Bible says that today is the day of salvation. None of us is guaranteed tomorrow. Ellie, the decision is too important for you to keep putting it off. Your eternal destiny is on the line."

"I know, I know. I'll think about it some more tonight, okay? I promise." Then she squeezed his hand and flashed a smile. "Please don't give up on me, okay?"

Caleb responded with conviction. "I'll never give up on you, Ellie. Never!"

It was a pleasant early December Sunday evening in Baxter, Georgia. The skies were a cloudless brilliant azure, and a slight southwesterly breeze provided cool comfort for the two figures on the wide veranda porch of the old Victorian house on Pine Street.

Ellie sat on the porch swing, enjoying a gingersnap with Miss Cora, who was seated in the wooden rocking chair set at an angle to the swing.

The elderly woman was reading to herself from the large, black Bible which sat open on her lap. Ellie watched her silently, enjoying the tranquility of the moment.

Miss Cora looked up from her reading and smiled. "Lovely evening, isn't it?"

Ellie returned her smile. "Yes, it's beautiful. I love late fall in the South." She eyed the frayed book in her landlady's lap. "You spend a lot of time reading the Bible, don't you?"

Miss Cora looked down at the dog-eared copy of God's Word in her slightly arthritic hands. The pages, once white and clean, were worn and well-marked. Faint vestiges of gold leaf was all that remained on the edges.

"Oh my, yes!" The wrinkles around her eyes increased and her eyes lit up. "It's my favorite book."

Ellie stopped the gentle motion of the porch swing with her foot and leaned forward. "Why is it your favorite book?"

"Why?" The old woman pursed her lips and tilted her head to the side as she contemplated her response. "Well, my dear, I'd have to say it's my favorite book because it's God's love letter to me. He chose to reveal Himself to all mankind through this book. And within these pages are the answers to all of life's mysteries. The beginning, the fall, the certainty of death, suffering, redemption, the ending, eternity. Everything."

Ellie scrunched her brow. "But how can you understand what it says? I've tried reading it from time to time, but I can't seem to make any sense of it."

Miss Cora looked over at her with a kind expression. "I have an idea. Didn't you say you have the Bible your mother gave you as a little girl?"

"Yes, it's up in my room."

"Why don't you go get it and bring it out here? I'd like you to read a few verses for yourself. That would be better than just hearing them from me."

"Okay." Ellie got off the swing and disappeared into the house. A few moments later, she reappeared in the doorway in time to hear the widow finishing a prayer.

" . . . and Lord, give me Your words to share with this precious young soul. May they not return to You void."

Ellie paused, and then cleared her throat and stepped around the corner with a little white Bible in her hand. "Here it is," she held up the small children's version of the Scriptures.

"That's a very pretty Bible. Did your mother ever read it to you?"

Ellie settled back on the swing. "Yes. I was about five or six when she gave it to me. I remember sitting on the porch swing listening to her read aloud from it. I can still recall some of the stories. Noah and the ark. Daniel and the lions. David and the giant."

"What a wonderful memory that is. That's something you must cherish very much."

Ellie smiled and nodded silently before Miss Cora continued. "Now, to answer your question about how to understand this book. Can you find First Corinthians?"

"I think so." Ellie began leafing through the pages.

"You can use the table of contents if you like," Miss Cora suggested gently. "First Corinthians is in the New Testament. Toward the end."

Ellie located the book. "I found it."

"Good. Now go to chapter two and verse fourteen." She paused. "Do you see it?"

"Yes. Here it is."

"Would you mind reading it to me?"

"Okay." Ellie hunched over her Bible and traced the words with her finger as she read. "The natural person does not accept the things of the Spirit of God, for they are folly to him, and he is not able to understand them because they are spiritually discerned."

"Thank you, dear. Now, the natural person here refers to anyone who has not been born again by God's Spirit. By that, I mean they haven't put their faith and trust in the Lord Jesus Christ to save them from their natural condition as a sinner estranged from God. We all come into this world as natural-born sinners. This book tells us that all have sinned and fall short of God's glory. Do you know what that means?"

"Yes. Caleb's talked to me about it several times."

"Good for him. Now then, this verse says that the natural person isn't even capable of understanding the spiritual truths of God. In fact, they seem like foolishness to him. That's because they are spiritual in nature—supernatural if you will—while he is only natural." She paused. "Do you understand that?"

"Yes, I think so. The natural person would have to be supernatural in order to understand it."

"Precisely!" The old woman thumped the arm of the rocker with obvious delight.

Ellie leaned forward. "So, are you saying a person has to become a Christian in order to fully understand the Bible?"

"Yes I am. They must first become a child of God in order for the Spirit of God to help them understand the truths of God."

As Ellie absorbed this statement, she grew perplexed. "But if you can't understand the truth without first becoming a Christian, how does anyone become a Christian in the first place? Don't they need to know the truth first?"

"That is a very good question, Miss Ellie. It takes faith to come to Him in the first place." Miss Cora tapped her Bible with her index finger. "God's Word says that without faith it is impossible to please Him. Abraham believed God, and it was assigned to him as righteousness. Look up Ephesians chapter two, will you?"

Ellie dove into her Bible and soon came upon the right page.

"Find it?" Miss Cora continued at Ellie's nod. "Good. Now read beginning around verse four or five and keep reading 'til I tell you to stop."

Ellie began reading, "But God, being rich in mercy, because of the great love with which he loved us, even when we were dead in our trespasses, made us alive together with Christ—by grace you have been saved—and raised us up with him and seated us with him in the heavenly places in Christ Jesus, so that in the coming ages he might show the immeasurable riches of his grace in kindness toward us in Christ Jesus. For by grace you have been saved through faith. And this is not your own doing; it is the gift of God, not a result of works, so that no one may boast."

"Stop right there." Miss Cora held up her hand. "How does verse eight say we are saved?"

"By grace."

"By grace through what?"

"Through faith." Ellie looked up at Miss Cora. The white-haired little woman was beaming.

"Through faith! By grace through faith. We are saved from God's wrath, which we naturally deserve because of our sin. Romans tells us 'For the wages of sin is death, but the free gift of God is eternal life in Christ Jesus our Lord'. And it is only because of God's grace, extending His favor to us when it is totally undeserved, that we can have that salvation. But it only comes through faith. Faith in His shed blood on the cross as payment for our sin." She paused to let her words take root. "And what does verse eight say is the source of that faith needed to believe?"

Ellie looked at her Bible. "Um . . . the gift of God?"

"Exactly!" Miss Cora thumped the arm of her rocker again. Ellie chuckled inwardly at her enthusiasm and fervor. "God even gives you the faith needed to believe in Him. And once you believe in Him, He gives you the power to become His child. That's in John's gospel. Chapter one and verse twelve, if I'm not mistaken. You can check me on that later if you'd like. You see, He provides everything you need. Child, when you put your trust in Him, a lot takes place in that moment. You have your sins forgiven, you are declared righteous and no longer condemned, you are restored to a right relationship with God, you are made a new creation, you are given eternal life, and you are given His Holy Spirit to live within you."

She paused to catch her breath. "It's that same Holy Spirit who will enable you to understand His truth. In fact, He promises to guide you in all the truth. And He does all this because He loves you."

She waited patiently for Ellie to respond. "I see what you're saying, Miss Cora. I didn't used to believe that God loved me, but now I see that He does. But I still don't understand something. If God is love, why doesn't everyone believe in Him? And why is there still pain and suffering in the world? Caleb tells me that being a Christian doesn't guarantee you won't have bad things happen to you. He told me about losing his brother a while back."

Miss Cora closed her eyes and nodded. "Yes, I remember when the Sawyers lost little Calvin. That was a hard time for their family. It was a hard time for our whole church family. We all suffered together through that tragedy. But, to answer your question, I have to tell you about the nature of true love. How can I best put it?" She looked up at the porch ceiling and tapped her chin before continuing. "Let me ask you this, you like Caleb a lot, don't you?"

Ellie was taken back by the seemingly sudden shift in the conversation. She replied shyly, "Well, yes, I do."

Miss Cora chuckled, "I thought so. I can see it in the way you look at him. And in the way you two interact." She leaned forward, placed a withered hand next to her mouth, and lowered her voice, as if divulging a secret she didn't want anyone else to hear. "I think the feeling is mutual."

Ellie looked away, trying to mask the crimson heat in her cheeks.

The elderly widow continued. "Now, would you rather he liked you because he wants to, or because he has to?"

"I suppose because he wants to."

"And that, my dear, is the very definition of love. Love is a choice, not a duty. It is voluntary for the giver as well as the receiver. That's where free will comes into play. When God created Adam and Eve in the garden, He chose to love them. And He gave them the same choice . . . the free will to love and obey Him in return. Only they chose to disobey instead. God doesn't force anyone to love or accept Him. He could, you know. After all, He is God. But then that wouldn't require love, would it?"

Ellie shook her head.

Miss Cora let out a sigh and closed her Bible before continuing. "Sadly, many people choose to reject God instead of accept Him. They choose their own ways over His. And it's because of that choice that we have sin and evil and misery in this world."

"That's exactly what Caleb told me." Ellie thought back to her own childhood. "I . . . I used to blame God for taking my mother away from me at such an early age. But that wasn't His choice, was it?"

"No, it wasn't. If mankind hadn't chosen to disobey God, there would be no suffering. No sin. And no death. We were created to live forever. But sin brought death. One man's disobedience brought death on all mankind, because we all have sinned. But isn't it wonderfully ironic that the death of one man, Jesus, brings life to all who believe?"

"That's pretty amazing." Ellie nodded in agreement.

"Yes, it is. That's amazing grace. Amazing love." Miss Cora stopped her rocking and leaned forward with a gentle smile. "My dear, wouldn't you like to experience that kind of love for yourself?"

Tears welled up in Ellie's eyes. Sniffling, she wiped them away with a sleeve. "Yes, I would. I really would. Only . . . I need to be alone for a while, if you don't mind. It's all so incredibly overwhelming."

Miss Cora smiled graciously. "Yes, it is, my dear. There is no greater love." She pulled the bookmark from her big Bible and held it out to Ellie. "Please take this and read it, won't you? It's a poem that will help you understand why this book is so special to me."

Ellie slid off the swing and accepted the strip of laminated paper offered her. She placed it inside the front cover of her white Bible. "Thank you, Miss Cora. I'll go up to my room and read it right now."

As the sun sank lower in the western sky, the shadow of the big white Victorian house crept across the lawn and into the street. Ellie sat on the edge of her bed and looked out her window at the approaching evening. A boy on a bicycle came into view, peddling furiously. He safely navigated the corner and sped off to some unknown destination. Probably a kid who had promised his mother to be home half an hour ago.

She opened her Bible and withdrew the bookmark. The poem's title caught her attention: "My Favorite Book."

That's what Miss Cora had called it. She began to read with interest.

The Bible is my favorite Book,
Its Author is divine;
His Spirit spoke through men of old
To reach this heart of mine.
I hear His voice when reading it,
He speaks to me Himself;
But it will never help at all
If left upon the shelf.

Within its pages, as I read,
I quickly come to see,
It's not the story of mankind,
But of God's love for me!
It tells me how the world began,
How stars were hung in space;
That God so longed for fellowship
He made the human race.

I read how man has fallen from
That perfect place of bliss;
Once close to God, now prodigal,
The truth is really this:
All we, like sheep, have gone astray,
We've turned to our own way;
So death has passed upon us all,
For all have sinned today.

But by God's grace He did not leave
Me in that dreadful state,
Estranged from Him, and all alone
To face a fiery fate.
Instead He came into a world

Corrupt with sin and strife,
To demonstrate His love for me
By laying down His life.

For God so loved the world He gave
His one and only Son,
That everlasting life can be
A gift for everyone!
He died, was buried, rose again
The third day as He said;
These words provide a living hope,
They are my daily bread.

Whoever asks for Him receives,
Believe and do not doubt;
The one who truly comes to Him
Will never be cast out!
The blood of Jesus on the cross
Completely paid my debts;
I serve Him now with gratitude,
And live without regrets.

Without this Book I'd never know
How wonderful it is
To have my sins forgiven, and
To be a child of His!
He's Alpha and Omega,
The beginning and the end;
Creator, Savior, Counselor,
My Father, Brother, Friend.

The more I read of His great love,
The clearer I can see
That all throughout these pages is

His perfect will for me.
He knows the plans He has for me,
To prosper, not to harm;
Removing all my fears and doubts,
And causes for alarm.

He always keeps his promises,
His word is very sure;
Because of this I'm confident,
In Him my life is secure.
If I but ask and seek and knock,
Then I will always find;
The door will open up to me
To know His heart and mind.

His Word is like a lamp to me,
A light that guides my way;
It keeps my feet from falling so
I will not go astray.
It shows me how I ought to live,
And teaches me to pray;
It fills me with a perfect peace
That never goes away!

It also says He's coming soon
To make all wrong things right;
He'll take me home to be with Him,
My faith will then be sight!
These things I know without a doubt,
Because His voice I've heard,
Communicating Truth to me
Through this, His written Word.

So why not give His Word a chance?
It's worth a second look;
The answer to your every need
Is right here in this Book!
Please don't ignore the Truth, my friend,
Or leave it on the shelf;
If you seek God within this Book,
You'll find Him for yourself!

Ellie placed the bookmark back into her Bible and stared out the window again. The evening shadow of the house had reached the other side of the street now. Twilight was imminent. But it was her past that she began thinking about, not the darkening night.

She was six years old, sitting on a green porch swing with her mother, a beautiful young woman with long, light-brown hair and beautiful, but tired hazel eyes. The two of them were singing "Jesus Loves the Little Children" in time with the swaying of the swing.

She heard her mother's voice, as if in a dream, saying, *"I'll always be there for you, Ellie."*

Then their laughter reverberated in her ears like a canyon's echo, until it faded away.

That happy scene was replaced by one of somber tones. She stood in a cemetery on a cold, gray, rainy day. A handful of people dressed in black huddled together under huge, black umbrellas as a clergyman droned on and on in a monotonous, unintelligible, distant voice.

As she was being led away from the casket, her mother's words echoed again, as if calling to her from the grave, *"I'll always be there for you, Ellie."*

Then, abruptly, she was in the state orphanage. Some little snot-nosed boy pushed her to the ground, where she sat in the dirt next to a merry-go-round, crying. A very big woman with very little patience was standing over her, hands on hips, scolding her for being such a baby. The woman dissolved, and a couple took her place. Ellie was now several years older, and in a cramped bedroom with four other children. They were all misbehaving badly, and laughing at her behind their parents' back, while she was getting punished for something relatively minor.

Her flashbacks took her through several more unpleasant child-hood memories until she found herself, now seventeen, in a heated argument with her disheveled and inebriated foster mother. Beverly was cursing and threatening her with all the venom of a coiled cobra.

Finally, in a fit of rage, the livid woman struck her across the face, knocking her back into the living room wall. The wall morphed into a row of school lockers, and Ellie was standing in front of one, using the open door to shield her bruised face from Caleb's inquisitive gaze.

When he saw the bruise, he took her face in his hands, and in a voice that sounded as pleasant as a gently-flowing steam, uttered the reassuring words, *"I'll never give up on you, Ellie. Never!"*

Ellie returned to the present with a jolt. A long, slow sigh escaped her lips as she glanced around the light blue room.

Her gaze fell on the little white Bible still clutched in her hands. She stared silently at it for a full minute. Then, letting it fall open in her lap, she began leafing through the pages until she found the gospel of John.

"The Gospel According to John . . . chapter one . . . verse twelve." Speaking in a half-whisper, she read the verse aloud. "But to all who did receive him, who believed in his name, he gave the right to become children of God."

Ellie turned and stared out the window again. Tears trickled down her cheeks, until they dropped one by one onto the open Bible. Quietly, she slipped to her knees beside the bed, and placed her hands together.

Looking up at the ceiling through watery eyes, she began talking to God in a soft, but shaky voice. "God, I don't know how to pray very well. But I believe in You. I believe that You love me and that You sent Jesus to die for me. Please forgive me for hating You and blaming You for everything that's happened to me. And please forgive me for my sins."

Sobs shook her body. She paused long enough to grab a tissue from the nightstand. After wiping her eyes and blowing her nose, she continued. "God, I really want to be one of Your children. I've never had a father before, but Your book says You're a good one, so I'm going to trust that You will always be there for me. Oh, and thank You for the eternal life You promised. I really appreciate that very much. Um . . . amen."

Ellie got to her feet and lay down on the bed, gazing upward. There was a lightness in her spirit that she had never known before. It was as if the weight of the world had been lifted from her shoulders.

Was this a new kind of happiness? No, not happiness.

She'd experienced that fleeting emotion before. Happiness was based on circumstances. This was something totally different. Something much more wonderful.

Was it joy? It was certainly that, but this was even better.

It was love.

True, undeniable love. Perfect love. God's love.

She stared at the ceiling, sure that her face reflected the newfound peace that emanated from deep within her soul.

After a while, Ellie turned to look at the clock beside the bed. A whole hour had gone by. She got up and went to the bathroom down the hall where she washed her face and brushed her teeth. Returning to her room she prepared for bed.

Then she slid under the covers and turned out the bedside lamp. The pale moonlight shone through the sheers on the window and cast a calm bluish haze across the bedspread.

In the near darkness, she clasped her hands again and addressed her heavenly Father. "God . . . Father . . . thank You for loving me. And thank You for bringing Caleb into my life. And Miss Cora, too. Without them, I don't think I would have found You. Amen." Then she added one final thought before falling asleep. "Oh, one more thing . . . good night!"

CHAPTER NINE

THE BLESSED ONES

CALEB BEGAN HIS MONDAY MORNING like every other Monday morning during the school year, by wishing it was Friday. The thought of sitting through another five consecutive days of classes did not meet his definition of an enjoyable use of time.

He didn't mind subjects that were challenging enough to hold his interest, such as calculus or biology. And he actually enjoyed his computer programming class. But it was subjects like economics and history that caused his days within the confines of the academic institution to drag by mercilessly.

Driving to school this particular morning, he wondered how his innate aversion to certain subjects might impact his college experience. A degree in architectural engineering would require courses that would be of no interest or apparent usefulness to him. But they were necessary for a well-rounded education, and he was determined to plow through them as best he knew how.

Angling his car into the parking space of Baxter High's senior lot, his thoughts turned to Ellie's upcoming birthday. In just six short days she would be turning eighteen, and he wanted to do something special for her.

Today, his plan was to recruit Kelli and Allison to organize a party for her after she finished work at the Pet Palace Saturday night. He figured Edwards would be the perfect place for a surprise birthday party, and hoped the girls could come up with some good ideas, the likes of which seemed to elude him. One thing was for sure, though.

He lacked the skills needed for planning and organizing any kind of social event. His past attempts to do so had rather confirmed that fact.

Caleb was unloading the contents of his backpack into the recesses of his already overcrowded locker when Ellie approached him.

"Good morning, Caleb."

He glanced up at her. "Oh, hi, Ellie. Ready for your English test first period?"

"I'm ready for anything today." The lightness in her voice caught his attention. There was an unusual sparkle in her eyes, and a poorly disguised grin on her face. Something seemed different about her.

He gave her a quizzical stare. "Everything okay?"

"Just fine," she replied, breaking into a smile. "Things couldn't be better."

"Well, you're sure in a good mood today," he exclaimed. He put a finger to his temple and looked at the ceiling as if deep in thought. "Let's see, now. When I last saw you yesterday afternoon, you were in a more . . . reflective mood. Why so cheerful all of a sudden? I wish I had your enthusiasm this early on a Monday morning."

Ellie laughed, "Well, you should have. You, of all people."

"What are you talking about?" She just stood there smiling secretively at him. "Well are you going to tell me what's making you so happy, or am I going to have to guess? After all, I'm just a guy, you know. I can't read your mind."

Ellie flashed a secretive grin. "I'll tell you at lunch. Meet me in the Senior Suite, okay?"

Without waiting for his reply, she flipped around lightly on her feet and floated off to her own locker, leaving Caleb shaking his head in bewilderment.

Throughout the morning, he tried to figure out the cause for Ellie's cheerfulness. Had she received her UGA acceptance letter, or better yet, a positive response to her academic scholarship application? Perhaps she'd been offered an art scholarship. It had to be one of those three.

At lunch he excused himself from their group of friends and went out the side door of the cafeteria into the courtyard. It was nearly full of seniors today. He found Ellie sitting alone at one of the tables and plopped his tray down beside her.

"Okay, now can you please tell me the good news?" he pleaded. "I haven't been able to concentrate in any of my classes, thanks to you."

"I'm sorry," Ellie laughed. She didn't look too sorry. "I did it, Caleb. I finally did it."

"Did what?"

"I became a Christian last night!" She beamed.

In Caleb's seventeen plus years, rarely had he been left speechless. He stared at her as if she had just walked on water.

"Well, aren't you going to say something?" she prompted, with a chuckle.

All he could do was parrot her previous announcement. "You became a Christian last night."

"Yes!" she continued excitedly. "After you left, I had a long talk with Miss Cora, and then I went to my room, and I prayed and asked God to make me one of His children."

"Wahoo!" Caleb shouted, as he simultaneously pumped his fist in the air.

The seniors at the surrounding tables stopped and stared at the source of the explosion. Laughter rippled across the courtyard. Even Ellie was tickled by his spontaneous reaction.

The other students gradually resumed their conversations.

"Ellie, that's wonderful. No, that's fantastic!" He could barely contain himself. "Do you know how long I've been praying for this?" She shook her head. "Since soon after I first met you."

She blinked in surprise. "Really? That long?" Ellie placed her hand over his as gratitude welled up in her eyes. "And you didn't give up on me. Thank you for caring so much. I've never known that kind of love." She paused and smiled sweetly. "Until now, that is."

"So, what finally prompted you to give your life to Jesus?" he wanted to know.

"Well, it was for the right reasons," she assured him. "I think I finally realized how much God really loves me, and how much I really need Him. I wasn't going to say anything about it just yet, because, you know . . . of what we talked about yesterday." She grinned shyly. "But I couldn't help myself. I just had to tell you."

"Well I'm glad you did. This is the best news ever. Does Miss Cora know?"

"Yes, I told her this morning before I left for school. And do you know what she did? She gave me a big hug, and then danced a little jig right there in the middle of the kitchen."

"I wish I could have seen that." Caleb tried to capture the image in his mind. "You know what? I think you ought to tell Kelli and Allison. And the rest of the kids at church. They've all been praying for you, too, you know. They'll be just as happy for you as I am."

"I hope they don't react quite as . . . as enthusiastically as you did." She laughed at the sheepish look on his face. Then she grew serious. "Caleb, do you suppose my mother knows what I've done?"

"Somewhere in the Bible it says there is joy in heaven when one sinner repents, so I expect she's heard about it by now."

"And now I know for sure that I'm going to see her again someday." Ellie had a happy, faraway look in her eyes.

"Yes, you are. I'll get to meet her, too. And you can meet Cal. We'll all be there together."

Before he knew what was happening, Ellie leaned over and kissed him on the cheek. One of the students at the next table gave a wolf whistle, and another let out a "Wahoo!"

"I'm sorry," she apologized. A red blush colored her cheeks. "I didn't plan to do that. Honest. It's just that I'm so . . . so happy. I hope you didn't mind."

Normally, under similar circumstances, Caleb also would have blushed. Instead, he grinned impishly as he touched the spot where her lips had made contact with his face.

"I didn't mind that at all."

———————————————————————

Following their shift at the Pet Palace that weekend, Caleb and Ellie drove to Edwards to meet up with the Saturday night crowd. Ellie looked forward to their usual good time involving tasty, but not-so-good-for-you food, fun music, and high-spirited talk. When she walked through the double glass doors into the diner she was pleasantly blindsided.

In the back corner, spanning several booths, hung a large banner bearing the words "HAPPY 18TH BIRTHDAY, ELLIE!" along with streamers and blue and white balloons. About a dozen kids, mostly from the church youth group, awaited her arrival.

They presented her with a birthday cake baked by Kelli and Allison. It had her name and the number 18 on it. Along with several cards, the group gave her a professional artist's easel and a nice leather case for storing her art supplies.

Ellie fought back tears as she thanked them.

"You all have no idea what this means to me," she said in a choked voice. "This is one of the most wonderful days of my life!" She dabbed at her eyes before she turned to Caleb and wagged an accusing finger at him. "Are you responsible for all this?"

Caleb held up both hands and declared his innocence. "Hey, don't look at me. I just came up with the idea. They're the ones who took it and ran with it."

Sunday morning during the youth hour, at the urging of Tony and Amanda, Ellie shared how she had given her life to Christ the previous Sunday night. And during the invitation following the morning worship service, she went forward to publicly profess her newfound faith.

Caleb was amazed at the boldness with which she openly shared her testimony. It was as if her shyness evaporated in those moments. Several other people publicly surrendered their lives to the Lord before Pastor Murphy closed the service and dismissed the congregation with prayer.

Caleb's parents invited Ellie to join them for Sunday dinner, and she accepted graciously. Following a delicious pot roast dinner prepared and served by his mom, Caleb drove Ellie back to Miss Cora's. The two of them relaxed on the porch swing, enjoying the moment but not saying much. After a while, Miss Cora came out of the house with a tray bearing a plate of gingersnap cookies and two glasses of sweetened sun tea.

"Mind if I join you out here?" she asked in her usual sweet way.

"Of course not." Ellie motioned to the empty wicker rocking chair. "You don't have to ask. It's your house."

Miss Cora placed the tray on the little round table between them, sat down in the rocker, and helped herself to a cookie.

"I know. But I also want to respect your privacy. You live here too, you know." She gave Ellie a knowing little wink, and then changed the subject. "I sure did enjoy your testimony at church this morning. I felt like jumping up and shouting 'Glory, Hallelujah!'" She chortled under her breath. "But I restrained myself."

Caleb and Ellie laughed.

The widow grew serious. "Miss Ellie, have you given any thought to being baptized?"

Ellie shook her head. "Um . . . no, not really. I've seen people do it before, but I'm not sure what it's all about. Is it something I'm supposed to do? Now that I'm a Christian?"

Miss Cora smiled. "Why don't we have that nice young man sitting next to you answer that for us? Caleb, would you care to tackle the question?"

Caleb grinned self-consciously. "I'll do my best, but I'm sure you could answer it much better than I can." He drew a breath. *Lord, help me say the right thing,* he prayed silently. "Ellie, when you accepted Christ last week, you became a new person. I guess you could say the old Ellie is gone, and the new Ellie has taken her place. Right, Miss Cora?"

"Go on. You're doing a fine job."

"Well, baptism is a public declaration that you are identifying with His death, burial, and resurrection. When you're placed under the water, that symbolizes that your old life is dead and buried with Him. And when you come up out of the water that symbolizes that you have been raised to a new life in Christ."

"What happens if I don't get baptized?" Ellie asked.

Caleb looked to Miss Cora for help.

"Your salvation and eternal life are secure, no matter what," the elderly woman emphasized. "Nothing can separate you from the love of God. In fact, in First Peter we're told that your eternal inheritance is guarded by Almighty God. Baptism isn't a requirement for salvation. But it is necessary if you want to be an obedient child of God. It's one of the first steps you should take to publicly declare your love and devotion to the One who transformed your life. Your identity is now in Christ Jesus. You don't belong to yourself anymore. You've been bought with a price. Therefore, you are to glorify God in your body and spirit, which belong to Him. First Corinthians six, I believe."

"I want to do the right thing. But I think I'm going to need a lot of help. I really don't know much at all about how to be a good Christian."

"Don't worry, my dear." The old woman leaned forward and patted Ellie on the knee. "You've got God's Word to light your path. And the Holy Spirit to guide you in the truth." She paused and winked slyly. "And then there's Caleb, here. Seems to me he's done a pretty good job of helping you along so far, wouldn't you say?"

Ellie glanced warmly at Caleb, and then returned her landlady's smile. "Yes he has. I think he's pretty amazing."

"Well what do you know? I do believe you've made him blush." Miss Cora cackled with obvious delight. She picked up the tray and held it out to Caleb. "Care for another cookie?"

───────────

"Miss Cora?" Ellie addressed the diminutive white haired woman who sat on the chintz print sofa knitting an afghan.

It was Monday morning, the week of Christmas. School was out for the two week winter break, and she had been up in her room reading.

The elderly landlady looked up from her knitting. "Yes, my dear? What is it?"

Ellie walked over to the sofa. She carried her white Bible in one hand and a printed brochure in the other.

"I found this pamphlet stuck between two pages in the back of my Bible. I never noticed it before now." She handed the folded paper to Miss Cora. "What do you make of it?"

Miss Cora slipped on her reading glasses and studied the brochure. Her eyebrows raised as she read the front. Removing her glasses, she looked at Ellie.

"You say you found this in your Bible? The one your mother gave you?"

"Yes. It's from a crisis pregnancy center. What would it be doing in my Bible?"

Miss Cora didn't answer. She replaced her glasses, and studied it again.

"Look on the back," Ellie urged her. "There's a handwritten note to someone named Katherine. What do you make of it?"

The old woman turned the brochure over, held it closer to her face, and read the note. She inhaled sharply. "Can it be?" she muttered under her breath. "Can it really be?" She glanced up at Ellie over the rims of her glasses. "What did you say your mother's name was, again?"

"Katherine Thompson. Do you think that note was addressed to her?"

Miss Cora didn't reply. Instead, she stared at Ellie in a way that made her uncomfortable.

"Miss Cora? Are you all right?"

Miss Cora broke into a broad smile. "The good Lord be praised. I should have known. I should have known."

"Known what?" she pressed, feeling like she'd missed something very important.

The old woman looked tenderly at her. "You look so much like your mother."

Ellie's jaw dropped. "My mother? You knew my mother?" She tried unsuccessfully to connect the dots. "But how . . . how's that possible?"

Miss Cora motioned for Ellie to sit down beside her and she complied as if in a trance.

"Yes, sweetheart. I knew your mother. Very briefly, but I knew her." She handed the brochure back to the confused teen. "That note was addressed to your mother. The reason I know that is because I'm the one who wrote it."

Ellie was astounded.

"Look at it again. Can you make out the signature?"

She squinted at the handwriting. "Mrs. Williams?"

"Yes, that's me." Miss Cora chuckled. "My penmanship never was very good."

"But how did you know my mother? And what was she doing with this pamphlet?"

"Miss Ellie, I'll tell you all of what I remember. Do you see the address on the front? That crisis pregnancy center is located in Chesapeake, Virginia. I used to volunteer there once a week when Henry and I lived in Portsmouth. He was a Communications Officer stationed in Norfolk at the time. Your mother came to the center one day. She was from a small town south of Chesapeake somewhere."

"Hickory!" Ellie interjected excitedly. "She lived in Hickory."

"Yes, that sounds familiar. I remember she was a very beautiful young lady. And very scared. She was still in high school then, and about your age, I think. She'd just found out she was pregnant, and wasn't sure if she should keep the baby or terminate the pregnancy."

"You mean, she wasn't sure if she wanted me?" Ellie was hurt by the news.

"I don't think it was that," Miss Cora assured her, "so much as it was the fact that she was young, unmarried, and without a family support system. At the time, she didn't think she could properly care for or provide for a child."

"I didn't know any of this!" Ellie was incredulous. "What else can you tell me about her?"

"Well, I met with her several times after that, to encourage her to keep the baby. I seem to recall that she was leaning toward an abortion, but she had some reservations about it. I wrote that note to her the last time she came in. She said she'd think about it. I never saw her again after that."

Ellie read the note out loud:

"Katherine, all lives are precious in the sight of God, both the born and the unborn. You may not understand it now, but He wants you both to be His children, and He has a plan for your lives. Please read these two Bible verses before making your decision: Deuteronomy 30:19, and Jeremiah 29:11. I will be praying that you choose life—eternal life for yourself, and physical life for your baby. No matter what happens, always remember that GOD LOVES YOU! -Mrs. Williams"

Ellie looked up at Miss Cora. The woman had a faraway look in her eyes, which were brimming with tears.

"Miss Cora? Miss Cora!" Her voice jolted the white-haired lady out of her thoughts.

"Miss Ellie, I must confess that I've sometimes wondered if my volunteering ever made much of a difference. Results aren't always immediate or visible. Perhaps it's a lack of faith on my part. In any case, I've learned that I'm to be faithful in doing what God has called me to do. The results are up to Him." Her face became radiant and she squeezed Ellie's soft hand with her wrinkled one. "And now He has been gracious enough to allow me the joy of seeing that my labor has not been in vain." Miss Cora raised her hands over her head. "Hallelujah!"

Later that afternoon, up in her room, Ellie set up the easel given to her as a birthday present.

She began a pencil sketch of a little girl sitting on a porch swing beside her mother. Standing behind them, pushing the swing, was the transparent, nearly invisible figure of a gentle-eyed, smiling, bearded man in a long, flowing robe.

Underneath the picture, in beautifully scripted calligraphy, were the words of Deuteronomy 30:19. " . . . I have set before you life and death, blessing and curse. Therefore choose life, that you and your offspring may live."

_____

The week of Christmas crept up on Caleb like a cat creeps up on a mouse. Silently, and without warning. He'd been so fixated on Ellie's move to Miss Cora's, and so joyous over her decision to become a Christian, that he'd all but forgotten his favorite time of year.

The town's holiday decorations, the tree in the living room, and the upcoming church Christmas program, had not garnered his attention or stirred his enthusiasm like they usually did every December. The holiday seemed to have simply materialized on his radar screen straight out of hyperspace.

When it dawned on him that he hadn't given a moment's thought to gift buying for his family and friends, he went into panic mode.

With the help of his mother, he made a list of what the other members of his family might like. He also included his close friends who had been so supportive the past couple of months. And then there was Ellie. He wanted to get her something very special, something that expressed how much he cared for her.

For the past week, Caleb had been praying about his relationship with the auburn haired girl who had not only captured his attention, but had commandeered his affection the past semester. Up to now he'd had to suppress his true feelings for her. But now, it seemed as if the Lord was giving him the green light to pursue a more serious relationship with her. And he wanted his Christmas gift to reflect his true feelings.

Caleb crisscrossed Baxter in search of the last minute gifts. He spent a fair amount of time at the Southridge mall, and even drove down Highway 84 to Cairo in order to find what he was looking for in the specialty shops there.

Since he didn't have a lot of money this year, he wanted to make sure the gifts were meaningful for each recipient. By Wednesday afternoon, he'd completed the purchases, and with a sigh of relief, tossed the list into the kitchen trash can.

He was especially excited about the necklace he'd bought for Ellie, and eagerly began planning how he would surprise her with it.

On Thursday evening, his family attended the annual Christmas Eve service, which had always been Caleb's favorite gathering of the year. It was a church tradition for entire families to sit together during this special meeting, and since many relatives and in-laws were in town for the holidays, some families occupied as many as two entire rows.

Caleb's parents had invited Miss Cora and Ellie to join their family tonight. Since Miss Cora didn't drive after dark, Caleb took his father's car to the house on Pine Street to pick them up instead. He pulled to the curb in front of the Victorian and got out of the car to go see if his passengers were ready. The always punctual Miss Cora and her boarder met him as he started up the front walk.

"Right on time, young man," the widow announced with a pleased smile.

Caleb held open the door and bowed deeply. "Sawyer Limousine Company at your service, ladies. 'On time every time'. That's our motto." Ellie rolled her eyes at him but couldn't help laughing.

As he approached the church property, Caleb noticed that the lot was nearly full, so he dropped off his passengers at the main entrance before finding a parking space several hundred feet away.

He walked up to the green lit building and stopped to admire the life sized nativity out front. It was the same one he'd been captivated by as a child. And this year was no different.

Once inside the church, he surveyed the foyer and auditorium. The walls were lined with wreaths and lights, the former exuding the heavenly scent of fresh pine. Golden candelabras with flickering filaments were mounted to the ends of the pews. The organist was softly playing Christmas music as people entered and stood in the aisles, greeting and conversing with one another, many of whom they hadn't seen since the previous Christmas Eve service.

Caleb located his family and sat down next to Ellie. She was wearing the same shimmering silver-gray dress and matching low-heeled shoes that she wore the first Sunday she'd visited. She'd said it was the only dress she owned, but even if she owned a hundred dresses, he couldn't imagine her looking any more beautiful than she did in this one tonight.

Following the service, which included the singing of Christmas carols, a brief message from Pastor Murphy, and communion, many of the families moved to the fellowship hall where refreshments were served. It was a time to catch up with family and friends who were in town for the holiday.

Miss Cora, however, appeared tired, and asked if Caleb might drive her home a bit early.

When they arrived at the old Victorian, the elderly lady excused herself and said she was going to bed. Ellie went upstairs to put on a sweater, and then joined Caleb on the porch.

Caleb had been waiting for this moment since the day he'd purchased Ellie's present. As the two sat looking at the twinkling lights adorning the houses up and down the street, he reached into his jacket pocket and pulled out a little red box with a gold ribbon and bow on it. He held it nonchalantly in his lap. After a while, Ellie looked down and noticed the object in his hand.

"What's that?" she asked.

"What's what?" He followed her gaze to the box in his hand. "Oh, this?" He held it up for her to see. "Oh . . . nothing. Just a little gift for a very special person, that's all."

It took a moment for Ellie to realize what he was saying. "You mean it's for me?"

"Well, it must be. I don't see any other special people around here, do you?" He handed her the box. "Merry Christmas, Ellie."

"Caleb! I wasn't expecting anything." She accepted the gift. "You really shouldn't have."

"Well, all right, then. I guess I can always return it." He made a move to take back the box, but she held it out of his reach.

"Not on your life, Mister," she laughed. "Don't you know a figure of speech when you hear one?"

He wagged a finger at her. "I thought you might feel that way. Go ahead . . . open it."

She carefully slid off the ribbon, and slowly opened the box. Tucked inside was a thin-chained white gold necklace with a small heart inside a larger one.

"Oh, it's gorgeous. I love it!" She disengaged the necklace from the velvet liner and held it in her palm, studying the details. "I've never had anything as nice as this." Then she turned to him with a question. "What's the significance of the two hearts?"

"Well, first of all, it's to remind you that you will always be safe in Jesus. He's the larger heart and you're the smaller one inside of His."

Ellie looked as if she were going to cry. "That's beautiful, Caleb. I'm going to always wear this." She unclasped the chain.

"Here, let me help you." Caleb took the necklace and she pulled back her hair so he could fasten it around her neck.

"Thank you." She looked down and quietly admired the double hearts for a moment. "You said first of all. Is there some other significance?"

Caleb thought he detected a hint of anticipation in her voice. Perhaps it was his own that he sensed. "Well, yes there is. It's to remind you that you will always be in my heart, too."

Tears welled up in Ellie's eyes, and then finally broke free and trickled down her cheeks. Blinking to hold back the flood, she gazed into his eyes.

"I've been waiting a long time to hear you say that." She wiped her eyes on the sleeve of her sweater.

"Well I've been waiting a long time to say it." His response elicited a lighthearted laugh from Ellie. "But now I have the freedom to tell you how I really feel about you."

He turned his body to face her, and their knees touched. Taking both her hands in his, he looked directly into her eager brown eyes and smiled. "Ellie, I can't think of anyone else I'd rather pursue a relationship with. Ever since I met you, you're all I've been able to think about. You've been on my mind, and now you're in my heart." He squeezed her hands. "You've changed my life. And I want you to continue changing it."

The tears resumed their path down her face. "Caleb, you've changed my life." She took a breath to steady her shaky voice, and a touch of the shyness that so appealed to him reappeared. "Maybe we can both continue changing each other's lives."

"I'd like that very much, Ellie."

She looked longingly at him. "Caleb Sawyer, I'm so lucky to have you in my life. No, wait. Not lucky. Blessed! I'm so blessed to have you in my life."

Caleb smiled. "You're right. It's blessed! But I'm the one who's blessed."

Ellie giggled. "No, I am."

They both laughed and timed their response. "Well, aren't we the blessed ones!"

With the Christmas lights from the house across the street reflecting in her eyes, Caleb grasped Ellie's hands in his and gazed longingly at her. She gazed back at him. The distance between them closed slowly, and the kiss that followed was one that he would never forget.

––––––––

Christmas break proved to be the best Caleb could ever remember. It even ranked above the year he received the new video game system he'd been dying to have. The joy of seeing Ellie put her trust in Jesus Christ as her personal Savior, and the prospect of beginning a new journey with her made this holiday season a most memorable one.

Even the air seemed fresher, the sky brighter, the sights and sounds more vibrant and clear than ever before. Never had each new day held so much promise, so much anticipation, so much enjoyment for him. But then, he had never known anyone like Ellie Thompson before. And it was wonderful.

On Christmas day, Ellie surprised him with a gift of her own, a framed pen and ink drawing of him wearing his #87 Bearcat jersey leaping high in the air to haul in a one-handed pass. She had obviously worked on it for some time, and he was as surprised with the gift as she had been with his.

He hung it on the wall of his bedroom where he could admire it from his bed while he daydreamed about the artist who had created it.

The second Sunday into the New Year Ellie was baptized at the conclusion of the morning worship service. When she came up out of the water with a huge smile on her face, the other teens erupted in spontaneous applause, and many of the adults joined them. In the midst of the celebration, Caleb was certain he heard a voice that sounded very much like Miss Cora's shout "Hallelujah!"

Amanda Sonnenberg expressed an interest in guiding Ellie in her new walk with Christ, and the new believer agreed to be mentored by her. She also became a regular at the Wednesday night youth meetings, and soon became good friends with Kelli and Allison.

Caleb was thrilled to see her continue to blossom and come out of her shell.

Every night before bed he thanked the Lord for all He'd done in Ellie's life, for using him to help her find peace with God, and for bringing her into his life. Never before had he seen God work in such wonderful ways, and as a result, his own faith grew by leaps and bounds.

One Tuesday evening toward the end of January, as he was preparing for bed, Caleb's cell phone beeped, indicating he had a text message. It was from Ellie.

All she said was, "Call me ASAP. Good news."

He couldn't hit her number on speed dial fast enough.

"Guess what!" the ecstatic voice on the other end dispensed with the usual greeting. "I just received my acceptance letter from the University of Georgia. Can you believe it?"

She squealed so loudly that he had to hold the phone away from his ear.

"I'm going to college this fall!"

"Ellie, that's terrific! I'm so happy for you. That's got to be a big relief."

"Tell me about it," she laughed, obviously over the moon about the news.

Caleb's mind raced ahead. "But I thought you had to prove financial ability before they would accept you."

Ellie's enthusiasm did not seem to diminish in the slightest by his back to earth inquiry.

"You do. But here's the best part, they're offering me a partial scholarship to the School of Art as a Drawing and Painting Major." She repeated her earlier exuberant question. "Can you believe it?"

Caleb had never heard her so excited. "That's fantastic. It's good to know those professors up there recognize real talent when they see it. Kinda renews my faith in the institution of higher learning."

Ellie laughed. "Oh, stop it." She chided him playfully. "Now if I can save up enough the rest of this year, I might be able to cover my entire first year."

"What about the FAFSA money you applied for? If that comes through, you'll be in good shape, won't you?"

"I was so excited about the scholarship, I completely forgot about that. But yes, that should cover just about everything else, I think." She paused to catch her breath. "Caleb, this is an answer to my prayers. God has been so good to me. In fact, looking back now, I can see His goodness even when I didn't recognize it before. He's always loved me, hasn't He?"

"Yes He has."

There was a momentary silence on the other end. "Hey, guess what I'm looking at right now."

"I don't know. What?"

"The necklace you gave me for Christmas. It reminds me of Him." She paused, then added with a sweetly flirtatious tone, "And it reminds me of you."

Before he could formulate an appropriate reply, she quickly tacked on, in a sing-song voice, "Goodnight, Caleb. See you in school tomorrow."

CHAPTER TEN

FULL OF SURPRISES

"WHERE DID THE TIME GO?" Caleb posed the question to Ellie one evening while the two were sitting on their favorite swing.

It was a warm Saturday in early May, and they had just completed their shifts at the Pet Palace and were enjoying some take-out burgers from the Dairy Shack they'd picked up on the way to Miss Cora's house.

Their senior year of high school was rapidly drawing to a close, and the semester had blown by to the pair like a bullet train to a couple of passengers standing stationary on the platform a few feet from the tracks. It was hard to believe that graduation was just around the corner. The entire second semester seemed to be compressed into a few short weeks, but a lot had transpired in that time.

In addition to his work hours at the pet store, Caleb picked up a half-dozen lawn mowing jobs to help pad his college savings account. Yet he still managed to find time to participate on the Baxter boys track team, where he competed in the 400-meter and 400-meter relay with a satisfactory measure of success.

Ellie continued to grow in her newfound faith, and not a youth meeting passed where she didn't come prepared with a list of questions for Tony or Amanda. In March her federal student aid application was approved, which, when coupled with the partial art scholarship she had received in January, completely covered her tuition and room and board at UGA.

On top of that good news, and out of the blue, Mrs. Sinclair informed her that an acquaintance of one of the art professors who had judged Ellie's entries in the art competition had seen her work and had been very impressed with her talent. He wanted to commission her to do a number of water color and ink drawings for the lobby of a large hotel he owned in downtown Atlanta. The amount he was offering to pay for her artwork was more than enough to purchase a new wardrobe for college.

Even though they were busier than ever, they still had time to spend with each other. Whether it was with the gang at Edwards or the Dairy Shack, or just the two of them alone on a date, they enjoyed every minute they were together.

It was becoming rather apparent to all their friends that there was something special going on between them, something wonderful developing in the relationship, something magical. They were falling in love.

Two weeks before graduation, Ellie was surprised to learn that she had been named class salutatorian, losing out to Monica Stedwell for valedictorian by only two hundredths of a grade point.

To celebrate this honor, Caleb took her to a fancy restaurant in Dothan the following Saturday night. The two enjoyed a delicious meal and a romantic walk in a nearby park.

"Thank you for planning such a wonderful evening," Ellie said, as they strolled hand in hand down the path. "You told me on my birthday that you weren't any good at planning things like this." She turned to face him with a twinkle in her eye. "Mister, you've been holding out on me."

They continued walking and soon came across a large decorative fountain in the middle of the park. He and Ellie sat down on the edge and ran their hands through the spray.

"Ellie," Caleb began, staring into the water, "there's something I've been meaning to say to you."

"Yes?" He detected the note of anticipation in her short response.

After drying his hands on his shirt, he took her hands in his. Looking intently into her eyes, he shared what was on his mind. "Ellie, I love you."

She responded with an affirmative—and very memorable—kiss.

Graduation came and went. During her salutatorian address, to the nervous consternation of the politically correct faculty adviser who had approved her speech, Ellie gave glory to God for all He had done in her life, and acknowledged the role her friends had played during the past year at Baxter High.

Once again, as he had observed during her baptism testimony before the church congregation, Caleb was amazed at how comfortable and confident she appeared standing before the packed auditorium of faculty, fellow students, and families. The withdrawn and isolated caterpillar he had first noticed in the fall seemed to have disappeared completely, only to be replaced by the beautiful butterfly that now stood with elegance and grace addressing the entire school community.

Following the commencement ceremony, Caleb and Ellie posed for group pictures with B.J. and Allison, Aaron and Kelli, and their other friends in their caps and gowns. After exchanging good-byes and well-wishes with their fellow classmates, the graduates who were in the church youth group attended a reception organized by their parents and youth leaders. It was one of those memorable nights that all high school graduates look back on for the rest of their lives, some with fond memories, and some with regrets.

That summer could best be described as a blurred blip on the radar screen. It almost seemed over before it started. The two worked as many hours as Mr. Pruitt would allow at the Pet Palace, sometimes picking up extra shifts for other employees who called in sick or took vacation time. Caleb continued to mow lawns, while Ellie concentrated on completing the drawings for the hotel owner who had commissioned her.

In late June, accompanied by Caleb's parents and sister, they made a trip to Athens to familiarize themselves with the UGA campus. And nearly every week, Caleb took Ellie shopping so she could assemble her wardrobe in preparation for college life.

Although Athens would be their home-away-from-home for nine months out of each of the next four years, Miss Cora assured Ellie that her residence would continue to be the house on Pine Street for as long as she wanted.

In spite of their busy work schedules and preparations for the late summer move to Athens, the two still found time to have some midsummer fun.

In July they went tubing down the Flint River, and twice they went boating on Lake Seminole with the church youth group. Aaron Johnson, whose dad owned the powerful red ski boat with the inboard small-block Chevy engine, was very popular on those outings.

Ellie had never been water skiing before, but on her second attempt managed to stay up for five minutes. During the second outing, Caleb and Ellie skied together behind the boat. At one point, he inched his way close and attempted to hold her hand while skiing side-by-side. Losing his balance, he took a rather awkward and awesome tumble that generated a huge splash, and to his chagrin, plenty of teasing that lasted the rest of the summer.

As the summer months drew to a close, Caleb found himself experiencing a mix of emotions. Although anticipating the start of college with Ellie, and eager to begin the next chapter in his life, he nonetheless felt a certain sadness that some things were changing forever. The friends he'd grown up with all seemed to be going in different directions.

B.J. and Allison were staying in Baxter to attend the local community college. He promised to stay in touch with his best friend as much as possible. Aaron would be attending Florida State, and Kelli was going to a Christian university in South Carolina. He couldn't help wondering if that separation would affect their relationship.

While bummed about the breakup of the long time group of friends, he was grateful that Ellie would be in Athens with him the next four years. Although unsure of how often they would be able to see each other, he knew it was going to be better than if they attended different schools in different states.

One early August evening, the two were discussing the upcoming school year as they sat on the porch swing. Ellie expressed a concern of hers.

"I'm worried that we won't see much of each other once classes start."

"Yeah, me too. It's gonna be difficult with our full schedules, but we'll figure it out." He patted her hand. "We'll eat lunch together, or study together in the library. Who knows, we might even have a few classes together. And don't forget the games on Saturdays."

"I know." She looked a little down. "But we won't have as much time together as we've had this past year."

Caleb took her face in his hands. "Ellie, whatever happens, I'll always be there for you. No matter what."

That discussion prompted him to ask Miss Cora if he could carve their initials in the other arm of the porch swing. The widow not only gave her wholehearted consent, she offered the very pocket knife Henry had used to carve the other arm as the tool to make the inscription.

Carefully, with Ellie looking over his shoulder, he carved the initials C.S. & E.T. surrounded by a heart. While he was working on the masterpiece, Miss Cora excused herself to get some cookies and lemonade to complete the celebration. As soon as she disappeared into the house, Ellie gave Caleb a kiss.

"I'm so blessed to have you in my life, Caleb."

"No, Ellie, I'm the blessed one."

Laughing, they completed the now-familiar routine. "Well aren't we the blessed ones!"

Then, underneath the heart, he added 4EVER.

***

Two weeks later, they loaded Caleb's car and made the trip up to Athens. After helping Ellie move into her dorm room and meeting her roommate, he found an empty cart and hauled his own things into the elevator and up to the third floor room that would be his home for the next year.

They registered for classes, received their schedules, and then went to the student center for a bite to eat and to pick up a copy of the fall football schedule.

Caleb was excited about the approaching season, and eager to attend all the home games at Sanford Stadium. The preseason polls had the Bulldogs cracking the top ten teams in the country, and the consensus was that the team might be contending for a national championship in the next year or two.

Classes began three days later, and Caleb threw himself into his studies. Certain subjects were going to be a challenge, but he'd set high goals for himself, and was determined to do well.

Whenever they could, he and Ellie would get together and share how school was going.

Ellie loved her art classes and said her instructors were very demanding, but encouraging at the same time. They attended games together, and enjoyed hanging out at the student center, playing ping pong, or just walking around campus holding hands.

During registration, they had picked up information about the various campus organizations, and began attending the weekly meetings of a Christian campus outreach ministry. There was even a church that met on Sunday mornings in one of the buildings, and they were soon worshiping and enjoying fellowship with other believers among the student population.

College life steamrolled on. Days turned into weeks, weeks into months. Winter and summer breaks came and went. Time rushed headlong into the future, picking up speed, faster and faster, much like the spinning night and day cycles of the time traveler in H.G. Wells' classic *The Time Machine*.

Amidst the blur of their college experience, some special moments stood out to Caleb.

For his nineteenth birthday, Ellie gave him a Bulldog jersey and a football that had been used in one of the home games. They became two of his most cherished possessions. The following year, she gave him a UGA football helmet, which he kept on display in his dorm room.

On Caleb's twenty-first birthday, Ellie outdid herself compared to his previous gifts. She made arrangements with the groundskeepers to allow the two of them half an hour in Sanford Stadium, reminiscent of how Rocky Balboa rented the empty ice rink for Adrian in the movie *Rocky*.

Caleb, dressed in his jersey and helmet, and holding the football, ran out of the tunnel onto the field and struck the Heisman pose as Ellie, laughing uncontrollably at his melodramatic posturing, took pictures in an effort to create the once-in-a-lifetime memories.

And he loved her all the more for it.

In June following their junior year, they attended B.J.'s and Allison's wedding. Caleb was the best man and Kelli, the maid of honor. Allison asked Ellie to be a bridesmaid, and she was happy to oblige. At the reception, Caleb learned that Kelli and Aaron had broken up, albeit amicably, and she was now dating a guy from Tennessee whom she'd met at school. Early into their senior year, Caleb and Ellie began talking about life after college.

They sat together at a small window table in an off-campus cafe late one Saturday afternoon following the season home opener. The Bulldogs had just defeated Alabama twenty-six to twenty-three in overtime, and the room was abuzz with excitement.

They were discussing the game when Ellie broached the subject of marriage.

"Caleb, there's something I've been thinking about a lot lately."

"What's that?" He took a long sip of his Coke.

She gave him a sly grin. "Getting married."

He pretended to be shocked. "You're getting married? Well, congratulations! Who's the lucky guy?"

Ellie laughed. "Well, it's going to be someone else if a certain person doesn't hurry up and do something about it."

He held up his hands in mock protest. "Hey, I'm workin' on it, okay? I'm workin' on it." He took her hands in his and became serious. "Look Ellie, we both know where our hearts are leading us. And I want you to know, I've been praying a lot about it already."

"So have I." Ellie smiled. "Do you think we should wait until after graduation? That seems so far away."

"Too far away," he groaned. "But yes, I think we should finish school first."

"Any particular reason why?"

Caleb hesitated. "Well, I hadn't planned on telling you just yet, but I talked with B.J. this week. He told me they're discovering that being newlyweds and full-time students is harder than they first thought. It's creating some stress in their relationship."

"Oh my!" Ellie looked alarmed. "It's not serious, is it?"

"They're having trouble trying to fit everything into their schedules and still find time for each other. But remember, B.J. works part-time, too. Anyway, he said not to worry. They're working it out."

"But our situation isn't quite as stressful. Neither of us has to work during the school year. Thank the Lord."

"That's true, but don't forget, we're just getting into some of our most difficult classes. The question is, do we want to risk introducing that kind of pressure into our own relationship right now?"

Ellie wrinkled her nose. "No, I suppose not. Being newlyweds on top of everything else might be too much." She paused. "But being engaged wouldn't be any trouble at all," she hinted playfully.

Caleb grinned. "Funny you should bring that up. I've been thinking about that."

Ellie looked surprised. "You have?" When he didn't reply right away, she prompted him. "And . . . ?"

He leaned back in his chair, crossed his arms, and smiled secretively. "I'm just waiting for the right moment."

Caleb started the ball rolling when they returned to Baxter for Thanksgiving. While Ellie was out shopping for Black Friday bargains with Kelli and Allison, Caleb did a little shopping himself.

He drove to the jewelry store near the Southridge Mall. Once inside, he glanced around the room at the gleaming glass cases. The sheer volume of gold and glittering gems overwhelmed him. How in the world would he ever pick out the perfect ring from among so many?

A professionally dressed woman in her mid-fifties approached him. "How may I assist you?" she asked politely.

"I'm here to buy a . . . to buy an engagement ring," he stammered, shaking his head, "and I have no clue where to begin."

The woman gave him a warm smile. "I'd be happy to walk you through that process."

She explained the four "C's" of gemstone purchasing to him: cut, color, clarity, and carat. Then she showed him a variety of stones and settings within his price range. There were so many options. Too many. How could he ever be expected to pick the right one?

This was the hardest decision he'd ever faced. Almost two hours later, after looking at what seemed like hundreds of rings, he made his final choice.

Driving home with the burgundy velvet box nestled in the seat beside him, he was ecstatic with anticipation. When should he give it to her? What should he say? How would she react?

For the remainder of the weekend he could barely mask his excitement. He was greatly tempted to give Ellie the ring right now, but he decided to wait and propose to her on her birthday instead. That would give him more time to properly plan the all-important event. But the suspense was killing him, and he was afraid he'd blow it. He'd never been very good at keeping secrets from Ellie.

Late in the afternoon on December nineteenth, Caleb, dressed in his finest suit and tie, drove his father's almost new car over to Miss Cora's to pick up Ellie. He'd made reservations for seven o'clock at La

Scala, a very upscale and highly-recommended Italian restaurant in Columbus nearly two hours to the north.

He wanted the night to be perfect.

Pulling to the curb in front of the old Victorian, Caleb got out of the car and walked up to the porch with a single red rose in his hand. The engagement ring was burning a hole through his inside breast pocket, and he hoped the shape of the box poking his ribs wouldn't give away his secret too soon. The deep peals of the doorbell brought back many happy memories as he waited for a response to his announced arrival.

Ellie opened the door. She was a picture of perfection. Her hair was pinned in a very attractive upswept style, and she wore a pair of sparkling earrings that complemented the two-heart necklace he'd given her their first Christmas together.

But it was the dress that caught his full attention. He'd never seen it before. It was an elegant, full length black dinner gown with a V-neckline. A thin silver belt and matching shoes completed the ensemble. She looked absolutely stunning in it.

He must have stared speechless for longer than he thought, because her words snapped him out of his trance.

"Well, are you going to come in, or are you just going to stand there gawking at me?" She tried to sound serious, but the poorly hidden grin on her face gave her away.

Caleb stepped sheepishly across the threshold into the foyer. "I don't know what to say. You look . . . you look absolutely amazing, Ellie."

"Why, thank you." She smiled sweetly at him. "And you look very handsome yourself tonight." She crossed the tiny room to fetch her clutch purse from the credenza against the stairway wall. He gave her the rose, and helped her on with the shawl that had been hanging on the coat tree next to the front door.

As they stepped out onto the porch, Caleb turned to her. "Ellie, I think you may have to drive to Columbus tonight."

She gave him a startled look. "What's the matter? Don't you feel well?"

He could contain himself no longer. "Oh I feel fine. It's just that I don't think I can take my eyes off you, that's all."

Ellie laughed and gave him a playful hug.

When they reached the curb, he held the door open for her, and then got into the driver's seat. As he started the car, he looked at her once again, shaking his head in amazement.

"I can't get over how beautiful you are tonight."

Ellie frowned. "You sure you don't want me to drive?"

―――――――――――――

"I've been looking forward to this evening ever since you suggested it," Ellie exclaimed, once they had merged onto Highway 27 for the two hour drive to Columbus.

She was obviously excited about the evening ahead.

He shot her a sideways glance. "So have I."

The pair drove in happy silence for a while.

Caleb felt a few butterflies in his stomach. He was eager to propose to the woman of his dreams. This was going to be a night they would never forget!

When they arrived at their destination, they were met by a valet. Caleb gave him the car key and then, with Ellie on his arm, escorted her inside. The host welcomed them and said their table was waiting. The maître d', dressed in a black tuxedo and bow tie, introduced himself and ushered them to an intimate damask draped table for two. After they were seated, he lit the centerpiece candle and said their waiter would be with them shortly.

Caleb glanced around at the Tuscan décor. Plaster statuettes graced small alcoves inset into the brick and stucco walls, which were lined with grapevines and elegantly framed portraits of the Italian country-side. The flickering wall sconces cast a warm, yellow light that reflected in the crystal goblets and highly polished silverware in front of them. His gaze returned to Ellie.

"Pretty fancy place, isn't it?"

She glanced around the room. "I've never been in such a fancy restaurant before. It's stunning." She flashed an impish grin. "I've got to admit, your taste in fine dining has greatly improved since we first met."

Their waiter arrived, introduced himself, and presented them with menus. After telling them about the evening's specials, he left them alone to make their dining selections. As they studied the menus, the sound of soothing violin music caught their attention. Across the room, a musician stood in front of another table, playing a song for its two occupants.

Ellie turned back to Caleb. "Not a strolling violinist, too! Do you think he'll come over here and play something for us?"

"Let's just say I've already made the necessary arrangements," he replied.

She looked lovingly at him. "Caleb, you're so romantic."

He seriously considered proposing to her right then and there, but decided to stick with his original plan to "pop the question" afterwards at the pond.

Their dining experience at La Scala proved to be *eccellente*. The fine dinner, the candlelight, and the strolling violinist created the perfect mood, and set the stage for what was to come.

It was sprinkling as they left the restaurant. Caleb borrowed an umbrella from the valet and held it over Ellie as they walked to the nearby park.

By the time they arrived, the skies had cleared. Strolling arm in arm, they reached the center of the park and stopped on the white arched bridge straddling the pond. They stood at the railing and gazed silently at the lights reflecting in the calm water below. Caleb slipped his arm around Ellie. She smiled and leaned into him.

"Thank you for such a wonderful evening. You're a real sweetheart." She turned and planted a kiss on his cheek. "I love you, Caleb Sawyer."

Caleb placed a hand over his jacket pocket to make sure the little box with its precious cargo was still there. Then he placed both hands on her shoulders and gently turned her so that they were facing each other. He gazed into her beautiful brown eyes. The dark orbs sparkled in the light of the old-fashioned lampposts on either side of the bridge.

"And I love you, Ellie Thompson." He cleared his throat and fought to regain his composure. "Want to know how much I love you?" he asked. Before she could answer, he pulled out the black box and knelt down on one knee. "I love you this much!"

Ellie sucked in her breath sharply, put both hands over her mouth, and took a step backward. "Caleb!"

Holding the box in front of him, he looked up into her eyes. They were glistening with anticipation. "Ellie, I want to spend the rest of my life with you." He slowly opened the lid to reveal the large solitaire diamond seated majestically in its white gold throne. "Will you marry me?"

She replied swiftly, eagerly, without hesitation. "Yes!"

Taking the ring from its container, he reached for her left hand. She was visibly trembling. He slipped the diamond onto her ring finger and stood to his feet. Tears trickled down her face, leaving faint streaks of mascara visible in the dim light.

Ellie wrapped both arms around his neck as he pulled her to him. Her lips met his in a long, passionate kiss. For several minutes, they stood in a silent embrace. Neither one of them spoke. Neither had to.

It was the most wonderful moment of Caleb's life, and he reveled in it. His emotions washed over him like the gentle swells of the ocean.

―――――――――――――

As they left the park arm in arm, joy seemed to float Caleb down the sidewalk. They headed blissfully back to the restaurant three blocks away.

Each time they passed a streetlamp, Ellie held up her hand to admire the rock that gleamed on her finger. And each time, Caleb let out a familiar "Wahoo!" that echoed off the buildings on either side of the street.

The faint sound of a police siren arrested Caleb's ears. It came from behind them. He glanced back as they came to an intersection, and he pushed the button to cross the side street. As the wailing siren grew louder and louder, the green "WALK" sign lit up and they stepped into the crosswalk.

They were nearly to the other side when the sharp screeching of tires caused them both to stop and whirl around.

A car slid into view around the corner and barreled down the street toward them, followed closely by a patrol car in hot pursuit, its red and blue strobes flashing ominously off the facades of the buildings. At the intersection, the fleeing driver lost control of the vehicle.

Caleb had only a split second to react. He threw himself at Ellie.

Then everything went black.

PART TWO

.

CHAPTER ELEVEN
MY FIANCÉE IS MISSING!

BEEP. BEEP. BEEP.

The rhythmic, soothing tone pierced the ghost-like fog in Caleb's brain. Faint, but steady.

Perhaps it was his cell phone informing him that he had a message. Ellie had probably called while he was asleep.

Now where was that phone? Why couldn't he find it?

And why was his room so dark?

He stirred slightly. Pain shot through him.

He lay still for a moment, trying to shake the haze that drifted through his mind. Stirring again, the pain returned, flooding his whole body.

I must've gotten beat up pretty good in last night's game, he thought.

Funny that he couldn't remember who the Bearcats' opponent was. The Arlington Tigers? Madison Central? He had no memory of the game whatsoever.

So this is what a concussion feels like! He blinked open his eyes and glanced around the semi-darkened room. Even his eyeballs ached.

Why was everything so blurry? And why was the bedroom window to the left of his bed instead of at the foot where it was supposed to be?

Beep. Beep. Beep.

My phone! Gotta find my phone and check Ellie's message. She'll be wanting to know how I'm doing this morning.

Caleb struggled to turn toward his nightstand where the beeping cell phone must be. Searing pain cut through his torso like a hot knife, and he fell back on the pillow with a gasp. As he waited for his head to clear, he became aware of movement in the room.

His parents' anxious faces appeared in front of him.

He was not in his bedroom. He was in a hospital room. And the steady beeping he'd mistaken for his cell phone was the sound of the monitor to which he was connected. He tried to sweep the remaining cobwebs from his brain.

The corners of his mother's mouth curled up in a soft, but relieved smile. "Don't try to move, Caleb. Just lie still."

The confusion in his mind manifested itself in the question that formed on his chapped lips. "I . . . I don't remember the game at all." The hoarseness of his own voice startled him. "Who did we play last night?"

His father leaned over and gently placed a hand on his shoulder. "It's okay if you don't remember, son. Things will start coming back soon enough."

A flash of panic shot across Caleb's mind. "Dad, why am I in the hospital? What happened?"

His father stole a quick glance at his mother before answering. "Uh . . . you were in an accident, Caleb."

"An accident?" The cobwebs began to evaporate. "Then it wasn't a football game? No, it couldn't be. That was way back in high school." He shook his head slightly, sending a twinge of pain down his spine. For the first time he felt the brace around his neck. "What kind of accident?"

This time he noticed the exchanged glances. "You were hit by a car, son," his father explained.

"A car? When? Where?"

At that moment the door opened and the nurse on duty entered the room in response to the call button which had been activated by his father. She went immediately to Caleb's side.

"Well, I see our patient is finally awake." She smiled at him and began checking the equipment to which he was attached. She addressed his anxious parents standing on the opposite side of the bed. "I've notified Dr. Cavanaugh. He's on his way. I'm just going to check your son's vitals here for a moment."

Caleb lay still, and silently watched her enter the data into the computer on the bedside cart. The door opened again, and a doctor with a stethoscope peeking out of his pocket entered the dimmed ICU room.

"Glad to have you back with us, young man." Dr. Cavanaugh smiled at his patient and introduced himself.

He asked Caleb and his parents a few questions as the nurse continued updating his information. Caleb answered each question patiently until, unable to stand it any longer, he interrupted the doctor with a question of his own.

"Dr. Cavanaugh, my dad told me I was in an accident. How bad was it? What are the extent of my injuries? "

The doctor studied the computer screen before speaking directly to his patient. "On the nineteenth you were struck by a car. I'm sure your parents can fill you in on those details better than I can. But I'll tell you this, you're lucky to be alive, given the level of trauma you've experienced. You sustained a severe concussion with some swelling of the brain, a broken left collarbone and left femur, three fractured ribs and left forearm, plus a number of lacerations and abrasions."

"Am I going to be all right?"

"It's a little early to be exact at this juncture. Your collarbone, ribs, and forearm should mend completely. However, your femur was shattered in two places. We had to perform a surgery called an open reduction internal fixation. That involves inserting a titanium rod into the center of the femur. It supports the bone so that it can heal properly." He pointed to the apparatus attached to Caleb's leg. "That external fixation device keeps your leg immobile. You'll want to remain as stationary as possible for now."

Caleb had two more questions for Dr. Cavanaugh, but it was the answer to the second he feared the most. "Is the rod permanent? And will I . . . will I be able to walk again?"

"Yes to both questions, Caleb," the doctor quickly replied, assuaging his fears. "The rod stays in place, but you won't even know it's there once the leg is fully mended. And I'm confident that with physical therapy you'll regain nearly full use of that leg. The worst case scenario is that you may walk with a slight limp. Only time will tell."

"What about the concussion?" Caleb asked anxiously.

"The brain trauma was our biggest concern upon your arrival. You experienced an intracerebral hemorrhage and some initial swelling of the surrounding tissue, which caused your coma. But thankfully your CT scans and MRIs determined that surgery was not necessary. Your EEGs and other diagnostics show no permanent damage. You should expect some headaches and blurred vision, and possibly nausea, but these symptoms should diminish over the next few weeks. At this point I don't foresee any long term effects. All things considered, I'd say you're doing fairly well for what you've been through. But given the severity of your injuries, I expect you'll be here for a while."

"What about my memory?" Caleb asked. "I don't remember the accident at all."

"Short term memory loss is typical for this type of trauma. But don't worry. That should come back to you. It could be all at once, but most likely it will be over the course of a few days, as your brain continues to heal. My advice is to be patient."

Caleb's mother spoke up. "He's already started asking questions about the accident. Should we answer them?"

Dr. Cavanaugh smiled reassuringly at her. "That's entirely up to you. As his parents, you're the best judges of how much information he can handle right now."

The doctor turned back to him. "Caleb, on a scale of one to ten, how's your pain right now?"

"Well, when I lay still, about a six, maybe. But if I try moving, definitely a ten."

"What should that tell you?" The doctor arched his brow.

"Lay still and don't move?" Caleb managed a grin.

"Good answer." Dr. Cavanaugh smiled and patted Caleb's shoulder. "I'll check in on you later this afternoon."

He shook hands with Caleb's parents before leaving the room. The nurse gave Caleb a sip of ice water from a foam cup with a straw through the lid, and then set the cup on the bedside tray.

"Don't hesitate to call again if you need anything. I'm right down the hall." She turned and left the room.

As soon as the door closed behind her, Caleb rephrased his previous question to his parents. "So, what happened? Where was I?"

His mother scooted her chair closer to the bed and sat down. His father stood beside her with his arm around her shoulders.

"It happened in Columbus. That's where we are now. You're in Good Samaritan Hospital."

"What was I doing in Columbus?" His father turned and stared out the window. Caleb urged him to continue. "It's okay, Dad. I can handle it."

"Well, son, you brought Ellie here to celebrate her birthday. And to . . . and to propose to her."

Ellie! For the first time since regaining consciousness, thoughts of his fiancée flooded his mind like waves crashing against a craggy shoreline.

"Where is she? Is she okay? Is she here in the hospital? Why isn't she here with me?" He looked from his father to his mother and back again. Their faces reflected strain and sadness. A tear broke free and trickled down his mother's face, and his father squeezed her shoulder.

As gently and briefly as possible, his father explained how the accident had occurred.

"Caleb, you and Ellie were apparently heading back to your car when it happened. The police were chasing a stolen vehicle and the driver lost control. From what we've been able to gather, you tried to shove her out of the way, but there wasn't time. The car hit you in the crosswalk and knocked you and Ellie onto the sidewalk. The police said you both narrowly avoided being crushed by the car when it jumped the curb and crashed into the corner building. You were both rushed here in critical condition."

Caleb tried putting all the pieces in place. Some of the details were emerging from the fog that still swirled in his brain. It was as if he were working on a difficult jigsaw puzzle without having the picture on the box to use as a guide.

"Ellie is here? In this hospital? How is she? Is she okay?"

Again, his father hesitated. Taking a deep breath, he answered his son carefully. "Well, Caleb, she . . . she was here. Earlier."

Caleb struggled with that explanation. "What do you mean she was here? Where is she now?" He repeated himself. "Is she okay?"

Panic rose within him. His mother stifled a sob that sent an icy chill down his spine. Suddenly, it felt as if a two hundred pound weight were sitting squarely on his chest.

He turned to his father. "Dad! She's not . . . she's not . . . is she . . . ?" He couldn't bring himself to finish the sentence. It was too painful to say out loud.

There were tears in his father's eyes, and his voice cracked as he spoke. "Caleb, I'm sorry, but we just don't know. She was in bad shape when they brought her here. She had some very serious injuries, like you. Your mom and I have been splitting our time between the two of you, sitting by your bedsides. But three days ago she was moved to another hospital, and we haven't been able to find out anything since then."

"Why not? Can't you find out how she is? Or where she is?"

His mother tag teamed for his father.

"Caleb, one day I went to her room and she was gone. I immediately ran down to the nurse's station, but all they could tell me was that she had been transferred elsewhere. For the past three days, your father and I have been desperately trying to get some news on her whereabouts and condition. But they said they can't give out that information."

Caleb's thoughts began to race, reminding him of how painful it was to even think. "Why not? Why can't they tell you anything? For crying out loud, she's my fiancée. I have a right to know. I have to know!" He struggled to sit up, but his pain, and his father, forced him into a prone position again.

"Son," his father's voice trembled as he spoke, "we talked with the hospital administrator himself, but all he could tell us was that Ellie had been moved to another facility. He was genuinely apologetic, but he said the hospital's confidentiality policy would not allow him to give us any more information."

Caleb didn't know a lot about confidentiality laws, but he'd had a few discussions about them with his father.

"Dad, doesn't the closest relative usually have the authority to make decisions for those unable to make decisions for themselves?"

"Yes, in most cases that's true."

"But Ellie has no close relatives. At least none that are involved in her life. We're the closest thing she has to family."

"I know, Caleb, I know. But we don't have legal power of attorney. Nor are we her appointed health care representatives."

Caleb's voice grew shrill. "Then who made the decision to move her to another hospital? And who made the decision to withhold the release of information to us?" The strain of the conversation was beginning to take its toll.

"Honey, perhaps you should rest now," his mother interjected, with a gentle pleading tone in her voice. "We can continue this discussion when you're a bit stronger."

"Yes, I think that's a good idea," his father quickly agreed. "Get some rest now, son. In the meantime, we'll do all we can to find some answers."

Perhaps it was his agitated state of mind, or the level of pain that affected his thinking in the moment, but before his parents could attempt any further persuasion, he reached determinedly for the call button dangling next to his pillow. With pain shooting up his arm and into his shoulder, he repeatedly pressed the red button on the end of the cord.

"Caleb!" his mother protested instinctively, but his father put his hand on her shoulder again and shook his head.

"Mom, I've got to get some answers for myself," Caleb insisted. "I just can't lay here and do nothing at all. I've got to know what happened to her."

The latch on the heavy wooden door turned with a loud click, and the nurse entered the room. He was still pushing the call button.

"How can I help you?" she asked cheerfully.

"I need some answers!" Caleb blurted out. "Answers about my fiancée. I need to know how she's doing and where you've taken her."

The smile drained from the nurse's face, and she looked as if she were going to fall over. But she maintained her professionalism and a look of compassion replaced her surprise. She responded to his outburst with a voice as gentle as his own mother's.

"Caleb, I understand how badly you want answers. How badly you need answers. And I wish I could give them to you." She shook her head. "But I can't. I just can't. I'm so sorry."

"I don't care about any stupid privacy laws. I have a right to know. She was my fiancée. We got engaged right before the accident. You don't have to say anything you're not supposed to say," he continued, pleading his case. "Just drop a hint or a clue. I'll figure out the rest. Please, I'm begging you. I need to know about Ellie."

The nurse tried to calm him down. "Caleb, even if I were allowed to tell you, I couldn't."

"And why not?" he demanded suspiciously.

"Because I honestly don't know her condition. Or where she is. I'm very sorry, Caleb."

Her best attempt to calm his rising agitation failed miserably.

"Well you could find out if you wanted to. There's got to be some-body here who will tell me. Call the head nurse. Call Doctor Cavanaugh. Get the hospital administrator in here. I've got to have answers. And I've got to have them now!"

By sheer willpower, Caleb managed to throw off the sheet and raise up on his good elbow, but the pain was so intense he gasped and nearly passed out. With the assistance of his father, the nurse forced him back onto his pillow. Too weak to resist, he sank back limply, his breath coming in short bursts. His parents held his hands and attempted to calm him as the nurse prepared a sedative.

She administered the shot to her hyperventilating patient. Soon his breathing became more regular, and he relaxed and sank into the mattress.

Caleb feebly turned his head toward his shaken parents.

"Mom, Dad," he whispered hoarsely. "I'm sorry. I didn't mean to get so . . . so riled up." Then he lapsed into unconsciousness.

———————

With a start, Caleb blinked and opened his eyes. A sudden chill sent shivers throughout his body. *What an odd sensation for such a hot, arid climate.*

He heard a faint, distant sound. It wafted toward him from across the dunes, as if carried aloft on the wind. He paused and listened. There it was again. This time it was much clearer. Closer. *Beep . . . beep . . . beep.*

His bleary eyes began to focus. He was not standing in a desert. The sound he heard was the soft, rhythmic beeping of the monitor to which he was attached. He glanced to his left. The blinds were drawn, yet slivers of sunlight had managed to find their way into the room and were casting their faint, parallel beams across his chest.

The sound of a chair scraping the floor came from his right. He turned his head in that direction. The sudden move proved to be a none-too-subtle reminder not to repeat the action.

His sister's worried face came into view. "Caleb?" Her voice sounded unusually shaky and high pitched.

He studied her face for a moment as his senses returned.

"Caleb, are you awake?" This time her voice was a tad stronger.

"Hey, Squirt. What are you doing here?"

Cassie broke into a broad, relieved grin. "Just keeping an eye on you. I've been sitting here for about an hour."

"Where're Mom and Dad?"

"They went down to the cafeteria to grab some lunch. I offered to stay here with you until they get back."

"Weren't you hungry?" he inquired.

"I'm fine. Mom said she'd bring me a sandwich." The look of concern returned to her face. "How do you feel?"

"Sore. And hungry." It was good to hear her laugh again.

He chatted with his sister for a while. Their conversation focused on the happier memories the two shared growing up. Caleb sensed Cassie was trying hard to avoid mentioning Ellie. Maybe his parents had put her up to that. In any case, the tactic took his mind off his fiancée. He joked around with her until their parents returned from the hospital's first-floor cafeteria.

"Cassie, I brought you a turkey on rye." His mother handed her a foil-wrapped sandwich.

"Thanks, Mom." Cassie started to unwrap her food.

"Honey, why don't you eat that outside," his father suggested. "I'll take the next watch. I'm sure you and your mother could use some fresh air."

"Okay." She re-wrapped the sandwich and headed for the door with her mother.

As soon as they were out of the room, Caleb brought up the taboo subject.

"Any news about Ellie?"

"I've been making some phone calls, but nothing concrete yet," his father replied. "But don't worry. I'm not going to give up. She had to be in stable condition or they wouldn't have released her. I know that much. But it's still very serious."

Caleb's frustration spilled out. "Dad, I feel so helpless. There's got to be something I can do besides lie here like a vegetable."

His father offered the best—and perhaps the only—course of action. "Caleb, why don't we pray about it together?" he suggested.

Caleb suddenly felt humbled. "I'm sorry, Dad. I don't know why I didn't think of that. I should know better. Remember all the times we prayed together for Ellie? When she needed a job, and a place to live? And when she needed the Lord?"

"Caleb, do you recall when we lost Cal? What was the one thing that made the hurt and heartache bearable during that time?"

Caleb thought for a moment. "I'd have to say it was prayer. That, and the love shown by our church family."

His father smiled and nodded in agreement. "I don't think we could have made it without either one. Taking our deepest needs and sorrows to a sovereign, loving Father is the best thing we can do. Sometimes it's the only thing we can do."

He pulled the chair closer to the bed and sat down. Placing his hand over Caleb's, he continued. "It seems to me that now is one of those times. Would you agree?"

Caleb nodded. "Yes. You know, Dad, not long after I met Ellie, I remember how hard it was for me to get out of the way so God could do His work in her life." He paused for a moment. "Why is it so much harder now? By now I should have enough faith for this."

His father fell silent for a few seconds before answering. "Caleb, perhaps it's not a matter of having enough faith at all. Or the lack of it. Let me ask you this, do you love Ellie more today than you did back then?"

Caleb didn't waste any time replying. "Of course I do. I love her with all my heart, Dad. Back in high school I cared a lot about her. I was infatuated with her, I suppose. But now we've had four years for our love to grow. Today it's stronger than it's ever been."

His father smiled. "Maybe that's why it's harder now for you to step out of the way and let God work. Your feelings are so much more intense. Stronger. Deeper. It's only natural that you would feel more helpless than ever before. But just remember, it's often when we're at our weakest that the Lord's power is most evident. His strength is made perfect in our weakness. Remember that verse?"

"Yeah, I do. Thanks, Dad. I really needed that."

Caleb prayed first. "Dear Lord, for whatever reason, I confess I'm having a really hard time giving this situation over to You. I know that every time I've done that before, You've always been faithful. As difficult as it is, I surrender this matter to You. Wherever Ellie is, would You please spare her life and heal her? And would You help us find her? Lead us to her. In Jesus' name, amen."

Then his father prayed. A deep sense of peace washed over Caleb. Of course he would continue to do all he could to find her. But the battle was the Lord's now. And he was ready to do whatever God directed him to do in the search for the love of his life.

Knock. Knock. Knock.

Someone's knuckles rapped on the door to Caleb's hospital room. With a mouthful of hospital food in his mouth, he managed a muffled "Come in."

The door opened, and B.J. peered around the corner. "Anybody home?"

The familiar face sent Caleb's spirits soaring.

"B.J.! Man, is it ever good to see you." Caleb held out the arm that was not encased in plaster and the two shared a heartfelt hug. "'Bout time you got here. What took you so long, bro?"

"Your dad said to wait until they moved you up here from ICU. Besides, you know the old saying, 'absence makes the heart grow fonder'." B.J. broke into a wide grin. "I thought the longer I stayed away, the more you'd miss me." He paused. "Dude, you did miss me, right?"

Caleb laughed. "Miss you? I didn't miss you at all. Of course, for a while there I didn't miss anybody. I was out of it for a week."

"That's what I heard. But you're looking pretty good now, though."

Caleb looked at the cast on his left arm and the contraption holding his left leg stationary. "You call this lookin' good?"

B.J. laughed. "Better, then." He pulled up a chair next to the bed and sat down. "But from what your dad told me, you looked pretty bad when he first saw you after the accident."

"Remember that bruise I got in the Arlington game our senior year?" Caleb asked. "You ought to see the bruises on me now. No comparison."

"Ouch." B.J. winced sympathetically. "So how are you feeling? What's it been, two weeks?"

"Just about. Got rid of that irritating neck brace yesterday. And the doc says my arm and leg are doing as well as can be expected. I still have some headaches and soreness, but all things considered, I'm feeling much better than even a few days ago."

"How long are they going to keep you incarcerated here?"

Caleb grinned. "Until I reform enough to take my place in society again. Which could be a while. Another week to ten days, maybe." He turned the interrogation on its head. "How's Allison?"

"Oh, she's fine. Sends her love. She would have come with me, but her grandpa's in the hospital."

"He is? Anything serious?"

"I don't think so. He's got A-fib, you know. They had to shock him to get his heart back in sync. They're keeping him overnight for observation, that's all."

"Well, tell Allison I'll be praying for him."

"Thanks. I will." B.J. grew quiet for a moment. Then he spoke haltingly, as if unsure about how to phrase his next question. "So . . . how's . . . how's Ellie doing, Caleb?"

Caleb expelled the air from his lungs through puffed cheeks. Then, taking a deep breath, he began to tell his friend about the situation.

B.J. shook in head in amazement. "So, you haven't even seen her or talked to her since the accident?"

"No. Nothing at all. When I woke up she had already been transferred. B.J., I could accept not being able to see her or talk to her if I only knew how she was doing. It's the not knowing that's killing me."

"Have you tried calling her cell phone?"

"Yeah, sure. Lots of times. I've left so many messages her mailbox is full. I keep asking myself, 'Why doesn't she answer? Doesn't she have access to her phone, or . . . or is she unable to respond?' That's what scares me the most."

"That's really tough, man." B.J. leaned back in his chair. "I feel your pain. Must be awful."

"I feel so helpless. But I still want to do something."

"Of course. I understand that completely. Is there anything I can do? Make phone calls, visit other hospitals, go to the police, anything at all?"

"Well, my parents are doing everything they can. And so am I." He nodded toward the table next to the bed. "My phone's been on that charger much of the past two days because I've called every hospital and care facility within a hundred miles. Nothing. They either say they have no information or they can't comment due to those stupid privacy laws." His voice was thick with exasperation. "It's a brick wall everywhere I turn, B.J."

"That's rough, man. Wish there was some way I could help." He scratched his head. "You know, most medical facilities won't give out information over the phone. But if someone was to pay them a visit in person, that might be different. I'd be happy to do whatever leg work you need done. Just name it." He grinned. "Doctor Watson at your service, Sherlock."

Caleb laughed out loud, releasing the tension that had been building inside. He was grateful for the offer. "Thanks, Doctor. I'll take you up on that, count on it."

The two friends spent the next half hour catching up on the latest news regarding mutual acquaintances, and reminiscing about old times and nearly forgotten shenanigans.

B.J.'s visit was just the diversion Caleb needed to take his mind off the things that weighed heavily on him.

During a brief lull in the conversation, a funny look came over B.J.'s face. "Oh, by the way, I've got some other news to share with you, dude."

"What kind of news? Good news or bad news?"

"Oh, for sure good. Definitely good." He crossed his arms and waited.

"Well?" Caleb cocked his eyebrow. "Are you going to tell me, or what?" B.J. just sat there grinning from ear to ear.

"Oh, I see. We're going to play the old 'Let's Make Caleb Wait' game again, are we?" He shook his head in playful disgust. "I'm really disappointed in you, B.J. That's such a childish game. I thought you'd be more mature than that by now." He could tell that B.J. thoroughly enjoyed having the upper hand.

"Well guess what it is. Take a guess."

"I have no idea," Caleb protested.

"Just take a guess."

"I can't."

His friend insisted. "Guess."

"Oh, alright, alright. Let me see." He thought for a minute. "Are you—"

"I'm going to be a father!" B.J. interrupted him.

It was Caleb's turn to be silent. His eyes widened. "You're kidding me. You're going to be a dad? When?"

"Mid-August. I just found out yesterday."

"That's awesome, pal. Congratulations." He high fived his friend with his free hand.

"Thanks. Needless to say, I'm really stoked about it."

Caleb suddenly became somber, and frowned. "Did you tell Allison yet?"

B.J. looked confused. "Allison? Why would I need to . . . Hey, what do you mean, 'tell Allison'?"

Unable to contain himself any longer, Caleb slapped the bed with his free hand and burst into peals of laughter. "Gotcha, pal!"

The look on his friend's face made the pain worthwhile.

"I've found out a few more details," Caleb's father informed him as he was finishing his hospital breakfast.

It had been three weeks since the accident, and in two days Caleb was scheduled to be transferred to a rehab center back in Baxter. He was dying to leave the hospital, and desperate for any news concerning Ellie.

"What is it, Dad?" he asked eagerly. "Did you find out where she is?"

"Well, no, not yet. But I've uncovered the reason for the stone wall."

"What is it?"

"The hospital spoke with a relative of Ellie's soon after she was brought here. They can't give us the person's name, but whoever it is showed up here and gave specific instructions not to share any information about her to anyone without their express permission."

Caleb was stunned. "A relative of Ellie's was here? In this hospital? But who? Her father? She doesn't even know who that is. And he's never made any effort to contact her. He might not even be alive, for that matter. And none of her other relatives ever showed any interest in her at all."

"I know that, son," his father offered gently. "But whoever it is apparently has the right to act on her behalf."

"But what possible reason could they have for not sharing her information with us? That's just plain wrong, Dad. Not to mention cruel."

"I agree with you, Caleb. I'm sure they must have been informed about her relationship to you. For the life of me I can't understand why they would want to cut us off completely."

"If I just knew that she's okay, I could deal with not knowing where she's at. Is there any way we can force them to tell us how she's doing?"

"I don't think so, son." His father's shoulders sagged wearily as he spoke. "Since the request to withhold information was made, there's nothing more we can do for now. But I'm going to contact a lawyer and have him look into it."

For the first time, Caleb noticed how tired and drawn his father's face looked. He must have spent countless hours exploring every possibility over the past two weeks.

"Dad, I really appreciate all you and mom have done . . . all you're doing. I'm sure it's as hard on you as it is on me."

"Thanks, Caleb. But we're not going to give up. It may seem next to impossible now, but remember this, we serve a God with whom nothing is impossible. You still believe that, don't you?"

Tears welled up in Caleb's eyes. "Yes, I still believe that. Although I have to admit, I haven't been acting like it."

"This has been very difficult for all of us, Caleb. But we've been through hardships like this before. And God has proven Himself faithful. We have to keep trusting Him." Caleb nodded in silent agreement. "Oh, there's one more thing I discovered. Ellie wasn't moved to another facility for medical reasons."

"What do you mean? I thought she was moved to another hospital that was better equipped to handle her injuries."

"I did, too. But that's not the case. Once she was stable enough, she was moved only because of this relative's insistence."

"But why?" Caleb blurted out. "Why would they want to move her if she was getting good care here?"

"I don't have the answer to that, either. We can speculate all we want about possible motives, but I don't think that would prove very helpful."

Caleb digested this latest bit of information. "Dad, can you bring my laptop with you next time? I want to start searching online for this relative of hers."

His father smiled patiently. "Do you suppose you can hold off until you get back to Baxter?" he suggested. "I think it might be better if you were settled in there first before you dive headlong into that pursuit. know how you tend to throw yourself at these kinds of things. A f more days rest here will do you good. What do you say?"

Caleb didn't want to wait two more days. That would mean two more days wasted when he could be searching instead. He wanted to act now.

But a familiar small voice seemed to whisper in his ear, *"Be patient, Caleb. Take a few days to pray. And wait on Me."*

"Okay, Dad," he surrendered. "I'll wait 'til we get back home."

CHAPTER TWELVE

SOME NEWS IS GOOD NEWS

TWO DAYS LATER, AS SCHEDULED, Caleb was released from Good Samaritan Hospital and, accompanied by his mother, endured the two hour ride back to Baxter. A few hours later he was settled in his room at the rehab center that would be his home for the next three weeks. If his recovery progressed as planned, he could expect to be transitioned to outpatient rehab and be back in his own bedroom by the end of the month.

When word got out that Caleb was back in town, a steady stream of friends and well-wishers began to flow through his room in between therapy sessions. So many, in fact, that the center had to limit the number of people per day. Pastor Murphy and the Sonnenbergs visited him on day two.

B.J. and Allison came by. Allison made sure to let him know that it was she who was having the baby. They had a good laugh over that one.

When Kelli and her sister Krystal paid him a visit, he learned that Kelli had gotten engaged over Christmas break to the young man she'd met in college. She hadn't planned on telling him about it yet, because the engagement had taken place on the same day as the accident. But he'd asked her about their relationship, and she finally told him.

Her hesitancy reminded him of just how thoughtful and caring she was, and he knew that whoever this guy from Tennessee might be, he was getting a great gal.

Although Caleb appreciated all the visits, they began to take their toll on him, not so much physically as emotionally. He grew weary of answering the same questions about Ellie over and over. It wasn't that he was unwilling to talk about her. It was just that with each explanation came a fresh reminder of the pain he felt within, re-opening the wound he knew would never properly heal until he was with her again.

He missed her terribly. He missed seeing her, talking to her, holding her. He longed to sit next to her on the porch swing and inhale the scent of her beautiful auburn hair as her head rested on his shoulder. The ache of her absence was almost unbearable.

On the third day of his rehab stay, Caleb had another visitor. He'd just completed his afternoon therapy session, and was back in his room, sitting in a wheelchair reading some get well cards that had come in that morning's mail, when Miss Cora appeared in the doorway.

"Hello, Caleb," she greeted him warmly.

"Miss Cora!" Caleb put down the card he was reading and motioned for her to enter. "Come in. It's good to see you." She slowly shuffled into the room, steadying herself with her cane. He noticed she carried a cookie tin in the other hand. He was sure he knew what it contained. Caleb pointed to the chair next to the window. "Please, have a seat, won't you?"

Miss Cora set the tin on the small round table between them, and with a grunt plopped into the chair. She leaned her cane against the table and turned toward his wheelchair. "I brought you some gingersnap cookies. I know how much you enjoy them."

"Thank you. I'm sure they won't last long."

She inclined toward him. "Now let me have a look at you, young man." She studied him for a moment. "You look as though you're doing well. How is your therapy going?"

"Pretty good, actually. My therapist says I'm making progress. I'm trying to regain my strength. They've got me doing stretching and mobility exercises, mostly." He glanced at his left leg, extended straight out in front of him. "But I should be walking again before too long."

"That's wonderful to hear," she said with genuine interest. "I'm sorry I wasn't able to make the trip up to Columbus to visit you in the hospital. I've had a flare up of this pesky arthritis lately and I'm afraid it's kept me close to home."

"Oh, that's quite alright," Caleb reassured her. "I understand. I haven't been very mobile myself lately," he added with a laugh.

Miss Cora chuckled. "Caleb, you and I are more alike than either one of us would care to admit." She grew serious. "I hear you've had a few visitors since you got back."

"That's an understatement," he declared.

"Well then, I'm sure you've had to answer the same questions over and over by now, so I'm not going to trouble you to do it again. Your parents have filled me in on everything they know. I just wanted to drop by and let you know that I'm praying for you and Ellie."

"Thank you. That really means a lot to me."

"Now don't you get discouraged, young man," she urged him, tapping a bony finger on the table for emphasis. "I'm convinced that God is not through with either you or Miss Ellie just yet. He has a plan for your lives. This is just a part of it. As difficult and painful as these circumstances must be for you right now, remember that God sees the end from the beginning. You're in a valley right now." She stared intently at him. "Do you know what a valley is?" Caleb shook his head, sure that her definition was right around the corner. "A valley is nothing more than a low spot between two high places. You don't stay in the valley, you walk through it! The psalmist said there may be tears in the night, but joy comes in the morning."

Caleb's eyes grew misty. "Thank you, Miss Cora. Those words are very comforting. I needed that reminder."

The elderly woman continued. "Whatever God has planned for you, Caleb, you can rest assured it's for your good and not your harm. You do have a future and a hope. And it's going to be wonderful."

Before she left, Miss Cora prayed for Caleb and Ellie, and then said her goodbyes. When she reached the door, she turned and addressed him one last time. "I know how much you miss her, Caleb. I miss her, too."

Then she hobbled out of the room.

Caleb wheeled himself around the table and stared out the window. A small yellow and black finch hopped from branch to branch in the courtyard tree a few feet away on the other side of the glass.

He reflected on the widow's words of encouragement. *"You do have a future and a hope. And it's going to be wonderful."*

Caleb bowed his head. "Father, forgive me for not trusting You like I should. I don't understand what's going on, or why it's happened, but I know You mean to use it for our good. Help me not to fear the future. It's in Your hands. Whatever happens, I'll trust You. But please take care of Ellie, wherever she is. And help me find her. In Jesus' name, amen."

Then he began his future by opening the tin of gingersnaps.

"Hey, I think I might have something!" B.J. exclaimed, leaning over his laptop and staring intently at the screen.

"Yeah? What is it?" Caleb glanced up from his computer at his friend sitting across the table.

"I've been pulling up newspaper accounts of your accident, beginning with the twentieth of December through the time you left the hospital. Here's a follow up story in the Columbus *Ledger-Inquirer* dated December twenty-third. It gives an account of the driver's arraignment as well as an update on the condition of the two people critically injured in the police chase on the evening of the nineteenth."

"What's it say?"

B.J. turned his laptop around and pushed it toward Caleb. "Here, read it for yourself. The first part is about the driver. Start about halfway down the column. The part that begins with 'The two pedestrians struck by the fleeing car . . .'"

Caleb pulled the computer to him and scanned the article until he found the paragraph B.J. had mentioned. Tracing the lines of type with his finger, he read the words out loud:

> "The two pedestrians struck by the fleeing car while crossing Chestnut Street on the evening of the 19th remain in critical but stable condition at Good Samaritan Hospital.
>
> One of the victims, Caleb Sawyer, a 21-year old college student from Baxter, remains in a coma due to head trauma suffered when struck by the speeding car, but a hospital spokesperson stated that his condition has improved slightly, and said that doctors are expressing optimism about his chances for recovery.
>
> The other person involved, Elinor Thompson, 22, also from Baxter, was admitted with similar injuries, but at the time of this report, no update was immediately available. A hospital spokesperson said he was unable to comment on her condition, and declined to give a reason. An attempt was made to speak with a relative of the injured woman, but he declined to comment as well."

"Did you catch that?" B.J. blurted out. "He saw this relative of hers, Caleb. He actually talked to the man."

"I've gotta get a hold of this reporter." Energized with renewed hope, Caleb grabbed a pen and wrote down the name of the article's author and the phone number of the newspaper. "Maybe he was able to get a name, or find out who he is. At least he can give us a description."

"Do you think it's Ellie's father?" B.J. asked.

"I don't know. If he's still around, he'd be her closest living relative. But I have no idea why he'd show up now. Or why he'd want to move her and not let us know where. In any case, this is the only lead we have at the moment, and I'm going to pursue it as far as I can."

He grabbed his cell phone and punched in the number for the main desk of the *Ledger-Inquirer.* After listening to several automated options, he selected one and waited for someone to answer.

"Yes, my name is Caleb Sawyer, and I need to speak with uh . . . with Jim McCready please. I believe he's one of your reporters." He paused as the person on the other end said something. "Well, he wrote an article that involved me in the December twenty-third edition of your paper, and I need to talk to him about it. It's rather urgent that I speak with him as soon as possible." Again he listened for a moment. "Do you have any idea when he might be able to return my call?" After a short pause, he was transferred to the newspaper's voice mail system where he left his number and a brief message for the reporter.

Caleb kept his phone within arm's reach the rest of the day, eagerly awaiting the call that was sure to come at any moment. The wait seemed like an eternity. Several times his phone rang, but the calls turned out to be friends checking in on him. By bedtime he was in such an anxious state that he knew sleep would be difficult. Picking up his Bible, he read a few chapters until he was too exhausted to keep his eyes open any longer.

The next day he clung to his phone even during the morning rehab session. He was just finishing lunch back in his room when the call came. As soon as he saw the caller's number, his heart began to pound. This was it. With trembling hands he took the call.

"Hello, this is Caleb."

"Caleb Sawyer? This is Jim McCready returning your call. I appreciate you contacting me. How are you doing?"

"Well, I'm making some progress. Slower than I'd like, but rehab's going well."

Instead of asking why he'd called, Mr. McCready began questioning him about the accident and what he remembered. Caleb responded politely, although somewhat impatiently, to his questions.

When the reporter asked how Ellie was doing, he was surprised to learn that she had been removed from the hospital without so much as a word to Caleb or his family. After asking a ton of questions about her disappearance, and how the family was coping with the situation, he said he wanted to do a follow up human interest article on their plight.

"Well, I don't know." Caleb hesitated. "I'm not so sure I want all the details made available to the public. We're kind of a private family. I don't think that's such a good idea."

"Sure it is." Undaunted, the reporter pressed him. "Look at it another way. It's bound to generate a lot of interest and sympathy, right? And that might lead to some new information about Ellie. That's what you're after, isn't it?"

"Yes, of course." He gave it a momentary thought. "All right. I guess you can go ahead with the article." He hoped he was making the right decision.

"Great. You won't regret it." The man launched into the possible responses to his story with all the enthusiasm of an adman pitching his brainchild to a CEO. Finally, Caleb was able to get around to explaining the purpose for his call.

"Mr. McCready, the reason I called is that your previous article mentioned that you spoke to one of Ellie's relatives. I was hoping you could give me some details about him."

"Sure. I'll tell you all I know, but it's not much. While I was at the hospital gathering information, I passed one of the doctors talking to this man in the hallway. From what little I overheard, he was related to Ellie somehow. As soon as the doctor left, I approached him and asked for an update on her condition. At first he looked startled, but then he scowled and issued a *no comment*. He hurried away but I followed him and kept asking more questions. He ignored me all the way to the main lobby. That's when he got in my face. 'If you don't stop harassing me, I'm gonna have you arrested!' Those were his exact words . . . give or take a few. Then he walked out the front door."

"Can you describe him?" Caleb asked eagerly.

"Well, I'd say he was in his mid-forties, about five-ten to six feet tall, short brown curly hair, and . . . oh, maybe weighed about two twenty to two forty."

"How was he dressed?"

"He had on a dark blue sport coat, a light blue shirt, and a bluish-gray tie. Paisley print, I think. With tan pants and brown loafers."

"Did he have any unusual features? Scars. Tattoos. Anything like that?"

"Not that I noticed. But I do recall that he had a small diamond stud earring in each ear."

"Thanks for the information. You've been a big help, Mr. McCready," Caleb acknowledged.

"No problem. I hope it makes a difference. I'll send you a link to the follow up story once it's released. Let's keep in touch, okay? I wish you well, Caleb."

Over the next three days, Caleb continued to focus on his rehab, which was progressing well, and on his search for Ellie, which wasn't.

He'd subscribed to a number of "people locator" search websites, most claiming to be able to find anyone anywhere. But he was greatly disappointed with the results.

Four days after his phone conversation with Jim McCready, the reporter sent him an email containing a link to the follow up story. Caleb immediately opened it and devoured its contents.

Jim had piled on the pathos this time, playing heavily on the sympathies of the reader. In the article, he wrote:

> What makes this an unusual tragedy is that the two young victims had just become engaged moments before the accident. They were returning from Ellerbee Park, where Mr. Sawyer had proposed to Miss Thompson, and were only a block from their destination when the fleeing vehicle struck them down.
>
> But what makes this an unthinkable tragedy is the heart-wrenching fact that the two are now, by another cruel twist of fate, unable to find one other. One minute they are united with the glowing prospect of a life together, the next, violently torn apart without so much as a single word or clue of explanation. The burning questions of 'why?', 'who?', and 'where?' remain unanswered. Why did this happen? Who is responsible for her disappearance? And where is Ellie Thompson?
>
> Put yourself in Caleb Sawyer's shoes for a moment. Imagine how he feels right now. He and his family desperately need your help. That is the purpose of this article. I ask you, I beg you, I implore you, if you have any information, no matter how insignificant, that might help reunite this hapless couple, please contact this reporter at the links below or call this newspaper, anonymously if necessary. Any person who is capable of reading this sad story without developing a deep sense of sympathy and compassion for this young couple's

plight must be a cold and heartless individual indeed. Let's bring Caleb and Ellie back together again.

———————————————

A week after the story was published in the Columbus *Ledger-Inquirer*, Jim McCready called Caleb with an update. He sounded very upbeat.

"The article is generating a huge response from the public," he told him. "In fact, there's been an avalanche of calls from people voicing their prayers and support for you, or offering to help locate Ellie. We've received a lot of tips on who's responsible for her disappearance, or where she might have been taken, or how she might be found. Most of those leads have been investigated, but so far they've turned out to be dead ends. But one person left me a voice message I thought should be passed along to you."

Caleb's heart skipped a beat. "Do you think it's legit?" he asked.

The reporter cautioned him. "Well, I can't verify anything this caller said. She didn't give her name, and her call back number was blocked, so I was unable to identify the source or substantiate the information. But I thought you ought to hear it for yourself. Maybe it will help."

The journalist placed Caleb on speaker phone so he could listen to the message. The female caller sounded hesitant, as though she were nervous or unsure about making the call.

"Hello? This call is for Jim McCready. It has to do with his article in Wednesday's paper. I have some information that may help Caleb Sawyer in the search for his fiancée. I'm afraid I can't give my name or number, because that could jeopardize my job. This may be nothing, but I want to help if I can. I know for certain that the person who ordered Ellie Thompson's transfer is her father. I can't tell you how I learned this, and I'm sorry I couldn't find out his name or where he took her. I know it's not much, but I hope it helps." The voice paused for a few seconds. "One more thing. Please don't try to trace this call. If you do, I'll have to deny everything."

"So, what do you think?" Jim asked him, after playing back the message.

Caleb didn't recognize the caller's voice. But it sounded familiar. "It's not much to go on," he replied. "Like you said, there's no way to verify the source. But if it's true, it confirms some of my suspicions. Thanks for sharing it with me."

"No problem. Glad to help."

After thanking the reporter again, Caleb ended the call. He felt a glimmer of hope. If the information provided by the anonymous caller was correct, then he should concentrate on locating Ellie's biological father. He and B.J. had explored that possibility earlier as part of their overall search, but now he would make the man his focus.

As he lay in the bed at the rehab center that night, Caleb replayed the woman's message over and over in his head. He was sure he'd heard her voice before. Sometime fairly recently. But where?

He was almost asleep when it hit him. He'd heard that voice while he was in the hospital. It was the nurse who'd said she couldn't tell him anything about Ellie.

CHAPTER THIRTEEN

DETECTIVES AND DONUTS

THE FOLLOWING MORNING CALEB DEVOTED himself to his rehab with renewed enthusiasm. The sooner he was able to reach the goals set by his therapist, the sooner he'd get to go home. And the sooner he got home, the sooner he'd be free to expand his efforts to locate Ellie's father, and ultimately, Ellie herself. In the meantime, he spent every free moment searching for online information. Every possible lead was followed up with a phone call. But each call ended in disappointment.

The next day, his last at the rehab center, Caleb unearthed another piece to the puzzle. As he was eating lunch he had a sudden inspiration. Ellie's birth announcement. Publications often printed a list of births, including the birth date, the baby's name, and the names of the baby's parents. Perhaps her father's name was on file in the Hickory, Virginia, newspaper.

A quick online search produced a website for the *Hickory County Courier*. It stated that the paper was published three times a week, on Tuesdays, Thursdays, and Saturdays. It didn't offer much in the way of information, but it did provide a phone number. He hoped he wouldn't have to suffer the agony of playing phone tag again.

He called the number listed. To his mild surprise, it was answered on the third ring by a live person.

"Hickory County Courier." The woman's voice had a pleasant tone to it, and a slight accent.

"Yes, my name is Caleb Sawyer. Does your paper publish birth announcements?"

"Yes we do. At the beginning of each month. But only for babies born in Hickory County. They're twenty-five dollars each and are limited to forty words or less. Would you like me to take your information over the phone?"

"Oh, um . . . I don't need to place an announcement. I'm just searching for one that would have been in your paper twenty-two years ago. Do you keep digital archives of old editions?"

"I'm sorry, but we don't have digital archives here. Our circulation is too small for that." Caleb's heart sank. "But we do keep actual hard copies of old newspapers in the basement. Do you have a specific date in mind?"

"Yes. The actual birth date was December nineteen, nineteen ninety-five. The mother was Katherine Thompson, and the baby's name was Elinor. I need the name of the father."

The woman wrote down the information. "Well, I can try to locate that announcement for you, but you need to be aware that we may not have that particular edition anymore. We lost a number of them a few years back due to a leaky water pipe, so I can't guarantee that the edition in question survived the mishap."

Caleb was undaunted. "I understand. But I'd appreciate anything you can do. It's very important that I find the information."

"I'll do what I can, but it may take a while. Can I call you back?"

He gave the woman his number. Another agonizing delay. Another anxious wait.

The afternoon seemed to drag by. As four o'clock came and went, Caleb began to fear that the newspaper office would close for the weekend and he'd have to wait until Monday to hear back from the woman. He resisted the urge to call her.

Finally, around a quarter to five, she returned his call.

"I'm sorry for the delay, Mr. Sawyer. I've had an unusually busy afternoon for a Friday. But you'll be pleased to know that I was able to locate the edition with the birth announcement in it. You're very lucky, though. It was in the area that was destroyed by the water leak, but we were able to save it. There are some minor water stains, but everything's still legible."

"Can you read it to me, please?" Caleb asked, hoping the impatience in his voice didn't come across as irritation.

"Here it is. Born December nineteenth, a baby girl, Elinor A. Thompson, to Katherine A. Thompson and John C. Smith."

"Is that all? Are there any other details?"

"No, that's it. Just your basic birth announcement. That's all we typically publish."

Caleb thanked her for retrieving the information and ended the call. He leaned back in the chair and stared at the name on the pad of paper in front of him.

"John C. Smith," he read out loud.

It was a common name. A very common name.

He groaned inwardly. Finding the right John C. Smith might turn out to be harder than finding the proverbial needle in a haystack. But at least it was a step in the right direction.

The search for Ellie was beginning to feel like a long, drawn out game of *Clue.*

One clue led to another clue which led to another which led to yet another. How many more clues were there between him and Ellie, anyway? But no matter how long it took, he was bound and determined to find her.

He'd promised early in their relationship to always be there for her. And he aimed to keep that promise.

Caleb entered the name John C. Smith and Virginia into the search parameters of one of the people finder websites. Fifty-eight names popped up. But none were listed as currently or previously living in Hickory.

Figuring it was unlikely that a person would remain in such a small, unincorporated town for twenty years, he methodically checked out all fifty-eight names. Eight were in their forties. One even had a relative named Catherine, with a "C," but her age was listed as sixty-seven.

Ellie had told him she didn't think her mom had ever married her father. If that were true, then the names Katherine Thompson or Elinor Thompson would not likely be associated with John C. Smith at all.

Fighting the temptation to get discouraged, Caleb pushed on. Armed with the knowledge that Katherine Thompson was eighteen when Ellie was born, and that she had met John Smith while in high school, he concluded that Ellie's father must now be between thirty-nine and forty-two. He narrowed his search to men in that age range. Then, since he was not sure that her father had been born in Hickory, or even Virginia for that matter, he began searching other states.

But there were thousands of John Smiths, and hundreds of John C. Smiths in each state. This was going to take a while.

There was a knock on the door. The cheerful face of his best friend peered into the room.

"Hey there, Hop-a-long. Thought I'd stop by on my way home and see how you were doing."

"Well don't just stand there, Jughead. Come on in and pull up a chair."

B.J. stepped into the room. He was carrying a box of Krispy Kremes in one hand. "Thought you might like something to help celebrate your parole tomorrow morning." He plopped the box of donuts on the table and sat facing Caleb. Then he opened the lid, and ate the first one himself.

Caleb gave him a disapproving look. "Thanks a lot, pal."

"What?" B.J. feigned innocence. "I'm just helping you get the party started."

Caleb grabbed a donut for himself. "Well, how's this for a party favor? I just found out the name of Ellie's father."

"No way!" B.J. exclaimed, his mouth full of pastry. "What is it?"

"John C. Smith."

"John C. Smith. Seriously? John Smith? There must be a million John Smiths in the world."

"Thousands, at least. It's going to take a lot of time and effort to find the right one."

B.J. grimaced. "Now why couldn't his name be more uncommon? Like . . . Arthur Flatbush? Or Victor Finnigan? Or . . . or Aloysius X. Mergatroid? Something like that," he bemoaned.

"Aloysius X. Mergatroid?" Caleb laughed out loud.

"Well that would be a lot easier to track down than John C. Smith. I wonder if he goes by J.C.?" he mused. Shaking his head, he reached for another donut. "Anyway, how'd you find his name?" Caleb recounted his phone conversation and his internet search.

B.J. agreed with his decision. "That sounds about right. Narrowing down the ages should help a lot. Trouble is, we don't know where he lives now. Shoot, we don't even know what state he lives in. Does this mean we're going to have to look at every John C. Smith in every state to see if there's a Hickory, Virginia, in his past?"

Caleb nodded. "'Fraid so. I don't see any way around it."

"But that could take weeks. Months, maybe."

"Yeah," Caleb sighed.

B.J.'s face lit up. "But . . ." He set his donut on the table, licked his sticky index finger, and waved it in the air. "But, if we could get a lot of people to help us search, finding the right John Smith might take only a week. Or a few days. Or even a few hours," he added with enthusiasm.

"Not a bad idea." Caleb grinned. "I knew there was a reason why I kept you as a friend all these years." He mulled over the suggestion. "We could assign three or four states to each person. Then we'd have the whole country covered."

"Yeah," B.J. agreed. "Let's divide up the states, beginning with those closest to Virginia. Chances are, if this guy has moved, it's not all the way to Oregon or Alaska, or Hawaii. As soon as I leave here, I'm going to contact our friends and give each of them a couple of states. Caleb, if this John C. Smith isn't from Timbuktu or somewhere like that, we'll find him."

Saturday morning, Caleb was discharged from the rehab center. Using a pair of crutches, he hobbled to his parents' waiting car for the short ride home. Although it would be a few weeks before he could try walking without them, he nevertheless relished the freedom of being in his own house again.

As soon as he was settled in, his search for John Smith resumed. He was dog tired, but felt driven to keep going. He just couldn't stop. It wasn't long before he developed a splitting headache and had to suspend his online activities. His parents urged him to take a break from the internet and rest throughout the weekend.

He reluctantly agreed, after estimating that he'd spent over sixty hours that week on the internet or making phone calls.

Sunday morning, Caleb went to church with his family. His mother thought he should stay home and rest, but when he promised to stay in bed for the rest of the day, minus the computer, she finally relented. He'd missed his caring Christian family, and Pastor Murphy's preaching.

As he hobbled his way into the building, he was warmly greeted. People he didn't even know all that well said they'd been praying for him and Ellie. He was amazed at the outpouring of love and support.

But for some reason, church today wasn't the same as it had been before. Perhaps it was because Ellie wasn't sitting in the pew next to him, sharing a hymn book or a Bible. As the service progressed, he felt her absence more and more, until it became so acutely painful that he wished he'd listened to his mother and stayed home.

Caleb spent the rest of the day in bed, too exhausted physically and emotionally to stay awake. He slept like the dead until ten the next morning.

When he finally awoke on Monday, he showered and ate a very late breakfast. He was sitting in the living room, reading his Bible when B.J. called with an update.

"Caleb, you won't believe the response I got from everybody. A lot of them said they'd recruit their friends, too. Everybody wants to help. There must be at least two or three people searching every state. Dude, we've got this thing covered from coast to coast."

"That's awesome, B.J. Thanks for doing this."

"No problem. I even made a contest out of it. The person who finds the right John C. Smith gets a month's supply of donuts."

Caleb couldn't help laughing. "For you that's about a semi load, isn't it? Some sacrifice you're making there, bro."

"Hey, whatever it takes, right? Didn't we say back in the fourth grade that we had each other's back?"

"Yeah," Caleb fired back, "but I didn't know that included donuts."

Wednesday night as he was preparing for bed, Caleb received a one word text from B.J.

All it said was "JACKPOT." Caleb couldn't hit the call back button fast enough.

"Jackpot!" B.J. shouted, as soon as the two friends were connected.

"You found him?" Caleb asked eagerly.

"Yeah. I mean, no. I mean, not me. It was Krystal. She's the one who found him."

"Where does he live?" Caleb scrambled for a pen and paper.

"You're not going to believe this. He lives in Atlanta. He's right here, Caleb. In Georgia."

"What's his address?" Caleb wrote it down and repeated it back to his friend. "Is there a phone number?"

"Yeah." B.J. read him the number slowly.

"Great. That's perfect. What else did she find out?"

"His profile shows previous addresses in Pascagoula, Mississippi, Hickory and Roanoke, Virginia, and three others in Atlanta. He's the only one so far with a Hickory in his past. It's got to be him, Caleb. How many John C. Smiths do you suppose lived in Hickory?"

"How old is he?"

"Forty-one. You were right on the money, dude. He must have been a year ahead of Ellie's mother in high school."

"What about relatives? Are there any listed?"

"Only three. A Thomas Smith, age seventy-six, and a Margaret Smith, age seventy-four. Must be his parents. And a Janet Robinson, age forty-nine. An older sister, maybe? Robinson might be her married name."

"Got it." Caleb had been writing furiously to keep up with his excited friend. "Thanks, B.J. This is an answer to prayer. You won't believe this, but just yesterday I felt God was telling me to get out of His way and let Him do His thing. So I do, and look what happens."

"Yeah. I wonder how many times I've gotten in the way, too. So, what are you going to do now? Give this guy a call? Track him down and pay him a little visit?"

"Uh . . . I think I'd better talk to my dad about it, first. I don't want to do anything that might jeopardize the situation."

"But aren't you dying to call him and find out where he took Ellie?"

"Of course I'm dying to find out. I'd drive up there in a heartbeat if I thought I'd find her. But remember, B.J., for whatever reason, this guy doesn't want us to know where she is. I think my dad will know the best approach to take."

"Well, let me know when you find out something, okay? I'm more than willing to drive you up there. Any time, day or night. All you gotta do is ask."

"Thanks. I promise you'll be the first to know."

"I guess I should call off the hounds, huh? No need for everyone to keep looking now that he's been located."

"I agree. Hey, please thank everyone for me, will you? I'll thank them myself as soon as I can."

"Consider it done."

Caleb was silent for a moment. "You know, B.J., it's a good thing that Krystal was the one who found him. You really lucked out on this one, pal."

"What are you talking about? Why Krystal? And how did I luck out?"

Caleb burst into laughter. "Don't you remember, you chucklehead? Krystal doesn't even like donuts."

────────────────────

Sleep made every effort to keep its distance from Caleb that night.

As he lay in bed, eyes wide open and staring into the darkness, his mind was a whirlwind of thoughts. What should he say to Mr. Smith? Would Ellie's father answer, or would he be forced to leave a message?

Would his calls even be returned? If not, should he drive up to Atlanta and go to the man's last known address? How would John Smith react if Caleb suddenly showed up on his doorstep?

How would he get the man to tell him where Ellie was or how she was doing?

And how *was* Ellie doing? All he knew was that she was in serious but stable condition when she disappeared from the hospital in Columbus nearly six weeks ago. Six weeks. Had she really been gone only six weeks?

It seemed like a lifetime ago that she was laughing and joking, her beautiful auburn hair bouncing as she walked hand-in-hand with him, her eyes sparkling as brightly as the princess cut diamond engagement ring on her finger.

Caleb let out a long sigh. "Wait for the lawyer's advice," his father had instructed him. Just another clue to follow.

Another piece to the puzzle.

Another delay to endure when he could be doing something. Another—he stopped mid-thought.

Another opportunity to practice waiting on the Lord.

He prayed for patience, and that the lawyer would know what to do. Sooner rather than later, if possible. Then, although he'd done it numerous times already that day, Caleb prayed for Ellie. And that's when sleep finally caught up to him.

━━━━━━━━━━━━━━━━

Caleb spent Thursday morning calling and texting his friends who had participated in the online blitz. He thanked them for their help in locating Ellie's father. Around five-thirty, his father came home from work with an update from the lawyer.

"Caleb, Mr. Thornberg called me at the office just before I left. He confirmed that John Smith is indeed Ellie's biological father. And because of her condition, he's within his legal rights as her next of kin to act as her proxy."

"I get that part, Dad. But what about denying us access to her information? What he's doing is wrong."

"Morally, perhaps. Or ethically. But so far there's no evidence that he's broken any laws. And because we're not related to Ellie, we can't force him to communicate with us if he chooses not to."

Caleb's heart sank. "Then where does that leave us?

"Well, I could have the lawyer pursue other legal options to get the information. But that might take time. Or . . . " His father hesitated. "Or we could try calling him ourselves."

Caleb was skeptical. "Come on, Dad. Do you really think he's going to talk to us now? After all the stonewalling he's done?"

"Perhaps not. But we can at least appeal to his sense of compassion. A personal heartfelt plea might get him to change his mind."

Caleb considered his father's suggestion. "Well, that appears to be the quickest way to get through to him at the moment. At least now we're free to contact him ourselves." He paused. "After all, I do have his phone number and address . . . "

CHAPTER FOURTEEN

DEAD END

CALEB'S HANDS TREMBLED AS HE placed the call to Atlanta. He sat by himself in his father's small, windowless office off the living room of the family residence. His parents had offered to be present while he made the call, but he'd wanted to be alone when he talked with Ellie's father.

The palms of his hands were so sweaty that he almost dropped the cell phone. Wiping them one at a time on his shirt, he steadied himself as the phone began to ring. He could hear his heart pounding in his ears. This was it. The moment of truth.

On the fourth ring, a voice answered the call. But it was not the voice of John C. Smith. It was female. And it was recorded.

"The number you have reached is currently not in service."

Caleb's heart sank like a stone. He sat motionless with the phone still to his ear, until the tone reminded him that the connection had ended. He shut off his phone and set it down on the pile of bills his father had been working on. He should have known.

But now what? If the phone number Krystal found was obsolete, then maybe the address was too. Where should he go from here? Caleb got up from the chair and went into the kitchen to get a drink.

As he was getting a glass of water from the dispenser in the refrigerator door, his mother came into the room carrying a basket of folded clothes from the laundry room. She glanced at her son.

"Is your phone call over already?" she asked, a look of mild surprise on her face.

"The number's not in service," Caleb muttered dejectedly. "Go figure."

"I'm sorry, Caleb. That's disappointing, I know." She set the basket of clothes on the counter, walked over to him, and gave him a hug. "It's not the end of the world. A minor setback, perhaps. Just a bump in the road, that's all."

"A bump?" Sarcasm dripped from his voice. "Mom, all it's been for the past six weeks is one bump after another. I'm sick and tired of bumps. This road I'm on is shaking me to pieces."

His mother looked him squarely in the eye. "Caleb, what makes you think you're the only one on this road right now?" The sharpness of her question pierced his grumbling spirit. "Have you seen your father lately? How tired he looks? How his shoulders sag? He's spent every bit as much time on this bumpy road as you have. Maybe even more. And he's not complained one time, to my knowledge."

Caleb felt ashamed for his self-pity. He'd seen the strain on his father's face, and the heartbreak and concern in his mother and sister. Ellie's disappearance was taking its toll on all of them. He reached out and grabbed his mother, enveloping her in his arms.

"Mom, I'm so sorry. I know it's been just as hard on you guys. And I know you love her as much as I do."

She smiled at him. "Yes I do. I think the world of Ellie. She's a real treasure." She picked up the basket of clothes. "Caleb, you remember Proverbs three, five and six, don't you?"

"Sure. 'Trust in the LORD with all your heart, and do not lean on your own understanding. In all your ways acknowledge him, and he will make straight your paths.'"

His mother tilted her head and raised her eyebrows. "Well?"

He thought about the verses. They were the words of King Solomon imparting wisdom to his son.

"I take it you're telling me that God is going to straighten out this bumpy road I'm on, right?"

"Yes, I am. And yes, He is. As long as you acknowledge Him in all your ways. Give God the glory when the road is smooth and when it's not. He's in control of it all."

Caleb couldn't help but grin at his mother. "Even the bumps?"

She laughed. "Even the bumps." Then she headed down the hallway to put away the laundry.

"Caleb, I have good news." His father was calling from his insurance office in downtown Baxter. "I talked to Mr. Thornberg this morning, and he just called me back. He's located the current phone number and address for Ellie's father."

"Really? That was fast," Caleb replied, somewhat out of breath. He was lying on the living room carpet doing his stretching exercises and upper body cardio when his father's call came. "Where did he find them?"

"The Fulton County Criminal Court records, of all places. Apparently Ellie's father is required to keep his contact information current with the county."

"Ellie's father has a criminal record? Did he say what for?" Caleb sat up on the floor with the phone to his ear.

"He mentioned public intoxication, petty theft, forgery, check kiting, and insurance fraud. Non-violent crimes. But he served time for the last three, though. And he's also got a number of DUIs in several states."

"Doesn't sound like a very nice guy. I hope he's treating Ellie right," Caleb muttered. "Dad, why would a man like that snatch away a daughter he hasn't seen or cared about in twenty years?"

"That's something we all want to know, son. And hopefully we'll have an answer soon. Are you ready for the information?"

"Just a minute." Mindful of his still-mending bones, Caleb reached carefully for his crutches and gingerly got on his feet. He hobbled into the office and grabbed a Post-it note and pen. "Okay, give it to me." He jotted down the phone number and address. "Got it. Thanks, Dad. Tell Mr. Thornberg thanks for me, too, will you?"

"I'll be sure to do that. But son, before you make the call, let me caution you. This man is a convicted criminal. So please be careful. And don't do anything illegal."

"I will. And I won't. Do anything illegal, that is."

His father chuckled over the phone. "That's good. Listen, Caleb, why don't we pray together before you make the call?"

Just as he had done the previous evening, Caleb placed a call to John C. Smith. Armed with the new number supplied by the lawyer, he was cautiously optimistic that he'd soon have the information about Ellie he'd so desperately pursued over the past six weeks.

The phone rang three times, and then was answered.

"This is John. I can't take your call. Leave your name and number. I'll call you back."

The gruff voice was flat, almost sullen, showing no emotion at all. Caleb tried pairing the voice with the description Jim McCready had given him, but the mental picture he came up with was a very vague one.

The *"bee-eep"* of the answering machine informed Caleb that it was his turn to speak. Finally, he was making first contact with the mystery man. With a slight tremble in his voice, he spoke into his phone.

"Um . . . Mr. Smith? My name is Caleb Sawyer. I'm your daughter's fiancé and I've been desperately trying to find her since the accident. Make that frantically trying to find her. I'm sure you have a very good reason for removing her from the hospital in Columbus, but I can't understand why you won't let me know how she is or where she is. If you could just put yourself in my shoes, you'd understand how awful the past six weeks have been. My family and I are really hurting right now. Please, if you would just return my call as soon as possible and let me know how Ellie's doing or where she's at, I'd be truly grateful. I love her and I really miss her. So does my family and all her friends. By the way, I'm not angry with you or anything. I just want to—"

"Bee-eep!" The tone interrupted him mid-sentence, informing him that the recording had ended.

Caleb slowly lowered his phone. Well, that was that. He'd done everything he could. Sometime soon, maybe within the next few minutes even, John C. Smith would discover how badly he missed Ellie. And how badly he needed to hear from her.

Hopefully, his appeal would find a soft spot in her father's heart and cause him to quickly return the call. That is, if there was a soft spot in the man's heart.

All afternoon and into the evening he nervously waited for his phone to ring. Perhaps Ellie's father was at work, or didn't have his cell phone with him.

A dozen possibilities ran through Caleb's head. In spite of the doubt that continually nibbled away at his optimism, he clung to the hope that John Smith might have been touched by his heartfelt plea, just as Ellie had been touched four years ago when she showed up at Edwards to meet him after reading the note he'd placed in her locker door.

Around eight o'clock, unable to stand the suspense any longer, he called a second time. Again, he was forced to leave a message.

Caleb tossed and turned that night. He found himself back in the hospital, bandaged from head to toe like a mummy, with just his face showing. Ellie passed by him in a wheelchair. She was battered and bruised.

He staggered after her down the long, eerily-lit corridor. Suddenly, a man with curly brown hair and diamond studs in both ears jumped out of the shadows. He grabbed the handles of the wheelchair and rushed her toward an elevator at the far end of the hall. He pushed the button and turned Ellie around to back in.

The doors opened. To Caleb's horror, there was no elevator. Only a gaping shaft. He shouted a warning, but no sound came out. Flashing a wicked grin, the man stepped back. Ellie reached out both hands toward Caleb, silently pleading for him to save her, but he couldn't reach her in time. The wheelchair toppled backward and disappeared down the shaft.

Caleb bolted upright and looked around. He was no longer wrapped in bandages, but entangled in bed sheets and drenched in sweat. He took a long, cool drink from the water bottle on his nightstand.

The nightmare had been so real. Too real. He glanced at the clock. 12:47 AM. This was going to be a long night.

Caleb awoke late Saturday morning, only to be greeted by a headache, chills, and a temperature of a hundred and two. His body ached all over, especially his left leg where the rod had been implanted. His mother gave him two ibuprofen and a cold washcloth for his forehead.

He slept off and on until three that afternoon, too exhausted to even get out of bed. But he kept his phone within reach, just in case.

By evening, the headache and chills were gone, and his temperature had dropped to one hundred point eight. He felt well enough to down some chicken soup, but he still ached. The tension of the past few days had finally overtaken him. At nine forty-five he was ready to call it a day. But before turning out the light, he made another attempt to reach John Smith. He was not surprised at all when the call went to voice mail. This time, however, he left a more forceful message.

Sunday morning, his mother wanted to stay home from church with him. His temperature had all but vanished, and the ibuprofen had done its job on the aches and pains.

"Mom, I'm fine, really," he insisted. "I don't need you to stay with me." He grinned at her. "I'm a big boy now."

"Alright," she conceded. "But can I get you a drink or some reading material before we go?"

"No thanks. I'll probably sleep the whole time anyway." His parents and Cassie left soon after that. Lying in bed, in the quietness of the empty house, he found himself wondering what he should do if John Smith continued to ignore his calls. No matter. He would keep knocking on the door until it opened. Literally, if he had to. He'd give Ellie's father one more day to respond, and then he'd pay the man a visit.

He'd have someone drive him to Atlanta. B.J. perhaps, or his father.

Caleb allowed his emotions to rise to the surface. But soon they boiled over.

The more he thought about John Smith, the more he detested him. The despicable low-life had, with cruel and malicious intent, spirited away his fiancée without so much as a shred of human decency. The man needed to be confronted. Held accountable for his actions. And justice for Ellie needed to be served.

Caleb reached for his cell phone and forcefully punched the redial button. This was the jerk's last chance!

The phone rang once and went straight to voice mail.

"Bee-eep."

"Mr. Smith, this is Caleb Sawyer again. I don't know why you haven't returned my calls, but I'm through with this little game you're playing. And I'm through being nice about it. I'm giving you until tonight to call me back, or else tomorrow morning I'm driving up to Atlanta, and I will track you down and I will confront you face-to-face. I'm not going to let this thing go, count on it. I'm going to find out where Ellie is, one way or another!" He paused for dramatic effect. "You have until tonight."

This time, Caleb disconnected the call before the recording ended.

The ring tone of Caleb's cell phone jarred him out of his daze. It was Sunday evening, and he was lying on the living room sofa, more asleep than awake.

His caller ID revealed the Atlanta number of John Smith. Aware that his hands were trembling, Caleb steeled himself and took the call.

"Hello?"

There was a short pause on the other end. Then the gruff sounding man from the voice mail recording spoke. "Are you Caleb Sawyer?"

"Yes."

"This is John Smith."

Caleb was primed and ready to restate his ultimatum to Ellie's father. To stand his ground and not back down. But the reality and relief that he was finally speaking with the real John Smith hit him hard, and gratitude overtook his anger.

"Mr. Smith, I really appreciate you calling me back. You can't even begin to imagine how much I've been wanting to talk to you."

To his utter surprise, the voice on the other end suddenly took on the same conciliatory tone. "You're right, I'm sure I can't. I apologize for not contacting you sooner."

Now that was unexpected. An apology up front? It knocked him back on his heels for a moment. He'd been prepared to demand answers and make threats. But now . . . now he wasn't so sure. With his dad's warning ringing in his ears, he decided to take a softer approach.

"Sir, why haven't you given us any information about Ellie?" he pleaded. "Where is she? Is she okay?"

John Smith hesitated again before replying. "I know you want answers. But would you allow me to explain myself first?"

Caleb sighed impatiently. At least the man was cooperating. That was more than he'd anticipated. "Go ahead. I'm listening."

Ellie's father launched into the reasons for his actions. It sounded rehearsed, almost as if he were reading his lines from a carefully crafted script.

"For the past few years, I've been wondering about my daughter, where she is and how she's doing. I've been feeling really guilty and ashamed for not stepping up and being a part of her life, and I've been thinking recently about trying to reconnect with her. Then one day, I was in the lobby of this hotel in downtown Atlanta, and I happened to be admiring a row of pictures on the wall. The artwork was incredible. I remember thinking that the artist must be very gifted. You can imagine my shock and amazement when I saw that the artist was Ellie Thompson, my own daughter! After that, I really wanted to find her. But I was hesitant because I knew she'd probably be angry with me for abandoning her. I was afraid she would want nothing to do with me if I contacted her.

"But then in December, I heard about the accident on the five o'clock news. When they mentioned her name as one of the victims, I felt compelled to finally do the right thing. I immediately drove down to Columbus to show my support for her. When I got to Good Sam and learned the extent of her injuries, I determined to take responsibility for her, hoping that through my show of compassion she might eventually allow me back into her life. My decision to transfer her to an Atlanta hospital was so that she could receive better care from the specialists there, and so I could be nearby to supervise her care and recovery."

Caleb interjected himself into John's explanation. "But why have you kept us in the dark all this time? Do you have any idea what that's done to me? To my family?"

Ellie's father sounded genuinely penitent. "I can only beg your forgiveness for that, now. You see, my guilt over not being in her life, and my fear of losing her again got the best of me. I wish I could give you a more legitimate reason than that, but I can't. When the hospital informed me that another family was there who were somehow involved in her life, I panicked. I was afraid they'd take her away from me and I'd lose my one chance to get back into her life. I assumed it must be one of her foster families. Yeah, I've heard all about them. I know how they treated her. But honestly, I didn't know she was engaged until you called a few days ago and identified yourself as her fiancé."

Caleb wasn't about to let him off the hook so easily. "Then why did you wait until now to return my calls? Why didn't you call me right back and tell me where she is? Explain that!" he demanded forcefully.

There was a long silence from John Smith. So long, in fact, that Caleb feared he'd crossed the line. Pushed the man too hard. Wasn't he finally being forthright and open up to now? What if he reacted by getting angry and shutting down altogether?

Caleb quickly backtracked. "I . . . I didn't mean to sound so demanding."

Ellie's father finally answered. He spoke haltingly, as if he didn't want to share what he was about to say. There was an alarming sadness in his voice.

"Ever since your first call, I, um . . . I've been trying to figure out how to explain this to you. How to prepare you for this."

A foreboding chill shot down Caleb's spine, and his heart beat faster. "Prepare me for what?" He wasn't sure he wanted to know the answer.

"When Ellie was brought to Atlanta, she was in serious condition. But after those first few weeks she started showing signs of improvement. Movement in her hands and feet, that sort of thing. The doctors said they were encouraged and cautiously optimistic about her chances for recovery. But then she took an unexpected turn for the worst. I was told it had to do with the type of trauma her brain had suffered. A delayed symptom of some sort. I don't remember the exact term for it."

He took a deep breath and exhaled before continuing. "Caleb, there's no good way to tell you this, but . . . but Ellie never regained consciousness." His voice choked up. "I'm afraid she didn't make it, son. She . . . she passed away two weeks ago."

The shock wave of that statement hit Caleb with the force of a nuclear bomb blast. His mind and body went numb. He couldn't think, couldn't move, couldn't speak.

The cell phone slipped from his hand and fell to the living room carpet with a muffled thud. Then the aftershock of reality hit.

"No . . . " he moaned softly. "No, no, no!" He violently shook his head in disbelief.

"That can't be true. It's not true!" He grabbed his hair with clenched fists.

From somewhere deep within him, a whimper rose. It grew and developed into a low, painful groan, slowly building in volume and intensity until at last, unable to carry the weight any longer, he delivered a full-term, agonizing wail.

"NO-O-O-O-O-O-O!"

Caleb's blood-curdling scream brought his parents rushing into the room. He sat hunched over on the edge of the sofa with his head in his hands, rocking back and forth violently, and moaning to himself. His terrified mother flew to his side and tried to cradle his head in her arms.

"Caleb, what is it? What's happened?" she cried.

He continued the rocking motion. Agonizing groans of "No, no, no!" spasmodically slipped past his lips.

His father noticed the cell phone on the floor and picked it up. He held it to his ear. "Hello! Hello?"

He knelt down on his knees and tried to remove Caleb's hands from his head.

"Was that Ellie's father on the phone just now?" he asked gently. "What did he say, son?" Caleb continued to rock without answering. "Bad news about Ellie?"

Still clutching his hair, Caleb managed a whisper. "Ellie's dead."

"What?"

"Ellie's dead," he repeated flatly.

His father's eyes darted to his mother, and then back again. "She's dead?" He grasped his son's shoulders. "Caleb, what did he tell you?"

"Brain trauma. She never woke up."

"Son, are you sure?" his mother asked in a quavering voice.

Caleb stopped rocking and let his hands drop limply onto the sofa. "He said she died. Two weeks ago." Tears flooded his eyes. "Ellie's gone. She's really gone!"

He turned and looked helplessly at his parents. "What am I going to do?"

Sobs racked his body. His father and mother wrapped their arms tightly around him. The three of them clung to each other and wept. Wept like they hadn't wept in nearly eleven years.

―――――――――――

Caleb awoke around nine thirty Monday morning. He'd had another awful nightmare. Still a bit groggy, he glanced around his room. His father was sitting in a chair next to the bed, dozing lightly.

Caleb stared blankly at him. What was he doing in his room? Shouldn't he be at the insurance office by now?

Then it dawned on him. Last night's phone call from John C. Smith. The awful news.

His father stirred and awoke with a start. Caleb propped himself up on one elbow.

"So it's true, then. About Ellie?" He studied his father's face for any clue that might indicate he was wrong.

His father rose wearily from his chair and sat on the edge of the bed. He placed his hand gently on his son's shoulder, the one with the mending collarbone.

"Caleb, at this point, we need to be prepared for the worst."

"What do you mean? Then, it's not confirmed yet?"

His father shook his head. "I haven't been able to verify it officially, no. After you fell asleep last night, I called her father back. I got his voice mail, but I told him to return my call right away, or I'd be driving up to Atlanta this morning to talk to him personally."

"Did he call back?" Caleb recalled his similar threat to the man the previous morning.

"Almost immediately. He told me everything he told you last night."

"But he said she died two weeks ago."

"I know he did, son. But so far, all we have to go on is his word. The word of a man we don't know and have never met. The word of a man who—at least in his past—has been unscrupulous and dishonest."

"Are you saying he might be lying to us?" Caleb struggled to a sitting position, a spark of hope welling up within him.

"Don't get your hopes up, Caleb," his father cautioned. "All I'm saying is we need proof to be sure. Mr. Smith sounded like he was telling the truth. I don't know why he would lie to us. He kept apologizing over and over for the pain he's caused by not informing us sooner."

"But like you said, Dad, so far all we've got is his word."

His father hesitated. "Son, he's going to send me a copy of her obituary and death certificate."

Caleb felt like a prize fighter who had just gotten the wind knocked out of him. But he wasn't about to throw in the towel just yet. He sucked it up and fought back.

"Couldn't those be forgeries? After all, this guy was in prison for fraud."

His father looked compassionately at him.

"Caleb, I wish I could give you the answer you want to hear. I thought of that, too. But there's another piece of evidence. He said he's ordered a headstone, and as soon as it's in place, he'll let us know so we can drive up to Atlanta and visit her gravesite ourselves." His father aged ten years right before his eyes. "I'm so sorry, son."

Caleb's rising hopes took a roller coaster plunge into despondency. He suddenly felt battered and bruised and bloody. This was the knock-out punch he'd feared. The bout was over, and he'd lost. Lost everything.

He embraced his father tightly. In that moment, grief flooded the room, drowning the two in a sea of sorrow. But even in the depths of his despair, Caleb stubbornly refused to concede the fight.

I'll believe it when I see it for myself, he promised himself.

Two days later his father received an email from John C. Smith. Attached was a copy of a short newspaper obituary dated January 28. It didn't say much:

ELINOR A. THOMPSON

ATLANTA—Elinor A. "Ellie" Thompson, 22, Baxter, passed away January 25 due to injuries sustained in an automobile accident on December 19 in Columbus.

Born in Hickory, Virginia, she was a senior art major at the University of Georgia, Athens. Burial arrangements are pending.

That was it. There was no picture or additional information. Mr. Smith said he was sending a copy of her death certificate via certified mail since he didn't want to forward such a personal document over the internet. Again, he apologized for all he'd put the Sawyer family through, and hoped that they could find it in their hearts to forgive him.

A certified envelope containing the copy of Ellie's death certificate arrived a few days later. Caleb sat with his father in the home office and studied the document. It appeared to be legitimate. He re-read John Smith's previous email and stared silently at Ellie's obituary.

Finally he spoke. "Dad, do you think you could ask him where Ellie is buried? I'd like to go visit her sometime this week. I need to tell her I love her one more time." His voice cracked. "And say goodbye to her."

His father's eyes misted over. "Of course, son. We'll all drive up there and visit her together."

They didn't hear back from John Smith for several days. Caleb's father sent another email, this time urging him to reply immediately so they could make the trip as soon as possible. He finally responded late the following day.

With his parents looking over his shoulder, Caleb read the email out loud.

"I apologize for not getting back to you sooner, but I was hoping to be able to give you the date when the headstone will be installed. Unfortunately, it's not going to be for a while yet. I know you're anxious to pay your respects, so I've attached a map with all the information you requested. I'll have a temporary marker set up so you know you're at the right place. When are you planning to come up here? I'd like to meet you at the cemetery. I feel I need to offer my condolences to you good folks in person."

Caleb looked up at his parents. "Do you think it would be alright if I asked B.J. to come with us? We've been through everything together."

His father glanced at his mother, who nodded her approval. "If that's what you want, then he's more than welcome to join us."

Friday morning at eight o'clock, the Sawyers and B.J left Baxter for the nearly four hour drive to Atlanta. B.J., always willing to support his best friend in any way possible, took the day off from classes at Baxter Community College to join the family for the trip north. It was a mild, sunny day, but nobody seemed to notice. A heavy black cloud hung over the small group.

When he'd first discovered that John Smith lived in Atlanta, Caleb had held onto the hope that he'd soon be making this joyous journey to finally be by Ellie's side.

Now, here he was, making the journey he'd longed for, but not for the reason or with the joy he'd imagined. Instead this was a somber drive, one of necessity, a trip which none of them wished to make.

The warm anticipation was but a faded memory now, and the cold, hard truth had set in. Reality cast its awful pall over the five subdued occupants in the car heading toward Interstate 75 North.

Almost four hours later, Caleb's father eased the family sedan off the highway and onto the road leading to their destination.

It was a few minutes before noon when they turned into the main entrance of the cemetery. Driving under the black metal arch bearing the name "Woodlawn" in scrolling iron letters, the car made its way through the maze of curved roads which separated the different burial sections, each with its own name.

Over a small rise near the back of the cemetery, they came to a section marked "Pine Hill." That was where Ellie was buried.

Caleb's father pulled to the side of the road and shut off the engine. He took his phone from the pocket of his suit jacket and placed a call to Mr. Smith. He had agreed to be there by eleven thirty to meet them, but he was nowhere in sight. And the call went to voicemail. Caleb's father left a message informing him of their arrival.

The quintet of melancholy mourners exited the car and respectfully navigated its way between the rows of markers and headstones toward the plot identified on the map.

His mother and Cassie, both dressed in black, carried bouquets of flowers. Caleb, wearing his best dark blue suit, clutched a single rose and a note he'd written to Ellie. Small twigs littered the grass, which needed mowing. Foxtails and thistles dotted the lawn, along with a few bare patches of red Georgia clay. Faded plastic flowers, placed next to graves long ago, had not been removed. Here and there a headstone rose angularly from the earth like the Tower of Pisa.

Straight ahead was an old, knotty pine. A blanket of dry, brown needles and rotting pine cones lay in a circle underneath. To the right of the tree, the ground had been freshly disturbed. The mound had recently been seeded, but the grass was only beginning to sprout from the red earth.

"This must be the place," his father said in a subdued voice, as he studied the map. A white plastic cross with a flower-covered wreath had been placed at the head of the grave.

Caleb, with the rose and note in his hands approached the marker. With his heart pounding rapidly in his chest he read the words on the cross.

"ELINOR A. THOMPSON"

There it was. The final piece of evidence he'd so desperately desired to will into non-existence. At last he'd found Ellie. Only to lose her all over again.

Caleb clenched his fists. His body stiffened. He felt dizzy and nauseous. He couldn't catch his breath. His head began to spin and he swayed unsteadily on his feet.

Before anyone could react, his knees buckled and he slumped to the ground. The others rushed to his side. A tiny spot of blood oozed from his hand where a thorn from the broken rose had pierced the flesh. A lone crimson drop splattered on the crumpled note that now lay in the dirt beside him. Agonizing sobs racked his body as he grieved for his lost love.

CHAPTER FIFTEEN

STARTING OVER

ABOUT A WEEK AFTER THE Atlanta trip, Caleb came downstairs and entered the kitchen. His father was seated at the table reading the morning paper. His mother glanced up from where she was loading the dishwasher.

"Caleb, you're up!" She looked surprised. "How's my Cherub? Feeling better?"

"A little." He slumped into a chair and spied the dirty dishes still on the table. "Where's Cassie?"

His father glanced up at him. "She's already eaten, Caleb. Her bus came about an hour ago."

"An hour ago? What time is it?"

His father checked his watch. "Five after eight."

"Oh." Caleb sat silently for a moment before turning to his mother.

"Mom, do you think you could make me some bacon and eggs?"

"Of course, honey." She scrambled to fulfill his request. "I'm glad your appetite's back."

His father looked him over. "I see you're dressed this morning. Are you planning to go out somewhere?"

"No, I'm just sick of laying around in my pajamas all day."

After downing a hearty breakfast, Caleb got up and left the table. In the doorway he turned back to his parents.

"Maybe I will go out for a while. I could use a change of scenery and some fresh air. I think I'll go over to Miss Cora's."

He caught the glance his parents gave each other.

"I thought I'd ask if I could sit on her porch for a while," he explained. "It might help clear my head so I can figure out what to do next. Maybe I'll spend some time in the Word. Ellie and I used to read and pray together there."

"Why don't you let your father drop you off on his way to the office," his mother urged. "You complained yesterday about your leg aching. Driving might aggravate it."

"Thanks, Mom, but I think I can handle it."

"I can pick you up whenever you're ready to come back," she added, refusing to give in.

"Mom," he protested, "I'm not a complete invalid, you know." He managed a faint grin. "At least, not anymore. I'll take it easy, I promise. I just need to get back to doing things on my own again."

His father came to his aid. "He'll be all right, dear. If he thinks it will do him good, then let him go."

His mother relented. "Alright. But, Caleb, if your leg starts hurting again or you need anything, you'll call me right away, won't you?"

"Yes, Mom." He went upstairs to his room for his wallet and keys. When he returned to the kitchen, his mother still looked uncertain. He smiled and gave her a hug.

"Thanks for breakfast. It was awesome." Then he kissed her forehead. "I love you, Mom."

He grabbed his jacket from the peg next to the back door.

With a slight limp he left the house and walked to his car, which had been parked next to the garage for the past eight weeks.

"Caleb! It's good to see you up and about. Please, do come in, won't you?" Miss Cora held open the door and he stepped into the foyer of the big old Victorian. "I see you've left the crutches at home. How's that leg doing?"

"Much better, thank you. It still aches a bit, but the doctor said it's okay to walk as long as I'm careful and take it easy."

"Would you like to sit down?" She motioned toward the living room off to the left.

"If you wouldn't mind, I'd like to sit out on the porch for a while."

"Of course. Whatever you like."

They stepped back outside and made their way to the end of the veranda porch. The old woman sat down in her rocker, and Caleb sat down on the porch swing.

She tilted her head to one side and studied him. "How are you holding up, Caleb? I've been praying for you and your family since I got the news."

Caleb let out a weary sigh. "Well, to be truthful, Miss Cora, not so good. I haven't done much of anything lately. All I seem to be able to do is lay around all day and sleep. And feel sorry for myself."

"That's quite understandable." She reached out and patted his knee. "You're mourning a deep and unexpected loss. But give yourself time. It takes a while to work through the grieving process."

"That's just it. I don't think I can get through it. Not this time."

Miss Cora smiled. "That's exactly how I felt when Henry passed away. We'd been together so long I could hardly remember life without him. I didn't think I could go on without him. I also felt that way when we learned we couldn't have children. That news took the wind right out of my sails for a while."

"So, how did you manage to get through those times?" he wondered.

"Well, about the same way you and your family got through the loss of Calvin. With a lot of prayer, the support of our church family, and a total reliance on God. Don't forget, He understands our deepest thoughts and feelings. That was a great comfort to me during those times of sorrow. Isaiah describes Jesus as '*a man of sorrows and acquainted with grief.*' While on earth, He was both fully God and fully man, and as such He experienced all the emotions we do. But He not only identifies with our pain and suffering, He carries it for us. Isaiah goes on to say that '*he has borne our griefs and carried our sorrows.*'"

"I know that's all true, but I just can't accept the fact that Ellie's gone. I'm not sure I can move on."

"Caleb," she said with a mother's tenderness, "this is where your faith gets tested. You know in your head that God loves you and knows what you're going through. But if you believe that with your heart, you'll cast your burdens on Him. This is much too heavy a load to carry all by yourself." She looked at the Bible in his hand. "I see you've brought your Bible with you. Did you want to spend some time out here alone with God?"

Caleb marveled at the godly woman's wisdom and insight. "How did you know?"

She smiled. "Just a hunch." Leaning heavily on her cane, she struggled to get out of her chair. He hurried to assist her. "Thank you, Caleb. I'll leave you alone for a while, then."

"Thanks, Miss Cora," he replied gratefully.

"You're welcome. But first, may I bring you some iced tea and cookies?"

―――――――――――――――――

Caleb sat alone on the porch swing, a glass of iced tea in one hand and his Bible and a plate of gingersnaps on the seat beside him. As he sipped the refreshing beverage, he stared at the heart he'd carved on the left arm of the swing three and a half years earlier. *C. S. & E. T. 4EVER*

Tracing those immortalized letters with his finger, he felt a stabbing pain in his heart as sharp as the pocket knife that had cut them. A bitter thought slithered its way into his mind. At first, he fought valiantly to suppress it, but in the end it overtook him.

Forever. Well, that didn't last very long, did it?

He remembered his promise to always be there for Ellie. That was supposed to be for a lifetime, not the short span of four years. And even then, he wasn't with her at the end.

Anger and resentment followed on the heels of the bitterness that he had allowed to access his mind. Why did Ellie have to die?

Why did God let him fall in love with her, only to take her away from him? Was this a test of faith, like Miss Cora suggested, or was God punishing him for something?

What had he done wrong? Nothing, as far as he knew.

He'd done his best to be faithful to the Lord. Gave up his job for Ellie, helped her find a home, shared God's love with her until she accepted Him for herself.

And for what? Only to have her ripped away from him? He didn't deserve this!

How could a loving and understanding God allow this to happen? Could it possibly be true that God really wasn't good all the time?

Did I really just think that?

The pity party in Caleb's mind came to a grinding halt. Resentment, anger, and bitterness exited as shame made its grand entrance.

He set down the glass of iced tea and picked up his Bible. In vain he tried to locate some verses of comfort and hope, but it was as if he were reading a book written in a foreign language.

Abandoning that plan, he decided to pray instead. But try as he might, no words came, and that pursuit proved to be futile as well.

This wasn't the result he'd hoped to gain by coming here. He'd come to find some peace, to gain some comfort, to get some direction. Not this!

He fought to hold back the onslaught of fear and panic that threatened to overwhelm his heart and mind. Finally, in desperation he leaned forward with his elbows on his knees and grabbed his head with both hands. His stomach churned and his head pounded from the tension. He felt as if he were losing the battle.

"Caleb?"

He straightened with a start. He hadn't heard his pastor come up the walk or onto the porch.

"Pastor Murphy? What are you doing here?"

"I thought you might need someone to talk to."

"But . . . but how did you know I was here?" he stammered.

Pastor Murphy chuckled. "Well, actually, Miss Cora called me, bless her heart. She said you seemed to be troubled and she was concerned about you. I hope you don't mind me taking the liberty of coming over here."

"No, I guess not. I probably should have called you myself."

"Not a problem." He smiled and sat down in the rocker adjacent to the swing. "Caleb, I know you've been through a lot lately, first with the accident, and now . . . this. Why don't you tell me what's going on, and I'll do my best to help you any way I can."

Tears welled up in Caleb's eyes. They broke free and ran down his face. He swiped at them with his sleeve but failed to erase their escape route. His body began shaking with silent sobs.

Pastor Murphy rose and put an arm around his shoulder.

"That's okay, Caleb. Go ahead and let it out." He remained quietly supportive until Caleb was able to regain control of his emotions. Then he returned to the rocker.

Caleb began to talk. At first, he spoke haltingly. But then the feelings and thoughts and words began to flow like water through a widening crack in a dam. For the next twenty minutes he opened up and poured out his heart to the man whose spiritual insight he had come to so highly respect. He shared his feelings of hopelessness, his fear of not being able to move past the loss of Ellie, his questioning of God, and his inability to find answers and to pray.

Pastor Murphy, ever the good listener, sat quietly, frequently nodding in agreement or understanding as Caleb revealed the pain and confusion and helplessness that had him tethered to despair. When his reservoir emptied, the preacher spoke up.

"Caleb, I want to thank you for feeling free enough with me to share all that's on your heart and mind."

"I didn't mean to go on and on like that," Caleb apologized, somewhat embarrassed.

"Don't apologize." His pastor held up one hand. "I wish everyone I counsel would be as transparent and honest with me as you are. Besides, it's good to get things off your chest and out in the open." He settled back in the rocker. "Caleb, telling me, and your parents, and others you trust can be very helpful. We all—to a certain extent—can help you shoulder the burden you're carrying. Jesus said we're to bear each other's burdens. Some can understand what you're going through more than others because they've experienced similar heartaches and trials. That can be a great source of comfort in times like this. But none of us is able to remove the burden for you.

"Only one Person can totally and completely do that. I'm sure you know this verse, but First Peter five seven says we're to cast all our cares—that's our anxieties, our fears, our burdens, our troubles, every last one of them—on Him, because He cares for us. It's an act of faith. It not only means we believe that He loves us, but that He's able and willing to remove our load and take it on Himself. If He was able to carry the sins of the whole world on the cross, don't you think He's able to carry your burdens as well?"

Caleb sighed. "I know that's true, and I've done that in the past, but for some reason, I'm finding it hard to do now. Maybe that's because I'm having trouble understanding why this happened. I mean, what purpose would God have for bringing Ellie and me together in the first place, only to take her away from me now? I thought He had a plan for us. You know, like the verse says, for our good and not our harm. To give us a future and a hope. I just can't make any sense out of it!"

Pastor Murphy took his time answering. "You're right, Caleb. God *does* have a plan for your life. And for Ellie's. And for all of us who put our trust in Him. And that plan includes an eternity with Him in heaven. That's our future. That's our hope. For Calvin, his future began, what, twelve years ago? For Mr. Williams, his future began nearly six years ago. And for Ellie, that future has just begun. Yours and mine is still to come. None of us is guaranteed another day in this life. But we are guaranteed an endless day in the next."

He paused and shook his head. "I can't tell you why God took Ellie when He did. But have you considered that He might have brought the two of you together so she could hear about Jesus from you? Without you, she might never have accepted Him as her Savior. And she might not be in heaven today. Maybe that was God's plan and purpose for the two of you all along."

Caleb pondered that possibility. "I . . . I hadn't really thought about that. I guess knowing that she's safe in heaven now, with her mother, helps some." He shook his head sadly. "But it still doesn't make me miss her any less."

"Caleb, I'm not going to preach a sermon, or quote a lot of verses to you." He smiled. "I'll save that for Sunday mornings. Yes, you will miss her. No doubt for the rest of your earthly life. And you're going to mourn for her. There's a time for that. But it's only temporary. Jesus promised that even our sorrow will turn into joy."

"But when will that happen? Does that promise apply now, or is it only for when we get to heaven?"

"I believe it applies to both. Caleb, do you remember that large picture hanging in the church hallway outside the fellowship room?"

"You mean the one of Daniel in the lion's den?"

"Yes. Have you ever noticed what Daniel is looking at?"

Caleb had to stop and think. "Is he looking up at heaven?"

Pastor Murphy nodded. "Yes. And he's not looking at the lions. In fact, he's got his back to them. If he were facing them, he'd no doubt give in to his fears. Instead, he's focused on the source of his strength and help. Not on his problems. Caleb, focus on the One who can carry your burden, not on the burden you carry. And when you think of Ellie, focus on her gain, not your loss."

Caleb dabbed at his eyes. Pastor Murphy was right. He'd been focusing on the lions instead of the Lord. And he was fearful, and helpless, and miserable because of it. He allowed the air to escape his lungs.

"Pastor, I think my focus has been in the wrong place." A wistful smile broke through the despair that had clouded his face. "Thank you for encouraging me to look up."

His pastor returned the smile. "You'd be surprised how many times God tells us to look up, or to look unto Him, or to lift up our eyes. He knows how often we need that reminder." He leaned forward and put his hand on Caleb's shoulder. "You're going to get through this. Go ahead and mourn for now. Grieve for a time. But keep your eyes on Jesus. He loves you and He's with you. And He'll see you through this crisis, just as He has in the past."

Pastor Murphy prayed with him and took his leave.

Caleb remained alone on the porch swing, reflecting on their conversation. He knew what he had to do. He would mourn a while longer. Then he would try to move forward.

It wasn't going to be easy. In fact, it was going to be impossible—without the Lord's help. In that moment, a thought that refused to leave planted itself in his mind: *"With God all things are possible."*

Caleb struggled to move beyond his grief. Some days proved to be better than others, but he did his best to focus on the One who had offered to bear his burdens, and that made all the difference. He still missed Ellie terribly, and felt the daily ache of her absence, but he was at last able to begin thinking about the rest of his life.

He attended Kelli's June wedding. She married the young man she'd become engaged to the night of the accident.

As he listened to the exchange of vows, an anguishing thought hit him. *This could have been Ellie and me standing up there, pledging to have and to hold from this day forward, 'til death do us part.*

Only for him, death had parted them before he could even make those vows.

As he congratulated the newlyweds, Kelli must have sensed his inner distress. She gave him a hug and whispered, "I miss her, too, Caleb. I wanted her to be one of my bridesmaids."

That was Kelli for you.

On August fifteenth, he got a call from an ecstatic B.J.

"Guess what, dude? I'm a father!" his friend announced.

"Congratulations, B.J. That's awesome. Is it a boy or a girl?"

"A boy. He was born at six forty-eight this morning. Weighed in at seven pounds fourteen ounces and measured twenty and a half inches long."

"Wow. That's great. How's Allison doing?"

"She's fine. Came through like the trooper she is. Guess what we named him."

"What? And don't play 'The Game' with me this time, pal."

B.J. laughed. "Okay, I won't. We named him Joshua Caleb Martin."

"Joshua Caleb?"

"Yep. We named him Caleb after you, dude. Aren't you impressed?"

Caleb couldn't pass up the opportunity. "After all we've been through together, and I only get the middle name?"

———————————————

Caleb held the painting up against the wall and eyeballed it. "That looks about right," he said.

Convinced that it was at the proper height, he hammered a small nail into the plaster, and hung the painting in place. Then he plopped down in his new recliner, and with great satisfaction surveyed the rest of Ellie's artwork that graced the walls of the small but cozy apartment.

Perfect!

At first he wondered if they might be too painful a reminder for him, but now, seeing them actually hanging there, they proved to be a source of comfort instead. It was as if a part of her was still with him.

Caleb stared at the diploma hanging next to Ellie's artwork and let his mind drift back. It was nothing short of a miracle that it was even there. Due to the accident, he'd been forced to withdraw from his final semester at UGA, and following Ellie's death, he'd lacked the motivation to go back to school.

But at his parents' urging, he'd enrolled in the community college and taken an internship with a small design firm in Baxter. The work had been challenging on both fronts, but had proven to be a much needed diversion.

Then, two weeks ago, he'd been offered a full-time position with Wilshire and Cunningham, a prestigious architectural design firm with an office here in Columbus, and headquartered in Atlanta.

Now, he was finally ready to begin this new chapter in his life. He was determined to devote himself to his new career with all the eagerness and enthusiasm of a rookie football player seeking the good graces of his new coach.

Six weeks into his job, the office manager announced that he was sending him to the company headquarters in Atlanta for a three-day training seminar required of all new employees. As he packed for the event, it dawned on him that this would be his first trip back to Atlanta since visiting Ellie's grave nearly nine months earlier. The memories of that painful day came flooding back, and he found himself wishing he didn't have to go.

But he was curious to see what kind of permanent marker Ellie's father had put in place, so he decided to face the challenge head on.

After the seminar, I'll swing by the cemetery and leave some fresh flowers on her headstone.

CHAPTER SIXTEEN

A RESURRECTION OF HOPE

DRIVING THE TWO-YEAR OLD METALLIC blue Camaro he'd purchased after landing the Wilshire and Cunningham position, Caleb headed north out of Columbus early on the morning of November tenth. This vehicle with very low miles, was all one color, had no dents or hail damage, and was quite an improvement from the old Sonata, which he had dubbed Old Faithful. As he merged onto I-85 North toward Atlanta, he couldn't stop thinking about Ellie. The feeling that she was somehow still with him had never fully faded, and he began to feel a bit guilty for harboring the idea for so long.

He hoped that this second visit to Woodlawn Cemetery would permanently lay those thoughts to rest. Arriving in Atlanta around nine, he checked into the Regency Towers Hotel which was within walking distance from the company headquarters. He headed toward the elevators to the left of the front desk, and pushed the button for his floor. As he waited for the doors to open, he glanced around the lobby.

A row of five framed drawings on one wall caught his attention. He stepped closer and studied the artwork. They were water color and ink drawings of the five hotels that had been purchased by the owner of the Regency. The detail of the renderings was exquisite.

Although he'd never seen the other hotels in person, the buildings looked awfully familiar. He searched for the signature of the artist.

These were the drawings Ellie had been commissioned to do when she was in high school!

A lump rose in Caleb's throat, and his eyes grew misty. A sense of happiness washed over him. Even in downtown Atlanta, right here where he was staying, a part of Ellie was with him.

Once in his room, he changed clothes and freshened up. Then he went back down to the lobby and out the main glass doors of the hotel. As he walked the block and a half to his company headquarters, he kept an eye out for restaurants he might want to try over the next few days. A number looked promising.

Upon entering the glass and steel lobby of Wilshire and Cunningham, he followed the signs down a side hallway to the meeting room. After registering at the table, he went in and took a seat with the other seminar attendees.

The three days in Atlanta passed quickly.

Caleb thoroughly enjoyed the seminar, and he learned a lot about the company and its high standards of excellence. In between sessions he got acquainted with several other attendees over lunch and dinner.

On Wednesday, the final day of the seminar, the last session wrapped up around four o'clock that afternoon. Caleb decided to hang around and try a little sidewalk cafe he'd spied the day before.

He planned to visit Ellie's grave before driving home that evening. Sitting alone at the small, round metal table on the sidewalk outside the cafe, Caleb enjoyed a cheesy bean and rice burrito as he relaxed in the shade of the large green and white striped umbrella. Rush hour in the city was just beginning. The sidewalks and streets were filling up with people and cars, all eager to get somewhere as quickly as possible.

From his sixth floor hotel room earlier that morning, he'd watched the throngs of people rushing to and fro, like so many ants going in all directions, each with a purpose and destination. While he enjoyed the city, with its sights and sounds and smells, he couldn't picture himself living in such a crowded, bustling area.

No, he would always be a small town boy at heart.

The sound of someone laying on a car horn caught his attention. Apparently a car had cut in front of another vehicle, and the offended driver was offering his opinion of the guilty party in no uncertain terms.

Caleb's attention drifted to the throngs of people on the sidewalk across the street. A homeless man sat on a low cement wall pounding on an overturned five gallon bucket with his palms. Although he couldn't hear the drumbeats over the din of the street, the man's playing must have been pretty good, because people would stop long enough to drop a few coins or a bill in the coffee can next to him. A young woman walking past the sidewalk musician caught his eye. It wasn't the way she was dressed, or the way she walked that grabbed his attention.

It was her hair.

The long, wavy, auburn hair that bounced as she walked. An icy chill shot down Caleb's spine. He sat upright in his seat, eyes frozen on the figure passing by on the crowded sidewalk across the busy street. Only one person he knew had hair that bounced like that.

"Ellie?" His mouth formed the word.

Dropping the unfinished burrito onto the open wrapper, Caleb stood up quickly, knocking over the metal chair in the process. Several cafe patrons at nearby tables turned to stare at him.

"Ellie?" His voice cracked. "Ellie!"

Adrenaline shot into his veins like an injection of nitrous oxide into a racing engine.

Dodging tables with moves worthy of a Heisman Trophy winning running back, and ignoring the pain in his left leg, Caleb hurdled the low iron railing that separated the cafe's seating area from the rest of the sidewalk's pedestrian traffic.

"ELLIE!" he shouted at the top of his lungs. "ELLIE, WAIT!"

Waving his arms to get her attention, he dashed into the street, dodging oncoming traffic. "ELLIE!"

The screech of brakes turned heads up and down the busy avenue. *Scree-eeeech!*

Something struck him on the right thigh. He tumbled to the pavement, narrowly avoiding hitting his head on a manhole cover in the center of the street.

People on the curb started toward him as he struggled to his hands and knees.

"Ellie!" he managed to peer around the vehicle blocking his view.

A man in a gray business suit was the first to reach him. He grabbed Caleb's arm and helped him to his feet. "Are you all right?"

"I'm okay," Caleb replied, as he tried to locate the receding figure on the opposite sidewalk.

"That was a nasty tumble," another man said. "You sure you're okay?"

Straining to see over the heads of those who'd gathered around him, Caleb brushed himself off. "I'm okay," he repeated.

"Sorry!" He quickly tossed the word in the direction of the driver who'd struck him, and limped to the opposite curb, leaving the small crowd of people standing in the middle of stopped traffic, shaking their heads and commenting to one another.

"That's one lucky guy."

"He must be crazy."

"What an idiot."

Caleb ignored their comments.

"ELLIE!" he yelled again as he reached the opposite curb.

Caleb looked around desperately, but the young woman with the bouncing auburn hair was nowhere in sight.

Dodging pedestrians on the crowded sidewalk, he hobbled as fast as he could in the direction she'd been heading. When he reached the busy corner, he looked in all directions. There were people everywhere. He started in several directions, but stopped. Which way should he go?

It was no use. She was gone, swallowed up in the sea of humanity.

Acutely aware of the pain in both legs now, he slowly limped back to the cafe to retrieve his brief case. Thankfully, it was still under the table where he'd left it.

He sat down to catch his breath. The waiter brought him a fresh glass of water and asked if he was all right. Assuring the man that he was, Caleb drained the glass in one long gulp. Then he pulled out his cell phone and called B.J.

"B.J.," Caleb shouted into his phone as soon as his friend answered. "I saw her!"

There was a pause on the other end. "Caleb? What are you talking about? Saw who?"

"Ellie. I just saw Ellie!"

There was an even longer pause. "Caleb, where are you? Are you still in Atlanta? At the cemetery?"

"Yeah, I'm in Atlanta. But not at the cemetery. I'm downtown. And I just saw Ellie across the street."

B.J.'s voice still seemed hesitant. "Um . . . you saw Ellie? What made you think it was her?"

"Are you kidding?" Caleb's voice rose an octave. "Of course it was her. I'd know her anywhere. That hair. The way it bounces. It was her, B.J. I'm telling you, it was her."

"Did you get a good look at her? I mean, if she was way across the street from you, maybe it was just someone who looked a lot like her."

Caleb fought back frustration. "I know it sounds strange, but it was her. I'm positive, B.J. She's alive!" His exclamation was met with a long silence. "B.J.? You still there?"

B.J. spoke slowly. "Um, Caleb, do you realize what you're saying? I'm afraid that couldn't have been Ellie you saw, pal. She's at the Woodlawn Cemetery, remember? We all visited her together."

Caleb placed his free hand over his other ear and leaned forward on both elbows. He fought to control his voice. "Listen, I know it sounds crazy, but I got a good look at her. Remember what I told you about her father? Maybe he really did fake her obituary and forge her death certificate."

"But what about her grave, Caleb? Are you telling me he faked her burial, too? You saw the marker yourself."

"I know I did. But what if that was a fake, too? It's possible. Anyway, I can't deny what I just saw with my own two eyes."

"I'm sure you saw someone who looked a lot like Ellie. The spitting image of her, maybe. I wish it could be her, too, pal. But we have to face the facts. Ellie's gone, and you need to move on. That's all there is to it. I'm sorry."

"Well, don't believe me, then," he huffed. "But I'm going to prove you wrong. You just wait and see." Caleb disconnected the call and leaned back in his chair. He slowly let the air escape from his lungs. *What now? What should he do?*

The waiter returned and refilled his glass. After taking another long drink, he sat there chewing his lower lip and pondering his next move. Suddenly his phone rang. It was his father.

"Caleb?" His father's voice sounded worried. "Son, are you all right? I just got a call from B.J. He said you seemed to be in some sort of crisis."

"Crisis? No, Dad, I'm not in a crisis. But you won't believe what just happened."

He told his father everything he had witnessed a few minutes earlier. "What do you make of it, Dad? What do you think I should do?"

"Well," his father began slowly, "why don't you go back to your hotel room for the time being and take it easy. I'll leave right away and drive up there to meet you."

"You don't need to do that," Caleb protested. "Besides, I'm already checked out."

"Then why don't you wait where you are and I'll meet you there."

"Dad, I'm fine. I'm not crazy," he assured his father. "I'm not having a mental or emotional breakdown. I know what I saw."

Always the diplomat, his father replied, "I believe you, son. But if you don't want me to come up there to Atlanta, maybe I could meet you at your apartment. When do you think you'll get back?"

"I'll call you when I'm about an hour out, okay? How's that?" His father reluctantly agreed.

Caleb limped back to his car in the underground parking lot. His legs were really hurting now. That car must have hit him harder than he first thought. As he got behind the wheel, he noticed the flowers he'd bought earlier that afternoon.

Maybe B.J. was right. Maybe it was only someone who looked like Ellie.

After all, isn't it true that every person in the world has a double?

But no, this was no double he'd seen. It was her, all right.

He wasn't going to let anyone convince him otherwise. And he would prove them wrong. Somehow. Instead of heading straight home, he decided to swing by the cemetery and place the flowers on Ellie's grave. After all, that's what he'd bought them for.

It was after six when Caleb drove into Woodlawn Cemetery and made his way up the winding road to the Pine Hill section. Parking where his father had parked the last time they were here, he grabbed the flowers and limped up the rise to Ellie's grave.

The first thing he noticed as he approached the plot was that the newly planted grass was now a thick luxurious carpet of grass and weeds. The second thing he noticed were the withered remains of the bouquets his family had left behind. No one had bothered to remove them.

The white cross with the wreath was gone. In its place was a black polished granite headstone set flush with the ground. It was nothing elaborate, but at least Ellie's father had kept his word.

As he stared at the inscription his blood ran cold.

AUBREY LYNN SELKIRK

March 7, 1936 – January 14, 2018

Stunned, Caleb stared at the block of stone under his feet.

That couldn't be right. He must have the wrong plot. He looked around. There was the old knotty pine to the left, now more dead than alive. No, this was the place. No mistake about it.

Then why had they replaced Ellie's marker with the headstone of a stranger? Was she somewhere else? In another section, perhaps? In an unmarked grave?

And what about seeing her downtown less than two hours ago? If that was really her, then she wouldn't be here anyway. He'd lost her in the rush hour crowd, and now he'd lost her in the cemetery as well.

Feeling extremely uneasy, he left the bouquet and got back in his car. He sat there for about five minutes, wondering what to do. Should he go home, like he promised? Or stay in Atlanta overnight and look into this latest mystery personally?

———————————————

Caleb left the motel around nine in the morning and drove back to the cemetery office. It was a small building off the frontage road about a quarter mile past the main entrance. As he pulled into the small gravel lot, he saw a sign on the door.

Office Hours: 9:00 AM to 5:00 PM

It was nine-fifteen, and no one was there. Go figure.

While waiting for someone to arrive, he thought about the call to his parents the previous evening. His father had not been happy with his decision to remain in Atlanta. But he'd convinced him that he needed to resolve this in person, now rather than later.

Twenty minutes passed before a small sedan pulled up next to the office. A woman in her mid-fifties with graying hair got out, and after glancing in his direction, disappeared into the building. He gave her a few minutes, and then he entered the office. The narrow room looked like it hadn't been updated since the seventies.

Wood paneling covered the walls, and the green sculptured carpet was faded and worn from years of sunlight and foot traffic. A faint odor of mildew hung over the room. After seeing the lack of maintenance outside, he wasn't surprised.

"May I help you?" The woman looked at him over a pair of gold reading glasses.

"Yes. I'm Caleb Sawyer, and I think there's been a mix up with a couple of headstones," he began. He went on to explain what he'd discovered the previous evening.

The woman cocked her head to one side and stared at him. "And where exactly did this alleged mix up take place?"

"Um . . . plot seventy-four. In the Pine Hill section."

She spun around in her chair and rummaged through a file cabinet against the wall behind her desk. She pulled out a single folder and turned back and plopped it down in front of her.

"What did you say the name of the deceased was again?" She leaned over and peered intently into the file.

"Elinor A. Thompson."

The woman frowned. She looked up at Caleb over the top of her glasses again. "You're sure about that?"

"Yes I'm sure." He returned her frown.

"And you're sure the location is in the Pine Hill section, plot number seventy-four?"

"Yes."

She stared at him. "Well I can assure you that no one by that name is buried there. Our records show that an Aubrey L. Selkirk was interred there on January fourteenth of this year. That plot and the one next to it were purchased by her family over twenty years ago."

Caleb couldn't believe his ears. "But I stood at that very plot on February twenty-first with my family and best friend. We all saw the marker. And it said 'Elinor A. Thompson.' There's got to be a mistake. Perhaps the grounds crew accidentally switched the headstones."

"Oh, I doubt that," the woman spoke up quickly. "Those kinds of things almost never happen in this business. We're required by state and federal law to keep very accurate records, you know."

"But there must be some mistake. All five of us couldn't have be wrong." He had a sudden inspiration. "Wait, I can prove it."

He pulled out his phone and scrolled through the photos. Showing her a close-up of Ellie's marker, he added excitedly, "See. I took this in February when we were all here."

The woman studied the picture through her readers, and then shook her head. "Well, I don't know. I see a white cross with that name all right. But there's not enough picture around it to prove that it was where you say it was. This photo could have been taken anywhere. Do you have any other pictures that show the surrounding area?"

"No," he answered, his shoulders slumping.

"Well, it doesn't matter." She clapped her hands. "If this Elinor Thompson is somewhere else in Woodlawn, our alphabetical files will tell us where." She opened the lower left desk drawer and pulled out a dog-eared list of names, held together by a half-dozen staples. Flipping back and forth through the pages, she searched for Ellie's name. "That's strange," she muttered.

"What? What is it?" he pushed.

The woman shook her head. "There's no record at all of an Elinor Thompson here in Woodlawn." She looked up and squinted. "Are you sure you have the right cemetery?"

Caleb returned to his car and sat in the parking lot for a while. What in the world was going on? Where was Ellie's headstone? He decided to pray.

"Lord, I just don't know what's going on here," he began. "I'm confused, and frustrated, and I don't know what to do. But I know You're in control. Please direct my steps and straighten out this mess. I need Your help."

Then he drove home.

His parents were waiting at his Columbus apartment when he got back. They spent the afternoon with him discussing the incredible events of the past twenty-four hours.

Later that evening, they took him out to dinner. At the restaurant, Caleb picked at his food. His appetite had left him, and he felt mentally and emotionally exhausted.

His mother voiced her concern. "Caleb, maybe we should stay here overnight." She smiled at him. "In the morning I could make your favorite breakfast if you like."

He stopped playing with his food. "Mom, that's really not necessary. I'm just tired after everything that's happened. I need a good night's rest, that's all. You guys go on home. I'll be fine in the morning."

"All right, if that's what you want," she relented.

His father agreed. "We'll go home tonight, but tomorrow I'd like to look into the missing headstone myself. Is that alright with you?"

"Sure, Dad. The sooner we get some answers the better."

After his parents left his apartment, Caleb collapsed on the sofa. But he awoke around one o'clock in the morning and couldn't go back to sleep, so he got up and made himself a snack in the kitchenette. Sitting at the small round table, his mind was a jumble of thoughts.

He knew he'd seen Ellie's grave at Pine Hill #74 in Woodlawn Cemetery in February. But he also knew he'd seen Ellie on the sidewalk in downtown Atlanta just two days ago.

Was there a logical explanation for both? Either Ellie was dead and buried in Woodlawn, or else she was alive and walking the streets of Atlanta. There was no middle ground.

His heart began to race. There was only one person who could explain this anomaly. One person who'd said Ellie was in Woodlawn when in fact she might not really be there. One person who knew for sure where she was right this very minute.

And that person was John C. Smith.

CHAPTER SEVENTEEN

THE CONFRONTATION

THE DARKNESS OF NIGHT WAS just beginning its metamorphosis into the grayness of dawn when Caleb's metallic blue Camaro pulled to the curb of the nearly deserted avenue in one of Atlanta's many residential suburbs. It was nearly six-thirty Friday morning. He'd been up since one-o-clock when he'd made the decision to return to Atlanta without notifying anyone.

Caleb turned on the car's reading light and picked up the scrap of paper he'd stuffed into the cup holder.

Elmwood Village Apartments

4391 W. Cannondale Avenue, Apt. 1C

Atlanta, GA 30310

That was the address for John Smith that his father had passed on to him. It matched the one that Krystal had located earlier on the internet. This had to be the right place.

He lowered his side window, and in the dim light of morning strained to read the numbers of the apartment buildings across the street. Through the evenly spaced trees that separated the east and westbound lanes of Cannondale Avenue, he made out the number 4389 on the building directly opposite him.

That must mean the one further down was 4391. Four ground level doors, labeled 1A to 1D respectively, faced the street in each building.

John Smith must live behind door number three of the next building. Sitting in his darkened car, Caleb tried to formulate a plan for confronting Mr. Smith.

Should he go to the man's door and talk to him there, or should he wait until he came out of the apartment and talk to him in the open?

He decided the latter would be the best option. He saw several lights come on here and there, but the windows of 1C remained dark. A person walked past on the sidewalk. As he waited, his eyelids grew heavy. He'd had only a couple hours of sleep before driving the two and a half hours to get here, and he'd already been exhausted before that.

He took a sip of coffee from the insulated foam cup he'd purchased when he reached the outskirts of the city, but the shot of caffeine failed to achieve its intended purpose.

The metallic squeal of brakes jerked Caleb awake. Dazed, he looked around to get his bearings. It was much lighter now. He glanced at his watch. The time was seven forty-five.

Across the avenue, a city bus had just pulled to the curb in front of John Smith's apartment building. In the early morning grayness, Caleb had failed to notice the Metro Stop sign on the pole by the curb.

As a half dozen people lined up to climb aboard, his eyes swept over the windows of John Smith's apartment. The lights were on.

It was almost time for the face-to-face meeting. The meeting he'd long desired—and feared. The door to 1C abruptly opened, and a beautiful young woman carrying a large canvas bag over one shoulder rushed down the steps toward the bus.

Transfixed, his eyes followed the bouncing auburn hair until the familiar head disappeared into the interior of the bus. The release of air from the buses' brakes snapped Caleb out of his trance. He flung open his car door, and limped across the eastbound lane of the Avenue, but not before looking both ways.

"ELLIE!" he shouted, trying to head off the bus. He frantically waved his arms to get the driver's attention, but the bus pulled away from him.

With aching legs, he hobbled back to the Camaro, nearly stumbling in the process. He started his car and fastened his seat belt in one fluid motion. Then, gunning the engine, he laid down rubber as he headed east toward a break in the median half a block away. With tires whining, he executed a U-turn and raced west down Cannondale Avenue, disregarding the speed limit in pursuit of the city bus, which was making a right hand turn three hundred yards ahead.

Caleb navigated the turn with all the skills of a professional drifter.

Don't lose sight of that bus!

Fortunately, traffic was light this time of morning. Rush hour wouldn't begin for another thirty minutes or so. He eased the Camaro in behind the bus and followed at a safe distance.

The bus made several more stops before leaving the neighborhood for the downtown business district. At each stop he was tempted to jump out of his car and get on the bus himself. But with only one or two people getting on each time, and his legs hurting the way they were, he was afraid it would turn into another scene like the one in front of the apartment.

Not wanting to risk it, he decided to wait until Ellie got off. Caleb tailed the bus all the way into the downtown area. Traffic was really beginning to pick up now. The bus made a right turn onto Second Street and eased to the curb next to a large, open air plaza.

They were only a block away from where he'd seen Ellie Wednesday afternoon. A car suddenly cut in front of him and pulled up behind the bus to let out its passenger.

Caleb braked hard and wheeled his Camaro to the curb within inches of the other car. People had begun to file off the bus and scatter in all directions.

As quickly as he could, he exited his car and limped to the side of the bus. It was more than half empty. He craned to see through the windows, but the glint of the morning sun on the tinted glass obstructed his view of the interior. When the stream of riders ceased, he clamored up the steps and looked down the aisle.

The bus was empty.

"Can I help you?" the middle-aged driver asked, looking at him suspiciously.

"Uh . . . I thought I saw someone I know get on a few miles back." Caleb made a hasty retreat and looked around the plaza.

There were hundreds of people going every which way. He felt a familiar sinking feeling in the pit of his stomach. He'd lost her again.

He was about to turn back to his car, which by now had drawn the attention of a city patrolman on a bicycle, when he spied the bouncing auburn hair in a group of people entering the revolving glass doors of the high rise office building to the far left of the plaza.

"ELLIE!" he shouted, waving his arms.

But the woman didn't turn around, and was swept along with the others into the open mouth of the hungry edifice.

He broke into a run, but it was more like an out-of-balance trot. His hips and legs were on fire. Ignoring the pain, he pushed into the crowd waiting to go single file through the doors. Caught up in the throng, he suddenly found himself in the noisy, cavernous lobby, surrounded by people who all seemed determined to get where they were going by the shortest route and in the least amount of time possible.

"ELLIE!" he shouted above the din, but only a few people walking past him even gave him a glance.

Looking around, he spied a large cluster of people waiting for the elevators to his far left. On the chance that she might be heading to one of the many upper floors, Caleb moved in that direction. The doors of three elevators opened, and the crowd surged forward. He frantically scanned the back of people's heads.

There were just too many people.

He'd have to pick one elevator. Throwing up a quick prayer, he focused on the closest door. One by one the people stepped through the opening and turned to face him. The last person stepped through and turned around.

It was Ellie.

Caleb lunged forward and grabbed the edge of the door just before it closed. He suddenly found himself staring into those familiar brown eyes. He looked at her and she looked back at him.

There was no doubt in his mind now. It was her. It was really her. Alive and well.

"Ellie!" he gasped, nearly out of breath. He stepped halfway into the opening. "Ellie, where have you been?"

Ellie stiffened and stared back at him with the look of a startled deer.

He took a step forward. "I've been looking for you everywhere."

She recoiled against the people behind her.

"I thought you were dead."

She shrank back further, her eyes wide with fear. "I . . . I don't . . . know you."

The voice was strangely fragile, but it was definitely Ellie's.

Blocking the door from closing, Caleb stared into her beautiful eyes. He'd never seen them full of terror like this. "Ellie, what's the matter? Don't you recognize me?"

The crowd behind her was becoming restless. Someone in the back corner muttered "Close the door."

A man in an expensive business suit and carrying an important looking brief case stepped forward and tapped Caleb lightly on the shoulder. "Sir, I think you need to step back and leave the young lady alone."

"But I've been looking for her for a long time. Ellie, it's me, Caleb."

Ellie looked like she was going to pass out. The scene in *It's a Wonderful Life* when Mary Hatch fails to recognize George Bailey because he'd never been born filtered through his mind.

"I don't . . . know anyone named . . . Caleb." Ellie shook her head. She stared intently at him and spoke firmly. "I've never seen you before in my life!" Ellie's words pierced his heart.

Stunned, he took a step back.

The last thing he saw was the mixture of fear and fierceness in her big brown eyes as she stared back at him.

Caleb stood frozen in front of the cold, polished steel door of the elevator. Gradually he became aware of the throng behind him. With plenty of suspicious and disparaging looks tossed his way, Caleb hobbled to the nearest bench and sat down.

He tried making sense of the scene that had just played out. What had happened to her? She seemed so distant. So fragile, so frail, so . . . frightened. Still dazed by the turn of events, he called his father.

As expected, he was both surprised and upset to learn that his son was back in Atlanta. "Son, I think it was very foolish of you to drive back up there this morning."

"I know, Dad. But wait 'til you hear what just happened!" His father listened with rapt attention as Caleb laid out the details of his latest encounter with Ellie.

"Son," he began when Caleb was through, "first of all, I want you to know that I believe everything you've told me is true, as incredible as it sounds. I'm convinced the person you saw Wednesday and this morning is really Ellie after all. And all I can say right now is praise the Lord she's alive."

"Amen to that!" Caleb raised his hand in the air. "This changes everything." He hesitated. "But it also raises a whole slew of issues I'm not sure how to deal with. And questions I don't have the answers for."

"You mean like, if she's alive, then why the elaborate hoax to convince us she was dead?"

"Exactly. Whatever his reason is, it can't be a good one."

"I agree one hundred percent, son. Mr. Smith's behavior leads me to believe that he's a desperate man. And desperate men are often dangerous men."

"Then Ellie might be in danger, too, Dad. She lives with him."

"Yes, you told me that. Caleb, when she first saw you in the elevator, did you detect any sign of recognition in her face at all?"

Caleb carefully replayed the moment of first contact in his mind. "No, Dad, none. It was like I was a complete stranger to her. She was startled at first, and then scared. Scared out of her wits. Like she was going to pass out or something."

"You said she seemed to be very fragile. Did you mean physically, mentally, emotionally, what?"

"I'd say definitely emotionally. Maybe mentally. I can't be sure. But she seemed to be okay physically. She was walking just fine, and I didn't notice any scars or anything from the accident. She looked just like she always has. Except for the blank stare and the fear in her eyes. I've never seen that before. Do you think she might have been pretending not to know me? Because of her father?"

"Caleb, anything's possible at this point. But I don't think she was pretending. When you surprised her, there would have been a brief moment when she recognized you before fear took over. No, I'm thinking she really doesn't know who you are."

"But why wouldn't she know who . . . " Caleb stopped short. "Amnesia? Do you think she's got amnesia from the accident?"

"That's very possible. In cases of severe trauma, people often have no memory of what caused it. But if she doesn't recognize you at all, then her memory loss must go back much further than the accident. And if that's the case, she probably is very fragile emotionally. That would explain a lot of things."

"Like why she hasn't tried to contact me all this time. I've asked myself that a hundred times since Wednesday."

"Yes, this raises all sorts of questions. But right now we know only two things for sure. Her father has apparently perpetrated an elaborate hoax by faking her death. And Ellie may have amnesia, in which case she's very fragile and should not be subjected to another strain like the one in the elevator just now."

"Are you saying I shouldn't try to contact her again for the time being?"

"That would seem prudent, don't you think? We don't want to run the risk of doing anything that might cause her more harm. I think you should wait until we're able to sort out this new information before you attempt any further contact with her. Son, this is a very delicate situation. The best thing for you to do is to drive down here to Baxter, and together we'll pray about it and seek advice from the proper authorities on how to proceed."

Caleb took his father's advice. "All right, Dad. But do you have any idea how hard it is for me to leave here, knowing she's somewhere in this very building with me?"

"I think I do. You know, I'm tempted to drive up there myself right now to help you solve this. But we need to be very careful. We've got to have clear, level heads for this one." He paused. "Will you promise me you won't try to contact her before you come home?"

Caleb sighed. "Yes, Dad. I promise."

"Good. I'll see you when you get here, then. Oh, and son, please drive carefully. If you get tired, pull over at a rest stop and call me, will you?"

Following the conversation with his father, Caleb got up and went looking for a vending machine. His mouth was dry and he needed something to wash away the fuzz. He located a soda machine around the corner from the elevators.

On his way back across the lobby, he noticed the business directory attached to the wall between two of the elevators. He stopped and studied it as he sipped his soda. One of those businesses must be where Ellie was headed. But which one? There were close to a hundred different listings.

He tried to recall what she was wearing, but drew a blank.

He'd been focused on her hair so as not to lose her in the crowd, and on her face in the elevator. But he did remember that she was carrying a large canvas bag over one shoulder. The kind she used to carry on her way to art classes at UGA.

Maybe she was working as a painter for an art gallery or studio. Or perhaps she was an artist for a design or marketing firm.

He ran down the alphabetical listing of company names. No art galleries or studios were listed, but three possibilities emerged from the search. A fashion design group. A marketing firm. And a publishing company. Maybe she was a magazine or book illustrator. He was tempted to check them out. After all, what harm would there be in asking the receptionists if they had an Ellie Thompson working for them?

That wouldn't be breaking the promise to his father. Technically.

At least then he could return to Baxter with something more specific than which building she worked in.

There must be thousands of people employed here. If he could just narrow his search down to one company.

Caleb, you idiot! Just get in your car and go home like your dad said, for once.

He headed across the lobby and out the revolving door to his car. A green piece of paper pinned against his windshield by the passenger side wiper blade greeted him. He'd been issued a parking ticket. Grateful that he hadn't been towed, Caleb climbed behind the wheel of the Camaro. He tossed the ticket into the center console and pulled away from the curb. Following the signs, he headed for the nearest I-85 South ramp. He should be home in about four hours.

He'd no sooner merged into traffic when he glanced at the fuel gauge. It showed less than a quarter tank. He'd have to stop for gas. And soon.

Exiting at the next interchange, he spied a gas station a few blocks away. He drove up to the pump and filled his tank. Then he went inside and bought another coffee and a sweet roll. That should hold him until he arrived in Baxter. Caleb was about to drive away from the pump when he spied the white scrap of paper lying on the passenger seat. He picked it up, intending to stuff it in with the parking ticket. Instead, he read it again.

Elmwood Village Apartments

4391 W. Cannondale Avenue, Apt. 1C

Atlanta, GA 30310

Hmm. Cannondale Avenue was only a few exits ahead. Maybe seven or eight miles to the apartment itself.

Should he stop there on his way out of Atlanta to see if John Smith was home? He'd promised not to contact Ellie, but he hadn't promised not to contact her father.

The man had caused immeasurable pain and suffering for him and his family. Caused a lot of grief for a lot of people. Wasted everyone's time and money. He'd gone to unbelievable extremes to convince them all that Ellie was dead.

And for what purpose? What motive did he have for keeping Ellie away from them? What diabolical scheme had he concocted? Was he somehow using Ellie in her fragile state of mind for personal or financial gain? Was he mistreating her? Abusing her even? If so, he needed to know now.

He had to have answers.

Answers he could take back to his parents and the authorities.

Besides, he'd promised to always be there for Ellie.

This was a chance to redeem himself for not being there after the accident. She needed him now more than ever.

It was time once again to confront John C. Smith. Caleb entered his destination into the GPS. Once the route came up on the screen, he started the car and headed back onto the highway.

Fifteen minutes later, Caleb pulled to the curb in nearly the same spot he had occupied a few hours before at dawn's early light. He shut off the engine and sat behind the wheel. Once again, he tried formulating a plan of attack, but his head was a jumble of unconnected thoughts.

He'd just have to be direct and come right to the point. He got out of his car, crossed both east and westbound lanes, and walked down the sidewalk until he stood in front of 1C.

Taking a deep breath to steady his emotions, he approached the residence. He rapped loudly on the steel door with his knuckles, ignoring the small button on the door frame.

No movement or sound came from within.

He knocked harder and waited. Still no response.

The third time he pounded with his fists so hard that a flake of peeling paint separated from the door frame and fluttered to the stoop at his feet.

Either John Smith was not home or he wasn't going to answer the door. Caleb fumed.

Why was this guy so hard to get a hold of? The man couldn't possibly be avoiding him. How could he know that Caleb was in town, much less that he had his address?

Caleb peered through the window to the left of the door. Through a gap in the heavy curtains, he could make out a sofa and recliner. He returned to his car, and, after finishing his coffee and pastry, reclined his seat and began the stakeout. He started to doze off again.

A car door slammed somewhere nearby. Caleb sat upright with a start and looked around. Across the street in front of apartment 1C, a man was unloading some groceries from the rear hatch of what looked like a brand new silver SUV. Caleb stared at him.

He appeared to be in his mid-forties, and had short, curly brown hair. When the man glanced up at a passing car, Caleb got a good look at his face. He was sporting a diamond stud in each ear.

Caleb sprang into action. He quickly exited his car and cut across the street. Coming around the front of the parked SUV, he approached the man on the sidewalk. "Mr. Smith," Caleb called out, "I need to talk to you!"

Startled, John Smith stopped in his tracks and stared at him.

"Who are you?" he demanded gruffly.

"I'm the person you've been trying to avoid. I'm Caleb Sawyer."

There was a momentary flash of recognition on the man's face. Then he deftly brushed it aside.

He began to walk toward the steps leading to the apartment, but Caleb stepped in front of him.

"You've spoken to me and my father several times on the phone."

John Smith stopped and sized him up for a minute. Then he set down his grocery bags on the sidewalk and took a step toward him. His demeanor instantly changed. He broke into a warm smile and extended a hand. "Caleb Sawyer. Of course. Now I remember who you are."

Caleb instinctively shook the man's hand.

"You caught me off guard there for a moment," John explained. "I'm sorry I didn't recognize you right away." He looked puzzled. "But how did you find me? And why are you here?"

There was no suspicion in his voice, just confusion. Either Mr. John C. Smith was a very transparent person, or he was a very good liar. Caleb didn't buy his act for a second. "I think you know very well why I'm here!"

He didn't bother to explain his presence. He didn't owe the man a thing. It was the other way around.

John scowled. "It's about Ellie, isn't it?" He sighed. "I was afraid this day would come. Somehow I knew it would, eventually. And I've been worried sick about what I was going to say to you if we ever met face-to-face," he said wistfully.

Ellie's father shook his head meekly. "Mr. Sawyer, I'm not a very brave man by nature. I've been afraid of how you might react to meeting me. And after all I've put you and your family through, I don't blame you one bit for being upset with me. I know I should have told you about her passing as soon as I found out you weren't from one of those awful foster families she had to put up with. I had hoped that you'd find it in your heart to forgive me."

Caleb stared at him in amazement. The man was good. Very good. If he hadn't come here armed with the truth, he'd probably have been taken in by the man's stellar performance. It was worthy of an Oscar.

"Mr. Smith, you're one of the biggest liars I've ever had the misfortune of running into!"

The color drained from John's face. His eyes flashed anger for a split second, but then he continued without breaking character. "I . . . I don't understand what you mean. I've done everything I could to assist you and your family. I sent the obituary and death certificate to your father. And I gave him the burial details." He feigned concern. "You did visit the gravesite, didn't you? I can only imagine how painful that trip must have been. I wanted to be there to meet you, but I thought you might want to be alone as a family. You know, to grieve in private."

Caleb felt like punching the man in the mouth. That wicked mouth that spewed forth lie after lie. It was obvious that John Smith had plenty of experience in the art of deception. His eyes narrowed, and his voice became like steel. "You can cut the act right now. You know full well that Ellie isn't lying there in Woodlawn at all. She's alive! You want to know how I know that? Because I saw her downtown on Wednesday afternoon, and I saw her again this morning."

John's face turned ashen, and his hands trembled. But the act wasn't over yet. "I . . . I don't know why you would say such a thing," he stammered. "I wish she were here as much as you do." He feigned suspicion. "Why did you really come here? Are you here for revenge?

Do you want some kind of compensation for your pain and suffering? Are you trying to extort money from me?"

"I'm here for one purpose and one purpose only." Caleb took a step toward the man. "To hear the truth from you so I can find out what you've done to Ellie. Those documents you sent my father were fakes. And so was that marker. The cemetery office confirmed that Ellie never was in Woodlawn!"

John's eyes narrowed, and he stared angrily at Caleb. His demeanor changed again. "Is this some kind of cruel hoax you're trying to pull on me? Telling me Ellie's still alive? You must be crazy. I was going to ignore your accusations and chalk them up as coming from someone who's been under a lot of stress and not thinking clearly. But now you're slandering me as the one perpetrating the hoax." He picked up the groceries. "Leave me alone to grieve in peace." Pushing past Caleb, he hurried up the steps to the front door of 1C.

Caleb bounded up the steps after him. "Hey, you're not gonna brush me off any longer. I'm not going away until you tell me what I need to know!"

Any traces of civility vanished. John set down the bags and fumbled for the keys to the apartment. His eyes were daggers. "You're trespassing, kid," he hissed. "If you know what's good for you, you'll get back on your high horse and ride out of here!"

Caleb didn't back down. "I came here for the truth, and I'm not leaving without it."

The man's teeth and fists were clenched. "You'll leave now, or you'll go away with something else you hadn't planned on." He turned and managed to open the apartment door.

Caleb's anger flared. He stepped forward and grabbed the man's arm. "Don't you walk away from me, you lying coward!"

Without warning, John's right fist connected with Caleb's left eye. Caleb staggered backward and nearly tumbled down the cement steps. Stunned and seeing stars, he doubled over and put a hand to his face. When he straightened up, John was standing in the doorway, cell phone in hand. "Like I said, boy, you're trespassing. One more step and I call nine-one-one."

Caleb decided to call his bluff.

With clenched fists, he stepped onto the stoop toward the man just inside the threshold. John quickly punched in the numbers.

Caleb heard the phone dialing and the emergency dispatcher's voice. "9-1-1. What's your emergency?"

John glared maliciously at Caleb as he responded to the question. This time, he played the part of the helpless victim. "Elmwood Village Apartments, 4391 West Cannondale Avenue, apartment one C," he spoke rapidly, fearfully, breathlessly. "I was just attacked by a stranger. He followed me from my car out front and jumped me on the porch as I was trying to open the door!"

The dispatcher said something unintelligible to Caleb.

"I'm in my apartment now. I was able to fight him off long enough to get inside, but he's still out there. I think he's crazy or high on something. He's got a wild look in his eyes and I think he's going to try and kick my front door in. Please hurry!" John placed a hand over his phone, and cursed Caleb in a low tone. It was more like the hiss of a rattlesnake than a human voice.

"I told you you'd be taking something home with you that you hadn't planned on. Now, if you don't leave right away, you won't be leaving Atlanta at all for a very long time!"

Caleb returned John's icy glare, and with balled fists responded with a threat of his own. "This isn't over. Not by a long shot."

He turned and deliberately walked slowly down the steps. At the curb he turned and looked back over his shoulder. There was an evil grin on the man's face.

Caleb fired a parting shot. "You'll be hearing from me again. You can count on it!"

Then he crossed the street and got into his car. He drove to the turn-around and headed back west. John Smith was still standing in the doorway, his phone in his hand, and his groceries on the stoop. In a final act of defiance, Caleb's Camaro left two long, black streaks on the pavement in front of apartment 1C. In the distance, he could hear sirens approaching.

CHAPTER EIGHTEEN

GETTING TO KNOW YOU

"I GUESS I WASN'T THINKING clearly." Caleb stood in the middle of his parents' living room with palms up.

His mother left her position in the doorway and took a seat on the sofa. His father lowered his head slightly, arched his right eyebrow, and stared at his son over the top of his black-rimmed readers.

Caleb remembered that look well. He could guarantee what was coming next.

"The better statement might be, 'I guess I wasn't thinking . . . period.'" His father shook his head. "Son, I can't believe you confronted him. You took an awful chance by going over there."

Caleb pursed his lips and hung his head. "Yeah, I know. I guess it was a pretty stupid decision on my part."

His mother spoke from her seated position on the sofa. "I'm grateful nothing worse happened. Caleb, what if he'd had a knife or a gun? What then?"

That thought hadn't crossed his mind. "Like Dad said, I wasn't thinking. But I am grateful. God was sure looking out for me. Even though it was a dumb idea."

"I hope you've learned a lesson from this," his father cautioned. "Always seek the Lord's will before making an important decision."

"Yeah, I should have. And I will from now on," Caleb promised.

He thought back to something his father had mentioned during their phone call that morning. "Dad, you said you were going to look into this hoax yourself. Have you talked to anyone about it yet?"

"I did. As soon as I got off the phone with you, I did some inquiring of my own. Forging a death certificate is definitely against the law, but the penalty depends on what type of crime was committed with it. If it was used to defraud an insurance company, for example, or offered in a state or federal court as an official document, then it could be considered a felony."

"What about the fake newspaper obituary?" Caleb wanted to know.

"Well, again, that depends on if it was used to perpetrate a crime. We still don't know her father's real purpose for trying to convince us of her death. I spoke with Lieutenant Jenkins at the police department, and he's going to contact the Atlanta fraud division to see if they will start an investigation into the matter."

"I was thinking about possible motives on the way home." Caleb sat down on the sofa next to his mother. "What if there's a life insurance policy on Ellie that we don't know about, or some distant relative's will that leaves an estate to her father in the event of her death? Those would be reasons enough for the hoax, wouldn't they?"

"I suppose those are possibilities. But right now they're nothing but conjecture and speculation. We're going to have to let the authorities do their job this time." He tilted his head and raised the eyebrow again. "Without our help."

Caleb spent the next two nights in Baxter with his parents and sister. He awoke around ten-thirty Saturday morning feeling remarkably rejuvenated, both physically and mentally.

His leg ached, but otherwise he felt fine. He got out of bed and went into the hall bathroom to wash his face.

He stared into the mirror. "Oh, great. Just great."

The face that stared back at him revealed a puffy and swollen eye socket, and sported the beginnings of a mammoth shiner. Following supper that evening, Caleb drove over to B.J. and Allison's to hang out with his friends and their baby boy.

"Dude, what a shiner," B.J. greeted him at the door of their small apartment. He followed Caleb into the living room. "You get into it with Chris Miller again?" he teased. "I had no idea you kept grudges this long."

Allison came into the room with the baby. Caleb gave her a hug and played with little Joshua.

"So, what happened?" B.J. pressed.

Caleb launched into a narrative of his encounter with Ellie and John Smith in Atlanta. When he finished, the couple stared back wide-eyed.

"That's unbelievable!" Allison declared. "Thank God Ellie's alive."

"Roger that," B.J. added. "But dude, what were you thinking, confronting her father like that?"

Caleb grinned sheepishly. "You guys sound just like my dad. But seriously, B.J., what would you have done under the circumstances?"

B.J. pondered the question. "I'd probably have done the exact same thing. Only I'd have gotten in a few jabs and right crosses before I left." He pummeled an invisible opponent with his fists.

Caleb laughed at his friend's antics. "I doubt you'd have been able to leave, pal."

"Do you think Ellie's in any danger?" Allison cast a worried expression his way.

"That's why I decided to confront her father in the first place," Caleb explained. "I learned he's definitely not a nice person. But that's about all. The police are investigating, but I'm supposed to stay out of the way and let them handle it."

B.J. eyed Caleb's shiner. "I'd do the same, pal," he chuckled. "But where do you go from here? With Ellie, I mean?"

Caleb shook his head ruefully. "I don't know what to do. My dad thinks it would be too stressful for her if I suddenly showed back up in her life right now. Plus, I promised not to contact her for the time being. At least until we can figure out how to move forward." A sudden fire flared up inside of him. "But I don't think I can stand being away from her much longer. In fact, now that I know she's alive, I miss her even more than I did when I thought she was dead."

"That's tough, man," B.J. sympathized. "Is there anything we can do?"

"Thanks, but there's nothing I can think of at the moment. Just pray, I guess."

"You can count on us for that," Allison assured him. "We've been praying since Wednesday morning when you told B.J. about seeing her in downtown Atlanta."

Caleb was humbled to have such faithful friends. "Thanks, guys. I appreciate that."

Sunday afternoon Caleb drove back to his apartment in Columbus. By noon Monday he'd grown so sick of explaining the black eye to his coworkers that he thought about running to the drugstore around the corner and buying some makeup to hide the discoloration. But he couldn't bring himself to do it. Explaining a black eye was one thing. Explaining makeup on a guy's face was something entirely different.

On Wednesday his office manager assigned him to a team of architects in charge of designing a new shopping mall on the far south side of Atlanta. The developer was wanting to begin construction in the next eight to ten months, and needed the final blueprints within the next ninety days. As a result of the project's urgency, the team planned to make several trips to the construction site in order to visualize the layout and land utilization. This news suited Caleb just fine.

Each day without Ellie seemed like an eternity, but hope remained alive and well that he would be able to see her again. How he'd go about doing that, and what he'd say to her eluded him, but he was confident it would be soon. Just not soon enough.

In the meantime, his father heard back from the Baxter Police Department. He relayed the information to his son in an email, which Caleb eagerly devoured.

"Caleb, I thought it would be better to put these details in writing for you. According to Lieutenant Jenkins, the Atlanta Fraud Division called in John Smith for questioning several days ago. In his written statement, he acknowledges some of his actions but denies any criminal intent. He insists his sole reason for the deception was purely a personal one. He claims to have panicked, fearing he would lose his only child again after just having had her reenter his life. They found no hard evidence of criminal motive, so he was dismissed on his own recognizance. However, some type of charges will likely be filed for forging the death certificate.

"While he was being interrogated at the precinct, another investigator went to the apartment to determine if Ellie is in any danger. He says she spoke well of her father, and expressed gratitude for his desire to care for her. According to Ellie, he told her she'd been involved in a car accident and he had taken responsibility for her. She was completely unaware of the hoax, and did not know who we were when asked by the detective. But he found no evidence that she is in harm's way. He did note that she appeared somewhat fragile, so he didn't tell her about us, the hoax, or the possible charges facing her father."

Caleb was disappointed with the news, but not surprised by it. Mr. John C. Smith, actor extraordinaire, was true to form, still portraying himself as the benevolent father with nothing but paternal intentions toward his mentally fragile daughter. At least Ellie was in no imminent danger from the man.

That was a huge relief. And there was some satisfaction to be had from the possibility that he would have to answer for his actions in court. But the investigation, which had just begun, left one thing unclear in Caleb's mind. If Mr. Smith's motives for the fraud weren't criminal in nature, or for illicit financial gain, just why had he gone to such extremes?

What did keeping Ellie away from him benefit the man? He didn't believe the story about the fearful, long lost father for one second.

Then what was his angle? He had to solve the mystery. Find the answer to that, and he'd find the way back to Ellie.

The following Monday, the four member design team traveled to the south Atlanta suburb of Riverdale to survey the proposed mall site. Caleb had a difficult time focusing on the project. All he could think of was how much closer he was to Ellie that day.

Where was she right now?

Somewhere within that hi-rise office complex?

What was she doing? Painting or designing something for her employer, whoever that was.

He pictured her, as he'd witnessed many times before, sitting on an artist's stool in front of her easel, head tilted to the side, that beautiful auburn hair captured by a purple scrunchie, humming happily as she masterfully turned the blank canvas into a majestic work of art with deft brushstrokes and dazzling colors.

A week later, the team made its second foray to the future site of the Riverdale mall. This time, Caleb drove by himself. When they broke for lunch, he drove the fifteen minutes into downtown, hoping to catch Ellie on her way to lunch.

He wasn't planning to speak to her at all, or even let her see him. But he had to see her. Just a glimpse of her might ease the heartache he carried with him every waking moment.

By eleven forty-five Caleb was in the lobby of the building where Ellie worked. He stood off to one side near a cluster of potted palms, where he would be inconspicuous but still able to see who came and went on the elevators. Pretending to read a pamphlet, he watched as the lunchtime crowd began to emerge from the three elevators and head for the revolving doors.

Every time an elevator unloaded, he searched the pod of people for that familiar auburn haired head. By noon, Ellie still hadn't shown up, and he began to second guess himself.

What if he'd missed her in the crowd?

What if she took a different elevator or a stairway elsewhere in the building?

What if she decided to eat lunch in her office?

What if she wasn't even at work today?

By ten past the hour he was ready to give up. Maybe this wasn't such a good idea after all. It was about time to head back to the job site.

Feeling his anticipation fading into discouragement, he fought back and decided to give it another five minutes.

The door to the middle elevator opened and the first person off was Ellie. His heart skipped a beat. She looked absolutely beautiful. He could almost smell the fragrance of her bouncing hair as she passed within thirty feet of him.

It was all he could do to keep from calling out her name and running up and taking her in his arms. Instead, he decided to follow her. Just the sight of her was salve for his aching heart.

He noticed she wasn't alone. A man maybe a few years older walked beside her. He was a nice looking guy, tall with blond hair, and dressed in a sport shirt and khaki slacks. One of the many young professionals who worked in the building, he guessed. She must be going to lunch with him.

Caleb followed the pair out onto the open air plaza, making sure to keep a few people between him and them. From his vantage point, he couldn't make out what they were saying, but they seemed to be having a good time. At the corner, while waiting to cross the street, the man leaned over and whispered something into Ellie's ear. She looked up at him and laughed.

The first time he'd heard that laugh was early in their senior year of high school.

It had stirred his heart then, and it stirred his heart now. Only this time it was sadness he felt. And loneliness.

It was he that she should be sharing laughs with, not this . . . this interloper.

The light turned red, and the crowd at the curb surged into the crosswalk. Ellie took the man's arm as they crossed. Riveted to the sidewalk, Caleb stared after them. For a brief instant, he wished a car would come careening down the street and run over the man on Ellie's arm.

"I can't take it anymore!" Caleb blurted out over the phone. "Dad, I can't stand being away from her any longer. It's just too painful. And now this guy shows up. I've got to do something. I just can't sit on the sidelines and let him cut in and take her away from me."

His father sighed on the other end. "Have you given any thought to how you're going to approach her?"

"I think it should be in a public place, so she feels less intimidated. I thought I'd apologize for startling her on the elevator. Let her know how bad I feel about what happened and that I'm not some lunatic."

"How are you planning to bring up the past to her? That's a very delicate issue."

"I've thought that through, too. I probably won't. At least, not right away. I'll drop a few hints here and there and see what she recalls."

"And what if she doesn't recall anything? Or even want to see you again? What then?"

"Here's what I've decided. I believe that if she fell in love with me once, she can fall in love with me again. I know it'll take time, but I'm willing to be patient. I don't plan to push anything on her. Hopefully, somewhere along the way, things will start coming back to her."

"Son, that sounds like a pretty good plan. But you've got to be prepared for the possibility that even though she looks the same, the accident may have changed her personality. She may not be the same Ellie you knew before."

"I realize that, Dad. But I've got to try."

"I have to agree with you." His father paused momentarily. "But may I suggest that you stay as far away from her father as possible? For now, anyway."

"Point taken," Caleb acknowledged. "But if things go as I hope they do, I don't see how I can avoid him forever."

"You may not have to," his father replied. "But Caleb, before you move ahead with Ellie, I think you need to find it in your heart to forgive her father."

"Forgive him?" Caleb paced back and forth, waving his hand wildly in the air. "Dad, you're asking the impossible! His actions are despicable. How can I forgive him after what he's put me through? After what he's put our family through?"

"Son, if you're harboring any bitterness toward him, you may be setting yourself up for a repeat of what happened the last time you confronted him. And the outcome could be worse this time. Much worse."

Caleb groaned loudly. "To be honest with you, I'm not sure I *want* to forgive him. If you ask me, he doesn't deserve my forgiveness."

"Caleb, remember that you didn't deserve forgiveness, either. God didn't forgive you because you were deserving of it. And now, as His follower, you're commanded to put away all bitterness and anger, and forgive even as God for Christ's sake has forgiven you. I urge you not only to forgive John Smith, but to pray for him as well. That will keep bitterness at bay, I can assure you."

Caleb sighed. "Yeah, I know. I guess you're right." Then he laughed and added, "As usual."

The next morning at work the branch manager announced that a position had become available at the Atlanta headquarters. Caleb took this as an opportunity from the Lord.

It would mean he could be near Ellie every day of the week, just a few blocks from her workplace. With a prayer in his heart, he submitted his transfer.

About a week later he was informed that he'd been awarded the position.

At the end of the month Caleb moved from Columbus into a high-rise downtown Atlanta apartment building. The rent was quite a bit higher than he'd hoped to pay, but the location allowed him to walk to the office. Besides, he now lived only six blocks from where Ellie worked.

Monday was his first day in the Wilshire and Cunningham headquarters. He spent the morning meeting his new coworkers and setting up his work station, and anticipating his lunch hour. By five after twelve he was in the lobby of the building where Ellie worked. He waited, as he'd done before, by the potted palms to the side of the elevators. A few minutes later, Ellie emerged and headed for the revolving glass doors. This time she was alone.

He followed her out onto the plaza, making sure to keep his distance. She turned the corner and walked a block to a sidewalk cafe. It was the same place where he'd first spied her across the street.

Getting in line several people behind her, he bought a half Reuben sandwich and a side salad. Ellie had already gone out to the sidewalk area and was sitting by herself at one of the tables.

Lord, give me the words to say, he prayed silently, but fervently. *Whatever happens, You're in control.*

Then he approached the table where she sat. "May I sit here?"

Ellie looked up from her lunch.

He smiled at her politely, "There doesn't seem to be anywhere else to sit at the moment."

"Be my guest," she shrugged, returning his smile.

So far so good.

He seated himself opposite her, unwrapped his Reuben, and after praying, took a bite.

When he glanced up at her, she was staring at him warily. "Wait, you . . . you're the guy who stopped me on the elevator last month." He could see the fear creeping into her eyes. She glanced around as if looking for a way to escape.

"Please," he held up a hand, "I owe you an apology. And an explanation, if you'll allow me."

Ellie hesitated, but she remained rooted to the edge of her chair.

He smiled again to reassure her. "I'm afraid it was a huge misunderstanding. On my part, that is. I mistook you for someone I once knew. Someone who looked very much like you. I'm really sorry I frightened you. That certainly wasn't my intention at all. Actually, I've felt terrible about it ever since it happened, and I was hoping for a chance to set things straight."

She exhaled slowly, but she still appeared unconvinced. With a slight smile, she replied, "Well that explains a few things. I guess that could happen to anyone." Then her eyes narrowed suspiciously. "But if it's a simple case of mistaken identity, how did you know my name?"

Caleb came prepared for that question. "This girl I used to know was named Elinor. But everyone called her Ellie."

Ellie studied him for a moment. "My name is Elinor. And I go by Ellie, too." She tilted her head to one side and raised an eyebrow. "So this girl not only looks like me, she's got my name, too? Pretty strange coincidence, wouldn't you say?"

He shrugged casually. "Well, Elinor isn't all that uncommon, I guess."

"Yeah, right. I meet women all the time named Ellie who look just like me."

Caleb wasn't sure how to take her sarcasm. Was she challenging him? Calling his bluff? Then he saw the familiar twinkle in her eye. His heart leaped in his chest.

Breaking into a grin, he responded. "Okay, so it's not all that common. But I'm telling you the truth. I did know a girl named Ellie who looked a lot like you. Honest."

"So where was this double of mine from?" Ellie inquired, still not fully convinced.

"Baxter. It's in the southwest part of the state. Near Lake Seminole." He hesitated, then decided to proceed with his next question. "Ever been there?"

"Baxter?" He held his breath. Then she shook her head. "No, I'm not even sure where that is, exactly." She took a sip of her beverage.

In that moment he noticed her ring finger. Where was the engagement ring? Had she lost it? Had her father hidden it from her? Had he pawned it?

He shook off those disturbing thoughts and returned to the conversation in progress. "So, where are you from?" he probed gently.

"Here in Atlanta. But I lived in Virginia and the Carolinas growing up."

"I was born and raised in Baxter, and after college I lived in Columbus for a short time. I just moved here to Atlanta this past week. Job transfer."

"What kind of work do you do?"

"I'm an architect for Wilshire and Cunningham. Their headquarters is just a few blocks from here."

"I know the place. It's a nice looking building."

"Yeah, I think so, too." Caleb flashed her another one of his grins. "But I didn't design it."

Her laugh nearly brought tears to his eyes. How he missed that wonderful sound. "What do you do?" he managed.

"I'm an illustrator for Beeson Publishing. I've been with them for about four months now."

"That's a pretty big company, isn't it? You must be very talented to have landed with an outfit like that."

"I'm very fortunate to be working for them, I suppose." She sighed. "But illustrating isn't what I want to do."

"No? What do you want to do?" He took a bite of his Reuben.

"I'd really like to be a freelance artist. That's where my heart is. Maybe have my own studio, someday. Anyway, I'd rather be outdoors painting and drawing for myself than cooped up in an office trying to capture other people's ideas."

"Must be hard getting started as a freelancer. Is that why you took the Beeson job? For the experience?"

Ellie hesitated. "Well, not exactly. My father sort of pushed me to take the position. He said we needed the income to—" She stopped short. "I'm sorry," she apologized, "I don't mean to bore you with personal stuff."

She hastily changed the subject. "So you said you just moved here?"

"Yeah, on Saturday. This is actually my first day at work."

"Well, then, welcome to Atlanta." She smiled at him with her big brown eyes. "I hope you like it here."

"Thanks. I'm sure I will."

"By the way, what did you say your name was?"

"Caleb Sawyer."

"Well, Mr. Sawyer, it was nice to meet you." The twinkle returned to her eyes. "This time, anyway."

Caleb rolled his eyes and grinned. "Hey, I'm grateful you were even willing to talk to me. So then, I'm forgiven? For the other time, I mean?"

"Sure. Like you said, it was just a misunderstanding. I can't hold that against you, can I?" She looked at her phone. "I need to be going. I've got to stop by the drugstore before I go back to work." She began to clean up her lunch.

Caleb longed to continue the conversation. "Thanks for letting me clear the air. I feel much better about it now."

Ellie looked relieved. "So do I. I hope the rest of your first day on the job goes well." She got to her feet.

"Thanks." He didn't want her to go. What if he never saw her again?

"Oh, by the way, my last name is Thompson. Maybe I'll see you around again sometime."

Caleb watched her walk away, her beautiful auburn hair bouncing in rhythm with his thumping heart. Then he hurriedly finished his lunch, and walked the few blocks back to work. He felt an incredible lightness in his spirit. Their first meeting had gone better than he'd hoped for. Much better!

———————————————

After keeping his distance for three days—three very long days—he decided it was safe to approach her again. He wanted it to appear like another chance encounter, and spent much of Thursday evening in his new apartment reviewing the possible scenarios.

The next day he positioned himself on the open air plaza where he had a good view of the twin revolving glass doors to the building where Ellie worked. With only one person exiting at a time, the chances of missing her would be minimal. A few minutes after twelve, Ellie emerged from the building and headed across the plaza in his direction.

He started walking towards her. She was looking down at her phone and bumped into him.

"I'm sorry!" she apologized quickly.

"My bad," he responded. "I wasn't looking where I was going."

Then she recognized him. The look was priceless. "Oh, it's you. How are you, Caleb?"

It was the first time he'd heard her call him by name since the accident.

"I'm doing well, thank you. And you?"

"I'm good. I was just on my way to lunch." She glanced around as if she were in a hurry to move on.

"Me, too. Hey, could you recommend any good places for me to try? I'm afraid I haven't had much time to scope out the area yet."

"Well, I know of a half dozen or so little delis and cafes within walking distance. They offer good food, they're reasonably priced, and they usually have quick service."

Caleb grinned at her. "You can't ask much more of a deli than that, can you? If you could just point me in the right direction, I'd really appreciate it."

"There's a little deli on Third Avenue called *Eat At Joe's*. They serve traditional American lunches. It's one of my favorites. I was just heading there myself." She looked at him and hesitated. "I . . . I suppose I could take you there if you like." She smiled a sweet little smile.

His heart leaped in his chest.

"That would be great. Any place good enough for you is good enough for me."

Together they headed up the sidewalk to the corner.

"So how's the new job going?" Ellie glanced sideways at him.

"I'm pretty much settled into my work station. But I'm still getting acquainted with my coworkers, though. All in all, it's a lot like the office in Columbus. Only bigger."

She laughed. "Well, that's Atlanta for you. Everything here is bigger and busier and faster and—"

"—and louder and more crowded," he finished the sentence for her.

"You've got that right," she laughed again. "Too loud and too crowded, if you ask me."

They came to the corner and waited for the light to change.

"Don't tell me you're a small town girl at heart," Caleb teased her.

Ellie shot him a wistful look. "Oh, I wish."

The light turned and they started across the street.

"Have you ever considered working in a smaller community? Out in the suburbs, maybe. Anyone who cranks out paintings like yours could have a successful career just about anywhere they chose to set up shop."

Ellie stopped in the middle of the crosswalk and stared at him. "How would you know about my paintings? You've never seen my work."

Uh-oh! He had to think fast. She was frowning with suspicion again. Guiding her safely to the opposite curb, he tried in vain to concoct a reply.

Suddenly he remembered something. "Well, actually, I *have* seen some of your work. Aren't you the artist who did the drawings in the lobby of the Regency Tower Hotel? I saw them when I stayed there a while back. You're the same Ellie Thompson, aren't you?"

The frown disappeared and her smile returned. "Oh, you saw those? Yes, I drew them."

He heaved a sigh of relief. He'd have to really watch what he said from now on.

They reached *Eat At Joe's* and ordered their food. Taking a seat at one of the red and white checkered tables, they began to eat their meal. Ellie picked up the conversation where they'd left off.

"It's a funny thing about those drawings, though. I remember working on them when I was in high school. My senior year, I think. But I can't remember where I was. Everything else is just a blur."

Careful, Caleb, he cautioned himself.

"I've heard that creative people often get in a zone like that. You know, they tune out all the distractions and nonessentials. You must have been very focused on your work at the time."

Ellie shook her head. "No, it's not that. I'm usually just the opposite. I'm very alert and aware of what's going on around me when I'm in my creative mood. Heightened senses and all that. My father says my memory is sometimes fuzzy because of the accident."

"Accident?" Caleb's heart skipped a beat. "You were in an accident?"

"Yes. I don't remember any of it, but he said I was struck by a car last December. I suffered a concussion and some memory loss, among other things. I was in a coma for nine days."

Caleb thought back to the accident. When he'd come out of his weeklong coma, Ellie's father had already moved her from the Columbus hospital. She was in another facility when she came out of hers.

"I'm sorry to hear that. That must have been a difficult time for you."

"Well, like I said, I don't remember it. Actually, I don't remember a lot of things from the past few years. The doctors say I have selective amnesia."

"We learned about that in Dr. Jacobson's psych class."

Ellie looked at him. "Dr. *Albert* Jacobson? Did you go to UGA, too?"

Caleb nodded. "I just finished my BA degree this past summer."

He didn't want to say any more about psych class with Dr. Jacobson. They had taken the same class together. But as long as Ellie was comfortable talking about her past, he decided to pry a bit.

"What kind of things do you remember?" he probed.

Ellie closed her eyes. "Well, I remember attending most of my classes, but I can't remember much of anything else about my college experience. You know, what extracurricular activities I was involved in, the friends I hung out with, that sort of thing. It's funny. Most students leave college remembering every detail about their social lives while forgetting some of what they learned. I'm just the opposite. Weird isn't it?"

Caleb smiled at her. "Well, at least you remember your education. I mean, that's what we all go to school for, isn't it?"

Ellie laughed. "I suppose you're right. But I'd sure like to know what else I did when I was in school besides attend class. Those activities make up an important part of who we are."

"Well maybe someday it will come back to you," he offered cheerfully.

"I hope so," she sighed. "It's like I'm missing big chunks of my life. It's all very unsettling."

Caleb ached to fill in the gaps for her. It was like they were assembling a puzzle together, only he was keeping some of the pieces hidden from her, and she was frustrated that she couldn't find them. "I can only imagine. So, how far back does your amnesia go? That you know of, I mean."

"Well, I lived with my mother until she died. I was only seven. After that, I spent the rest of my childhood and adolescent years with different foster families. I remember everything up to the end of my junior year in high school, but not much after that. My father wasn't a part of my life at all until my senior year. That's when he says he decided to finally step up and take responsibility for me. I can't recall the details, but I think he must have felt guilty for not being there for me when I was growing up. Anyway, he says I have him to thank for rescuing me from a bad foster family. And for helping me through college, and taking care of me after the accident."

Caleb felt his face flush with anger. The nerve of the man. Telling Ellie he'd rescued her. Kidnapped her was more like it.

If Ellie ever had a rescuer, it was him. He'd been the one who'd stood up for her, who'd given up a job for her, who'd found a safe place for her to live. And now her father, Mr. John Come Lately, had the audacity to claim that title for himself.

He was nothing but a fraud. A liar and a crook. A charlatan and a scammer.

It was beginning to make sense now. Why her father had spirited her away. He was a no good bum who'd seen an opportunity to cash in on the situation. Pretending to be the remorseful, absentee father who wanted to make up for lost time, he'd convinced his vulnerable daughter that she was a lonely damsel in distress and he was her knight in shining armor. He'd come riding in on a white horse, slain the dragon, and rescued her from all her perils, and now she was fortunate to have him as her magnanimous protector and gracious caregiver.

During their first lunchtime meeting, Ellie had mentioned that her father had pushed her to take the Beeson job because of the money. He recalled seeing her father's new silver SUV parked outside the apartment on Cannondale Avenue—no doubt purchased with Ellie's money. The man didn't care about her well-being at all. Only the income she was capable of bringing into the household.

Ellie had not been rescued. She was still a damsel in distress. And he was going to rescue her!

Caleb suddenly realized that Ellie was staring at him with a strange look on her face.

"Are you all right?" she asked, tilting her head to one side and looking at him quizzically. "You look like you kind of . . . zoned out there for a minute."

Caleb masked his anger with a grin. "Sorry about that. I do that sometimes when I'm thinking. I was just processing what you're telling me. It sounds like there have been some pretty rough times in your life."

Ellie blushed. "I'm so sorry. I didn't mean for a simple lunchtime conversation to turn into True Confessions."

Caleb quickly replied. "No need to apologize. In fact, I'm glad you feel comfortable enough to share a bit of your life with me."

Ellie put her elbows on the table, clasped her hands under her chin, and studied him for a moment. The corners of her mouth upturned slightly. "You know something? I do feel comfortable talking with you. And that's a strange thing for me to say, because I'm not one who usually finds that easy to do. Especially having just met a person. But, and I don't know how to explain this, but I feel like . . . like I know you already." She let out a little nervous laugh.

Caleb smiled and shrugged. "I guess some people just happen to communicate on the same wavelength, that's all."

Ellie arched her eyebrows. "You call this one sided conversation communicating? Here I am rambling on about my life, and I still don't know much about you." She grinned. "Well, Mr. Sawyer, now it's your turn."

In the few minutes they had left, Caleb told Ellie what it was like growing up in Baxter, hoping that some of their shared experiences there might trigger her memory. He was disappointed when that didn't happen.

"Thanks for suggesting this place," he said as they returned their trays. "I see why it's one of your favorites."

"Not a problem. I enjoyed the conversation."

"Me too. Maybe we'll bump into each other again sometime," he hinted.

Ellie flashed a shy grin. "Maybe."

———————————

Early the next week, he just happened to run into her again, this time while waiting in line at a Mexican taco stand in the food court.

"Hi, Ellie," he called out as she passed by.

She recognized him and smiled. "Oh, hi Caleb."

"Care to join me for lunch?" he asked casually.

Ellie looked around and hesitated. "Well . . . alright, I guess."

He made a mental note of her reluctance as they searched for an empty table. Was he pushing too hard? Should he back off a bit?

Gotta keep things light and easy. Slow and steady. And have patience. Lots of patience, he reminded himself.

His concerns vanished once they found a table and began eating. Their conversation was as easy and free-flowing as it had been the previous week. By the end of lunch, he'd forgotten all about her reservations.

"Ellie, I really enjoy having lunch with you," he began, as they left the food court. "I was wondering, would you like to go out with me some weekend? Maybe to a ball game, or a play? Or the Museum of Art?" He grinned. "Although you've probably been there a zillion times already."

Ellie laughed. "Let's just say I've been there more than once."

A look of uncertainty clouded her face.

He got the sudden feeling that he'd moved in on her a little too fast.

"Caleb," she began, "I've enjoyed our lunches too, and I think you're a really nice guy. But . . . " she hesitated. Caleb steeled himself for the shoot down.

"Boyfriend?" he offered, remembering the young man he'd seen her with at lunch earlier.

"Boyfriend? No, I'm not seeing anyone at the moment. It's just that . . . well, how do I explain this? You see, I'm a Christian, and I made a vow to God that I would only go out with other believers. You know, only guys who've put their trust in Jesus Christ as their Savior and Lord."

Caleb caught himself staring at her in stunned silence. That certainly wasn't what he'd expected. He felt his spirits rise and his face flush with excitement.

Breaking into a knowing smile, he blurted out, "The unequal yoke principle, right? Second Corinthians six."

It was Ellie's turn to stare. "You . . . you know about that?"

"Of course I do. I took that pledge at a church youth meeting when I was fifteen."

Ellie's eyes grew wide. "Then, you're a Christian, too?"

"Yes I am!" he replied excitedly. "I accepted Christ when I was in the eighth grade."

She gave him what appeared to be a relieved smile. "That's wonderful, Caleb. I'm happy for you." She paused, bewildered. "But if you took that pledge, how come you asked me out without knowing whether or not I was a Christian?"

In his exuberance Caleb responded without hesitation. Or thinking. "Because I knew you were a Christian when I met you."

Her frown made him painfully aware that he'd put his foot in his mouth again. "How could you have known that? I don't think I mentioned it in any of our conversations."

Oh, how he wanted to tell her how he knew. How he knew all about her surrender to the Lord that Sunday night in Baxter up in her bedroom in Miss Cora's house on Pine Street. Instead, he fumbled for a believable, yet truthful reply. "Well, you know how sometimes you run into a person, and you have this . . . this unspoken connection with them? Like you just somehow know that they're different? Well that's how I felt about you. Maybe it's the Holy Spirit living in us that gives us that discernment. I don't know how else to explain it."

Ellie considered his explanation and to his relief, agreed. "That makes sense. But I've got to tell you, I feel like it's more than that. There are things about you that feel so . . . familiar. Remember last Friday when I told you I felt like I've known you a long time? It's more than two people recognizing each other as a child of God. I get that. But this goes deeper than that. Only, I can't explain it. Does that sound crazy or what?"

Caleb's heart was singing. "Not at all, Ellie. Truth is, I feel it, too. But I'm not sure just what to make of it at the moment."

Ellie stopped in the middle of the sidewalk, put her hands on her hips, and grinned playfully at him. "Then let's not make anything of it for the time being. Let's just accept it for what it is and enjoy it. What do you say?"

He fought the urge to gather her in his arms and kiss those smiling lips. Practicing incredible self-control, he replied, "I say 'Amen' to that!"

He raised one eyebrow flirtatiously at her. "So then, does this mean you'll go out with me?"

CHAPTER NINETEEN

THE FRUIT OF FORGIVENESS

CALEB HAD ALWAYS LOVED WEEKENDS for a variety of reasons. Two days with no school, Bulldog football games in Sanford Stadium, hanging with friends, church, and a well-deserved day of rest. But this week, he was impatient for the weekend to roll around. On Saturday, he was going to go out with his long-time girlfriend and fiancée for the very first time. More or less.

He decided to keep things casual for their first date. A nice meal at a trendy restaurant before catching a Hawks game at Philips Arena. Not the most original of evenings, but a simple and safe one to be sure. The only thing he'd been concerned about was the prospect of running into Ellie's father.

But she'd solved that problem for him by suggesting they meet at the restaurant instead of her home. They agreed to meet at five-thirty. Caleb was there fifteen minutes early to make sure she didn't have to wait for him. Ellie pulled into the parking lot right on time.

She was driving the silver SUV her father had been using the day Caleb confronted him at their apartment. He wondered what her father thought about her going out on a date. Would he try to discourage any serious relationship from developing since that might eventually take her away from him? Had she told him who she was going out with? If so, what had his reaction been when he learned it was with the young man he'd stolen her away from and punched in the face?

Surprisingly, he felt no hatred for the man. Only pity. After being seated, the pair put in their order, and started in on the appetizer.

"I've never been here before," Ellie began, glancing around the room. "How did you hear about this place?"

Caleb grinned. "Online reviews. It sounded like a sure bet. Nothing like a bad dining experience to ruin a first date."

Ellie laughed. "Well you're safe with me. I'm not particular when it comes to food. I enjoy most anything."

"Do you have a favorite?"

She thought for a minute. "Well, not really. I do like Italian food, though, or a good steak. And sometimes I get a real craving for a big tenderloin sandwich and a side of onion rings. Isn't that funny? I don't even remember the last time I had one."

Caleb felt a chill go down his spine. Could she be thinking about Edwards?

"There's this little 50s diner in Baxter that serves the best tenderloins you'll ever find," he hinted. "The meat hangs over the bun so far you're almost full before you reach the bread. And they serve killer onion rings and genuine draft root beer."

"Sounds like my kind of place. If I'm ever down that way, I'll have to try it out."

"It was our favorite hangout in high school. That and the Dairy Shack. There aren't too many other places in town."

"It must have been wonderful, growing up in a small town where everyone knows everyone else." She looked wistfully at him. "Unfortunately, I can't lay claim to such an idyllic childhood myself."

"I'm not sure I'd call my childhood idyllic. In a small town, you can't get away with anything." He chuckled. "You get into any kind of trouble and the news gets back to your parents before you do."

Ellie laughed. "Somehow I can't picture you getting into trouble. Did you have a rebellious streak?"

Caleb shook his head vigorously. "Oh no, not at all. Well, not much of one, anyway." He grinned. "I was too afraid of what would happen when I got home. My dad kept a pretty tight rein on me, I guess. But looking back, that was a good thing. It kept me from making all sorts of bad decisions." He looked at Ellie and thought about her hollow childhood. "So, how do you feel about your father, now that he's back in the picture?"

She paused thoughtfully. "Well, I'm grateful that he finally stepped up and took responsibility, I guess. You know what they say, 'Better late than never'. I can't recall the details of how he reentered my life, or how he helped me when I was at UGA, but I do appreciate how he's taken care of me after the accident, and what he does for me now. He handles all my finances for me and takes care of all the details like paying bills and buying groceries."

Caleb was tempted to add, *and uses you for his own selfish purposes.*

It was painful to hear her praise the man for something he'd never done. For something he wasn't even around to do. And for what he was doing to her now.

He crossed his arms and leaned back in his chair. "Well you certainly have a good attitude toward him. I'm afraid I might have had a . . . a less honorable one if that had been me."

Ellie studied him for a moment. "I did have a lot of bitterness and resentment toward him earlier in my life. But that was before I gave my life to Christ. He's the One who helped me put those feelings behind me. But it wasn't easy, that's for sure."

Caleb felt ashamed. "When did you make the decision to accept Christ?"

She frowned slightly and shook her head. "Honestly, I don't know when it was. I have no real recollection of the actual moment. It must have been within the past three or four years, though. That's the period I have the most trouble recalling. All I know is I despised my father before then, and now I don't . . . even though he still does things I don't like. That has to be the Lord. I couldn't have done that on my own. You know, even though I can't remember the circumstances surrounding my salvation, I know that I'm a child of God. I have His love and peace in my life, and the Holy Spirit gives me that assurance."

"That's the important thing, isn't it?" Caleb concurred. "To know for sure now." He thought of something she'd mentioned. "You said your father still does things you don't like. I don't mean to pry—and stop me if I am—but what exactly did you mean by that?"

Ellie seemed to be conflicted. "Well, I don't want to speak ill of him, and I don't mean to sound ungrateful. But I sometimes feel like he's . . . he's too manipulative and controlling. Like not letting me finish my degree, and pushing me to take this job because of the money, even when I didn't really want to. Demanding to know where I am and what I'm doing all the time. Things like that. Take tonight, for example. He wasn't at all happy that I was going out on a date with someone. Sometimes he treats me like I'm fifteen or something. And then there's the drinking. He's a borderline alcoholic, I think." She gave a sad little sigh. "But, he's not a Christian, and I'm praying he'll see that Jesus is his only hope." She suddenly brightened and flashed him a smile. "I guess that's one example of the difference Jesus has made in my life."

The waiter came with their food, and after praying together, they began to eat their meal.

Ellie suddenly changed the subject. "Have you ever had a reoccurring dream?"

Caleb finished a mouthful of chicken cordon bleu before replying. "You mean, have I ever dreamed the same dream over and over again?"

"Yes. Like that."

He thought back to his childhood. "Well, I remember this one dream I used to have when I was in grade school. I must have dreamed it eight or nine times before it went away. It always scared me."

"What was it?" Ellie leaned in eagerly.

"All I remember is that we were living in some creepy old farmhouse out in the boonies somewhere, and I had to spend the night on an old, musty army cot in the middle of the kitchen. There were three doors next to each other. The one on the right led to a small bathroom, the one on the left led to the rest of the house, and the one in the middle led to a dark, damp cellar."

"Let me guess," Ellie interjected. "You were afraid of the door in the middle, right?"

"Pretty predictable, aren't I?" he chuckled. "I remember lying on the cot in the shadowy moonlight and staring at the cellar door. Something seemed to be calling me, so I finally got up the nerve to open the door to see what was down there. I remember slowly descending the creaky wooden steps, fearful of what was waiting for me in the darkness below. But I always woke up before I reached the bottom." He held up his hands and shrugged. "The end."

Ellie laughed. "That's it? You never discovered what was down there?"

"Nope. I never did. And I have no idea where that dream came from, either. Unless it was the time in the fourth grade when I spent the night at my best friend's house, and we stayed up late watching Nightmare Theater. That was a local TV program that came on Friday nights around midnight. The host was made up to look like Dracula, and he rose up out of a coffin at the beginning of every show to announce the feature movie. It was usually an old black and white horror film like *Creature from the Black Lagoon* or *Frankenstein*." He grinned. "Scary stuff for a couple of nine-year old kids staying up way past their bedtimes."

Ellie laughed. "I can imagine."

"So, why do you ask? Did you have a reoccurring dream, too?"

"Well, not that I can remember as a child. But I have one now. I've had it maybe five or six times. All within the past year."

"A nightmare?"

"No. Just the opposite. It's very tranquil and serene. But I can't figure out what it means. Don't get me wrong, I don't put any stock in dreams. I just wonder why I keep having the same one, that's all."

"Okay, now I'm the curious one. What's it about?"

Ellie set down her fork, wiped her mouth with her napkin, and launched into her narrative. "It always starts with my mother and me sitting on a green swing on the small porch of a tiny bungalow. I get that part. That's a favorite childhood memory of mine before she died. But then she goes into the house, and this old woman comes out instead. I don't know who she is or why she replaces my mother."

"Are you afraid of her?"

"No, she's very sweet. What you'd expect a kindly old grandmother to be like. And she always brings me cookies."

Caleb felt a familiar chill run down his spine. "Then what?" he asked.

"Well, when she sets the tray of cookies down next to me, I look around, and I'm no longer at the same tiny bungalow. I'm on this big porch of an old three-story home. You know the kind. White gingerbread trim and everything. Anyway, as I take a cookie, I notice that I'm not alone on the swing any more. There's a guy sitting next to me. But I don't know how old he is or what he looks like. His face is always in the shadows. I can never quite make it out."

Caleb sat up straight and leaned forward. "Does this guy say anything to you?"

Ellie caught the anticipation in his voice and shot him a look of amazement. "Why, yes he does, actually. It's the only dialogue in the whole dream sequence. He says, 'I'll always be there for you, Ellie!' I remember that because he calls me by name. And then he simply vanishes right before my eyes. That's when I wake up."

"Wow, that's interesting. You say the first part is a memory you shared with your mother?"

"Yes, I've had that memory long before the dreams started. What I don't understand is the significance of the old woman or the guy. Do you suppose they're memories, too? Or just general representations of some sort of . . . some sort of theme or something?"

Caleb shifted uneasily in his seat. "I'm not sure. I'm no expert on the subject of dreams, but I've heard that sometimes they're the subconscious mind's way of working out a conflict or a stress from real life. What do you think?"

"I think it might be related to the trauma of the accident in some way. I don't recall having this dream before then. I don't know." She shook her head in frustration. "I hate not being able to remember things."

Caleb desperately wanted to tell her that it wasn't a dream she was having, but a memory. All of it.

"You're probably right about it being related to the accident," he nodded in agreement. Then, to ease her frustration, he added with a grin, "Just be glad there's no boogey man in your dream waiting to grab you at the bottom of the stairs."

―――――――――――

Caleb and Ellie's first date went very well. Both enjoyed each other's company so much that neither paid much attention to the action on the hardwood seventeen rows below them. During the game, he learned that Ellie had begun attending a small church a few miles from the apartment where she lived. Since he hadn't yet had time to find a church home in Atlanta, he asked if he could attend with her on Sunday. She was pleased that he was interested, and readily agreed.

He offered to pick her up, but she said she'd rather meet him there. He wondered if that was because she was hesitant about him meeting her father, just as she'd been hesitant about him meeting the Markles during their senior year. And just as he'd wanted then to help her escape her foster parents' cruelties, he wanted now, more than ever, to help her escape her father's clutches.

As the two began to see more of each other, Caleb continued praying about their future. When the opportunity presented itself, he mentioned people and places and events from the last four years, hoping that those specifics might trigger Ellie's memories of their past relationship. But she seemed no closer to recalling their former life than she did when he surprised her on the elevator.

Discouragement often lurked in the shadows of his spirit following those conversations, but he accepted the fact that she might never recall those lost years, and was grateful for the new beginning God was allowing them to experience together. Several weeks later, before a Friday night date, Ellie texted him.

"Can you pick me up? My father needs the SUV tonight."

"Sure. I'll be there at six," he responded.

Caleb eased his Camaro to the curb in front of 4391 Cannondale Avenue at exactly six o'clock.

He shot Ellie a text letting her know he was out front. When she didn't reply, he texted her again.

A few minutes later she answered. *"Just out of shower. Held over @ work. Shoulda called earlier. Sorry! Come in & meet my father. Ready in 20."*

He wanted to tell her he'd rather wait outside, but he didn't know how to explain his reluctance for meeting the man. Besides, he'd have to face him sooner or later anyway. It might as well be now.

"OK. Take your time. No rush," he texted back.

Offering up a quick prayer, he got out of his car and walked up the steps to the front door of Apartment 1C. His previous meeting with John Smith was very much on his mind.

Although his face bore no trace of the deep purple shiner, his left eye socket was still sensitive to the touch.

Caleb rang the bell.

John Smith, holding a beer in one hand, answered the door wearing an old pair of jeans and a muscle shirt. He stared at Caleb in slack jawed disbelief for what seemed like an eternity.

"You! You're her date?" Slowly, like fog creeping across a harbor, crimson crept across his pallid face. His eyes became smoldering reptilian slits of pure evil. Shooting a quick glance over his shoulder, he turned on Caleb with all the venom of a poisonous serpent. "You've got a lot of nerve showing your face here!" he hissed. "I warned you what might happen if you came around here again. What's the matter, boy? Can't you take a hint?"

Caleb stared back into those dark, hate filled eyes. He felt no animosity towards the man whatsoever. Only pity.

"I expected you to be surprised to see me again," Caleb began. "Even angry. But listen, can't we set aside our differences for the time being? At least for Ellie's sake? She knows nothing about our last meeting."

John looked at him suspiciously. "You mean you haven't told her? Why not?"

"Because I don't think she's ready for the truth. She's too fragile right now."

"Just what have you told her?" her father demanded.

Caleb made sure to keep his voice low. "You mean about all the other stuff? The lies and deception? Nothing. I've told her nothing at all. Not even who I am. Mr. Smith, as far as she's concerned, I'm just a guy she met a few weeks ago. She doesn't know anything about our past together."

"Do you plan on telling her?"

"At some point in the future, maybe. If and when I think she can handle it."

Ellie's father stared silently at him. Caleb could see the wheels turning in the man's mind. A sudden shiver came over him. Had he said too much? What would the man do now that he knew that his daughter was still in the dark about his deceptive schemes against Caleb and his family? That she still knew nothing of her past relationship with Caleb? What lengths would he go to in order to keep that information from her, so that he could continue cashing in on her misfortune? What was Mr. Smith capable of?

An icy fear gripped Caleb. In his mind's eye he pictured the man smoothing things over for the moment with his slick acting talents, only to buy time to formulate a plan for Caleb's cold and calculated demise. He would have to be on his guard.

John suddenly changed his tone. "I think you're right not to tell her anything. Like you said, for her sake." It sounded like he really meant those words.

Caleb gave him the benefit of the doubt. "I'm glad you see it that way too."

The man, however, was not finished. "I can't do anything about tonight. Not without upsetting her, anyway." He stepped across the threshold and leaned in closer. Caleb smelled the alcohol on his breath. "But I can do something about tomorrow. And the next day. And the next."

"What do you mean?"

"I said I agreed she's not ready for the truth right now. The fact is, I don't think she'll ever be ready for the truth. The doctors tell me it's likely she'll never remember the past."

John Smith's words hit Caleb harder than his fist had. But he refused to go down without a fight. "But as long as there's still the chance that she will—"

"Forget it, boy!" Dropping the benevolent father act, the man cut him off midstream. "Her amnesia is permanent. You're going to have to accept that fact."

As Caleb wrestled with how to respond, John issued an ultimatum. "I want you to stop seeing my daughter. I don't care how you do it or what excuse you come up with. But I want this thing ended for good after tonight. I can't run the risk of her finding out. Like you said, it's for her protection." He squinted menacingly into Caleb's face. "If you don't take my advice this time, I predict something worse than a black eye will be in your future. You got that?"

So there it was.

He'd just been struck in the face with the gauntlet. He was being challenged to a dual. But Caleb refused to back down. Instead, he met her father's gaze with unwavering boldness.

"Mr. Smith, you can threaten me all you want, but I'm going to keep on seeing Ellie no matter what you say or do. I promised her a long time ago that I would always be here for her, and I mean to keep that promise!" He shook his head. "But you don't have to worry. If what you say about her memory proves to be true, then I don't plan on telling her. Ever. To her I will always be the new guy she met a few weeks ago."

Ellie's father was not convinced. "I don't believe you. You'll never keep the truth to yourself. If I was in your shoes, I'd have told her everything by now. Just to get even."

The real character of John C. Smith finally revealed itself. But Caleb was prepared for him this time.

"Mr. Smith, I can't get even with you because I hold no grudges against you. None whatsoever."

Ellie's father glared at him. "That's just not possible. Not after what's happened between us."

Caleb was quick to respond, "Oh, but it is. It's possible because I've already forgiven you for what you've done to me. For keeping Ellie away from me, for deceiving my family and me . . . and Ellie, and for punching me in the face. Everything."

The man was stunned, but still unconvinced. "Why . . . why would you even do that?" he muttered.

Caleb smiled at him. "It's simple. You see, when Jesus was hanging on the cross, He forgave those who nailed Him there. He also forgave me. And He's forgiven Ellie. By now I'm sure you've seen evidence of that in her life. And He says we're to forgive others in the same way He's forgiven us. That's why I've chosen to forgive you."

For the first time Caleb could recount, and probably for the first time in John Smith's entire life, the man was at a loss for words.

"I see you two have met." John spun around and stared as Ellie approached them on the front stoop. She stopped in the doorway and glanced between Caleb and her father. There was an awkward silence.

"Is . . . is everything all right?" She looked first to her father, and then to Caleb.

Caleb glanced at John and nodded. "Yes. Everything's fine. We were just talking."

"Yeah, just talking," her father murmured, managing a forced little smile.

Caleb turned his attention to Ellie. Her auburn hair was full bodied and had that just-washed silky sheen to it. She wore a simple pair of silver hoop earrings and was dressed to go out for the evening. She looked as beautiful as ever to him.

"I see you're ready," he smiled reassuringly. Then he offered his arm. "Shall we go?"

"What were you and my father talking about?" Ellie asked, once they were in the car heading to their destination. "There seemed to be some tension between you two."

Caleb shot her a sideways glance. She had a puzzled frown on her face. "Oh, you know. We were just having a conversation. About you." He sighed. "I wouldn't say your father was exactly overjoyed with the idea of me taking you out," he stated truthfully.

Ellie scowled. "You see what I mean? He treats me like that all the time. Like I'm not even old enough to go on dates. I can't decide if he's afraid of me getting hurt or if he's just plain selfish. Sometimes I get the feeling he only cares about my money and not about me."

Caleb and Ellie's budding relationship began to blossom. They saw one another regularly in spite of her father's objections. They met for lunch three or four days a week, went on dates nearly every weekend, and attended the little church together on Sundays.

One day over lunch, Ellie told Caleb that she no longer had use of the SUV. When her father learned she was still seeing him, he became so angry that he refused to let her drive it. He said she needed to trust that he had her best interests at heart. When that tactic failed to quell her anger, he reminded her that even though the vehicle had been purchased with her money, it was titled in his name, and therefore he had every right to decide who could or couldn't drive it.

Caleb shared Ellie's pain. He could see her being sucked into the same stressful vortex of emotional and mental abuse that had nearly broken her while in the foster care system. He'd been pleasantly surprised to see some of the old fire in her eyes recently, but he could tell the conflict with her father was taking its toll.

John Smith was unable to stop his adult daughter from leaving the apartment on foot, so Caleb resorted to picking her up around the corner whenever they wanted to go out together. At times he felt downright cowardly about it, but he knew it wasn't a matter of fear. He was just trying to avoid unnecessary stress between them and her father.

One Saturday afternoon, following a visit to a local art exhibit, Caleb and Ellie took a stroll through the gardens adjacent to the gallery. As they enjoyed a treat from a sidewalk vendor, Ellie caught him off guard.

"I've decided to start looking for an apartment," she announced out of the blue.

He turned and stared at her. "Has it gotten that bad at home?"

Her eyes misted over. She turned away and watched two nearby children tossing a Frisbee. "Yes it has. It's gotten to the point where it's just about unbearable." She turned back to him and declared, "Caleb, I don't think I can stand to live another day with him!"

Caleb's mind flashed back to her struggles with the Markles during their senior year in high school. She'd expressed the same sentiment then. He grew alarmed.

"What's he done? Has he hurt you?" Anger welled up inside him. "Because if he's so much as laid a finger on you, I'll—"

Ellie grabbed his arm. "Oh no, nothing like that. He knows better." She sighed deeply. "But it's just as painful as that. Ever since he learned I was going out with you, he's become extremely manipulative and controlling. Remember what I told you about him refusing to let me use the car?"

Caleb nodded.

"Well, it's gotten worse since then. He's always agitated now. Irritable. Angry, even. He yells a lot and threatens me if I don't stop seeing you. And he's drinking heavily all the time. Most days he's already sloshed when I come home from work."

"Ellie, I'm so sorry," Caleb empathized with her. A knot formed in his stomach.

This self-centered man is taking out his hostility toward me on his own daughter, he thought to himself. *He doesn't care about losing her. Only her income.*

He put his hand on hers. "Is there anything I can do to help?"

Ellie's face brightened and she smiled at him. "As a matter of fact, there is. Can you help me look for a place to live?"

"Absolutely. I'd be happy to. The sooner you get away from him, the better. I'll take you anywhere you need to go to look for an apartment." He grinned to lighten the mood. "I don't think your father is gonna do that for you."

Ellie laughed out loud. "I seriously doubt it."

Together they began the search for an apartment for Ellie. Caleb took her to look at several possibilities, but for one reason or another, those didn't pan out. Undaunted, they kept looking. Something was bound to open up soon.

He continued clinging to the hope that she would someday regain her memory of him and their four years together. That, and Ellie's desire for a small-town lifestyle and a less stressful work environment were at the core of the plan forming in his mind. If he could just get her to visit Baxter with him, perhaps the experience would help jar her memory of their life together there.

The search for an apartment continued in earnest, but strangely, they couldn't find an available place suitable for Ellie. The two of them were faithfully praying together about the move, but it seemed as if every door on which they knocked stayed tightly closed. In spite of this, they remained encouraged, believing that God would provide the right place at the right time.

It was the first week in February when Caleb began thinking about Valentine's Day. Their relationship had been growing steadily ever since that first lunch encounter, and he wanted to do something special for her. Something besides flowers and chocolates.

So he asked her to accompany him to Baxter for the Valentines weekend. It would be good for her to get away from the caustic environment in apartment 1C and get out of Atlanta for a few days.

———

Caleb parked his Camaro in front of 4391 Cannondale Avenue. It was five o'clock. Ellie was not only eager to get away from her father and the city, she was anxious to see the small town where Caleb had grown up.

After sharing his plans with his parents, he'd called Miss Cora to ask if Ellie could stay with her Friday and Saturday night. The widow had been ecstatic with the news that Ellie was coming back to town, and happily offered her former bedroom. The old woman had not been able to bring herself to seek another boarder, saying she would always consider that room to be Ellie's. Other than Ellie's personal effects, which were still being stored in the Sawyer's garage, Miss Cora had left the room untouched.

The double bed with its worn brass head and foot boards, the nightstand with its small reading lamp, the dresser with its arched-top mirror, the small table with its lone wooden chair, all were left exactly as they had been when Ellie lived there.

Caleb got out of his car and walked up to the apartment. He did not relish another confrontation with Mr. Smith, but Ellie had assured him that as long as she was there, her father would likely behave himself.

Caleb wasn't so sure. The man had been getting drunk a lot lately. He had not been able to keep his daughter away from Caleb. No telling what frame of mind he'd be in today.

To his relief, Ellie answered the door. He was glad to see her bags packed and ready in the middle of the room.

"Hi, come on in. I'm ready to go." She noticed his hesitation. "It's all right." She leaned in and lowered her voice. "He's in the kitchen sitting at the table drinking. But don't worry. I don't think he's in any condition to walk out here."

Caleb caught her wink and grinned back at her. "Okay."

He looked at the pile in the middle of the living room floor. His lone medium sized soft shell suitcase would have plenty of company on the four-hour trip to Baxter.

Ellie surveyed her bags. "If you wouldn't mind grabbing the larger one, I can manage the rest."

"Sure. No problem." He headed for the pile.

"Oh, shoot!" Ellie exclaimed, snapping her fingers. "I forgot to pack my makeup. It's all still on the dresser up in my bedroom."

"What do you need that for?" he teased. "You don't need to cover up perfection."

Ellie laughed and gave him a playfully sarcastic eye. "Ha ha. You should do stand up at the *Improv*." She patted his arm. "I'll be only a minute." Then she hurried up the stairs and disappeared around the corner.

Caleb picked up the suitcase and turned toward the front door.

"And jus' where d'ya think you're goin'?" The gravelly voice of John Smith stopped him in his tracks.

Caleb turned around and saw Ellie's father in the kitchen doorway, staring at him. He was leaning against the jam for support, clearly drunk as a skunk.

"Oh, hello, Mr. Smith," Caleb politely greeted her father. "Sorry to have bothered you. We'll be out of your hair in a minute."

There was no way he was going to leave Ellie alone with the inebriated man, even for a second. John looked at him through blood-shot eyes. He had not shaved in two or three days. His hair was uncombed and his shirt was half tucked into a beltless pair of dirty khaki shorts. He was shoeless, sporting a pair of stretched-out black socks that had succumbed to gravity. Caleb could smell the alcohol from where he stood.

"I have somethin' for ya." Caleb detected a sly, devilish grin on the man's ashen face. "And yer not gonna leave here until I give it to ya!" He lurched away from the doorway, nearly losing his balance in the process. Steadying himself, he stumbled toward Caleb.

Caleb set down the suitcase to free up his hands, just in case. "We were just leaving." He held up his open palms in a show of conciliation. "Like I told you last time we spoke, I have no quarrel with you anymore."

John maneuvered around the pile of travel bags and shuffled up to him. Caleb braced to defend himself. His open hands transformed into balled fists.

"I want you to have this!" John reached into his pants pocket and pulled out a crumpled white piece of paper. It had once been a busi-ness size envelope, now torn in half, and sealed with a small piece of cellophane tape. He held it out with an unsteady hand.

Without flinching, Caleb glanced at it, keeping a wary eye on the man.

Ellie's father grew impatient. "Well don't jus' stand there like a danged fool! Take it, boy. I'm givin' it to ya."

Caleb put out his left hand and cautiously took the envelope from him. His right hand was still clenched. Before he could reply, John turned and fell over Ellie's bags.

Frozen in place, all he could do was watch as the man rather comically extricated himself from the obstacles in his path, staggered back to the kitchen, and disappeared through the doorway. He'd expected the man to at least take a swing at him. He'd been ready for that.

This was a total surprise. As he looked down at the crumpled envelope in his hand, he realized that his heart was pounding fiercely in his chest.

What was John Smith wanting to give him? His mind raced like the wind.

Had he put poison in the envelope? Anthrax?

Deadly laced heroin?

He gingerly probed the contents of the envelope with his fingers. There was something hard inside.

An explosive cap, or incendiary device, perhaps? He should call the police!

Caleb, you've been watching too many murder mysteries, he chided himself.

He was being ridiculous. The man wouldn't do anything that stupid. Not in his own living room.

Or would he? Hadn't he threatened something worse than a black eye if Caleb continued seeing his daughter? And now, fueled by an alcoholic mindset, what if he really was that desperate? Perhaps it wouldn't be a bad idea to call the police after all. Just in case.

He switched the envelope to his right hand so he could reach for the cell phone in his left pants pocket. In doing so, the tape popped loose on the envelope, and he felt the contents slide out into his palm.

Panic shot through him like a bolt of lightning. He looked at the object in his hand. It was not coated in some mysterious white powder, nor did it resemble some type of explosive device. It was metallic and round and shiny.

It was a ring.

Ellie's engagement ring.

CHAPTER TWENTY

DÉJÀ VU ALL OVER AGAIN

CALEB PULLED INTO THE DRIVEWAY of his parent's modest cape cod three and a half hours after leaving Atlanta. He shut off the engine and glanced over at his passenger.

"You ready to meet my family?"

"Do you think they'll like me?" Ellie sounded unsure of herself.

Caleb smiled confidently. "I think they're going to love you." He reached over and squeezed her hand. "Trust me."

They got out of the car and together walked up the curved brick pathway to the front door.

"Do I look alright?" Ellie brushed off her blouse and ran her hand through her hair.

Caleb stepped back and gave her the once over. "Ellie, if you looked any better, I couldn't stand it." Her laughter steadied her nerves.

The front door opened.

"Caleb!" His father stepped onto the stoop and grabbed him in a bear hug. "Good to see you, son."

"Dad," Caleb began, once he'd extricated himself from his father's embrace, "I'd like you to meet Ellie Thompson. Ellie, this is my father."

"Hello, Ellie. I'm glad to meet you." His father smiled and offered his hand to the beauty on his doorstep.

"Hello, Mr. Sawyer." Ellie took his hand and returned his smile. "I've been looking forward to meeting you and your family."

"Please, come in." Caleb's father held open the door and the two stepped into the living room. His mother and Cassie stood up from where they'd been sitting on the sofa.

After the introductions, Caleb and Ellie sat down on the love seat and his father sunk into his overstuffed recliner.

"Did you have a nice trip?" his mother asked Ellie.

"Yes," Ellie replied. She shot a sideways glance at Caleb and smiled shyly. "I think we talked the whole way down here."

It was that same shyness that had greatly contributed to her being irresistible to him from the beginning.

"Good conversation always makes a road trip go faster," his mother acknowledged.

Caleb interjected with a sheepish grin. "That, and the fact that I pushed it a bit on the interstate."

His father raised an eyebrow and gave him a knowing look, but there was a twinkle in his eye. "It's that Camaro." Shaking his head, he turned to Ellie. "That car is going to generate a sizable increase in revenue for the Georgia State Patrol."

It was dusk when they turned onto East Pine Street. The sun cast a faint orange glow in the rear view mirror as Caleb parked in front of the old Victorian. He popped the trunk and went around to the back of the car to get Ellie's bags. Reaching in, he rummaged through the mess. He was definitely not a neat packer.

"Here, you take these. I'll get the rest, okay?" With his head still in the trunk, Caleb handed a couple of smaller bags back to Ellie, who was standing behind him.

"No way," she exclaimed, without taking the luggage.

"What?" Puzzled by her response, he stood up, banging his head on the open trunk lid. "Ow!"

He rubbed the top of his skull and glanced back at her. She stared at the house. "What's the matter? Haven't you ever seen an old house before?" he teased.

Ellie ignored him. "I don't believe this."

"Don't believe what?"

She grabbed his arm. "Caleb, it's . . . it's the house in my dreams!"

Caleb's heart skipped a beat. He pretended to be surprised. "Really?"

"Yes!" she replied excitedly. "See, there's the wrap around porch, and the gingerbread trim, and . . . and there's the porch swing. Caleb, it's exactly like the house I saw in the dream I told you about." She suddenly looked bewildered. "How weird is that?"

"Coincidence?" he suggested with a shrug, unable to come up with anything better.

"Coincidence? That's impossible. Okay, I'll grant that you could have found a similar house for me to stay in, but to find one exactly as I dreamed it? Come on. That can't be a coincidence." She suddenly looked confused. "Can it?"

Caleb avoided her question. "Don't most Victorian style homes have veranda porches and gingerbread trim? I suspect many have porch swings out front, too. Anyway, I knew you liked old houses, and Miss Cora had one with a furnished room. So I made arrangements for you to stay here. She used to have a boarder living with her, but it just so happened that the room was available this weekend."

His attempt to redirect her attention away from her dream house succeeded.

"That was very thoughtful of you." She smiled flirtatiously at him. "And very sweet."

Caleb discovered she could still make him blush.

They grabbed the luggage and made their way to the front door. The bell's tones, though not as rich and resonant as they once had been, still brought back memories to Caleb. Childhood memories of when he'd been barely able to reach the button, as well as more recent memories of when he'd rung that bell to call on Ellie.

It was some time before Miss Cora answered the door. When she did, Caleb realized the reason for the delay. The kindly widow appeared tired and frail. Her wrinkled face was thinner, her hair whiter, and her shoulders more stooped than when he'd last seen her. To support and steady herself, she leaned heavily on her cane, which was no longer the knotty pine stick she'd had for years, but an aluminum shaft with a foam rubber handle and a four pronged base.

But there was nothing feeble about her eyes. They still had the flash and sparkle of a woman thirty years her junior. "Come in. Come in. I've been expecting you."

They stepped into the foyer of the old house. Caleb looked around, catching a glimpse of the living room through the wide doorway on the left. Nothing had changed.

"It's good to see you again, Miss Cora." Caleb gave her a gentle hug. Then he turned to the house guest. "Miss Cora, I'd like you to meet Ellie Thompson. Ellie, this is Mrs. Williams."

"Miss Cora," she scolded, wagging a bony finger at him. "It's Miss Cora to my friends." Her eyes twinkled as she looked at Ellie. "And it's Miss Cora to everyone else, too. Sooner or later, we all become friends anyway, so why not get used to it from the start?"

Ellie laughed as she shook the widow's thin hand. "It's really nice to meet you, Mrs. Will—Miss Cora."

"And it's really nice to see you, young lady." Miss Cora shut and locked the door.

Caleb was relieved that she didn't say *again*. He'd been worried that Ellie's former landlady might accidentally slip up and forget that she was supposed to be acting like she had never met her former boarder before.

"I'm sorry we're a bit late," Caleb apologized. "We stopped at Mom and Dad's before coming over here."

"No need for apologies, young man. I imagine you're both pretty tired after such a long trip. But before I show Miss Ellie to her room, perhaps you'd like some warm cookies and a glass of milk?" She turned to Ellie and smiled. "I do hope you like gingersnaps, my dear."

The next morning, Caleb left his parents' house for Miss Cora's. She had insisted he come over and join her and Ellie for breakfast, and there was no way he was going to miss that.

After a wonderful meal of scrambled eggs, bacon, toast, and orange juice, Miss Cora invited her guests to set a spell out on the front porch. Caleb sat with Ellie on the porch swing, and Miss Cora eased herself into the wooden rocker.

"What a beautiful morning," the old woman began. "Just another reason why Henry and I picked South Georgia to settle down in."

"Yes, it is." Ellie placed her hand on the arm of the swing and noticed the marking there. "Somebody carved a heart in your swing."

Miss Cora glanced quickly at Caleb before replying. "Why, yes. My husband, Henry, did that for our anniversary one year. At first, I told him it would ruin the swing, but now I'm glad he did it. It brings back a lot of happy memories we shared together."

Ellie traced the initials with her fingers. "H.W. and C.W. That's so sweet."

Caleb suddenly realized that the artwork on his side of the swing was also in plain view.

"You have such a lovely house," Ellie complimented her hostess.

"Why thank you, my dear. I've enjoyed living here all these years. God has been very good to me."

"I could see myself living in a place like this someday," Ellie announced, as she glanced around at the gingerbread trim on the porch. "And I'd have a swing just like this one. It reminds me of the one my mother and I used to have when I was a little girl."

"There are lots of precious memories attached to that swing," Miss Cora replied. The old woman got a faraway look in her eyes, and was soon lost to reminiscing.

Caleb silently prayed that she wouldn't say too much.

"Henry and I spent nearly every evening together out here," she began. "And after he went to glory, I'd sit and read my Bible there. It's been a very popular spot down through the years. Why, even Caleb and the girl who used to live here spent a lot of time on that swing."

"What did Miss Cora mean when she mentioned you and the girl who used to live there?" Ellie wondered, as they drove away from the house. "Was she your girlfriend or something?"

"Um, I think she meant that we were just two of the many people who've spent time there. Not necessarily together." His conscience made its presence felt.

"Oh. She made it sound like you've been over there a lot."

"I have, I guess. Over the years. My family used to visit the Williams all the time. They were very hospitable people. Miss Cora still is, obviously."

"She's such a thoughtful person. It must have exhausted her making breakfast for us. But it was so good."

"I don't think I've ever been to Miss Cora's without food being involved in some form or another."

Ellie laughed. "Like last night. Cookies and milk. She's got a real heart for people, doesn't she?"

"Yeah, she sure does."

They drove in silence for a while.

"Caleb," Ellie turned toward him. "Do you know what déjà vu is?"

"Sure." He gave her a quick glance. "Why do you ask?"

"I don't know. It just seems like I've been experiencing it a lot recently."

"How recently?"

"Oh, the past three or four months, I'd say. Like when we ran into each other and went to lunch at that little sidewalk cafe. I had the strangest feeling that I already knew you. I didn't mention it then, but it kind of made me uncomfortable."

"I remember you telling me that." He grinned. "Do I still make you uncomfortable now?"

"What? Oh no. I didn't mean you personally. I meant the idea of feeling that way around someone I've just met. It usually takes me a while to warm up to people. You know, trust issues and everything. Because of my past."

"I get that. But why bring it up now?"

"Because the more I'm with you, the more I have those feelings. Like when we got to Miss Cora's. I felt like I'd seen her house before."

"That's because it reminded you of the one in your dreams."

"I know. But it doesn't stop there. I had the same feeling when Miss Cora showed me to my room last night. I felt like I'd been in it before. And just now, when we were sitting on her porch swing . . . that same sensation again. And then there's Miss Cora herself. Doesn't she remind you of the old woman in my dreams?"

Caleb grinned impishly. "I wouldn't know. It wasn't my dream, remember?"

Ellie laughed. "No, of course not. But isn't it weird, though?" She repositioned herself in the seat. "And then there's the coincidences on top of all that."

"What coincidences?"

"Well, like you mistaking me for another Ellie in the elevator. And you seeing my paintings in that hotel lobby. And us both liking small towns and . . . and tenderloin sandwiches."

"Tenderloin sandwiches?" Caleb laughed. "What's so unusual about that? Lots of people like tenderloin sandwiches. If they didn't, places like Edwards would go out of business."

"You know what I mean. It's not each individual coincidence that makes this so strange, it's the sum of them. They all add up to one thing, near as I can figure out."

"And what's that?" he asked, hoping the eagerness didn't reflect in his voice.

"I thought about it a lot last night. I think it means that all these things remind me of places and people from my past. The part of my past I can't remember."

"That sounds possible," he agreed. "Maybe Miss Cora's place reminds you of a house you've been to before. And she might remind you of an older woman you once knew."

"Maybe. But it happens all the time. I wish those feelings would go away. I'm so confused." Her frustration spilled over. "Why can't I remember things from the past four years? Sometimes I feel downright helpless and lost. I just hate it!"

"Well, look on the bright side. You said those feelings began a few months ago, right? Maybe that means your memories are starting to come back. I'd be patient and give it some more time. "

"I suppose you're right." She sighed deeply. Then she frowned and studied him.

Even with his eyes on the road he could feel her intense stare.

"But how do you explain the feelings I've had about you? Is it possible that even you remind me of someone I once knew?"

Caleb stared at her long enough that he had to swerve to stay in his lane. His heart beat faster. He wanted to cry out "Yes! Yes! I remind you of me!"

Showing great restraint, he smiled reassuringly. "It's possible."

They reached the downtown section of Baxter and turned onto Main Street. Grateful for the distraction, Caleb began the grand tour of his home town.

He showed Ellie the courthouse and other landmarks, the park down by the river, his former high school, and the pet store where he used to work. Although she didn't mention it, he could tell she was experiencing more feelings of déjà vu. He prayed throughout the afternoon that their return to these familiar places would jog her memory of her past life in Baxter—and with him.

Around five o'clock they pulled into the parking lot of Edwards Drive-In to join B.J. and Allison for dinner. He was anxious for Ellie to meet them. Of all their mutual friends, she'd spent more time with them than anyone else.

If anything can bring back her memory, it's B.J. and Edwards Drive-In!

Ellie was immediately smitten by Joshua Caleb. She held him and played with him as they waited on their order. Once they began the meal, she readily agreed with Caleb's earlier assessment that the tenderloins at Edwards were the best ever.

On the ride back to Miss Cora's, however, Ellie was unusually withdrawn. She stared silently out the passenger window and fiddled absentmindedly with her hair. She seemed to be lost in a world of deep thoughts.

As the two walked up to the old Victorian, Caleb asked if she'd like to sit on the front porch for a while.

As if in a trance, she headed for the swing without replying. He sat down next to her, and the two of them began rocking back and forth. Neither spoke for several minutes.

"Did you have a nice time today?" he inquired, gently breaking the silence.

"What?" His question seemed to jolt her from her thoughts. "Oh, yes. I enjoyed everything. Baxter is a lovely little town. And you're very blessed to have such nice friends."

She smiled, but he noticed that it was forced. Something was definitely troubling her. "You've been awfully quiet since we left Edwards. Is something wrong?"

She looked at him. "Wrong? No, nothing's wrong, really." She hesitated. "But something is bothering me. It's those feelings. You know, the one's we discussed earlier this morning. I've had them nearly everywhere we went today. They were especially strong when you took me to the high school and the Pet Palace. And when we went to Edwards, I could have sworn I'd been there before. Even your friends looked familiar. And that's not all. I've gotten the distinct impression that people have been tiptoeing around me since we got here." She sounded stressed about it.

Had the time come to tell her the full truth? Would she be able to handle it? He didn't know what to do or say.

"I um . . . I think it's what you said earlier. You might be starting to remember things from before. "

"But why does everything here have that effect on me? What are the chances that everything and everyone in Baxter could remind me of different places and people from my past? That's impossible. Unless . . ." her voice trailed off. "Unless I've been here before."

How should he reply to that? Caleb nervously ran his hand through his hair.

"What's that?" Ellie leaned across him and stared at the artwork peeking out from beneath his forearm. She grabbed his arm and pulled it away. "It's another heart. Like the one Miss Cora's husband carved on this side."

She read the inscription. "C.S and E.T. 4EVER. C.S. and E.T?" She looked puzzled. "Someone else carved their initials in this swing!"

He watched her and waited breathlessly. "C.S. Those are your initials, Caleb! And E.T." She frowned skeptically. "You said I reminded you of someone you once knew. Someone else named Ellie." She put her palm on her forehead as if trying to remember. "And that day you stopped me in the elevator, didn't you say something about looking all over for her? That you thought she was . . . she was dead?"

"Yes . . ."

Ellie's voice rose in pitch. "Caleb, what's going on? I feel like I'm in the Twilight Zone or something! Am I . . . do you think I'm having a nervous breakdown?"

Caleb looked away, afraid she'd see the moisture in his eyes. He let the air he'd been holding in his lungs slowly escape. "No, you're not having a nervous breakdown. This girl, she was . . . she meant everything to me. We were in love. We were going to be married." He looked her full in the face. "But then, she was suddenly taken away from me."

Ellie's eyes widened. "No wonder you were so shocked to see me in that elevator! I can't imagine what you were thinking at the time. Or feeling."

Caleb didn't reply. He was searching for the right words, ones to tell her that *she* was the other girl. The one who meant everything to him. The one he was in love with. The one he planned to marry.

"Caleb, I'm so sorry. I had no idea. You never mentioned this to me before." She placed her hand over his.

Caleb looked away. "I . . . I didn't know how to tell you about it."

"You don't have to," she assured him. "I don't need to know the details." She squeezed his hand. "Caleb, whoever she was, I think she was very blessed to have someone like you in her life."

Caleb's eyes widened. He'd heard similar words from her before. He turned to her and shook his head vehemently. "No. No, Ellie, you've got it wrong. I'm the blessed one to have *you* in my life."

Ellie brightened, and smiled shyly. "No, Caleb, you're the one who's got it wrong. I'm the blessed one to have you in my life."

He caught the hint of playfulness in her voice. "Nope. It's me who's the blessed one," he responded, breaking into a grin.

"No, I'm the blessed one," she insisted, laughing out loud.

They looked each other squarely in the eye. "Well, aren't we the blessed ones!"

The phrase escaped their lips simultaneously. Caleb stared at Ellie. Ellie stared at Caleb. Neither moved a muscle.

Then suddenly, Ellie grabbed her head with her hands.

He instinctively reached out and touched her shoulder. "Ellie, what's wrong? Are you all right?"

After what seemed like an eternity, she looked up at him with a faraway look in her eyes. "I . . . I remember."

"You what?"

"I remember. Caleb, I remember!" She shook her head. "It's coming back to me." Caleb waited anxiously. "My memory of this place. I remember Baxter. I used to live here. I remember going to high school . . . and working at the Pet Palace . . . and . . . and living in this house!" She looked around in wide-eyed wonder. "That's my old bedroom upstairs." Raising both hands to her face, she exclaimed, "I gave my life to Jesus in that room, didn't I?"

Her face shown like an angel. He could only nod. The lump in his throat denied him speech.

"And that." She pointed to the heart. "Those are our initials, aren't they? You carved them there. With Henry's pocket knife." Her brown eyes were wide and shining and more beautiful than ever. "And you. I remember you." She softly brushed his face with her fingertips. "You're the guy in my dreams!"

Tears rimmed Caleb's eyes. "Yes I am."

He gathered her in his arms and pulled her tightly to him. The two clung to each other in a long, emotional embrace. He did not want to let her go, for fear she might once again slip from his grasp.

Ellie pressed her face against his. "Oh, Caleb, thank you for not giving up on me." Tears were streaming down her cheeks now. He could feel their wetness against his face as they mingled with his own.

And he was not ashamed of them.

"I told you I'd always be here for you," he whispered in her ear.

She pulled back and gazed tenderly at him with her beautiful brown eyes. "I just love a man who keeps his word!"

Placing both hands on the back of his neck, she drew him into a long and passionate kiss.

Ellie sat back in the swing and laid her head on Caleb's shoulder. He put his arm around her and inhaled the intoxicating scent of her beautiful auburn hair. For several minutes, they rocked back and forth on the porch swing. Neither one of them spoke. Neither had to.

Ellie had a faraway look in her eyes. She finally broke the silence. "It's so good to be back, Caleb."

He squeezed her shoulder. "It's so good to have you back, Ellie." His voice cracked.

She looked up at him and smiled lovingly through watery eyes. Her lips brushed his cheek.

He returned her smile and her kiss. "Welcome home!"

CHAPTER TWENTY-ONE

FULL CIRCLE

CALEB OPENED THE FRONT DOOR of the old Victorian house at 401 East Pine Street and stepped onto the veranda porch. He yawned and stretched.

Patting his stomach, he announced to no one in particular, "That was one good Sunday dinner!"

He ambled around the corner and plunked down on the porch swing. It was a warm, sunny day in southwest Georgia, and the magnolias were in full bloom. The scent of lilacs and honeysuckle, and the sounds of cicadas and song birds filled the air. As he drank in the ambient tranquility of the moment, his mind began to drift.

Six years ago, on this very swing, Ellie's memory had come back to her. For a moment, he allowed himself to relive the emotions of that incredible day. Soon after that, he'd proposed to her all over again with the same ring he'd slipped onto her finger the first time.

They'd been married three months later. It had been a beautiful, joyous affair, a testament to their undying love for each other, as well as to their Savior's eternal love for both.

He suddenly chuckled out loud, recalling the wave of laughter that had swept through the church as he knelt with Ellie at the altar. On the soles of his black patent-leather shoes, compliments of the best man, the word "WA-HOO!" had been written in white paint.

His mind fast forwarded to when they'd received the news that Miss Cora had gone home to be with the Lord. Her funeral had been a celebration of a life well lived. The eighty-six year old widow had touched countless lives.

He stopped swinging for a moment and glanced around the porch, recalling the certified letter informing them that Miss Cora had willed her house to them. They had rejoiced at the news, and Ellie had cried over it. She had always wanted a house like this, and God had seen fit to bless them with the very one that held so many wonderful memories for both of them.

Not long after that, they'd moved back to Baxter. He reflected on how that decision had changed their lives. He was now working for the design firm he'd interned with after graduation, and Ellie was living her dream of having her own art studio in a small town. And the two of them couldn't be any happier.

The front door of the house opened again, and an auburn haired little girl wearing a frilly yellow dress darted out onto the porch.

From his seat around the corner, Caleb could hear Ellie's voice calling after the fleeing four-year old. "Savannah! Where are you going?"

"I'm going to sit with Daddy on the swing," the little girl replied. She rounded the corner and climbed onto the swing next to her father.

"Swing me, Daddy," she begged, patting his arm with her tiny hand.

Caleb put an arm around his daughter and smiled at her. "Okay, honey. But did you close the door?"

She squinted her big brown eyes. "I think so."

"No she didn't," Ellie laughed, rounding the corner of the porch with a cup of coffee in her hand. She was very pregnant. "Savannah dear, you need to remember to shut the door behind you next time, okay sweetie?"

"Okay, Mommy. I will do it next time. I promise!"

Ellie eased herself into the padded wooden rocker that had been Miss Cora's favorite and took a sip of her coffee.

"I like swinging with Daddy!" Savannah announced, with her feet sticking straight out in front of her.

Ellie smiled at her. "I know you do, sweetie. You're just like me when I was a little girl. I used to like swinging with my mother, too. Only my swing was green and your swing is white."

She watched Caleb rock back and forth with their daughter for a while. Savannah suddenly slid off the swing and lay down with her back on the floorboards.

Caleb looked down at his daughter in amazement. Four years old, and she was still unpredictable.

"Savannah, what in the world are you doing?" he chuckled, glancing at his wife and shaking his head.

"I want to push you, Daddy," his precocious daughter replied. Instead of going around, she began scooting under the swing.

"Savannah! Get up off the porch," Ellie scolded. "You're going to get your Sunday dress all dirty."

Savannah stopped halfway under the swing and lay there for a moment. "Savannah, did you hear me?"

The little girl ignored her mother's question. "Mommy, there's a heart on the swing."

"Yes, I know, sweetie. There are two hearts, actually. One on each arm. Now, please get up."

"No, there's another heart on the swing."

"What is she talking about?" He got up, pulled Savannah out from under the swing and dusted off the back of her yellow dress. "Another heart? Where?"

"On the bottom. I'll show you." She started to crawl under the swing again.

"Whoa, princess." Caleb scooped her up and deposited her with her mother. "I'll check it out myself." He tipped the swing back so he could see the underside of the seat. "Well, what do you know, there *is* another heart under here."

"There is?" Ellie struggled to get out of the rocker. "Let me see."

"Hold on. I'll unhook the chains so you don't have to get up." Caleb reached up and unfastened the S-hooks from the eye bolts screwed into the rafters. He tipped the swing over and laid it on the floor, turning it to face her.

There on the underside, was a heart, painted on the slats with what must have been a small artist's brush. The white paint stood out in stark contrast to the dark green bottom of the swing.

Caleb stared at the initials. "Uh, Ellie . . . "

"K.T. and E.T. BFFs," Ellie read the letters out loud. "Who do you suppose that was? The people who owned the swing before the Williams?"

"Where did Miss Cora say they found this swing? Do you remember?"

"Um . . . she said they bought it at a garage sale. Somewhere near Chesapeake, I think. Why?"

"A green porch swing . . . bought about twenty years ago . . . near Chesapeake, Virginia. Does that ring any bells?"

Ellie looked at him. "K.T. and E.T. That must have been the people who . . . " her voice trailed off. Staring at the letters, she shook her head. "No. No, it can't be."

She glanced up at him. "Caleb, is that possible?"

"Katherine Thompson and Ellie Thompson." He said it for her.

Ellie stared at him in disbelief. "BFFs. Best Friends Forever. That's what my mother and I used to pinkie promise each other when she tucked me in bed every night."

Caleb knelt down in front of his wife and gently took her face in his hands. "Ellie, this is the swing you and your mother used to sit on when you lived in Hickory."

"I can't believe it! Caleb, I've been sitting on that swing since our senior year of high school. And all this time, I didn't know . . . " Ellie was crying now.

"What's the matter, Mommy? Why are you crying?" Savannah reached up and gave her mother a hug. "Don't be sad, Mommy. It's okay." She patted her arm.

Ellie wiped her eyes and pulled Savannah tightly to her. "Thank you, sweetie. I'm not sad."

Caleb got to his feet. "Would you like some more coffee?" he asked his wife.

Ellie nodded through her tears, and with a smile handed him the nearly empty cup.

He took it from her hands and disappeared around the corner of the porch. On his way to the kitchen, he made a detour into the living room. Standing in front of the fireplace with its smoke stained brick and dark, aged wood, he surveyed the items on the mantel.

The old German clock was still ticking faithfully and keeping excellent time. A small Bible lay beside it, a wrinkled brochure and a dog-eared bookmark peeking out from beneath its white cover. He stared at the large acrylic painting in the beautiful antique frame hanging above the mantel. Done in all sepia tones, it depicted an auburn-haired young woman and a tall young man, both wearing old fashioned turn-of-the-century clothing, sitting arm-in-arm on the porch swing of a large old Victorian house.

The artist had signed it in the lower right-hand corner, *Ellie Thompson Sawyer.* Attached to the frame was a brass plaque inscribed with the words of Jeremiah 29:11.

He read them out loud. "For I know the plans I have for you, declares the LORD, plans for welfare and not for evil, to give you a future and a hope."

Caleb looked upward and smiled. In a sudden rush of emotion, he uttered a familiar word.

"Wahoo!"

Then he turned and headed for the kitchen.

It must have been his imagination, but for a brief second he caught the sweet scent of warm ginger.

And he could have sworn he heard a faint, barely audible voice.

"Hallelujah!" it said.

THE END

ABOUT THE AUTHOR

David Mathews was born in the small mid-western town of Friend, Nebraska, a community of 1100 people once listed in *Ripley's Believe It or Not* for having the world's smallest police station—a tiny tool shed previously used by highway construction crews. He grew up in small towns in Kansas and Indiana before settling in Indianapolis after college.

He describes himself as a big dreamer with an overactive imagination. As a child without a TV in the home, he managed to find a variety of ways to avoid boredom. Whether it was putting on puppet shows, producing radio plays, drawing cartoons, or making home movies, he always found something creative to occupy his time.

Now living in Xenia, Ohio, David and his wife, Donna, have six children between them, along with a son-in-law, daughter-in-law, three granddaughters, and two Boston Terriers. He enjoys home remodeling, woodworking, bicycling, camping, and writing. He also serves in their local church, loves being a grandfather, and never grows tired of watching Andy Griffith reruns.

Always up for an adventure together, David and Donna went spelunking on their honeymoon, tent camping with bears on their anniversary, and skydiving on his sixtieth birthday.

For more information about
David Mathews
&
A Future and a Hope
please visit:

www.davidjmathews.com
www.facebook.com/davidmathews.author
davidmathews.author@yahoo.com
@davidmathewsau1

For more information about
AMBASSADOR INTERNATIONAL
please visit:

www.ambassador-international.com
@AmbassadorIntl
www.facebook.com/AmbassadorIntl

If you enjoyed this book, please consider leaving us a review on
Amazon, Goodreads, or our website.